RIVER CHILD

ELEANOR MILLARD

Order this book online at www.trafford.com
or email orders@trafford.com

Most Trafford titles are also available at major online book retailers.

Printed in the United States of America.

ISBN: 978-1-4269-9257-5 (sc)
ISBN: 978-1-4269-9258-2 (e)

Library of Congress Control Number: 2011914530

Trafford rev. 09/27/2011

 www.trafford.com

North America & international
toll-free: 1 888 232 4444 (USA & Canada)
phone: 250 383 6864 ♦ fax: 812 355 4082

CONTENTS

LEAVING HOME

The stream of light from Dave Maclean's flashlight pierced the murky corners of the lean-to woodshed and climbed up the rough wooden shelves. "Now, where did I put the damn thing?" he asked himself, stepping over the chopping block. His foot caught in a broken dogsled he had promised a neighbour he would fix before winter. He swore and rubbed away the cobwebs clinging to his beard. Glass jars accumulated over the years rattled as he pulled down wooden boxes once used for butter and oranges. Finally from the back of the top shelf he dug out a tan-coloured cardboard suitcase covered in years of dust. He had last used it when he left Saskatchewan and came North. 1925. The rapidity of time passing struck him. Twenty years had flown past as if they were a dream. Who could have told him when he put the suitcase in the shed that he would need it again for his little daughter sleeping on the other side of the wall? To send her away?

Back in the kitchen, Dave dampened a dishcloth to meticulously wipe dust from the inside of the suitcase and then from the outside. He covered two gouges on the sides with adhesive tape. In his elaborate script, in dark blue ink near the handle, he labelled it: *Eliza Maclean Dawson City*. He filled it with a few of Eliza's clothes, carefully folded, and her favourite doll. The latch wasn't much good. He took one of his old belts and secured the lid with it.

While it was still dark, early the next morning, Eliza woke up and ran into Dave's bedroom. She shook his shoulder, and shouted, "Daddy! Can I get dressed now? Before I eat?"

Dave sat up, squinting at her smile. "OK, little one. Whatever you like," he said. She hurried to her room, pulled on her long white stockings, and stepped into the new patent leather shoes from Grander's store. She had left her dress, the one she liked best, on her bed the night before. It was red cotton, printed with bright flowers, trimmed with white lace around the collar and on the cuffs of the long sleeves. Daddy always called her his little princess when she wore it.

For the first time in her almost ten years, Eliza was leaving home. She would take a paddlewheeler, the *SS Klondike*, south on the Yukon River to Whitehorse. The steamer left at 6:00 a.m. near the Bank of Commerce. After the trip on the steamer, she would even take a train! She would go to a big school with lots of other girls and boys. It was in Carcross, a long ways from Dawson City.

They ate a hurried breakfast and were soon walking along Church to Front Street in the early morning darkness. The cries of gulls pierced the translucent August fog curling upwards off the river, answered by *caw-plunk* from a raven watching them from the steeple of the Anglican Church. One of the church ladies had given Eliza a green corduroy jacket of her daughter's that she had outgrown. Although it was cold enough to wear it, Eliza carried it over her arm. She wanted to show off the lace on her dress. In her hand was a wrinkled paper bag from Stewart's store with a lunch of three moose meat sandwiches, dried meat, and her favourite home-made cookies. Dave had two good oranges in his overcoat pocket that he had found at the Alaska Commercial store. He would give them to her as a special treat when he had to say good-bye. He swung the suitcase by his side. Somehow it was heavier than it should be.

"Daddy, tell me again about school," Eliza said, eagerly looking up at him.

Dave forced his enthusiasm. "Oh," he said, "you'll learn a lot of good things. Like how to do fractions. And you'll read lots of books and you'll meet new friends..."

"When can I see you?"

"I told you, sweetheart. I'll try to get enough money together to bring you home for Christmas on the plane. I'll be able to trap this winter. Prices are good for a change. And next summer you can come home with the others on the steamer. You'll be here the whole summer with me. We'll go downriver and fish."

"You can write letters to me, too, eh?"

"Of course, little princess."

They joined the crowd of people milling around Front Street near the SS *Klondike*. It had come in overnight. The steamer was like a huge animal tied up, anxious to run, grunting and moaning in an uneven rhythm. Dark smoke belched from her smokestack, metal chains clanged and people shouted as they loaded her belly. Her whistle screamed shrilly three times to let the town know she was leaving in half an hour. Eliza took her father's free hand, even though she had stopped doing that the year before.

In front of the Bank of Commerce Eliza saw a small gathering of Indian children and their parents. They were mostly strangers to her because they lived away from Dawson every winter, in the bush. In the summer they were on the rivers fishing. A man and a woman wearing blue blazers with official-looking crests on the pockets were moving around amongst the children. The woman had a list of names that she was checking. She blew a whistle twice and called, "Gladys Charlie? Where's Gladys? Oh, there you are." She beckoned with a nod and said, "Come over here, Gladys, get in line with the other girls now. You're not supposed to be over there with the boys." Gladys walked over, dragging her feet. "But I want to be with my brother."

"Nonsense! You'll have to get used to not seeing him again. You remember that, don't you? At school he'll always be with his own friends, with the other boys. He doesn't want a silly little girl tagging along, now, does he?"

The blue blazer woman noticed Dave and Eliza coming up to her. Smiling and leaning down to Eliza, she asked, "Now who is this? A new little girl, I see."

Dave said, "Eliza Maclean. Band Number 59."

The woman looked at the list on her clipboard. "Oh, yes, I remember," she said. "Here we are. Number 94." She checked Eliza's name off.

"No. Not 94...59," Dave said.

Laughing, the woman said, "Oh, no, Mr. Maclean, this is *our* number. At the school. She'll have it the whole time she's there. Just leave her suitcase over there with the rest. We'll see she has it when she gets there."

Clutching her lunch and jacket, Eliza skipped over to the loading ramp and ran up confidently. Dave followed. He took her around everywhere and showed her where all the important things were. She would share a bed with another girl for the four-day trip, in a tiny room with five other girls. Eliza recognized one of the girls as Gladys Charlie. "Hi, Gladys," she said, but the girl looked blankly at her. All the other girls in the room had gone to the school before. They didn't seem very friendly. It was probably because they were older. They didn't want to be bothered with someone as young as she was. Dave told her to leave her lunch under her pillow, and they went up on deck.

When the *SS Klondike* blew her final whistle for a full minute, Dave took Eliza's jacket and put her arms through it. He buttoned it up. She could do that herself, but she knew he liked to do it. He lifted her up in a hug that made her feet come off the deck and she smelled his familiar sweet pipe tobacco. His beard tickled her ear. "I love you, sweetheart. Be a good little girl," he whispered, turned quickly, and left her standing on the deck.

Wavering a little, the *Klondike* grumbled, pulling away from shore. Men shouted orders and jokes at each other on the deck beneath Eliza's feet. Behind her, the giant paddlewheel creaked and splashed as it turned methodically in the muddy water. She ran over to hang onto the railing with both hands and watched her father walking quickly along the river bank with the crowd waving good-bye to the passengers. Then he was standing alone at the mouth of the Klondike River. She wanted to wave back to him, but she was afraid that if she let go of the railing, she would fall over into the river. The steamer finally turned the bend and he disappeared.

The blue blazer lady came and took Eliza's hands off the railing, silently leading her away. Eliza remembered that while they were walking to Front Street, her Daddy had said that he had a surprise for her. Maybe it was waiting for her in the cabin. Looking up, she asked, "Did Daddy leave me something?"

"Not that I know of," the woman said. "Now you be a good girl and just stay in the cabin with Gladys and the other girls until lunch."

"But Daddy said he had a surprise he would give me."

"Maybe your father forgot."

When the blue blazer lady left her in the cabin, Eliza looked for her lunch under the pillow. It was gone.

****

Three weeks before Eliza left home, the ladies of the Wednesday afternoon Anglican prayer group had gathered to have tea, cakes, and a tiny drink after their meeting. They met at the home of Angelina White, current Regent of the Imperial Order of the Daughters of the Empire, Dawson City Chapter, and wife of the Territorial Councillor, Samuel White.

Angelina had requested that their priest, Father Malcolm Pandergast, join them for refreshments to help "settle their minds," she said. They were concerned about a proposed move into town of several Indian families from the village of Moosehide downstream on the Yukon River. Two blocks of

Crown land on Front Street had recently been selected for the move by the new Indian Superintendent, who was also the Anglican Bishop.

The ladies were relieved to be thinking about something besides the distant European War. Again this day, as they had every meeting for five years, the ladies had prayed for their boys fighting overseas. Thanks to God and the fine fighting force from Canada, it was now just a matter of wiping up in Europe and helping the Americans settle the Pacific.

Shifting his black cassock up to reveal a grey shirt sleeve, Father Malcolm leaned forward to accept another slice of Mrs. White's excellent wild cranberry bread. He always wore his cassock in public out of respect for the seriousness of his calling at St. Paul's, in sober contrast to the floral dresses worn by the rouged and powdered trio of women.

Decisively, Father Malcolm swallowed a bite of the sweet buttered loaf. He said in his fading English accent, "Moosehide is a much better home for them than here, I do agree. But it is the Bishop's wish." He glanced around the cluster of women, smiled, and said: "I'd be happy to live in Moosehide myself." The ladies giggled protectively at the thought of their lanky bachelor priest managing to live in the Indian village without his housekeeper, let alone the electricity, water, and sewer that Dawsonites had enjoyed since the days of the Klondike Gold Rush, nearly fifty years before.

Maude Grander, four-term president of St. Paul's Women's Auxiliary, shifted her short plump figure. She accepted "just a smidge, dear, in my cup" of Benedictine from the crystal decanter Angelina held. Maude announced: "Well, Father, I firmly believe the move from Moosehide to be downright un-Christian."

Father Malcolm's left eyebrow raised. "I have thought this through very thoroughly, Father," Maude said, "and I have even discussed it with our Indian W.A. president, Mrs. Thomas, the last time she was in town. She doesn't totally agree, but in my opinion, it deprives them of their livelihood in the wild. It will turn them into beggars on our streets." Father Malcolm gave Mrs. Grander his full attention. "Furthermore," she stated loudly, taking a sip of her tea, "moving them into town exposes them to...to...well, moral degradation is the only decent way to put it." Encouraging nods and hums of approval came from the other two women. These good wives and mothers were acutely aware of the evil influence of the six hotels with bars and live music. They were particularly disgusted by the two houses with so-called good time girls that somehow still remained so many years after the Gold Rush. There was no need for them now.

Angelina turned to her friend, wire-rimmed glasses sparkling as she nodded and said, "Oh yes, Maudie, I agree. It surely does leave them open to all kinds of negative influences if they come into town. We've all seen the results when we mix them with our more sophisticated Dawson society." She leaned toward Father Malcolm and he sat back. "Father," she said, "don't you agree that maybe they were better off in the bush, like my Sammy says?"

"Yes, Mrs. White," Father Malcolm said. He never failed to address the members of his congregation formally. "You could say we were somewhat at fault for establishing them as a community when normally they would have been nomadic, in the bush, along the river, and so on." He touched his lips with his napkin, and looked deliberately around the circle. "Of course, as we all know, the biggest problem is alcohol." He was a total abstainer.

Maude forced a smile. Everyone knew that her husband was decidedly not an abstainer.

"Of course it certainly isn't the same for everyone," Father Malcolm said, glancing at Maude. "We all know what drinking does to the Indians. They're very much like children, aren't they, not physically disposed to cope with it. It seems it takes generations to adapt to alcohol," he said, trying to keep the conversation away from the Bishop's decision which he had objected to in several letters.

Angelina's newly arrived girdle from Eaton's catalogue was a shade too small. It was pinching her waist badly and she shifted her weight. "Well, there you are," she declared for no apparent reason, putting the teapot on the coffee table. "To sum it up, then, we all know that Moosehide is a better choice for them than town. After all, it is their home. Imagine being told to leave home! Marched into Dawson - just like that." Her eyes were open wide and searched the ceiling.

Father Malcolm said, "They will have to learn to be a part of our White society eventually, of course." Everyone nodded. "But it must come more slowly and naturally, over time. Do I understand you correctly, Mrs. White?" He leaned back in the sofa chair, reaching down with his free hand to play with his thin grey-brown beard. He flipped it up to reveal the heavy chain that held an ornate gold cross that hung to his waist.

"Precisely," she said.

Maude turned to the silent Irene Ward across the room. She was the wife of the Federal Government's Mining Recorder, one of the most important posts in the gold mining town. "And what do you think your husband would recommend that we do about this tragedy, Irene?"

Irene's pale face, all bones and angles, turned to Maude. She was sitting on the only hard chair in the room. Her lower back and one leg were aching from sitting and a roaming cramp reminded her that her period would be coming soon. Maude was once again making her say something she might later regret. She folded her napkin, placed it on the table, and reached for her tiny liqueur glass of French brandy. Pulling her flat torso up gave her some relief. She said in a murmur, "I suppose Father Malcolm could talk to my husband about..."

"Nonsense!" Everyone turned to Maude as she snorted. Irene brought the liqueur glass up to her lips and took a sip for courage.

Father Malcolm pulled his pocket watch out. He frowned, picking his prayer book up from the table and offered what he hoped were his final conclusions: "This government in Ottawa, getting so involved with Indian concerns in the Yukon - it's ruining all the good that the Yukon Diocese has done for them. Confidentially, we are stressing to the government that they should leave these important decisions of a local nature, like moving them into Dawson, completley up to the local congregations."

Angelina threw her napkin on top of her plate on the table. She stood up. "I'm much more concerned about an immediate situation," she said. She reached for the teapot. Leaning over, she silently poured the priest and Irene more tea, gaining the attention of the room.

Father Malcolm put his prayer book back on the table. "And what is that situation, Mrs. White?" he asked calmly.

"A certain Moosehide family who are already in Dawson," Angelina said. She sat down, holding the teapot in her lap. Forcing herself to look as if she were actually seeking information, she asked, "Father, I would like to know why there are Indian children living in Dawson who are not sent away to school."

"And who are you thinking of, Angie?" Maude prompted.

Angelina placed the teapot on the table and smiled. "You remember, Maudie? We talked about it. The situation with that White man everyone calls Indian Dave. He moved into town from Moosehide with his daughter a couple of years ago."

"Perhaps I am wrong, but I understood it is mandatory, is it not, Father, to send all the Indian children to residential school?" Maude asked.

"You mean little Eliza Maclean?" Father Malcolm said pleasantly. He wanted to sound informed and on top of the problem. "Didn't the mother die of tuberculosis?"

"Yes, that's the family," Angelina said. She poured herself a second orange liqueur and sat back in her chair, looking away from a reproachful glance from her priest.

Father Malcolm said, "Well then, to answer your question, Mrs. Grander, yes, it is compulsory to send them to school. The Indian Act was changed--as early as 1920 or thereabouts I believe--to make certain that all Indian children get the opportunity to go to a good school. Some are taken away from their homes - the ones we know where the environment is not appropriate. It is unfortunate that not all of them can go, but the Federal Government simply won't pay to provide the service our Diocese gives to these poor unfortunate children."

With both feet flat on the floor, knees together, and her back straight, Angelina eased the tightness around her waist. She said, "I'll get straight to the point, Father. Eliza Maclean is a worry to all of us." She looked directly at Father Malcolm, "You must admit," she said, "it's pretty...um...*unusual* to have a man looking after his daughter like that. Alone."

"It's just not done," Maude said cryptically, "And not very healthy, either. A little girl living with a grown man is downright dangerous."

"Dangerous?" Father Malcolm asked.

Angelina sighed. "Yes, Father," she said. "You are surely aware of that poor little girl in Moosehide who was living with her aunt and...well, was being used by her uncle for his own...ah...pleasure. She had been made to suffer terribly, up until that evil man drowned just last week. I understand it might have been a case of family revenge, his death, by the way."

"Really?" Father Malcolm said, hoping he sounded shocked. "God's justice," he murmured.

"Well, we certainly don't want an episode like that to happen in Dawson, do we?" Maude said. "We need to nip it in the bud, get rid of any possibility of it happening here! Their animal instincts are just not under control. It's quite possible that Eliza has already had some unsavoury experiences, poor thing."

Angelina turned to Irene. "Now, Irene," she asked, "isn't it true that to go to an industrial...a...residential school, whatever they call it--that the girl must be registered as an Indian with the government?" Irene was expected to absorb all the Federal Government red tape and legalities from her civil servant husband.

"Well, a lot of these White men don't ever marry their Indian women, you know," Irene said. She reached for her glass of brandy and said, "If they do marry them, you realize, the wife and any children born after the marriage are automatically recognized as White status, but if they don't, they are still Indians."

Maude was getting impatient. Sometimes Irene could be so evasive. "Yes, yes, I think we all know that. But what about the Macleans?"

Irene blinked. "I don't believe that Dave Maclean ever married her. But I'm afraid I don't know anything as confidential as that."

"Then she could go to a church industrial school," Maude concluded for her.

"Of course she could go!" Angelina said with a exasperated laugh. She looked pointedly at Father Malcolm, "and I'm sure Father Malcolm would agree that she *should* go."

"I think I'm right when I say that we are all aware, as Christian women," Maude said through her nose, looking away from Father Malcolm to the other two, "that a growing girl simply should not be left alone to live with her father. Besides terrible things like that dreadful case in Moosehide, as she becomes adolescent there are, ah...well...*physical things* that are important for her to know. Isn't that right?"

The other two nodded.

Father Malcolm reddened behind his beard. Clearing his throat, he grasped the opportunity to talk about something he knew more about than girls and women. He said, "Mrs. White, you, I think, were asking if Eliza has to be a registered Indian to be sent away? It's true. We accept only Indian status children at our Anglican residential schools. We have a place for half breeds too of course. Our local hostel here at St. Paul's provides quite adequately for them."

The priest had never visited the residential school, but he said, "It is truly remarkable, our little Chooutla school in Carcross, founded as you know by that saint, Bishop Bompas in 1903, whose whole mission in life was a good education for our Indians. We provide five full years of schooling. That's actually the equivalent of only the first three grades in the regular school but that's because of the language problem." He looked around to be certain all the ladies were listening. "As you know, most of them don't speak English very well, if at all. We immerse them in good solid Standard English from the very first day and are forced to punish them if they speak Indian. We separate siblings. In that way, they don't have someone they are able to talk their own Indian language with. Pedagogically, complete immersion is the only reliable and effective way to teach languages."

Maude wanted less philosophy. "Just how many children are there in the school, Father? It seems to me there are a lot of Indians who could use it that aren't going."

Father Malcolm hesitated. Five children had died the year before at the school and the clergy had been told to recruit only the most healthy of children to avoid controversy. "I believe the latest news from the school was that this year the Bishop will select nearly fifty boys and girls, ages eight to sixteen, from all over the Territory."

"Select them? Only fifty?" Maude asked. "Don't they all just go?"

"No, not everyone who wants to can go," Father Malcolm said. "They are the chosen few you might say. We are restricting our numbers for awhile since the old school burned down, due to lack of space. The Bishop in his wisdom, advised by our long-time principal of course, finds and educates only the healthiest and most promising--the leaders. The object is of course to have them eventually return home and civilize their villages. Our unfortunate little Eliza Maclean may not be one of them, sad to say."

"Well, Eliza does have a good start already," Angelina said. "She's always clean and looks pretty bright. She should be good material, don't you think?"

Father Malcolm cleared his throat and said cheerily, "To conclude, then: I pray that we are fulfilling the Church's purpose, to assimilate the younger generation into our White civilization as quickly as possible, in a faithful Christian way. All the staff who work there are very devoted to the children," he smiled, "...and of course devoted to the Church, as missionaries."

The women listened silently while the grandfather clock on the dining room wall bonged five times. Rayon skirts and silk stockings were smoothed in preparation for leaving. Cups and plates were clattered together on the table.

Standing up, Maude said, "Well, I for one am absolutely convinced that our Church is doing a very fine job with the schools, Father. And that poor little Maclean girl should be given the decent English education that she would get there, to learn to make her way in the White world. Not to mention the fact that a man like Indian Dave should never be looking after a growing girl, whether she's his daughter or not."

Heads shook as Father Malcolm led the way to the door. "A White man living alone like that"..."with those Indians all the time"..."never in church, either, you notice." The women gathered around the priest, accepting coats from Angelina.

"Thank you for all your support and prayers today, Father," Angelina said, her hand on his arm. "You have been a wonderful help to us as usual. And I believe Eliza Maclean has fine potential, given the opportunity, don't you? You will see to that matter soon, won't you? She must be taken out of any potential danger in that situation with her father."

"Yes, yes, of course. I'll check the Church records first to see if there ever was a marriage with the woman at Moosehide. If Eliza passes that test, I should have just enough time to meet with Bishop Folwell before the steamer leaves with the school children in three weeks. It is his final decision of course."

Maude smiled and summed it up for all of them as Angelina opened the door. "I believe the protection of the school in Carcross will be a decent substitute for a good Christian home for the poor little thing." All nodded, murmuring approval as they left.

Angelina sighed. "She will be in all our prayers tonight," she said, and closed the door.

****

Two days after the prayer meeting, Father Malcolm glanced at the man called Indian Dave and showed him to the uncushioned bench against the wall in St. Paul's rectory office. Without preliminaries, he asked in a loud voice, "You do know why I called you in, do you, Mr. Maclean?" The priest had sent a note through one of Mrs. Grander's children, but he was never certain if people could read or not.

"Yes, sir. In your note you said you wanted to talk to me about my daughter Eliza?" Dave was a tall, muscular man of forty-odd years with a beard that could have used a trim. His large hands pushed his cap under his thigh and he shoved his feet beneath the bench. He had never been inside the rectory before. The hardwood floor shone as if it had never been walked on. He was glad he had had sense enough to take his boots off at the door, even though one of his woolen socks had a hole in the heel.

Father Malcolm leaned back comfortably into the plush covering of the high-backed chair behind the wide mahogany desk. "What do you want for Eliza, Mr. Maclean?" he asked abruptly.

"Well, sir, I guess I want the best that I can offer my daughter, of course."

Father Malcolm twisted the tip of his long, fine beard into a point and said, "Well, Mr. Maclean, I believe that the best you can do for her is to give her a decent education, with the right people." With a humourless smile, he added, "Don't you agree?"

"Yes. She's in the day school. Goes every day. It's better than the one in Moosehide."

"Oh, yes, of course it is. But perhaps she should be with...um...with her own kind, with the others...?"

"Well, we're not going to be moving back to Moosehide. Since her mother died, I had to give up trapping to look after her, and the jobs are here in town." Dave felt his mild resentment return, remembering how little money they needed when he was trapping and living in Moosehide. Now he had to spend a lot more. And how independent he had been in Moosehide! Now he had to ask for work from other people to make a living and had much less in his pocket.

"I am so sorry for the loss of your dear...ah...companion. It was Maggie Taylor, was it not?" Dave nodded. "I hope you will some day bring your grief and sorrow to God in our congregation?" Dave swallowed silently. He hadn't been inside a church in his life except for three funerals: his father's, his mother's, and his wife's. He wasn't about to start now.

"But let's talk about Eliza," the priest said. "I'm not suggesting that you take her back to Moosehide. No indeed. Not at all. That may not be the proper place for either of you any more." He flipped his beard out of the way, and leaned forward. "You know, some selected Indian children from here go to our school at Carcross. The Chooutla School. Started by our dear Bishop Bompas. They get a fine education and they learn how to make a living in this new world as they quite literally come out of the wilderness. And they are with other Indian children from all over the Territory. How old is Eliza now?"

"She'll be ten next month."

"Ten! Then she's getting old enough to learn how to cook, how to sew... be a young lady."

Dave's proud smile lit his eyes. He had been surprised that Eliza had adjusted so well to town, without Maggie, too. Maggie had been in the hospital in Dawson so much, and when she came home, she was a thin ghostly presence, seldom seen out of the bedroom. "Eliza helps me a lot around the house already. I'm teaching her how to cook, and she's a pretty good little housekeeper. Seems happy, too."

"Do you think you can teach her everything about her future role as a woman?" Father Malcolm said carefully. "Have you thought about that?"

"Well...maybe not." What did he know about female things? And he had no women around to help, either.

"Let me tell you a little about the school in Carcross..." Father Malcolm praised the staff, the buildings, the education system. He instinctively knew that stressing the religious training was not an argument with Dave. That was all the more reason for him to try to salvage this young girl's life. "Our Anglican schools are just like the public schools in the old country, and people there have to pay a lot of money to send their children to them, like my father did." Father Malcolm leaned forward. "Think about when Eliza gets a little older and is looking to get married. How will she ever be acceptable to the young men in Dawson, without proper training? They may even treat her badly -you know, physically I mean."

It was true that Eliza had already complained to Dave about the boys at school. Every day, she faced White boys who called her *flat face* and who told her she should go back to Moosehide and catch fish because that was what she smelled like. She was small for her age, and had been beaten or chased home the few times she defied them. Sometimes even the girls would chase her.

"But when would I see her again? Don't they go away for years at a time?"

"She will stay there for the school months and she can come home for all the holidays. It depends on you, on how much you want to see her and what you can pay towards the cost of getting her home. Most of the others don't pay anything and so it is quite a long stretch before their children are home, that's true, but that is entirely their choice. We provide for the cost of leaving home, but not to come back unless they are returning permanently or under very unusual circumstances. We simply cannot afford to pay for frequent visits back and forth. Remember it is nearly 400 miles away and there is no road. But you should be able to save enough to have her home almost whenever you want."

With Eliza gone, he could go back to trapping, save money for their future together, even fix up the cabin a little. And have his independent life back again. She already has two years schooling. It would only be a couple of years more.

Pressing his hands together in front of his chest in a prayerful attitude, Father Malcolm asked, "You don't want to keep her here just for your own sake, do you? That would hardly be fair to her and her future." Dave had never thought of it that way. Maybe he was being selfish. He should think about Eliza's needs as a young lady, things he couldn't give her no matter how hard he worked. He did want her to have every advantage, especially a good education.

"You know, the Bishop chooses only certain children to have the opportunity to go to the school. They must be of healthy stock, and have the potential to become the future leaders of their people. I believe I can convince him that your daughter is one of those children." Dave knew Eliza was smart enough to make the most of a good education. Maybe she could make a difference with other Indians in the years ahead, when times were sure to be difficult for them, coming out of the bush. That was one of his unspoken dreams for her, that she would some day be proud of her heritage, and maybe help her people.

Dave said, "I'll think about it. Have to talk it over with her, though." He stood up and leaned over the desk to offer his hand to Father Malcolm who stayed sitting. Seeing the priest hesitate, Dave stepped back, rubbed his hand on his pant leg, nodded once, and said, "Thanks for your concern." He shuffled his stockinged feet toward the door, shoving his cap on his head.

Father Malcolm stood up behind the desk. "Remember the steamer leaves for school next Monday, Mr. Maclean. Let me know by Saturday and we can make sure she gets on it." His voice took on a warning tone: "Otherwise, she'll miss this chance, and we wouldn't want that, would we?"

Something in Dave's chest churned as he walked home. He knew some Indian families took their kids into the bush with them at the end of summer so they wouldn't be taken away to residential school. They said that school made them no good in the bush, that they couldn't hunt or trap properly, didn't even know how to snare a rabbit, kids' work. The RCMP would have a list of the missing children. The kids were usually discovered when the families made a trip to town for supplies and they were made to go to the Mission School in Moosehide. The mothers would have to stay with them. It meant that the fathers had to trap alone, making it very hard on everyone. Well, Eliza wouldn't be in the bush much anyway in her lifetime. Those days were over for the younger generation.

Dave opened the door to their cabin. He tried to imagine life there without Eliza's chatter and silly jokes, but made himself dismiss the prospect from his mind. Maybe she would just not want to go. That would decide it for him. Let her make up her own mind.

Eliza cried a little that night when they talked about it. She said she would miss her Daddy too much. But the next morning, with the resiliency and optimism of the young, she was thrilled to go. She was full of questions: "When am I going, Daddy? Can I get those black shoes in Grander's store? Do I get to go on the steamer? How long will it be before I get there?"

Dave lifted her up to stand on a chair in front of him, looked her straight in the eye, and asked, "You really want to go?"

"Oh, yes, Daddy!" She threw her arms around his neck and bounced up and down on the chair.

Dave's throat tightened. All he could say was, "OK, then, little one."

****

The *SS Klondike* stopped several times along the Yukon River to load wood for the boilers and to pick up passengers for one of her last trips upriver that season. Every stop brought old friends together. They chatted and laughed, anticipating the long days and nights on board the floating hotel with nothing to do but enjoy themselves. Trips on the steamer were times for fun: good food, drinking, gambling, and laughter. Many of the passengers would stay Outside for the winter, a holiday from the unforgiving toil of placer mining. And this year was special. The end of the war in Europe was in sight. They would see some of their boys in Vancouver and Seattle who were coming home. What a party they would have then!

On the second night most of the Indian children were taken out of their cabins to make room for new passengers. They were each given a blanket and told to sleep on the benches or on the boxes of freight. There was no heat on the lower deck. The wind coming through the wide doors blew Eliza's hair away from her face and made her ears tingle. Her thin jacket was not enough to keep her warm, so she wrapped herself all day long in the blanket. They were told not to move around, that it was dangerous. They were given apples for breakfast and cold sandwiches for lunch and supper, to be eaten where they sat. Herded in groups to the toilet after meals, they were not allowed to go in between times. Eliza didn't know where her suitcase was to change her clothes. Maybe it was lost. What she would do for clothes at the school? She wanted to look nice.

One of the older boys who was returning spent the long boring days telling terrible tales of torture and starvation at the Chooutla school. He said to a small group of girls new to the school, "There's graves of two boys. Behind where the old school was, in the dirt. I saw them, the graves. The janitor chased me away, but I saw. Them kids were killed when they ran away one time, long time ago. My father, he was in the old Chooutla school then, before it burned down. He told me. They haunt our building, them boys. They come up to your bed at night, specially if you're bad. You're lucky you're girls. You don't live close to them two dead boys, like we do." Eliza was standing by a younger girl that she knew only as one of the Johnsons. She took the girl by the hand, leading her away from the storytellers, and said, "Don't worry. My Daddy wouldn't send me to a place like that. I just know it." Eliza and the others had heard some of the stories before. They didn't really believe them. But their apprehension grew with their exhaustion.

Nearly five days after leaving home, thirty-four children walked off the ramp of the SS *Klondike* in Whitehorse into a chilly late afternoon rain. Lined up into two straggling lines, one for boys and one for girls, they were marched along a muddy path on the bank of the Yukon River toward the railroad station. The waiting White Pass engine with its fat black body and its wheels taller than Eliza looked evil. Snorting steam and clanging a bell in an off-beat rhythm, it sat on steel tracks that stretched forever. Its whistle pierced the air and everyone jumped. Someone started crying.

The shivering girls were loaded into the coach behind the engine and the boys in the one behind them. As they passed the first seats, the blue blazer lady handed them each an apple, saying, "Quiet, now, girls, quiet. We're nearly there. Try to sleep."

Eliza found a hard wooden seat. She clutched her apple with both hands, too cold to eat or to sleep. A skinny girl younger than Eliza stood in the aisle without speaking. She looked at Eliza meaningfully through wet hair streaming over her eyes. It was the little Johnson girl that she had led away from hearing the boys' stories. Eliza couldn't remember her first name. The girl said without emotion, "My sister's home in Dawson. Can you be my sister?" Eliza moved over by the window to give her room. The engine gave three screams of its whistle, the train shuddered and pulled them away from the station with a clattering jerk. The Johnson girl lay her head in Eliza's lap, put her thumb in her mouth, and fell asleep before Eliza could ask her name. Eliza looked around the coach. She couldn't see anything that looked like the outhouse at home and was too frightened to ask anyone. She had to pee. She kept her hand on the girl's back through the long darkening afternoon and the girl's warmth seeped into her.

Where were they taking them? All Eliza could see were tall black trees scratching the starry sky as the train groaned and swayed, clacking along the tracks. Eliza made herself pretend that she was on one of the long hypnotic boat rides she had taken with Daddy on the Yukon River when she would quickly fall asleep. But she couldn't sleep in the train even when she closed her eyes. She tried to forget that she needed the toilet; she was too afraid to ask where it was. In a daze, she felt as if she were inside some huge animal that had swallowed her. She remembered Daddy reading her a story with pictures about Jonah and the whale. Maybe that's what had happened. They were inside a whale's stomach. They were its food. They were just waiting to die. They would be taken to disappear somewhere down its long body, there in the back where the boys were. It was eating the boys first.

Three hours later, the train pulled into the Carcross railway station and stopped with a final shudder. Eliza took the Johnson girl's hand, relieved to get off. It wasn't raining, but gusts of wind whipped around the swarm of dirty, tired children. The girls were herded into one of the small white vans waiting for them. Some of the older ones had to stand as they were silently driven a short distance, bouncing off the main road onto the floodlit school grounds. When the van stopped, Eliza sat still. She took a deep breath. Her heart sank as she felt a warm trickle go down her legs. She was wetting her pants. Her good red dress would be soaked at the back. The Johnson girl pushed past Eliza's wet legs, and disappeared into the cluster of girls. Eliza was the last to leave. She stood close to the van behind two big girls. She hoped she didn't smell.

The blue blazers who had come with them disappeared into the dark. Eliza could see three buildings with half-circle rounded roofs. They looked like huge black pipes cut in half with a door in the wall at the front. "Shit. We're still in those damned Quonsets," one of the older girls said. Quonset huts were pre-fabricated American Army barracks, left from the building of the Alaska Highway three years before.

Four women dressed in white uniforms pulled coloured cardigans close to their bodies to ward off the wind. They paced through the children, took some by the hand, greeting them, and gently pushed others into line. A whistle shrieked. Eliza's heart thumped. Two more blasts of the whistle shot through her body. One of the women shouted "Quiet! Quiet! Three whistles means quiet!" A metallic male voice coming through a megaphone bellowed: "You returning kids. Pick up your things over there behind the van. Then you go straight ahead to your huts. Understand? Now! Speed it up!" Moving through the scrambling crowd, he shouted, "The rest of you, new kids--line up in front of me! Single file! Boys here. Girls there."

Eliza needed her suitcase first. She had to change her dress. She rubbed her eyes in the bright light. Maybe her suitcase was in that pile of boxes and bags she could see behind the van. Maybe it wasn't lost after all. She started toward the van, but a man yelled at her, "Come on, lass, get in line with th'others!" She turned around to do as he said. She knew he could see the lower part of her dress sticking to her legs with a dark wet stain. Without speaking, he took her by the shoulders with both his hands and pushed her ahead of him into the dark across a grassy field towards a small log building. They left unnoticed in the confusion. Eliza nearly fell twice, but she could see that he knew what he was doing. He was strong, like her Daddy. Maybe he would find her suitcase for her.

They stopped in front of the door of the small building. The man opened it with a key. He pushed her inside and followed, closing the door. Pulling a string in the middle of the room, he switched on a bare electric bulb. Three metal compartments with white curtains stood along one side of the room.

The man grabbed Eliza's upper arm and pulled her to the middle of the room. He demanded: "Strip off yer clothes." Eliza had never undressed in front of anyone before. Confused, she stood with her arms stiff by her sides, staring up at him, unmoving and unbelieving. She felt paralyzed. The man leaned his bulk into a shower stall and turned the taps. The water hit the metal floor with a bang that made Eliza blink. They didn't have running water at home and she had never had a shower before. With a sigh, the man leaned over her from behind and pulled off her jacket. He lifted each leg to remove her shoes and turned her around. He knelt in front of her, his pudgy fingers fumbling with the tiny buttons on the front of her dress. His full curly beard scratched her arm. The sickening smell of cigar smoke and whiskey drifted around her.

"No! No! I can do it," she protested. She pushed at his hands and stepped away. She turned her back to him and carefully took off her stockings, dress, and underwear. She folded the clothes over her arm and held them in front of her. The man grabbed her clothes and threw them to the floor. She stared up at him in silent terror. What did he want her to do now? Her legs could not move. He put his hands under her arms and lifted her easily into the air. Eliza gasped when he set her under the stream of cold water and snapped the curtain across the opening. Sobbing, tears mixing with the water running down her face, she crouched in the corner of the shower stall, her arms wrapped around her waist. Her whole body was shaking.

For the five years she was in the Chooutla school, Eliza would wake up in the night, struggling to scream but unable to. A repeating dream would not allow her to forget what happened next in that shower room. She would relive it through many dark nights.

A man stands outside the shower curtain, loudly complaining. He has a thick accent which puzzles Eliza; she can hardly understand him. "Y'know yer keepin' me from me sleepin', lassie. Hurry it up naw!"

He throws a towel over the curtain rod, and his huge bare arm reaches into the shower stall. Even her Daddy doesn't have that much hair on his arms. He turns off the taps. She struggles to dry herself with her stiff hands that won't work properly. She is shivering. But she's glad she has stopped crying.

He abruptly throws open the curtain, and suddenly more calm, his gaze passes over her body. She tries to cover herself with the towel. He grabs it from her, throws it over by the door, and kneels onto the wet floor. He looks down to her feet. His hand slowly moves from her ankle upwards on the inside of her leg until it can't go any farther. She can't breathe. She stands frozen. It's only when she starts screaming that he stops.

The man reached over to a box of old clothes in the corner of the shower room. He threw a clean cotton dress and a pair of panties at her and left without a word, slamming the door. Eliza dressed hurriedly and slipped her wet feet into her shoes. She put on her jacket and felt a little warmer. With her clothes bundled under her arm, she waited for long minutes, staring at the door. She didn't know if she was supposed to stay or go. She tested the door. It wasn't locked. Finally she opened it, her heart pounding. Her legs were shaking, but with her clothes clutched to her chest, she made herself run across the wide yard to the lighted part.

Eliza was met by a sudden explosion of girls bursting outdoors through a door at the end of one of the huts. They were chattering and giggling with each other. Whistles and loud calls from two women to keep quiet added to the chaos. She melted into the group of girls and decided to follow wherever they were going. They moved across the field. A supervisor stood at the top of the wooden stairs at the end of one of the huts and blew her whistle twice. She said hello and that her name was Marsha. She ordered the girls of Eliza's size into a line in front of her. The older girls were separated from the rest and taken away somewhere. "Hush now. Listen to me. Quiet over there!" Marsha frowned. Then with a tired smile, she said, "This is your home now, girls. Be sure to keep it clean and we'll all be happy here."

They filed up the stairs through the door into a room with a high round ceiling. They were inside Quonset Hut number 3. It was larger and brighter than anything Eliza had ever been inside of before. On both sides, in strict rows, were two dozen identical small beds covered in white. A girl who looked as if she had some authority came up to Eliza and asked her name. Eliza looked up at her blankly, her lips moving. No sound came out. "That's Eliza Maclean, Dawson City," Marsha called to the older girl, "She's Number 94." Silently, the girl pointed to the space that would be Eliza's and disappeared. Eliza sat uncertainly on the edge of the hard narrow bed, noise and girls all around her. Her head was spinning.

"Prayers, girls, evening prayers!" Marsha stood at one end of the room, clapped her hands together, and called, "Number 72, cut that out! I saw you! Now kneel beside your beds, girls!" Eliza had never prayed before. She looked at the other girls in the row ahead of her and did what they did. She kept her eyes open, although she could see that most of the others squeezed theirs tight. When they were silent, Marsha said, "55, it's your turn." One of the older girls loudly and emotionlessly recited a bedtime prayer with big words that Eliza could not understand like "obedience" and "diligence" and "industry".

After the "amen", Eliza saw the girl next to her shove a cardboard box under her bed. Eliza leaned over to look under her own. Her suitcase was miraculously there! She pulled it out. It had a large number in yellow crayon on the lid: 94. But *Eliza Maclean Dawson City* was still there near the handle, too. That's who I am, she thought, *that's me*. She told herself to memorize the number: 94. It must be important, it was so big, and Marsha had called her that, Number 94. She undid the buckle of her Daddy's old belt, and carefully folded her good red print dress and underwear into the suitcase. She would have to wash them in the morning.

There was a nightgown on the pillow but she simply took off her shoes and crawled under the blanket, covering her wet hair to keep warm. She tried to think about Daddy telling her stories about the olden days with Mommy, bringing her cookies in bed before she went to sleep. He was so far away. But something else kept her from remembering. There was a new thing she hadn't felt before: shame. She was terribly ashamed.

In her sleep, the sour smell of cigars and whiskey surrounded her and made her nauseous.

FINDING HOME

It was after 1:00 in the morning when Eliza pulled the old cardboard suitcase out from under her bed. The words her father had written in ink near the handle were hardly visible. Taking a pencil stub she kept in the drawer of her bedside table, she marked it more clearly: *Eliza Maclean Dawson City.* She had long ago scrubbed off the *94* someone had written with yellow crayon on the lid. Five years before, she had been taken to the Chooutla Residential School in Carcross, given that number, and told to put it on all her things. She was going home.

Eliza was safe moving around while the other girls slept. At almost fifteen, she was one of the group of older girls. They didn't have a supervisor with them at night. Earlier that evening, after she finished her assigned chore--washing the supper dishes --she had stolen the end of a loaf of bread, two apples, and some cheese from the kitchen. She stuffed the food in the suitcase with its few items of clothing and put on her heavy blue wool skirt with her green pullover sweater. "Blue and green should never be seen", one of the supervisors had told her, but she didn't care. It was early April, snow still on the ground, and she had to keep warm.

Eliza tossed the blankets on her bed to look as if she was still in it. With her suitcase in one hand and her jacket and shoes in the other, she took one last look at the pillow on the bed where she had smothered so many tears late at night. Some little girl from a village in the Yukon would be sleeping there next, maybe even at that moment in her own bed awake, worried about leaving home. Eliza was excited to finally be going home, but somehow sad, and not a little frightened.

The residential school was in a small cove on Nares Lake. It was a collection of several American Army huts left from building the Alaska Highway during the Second World War a few years before. Shallow Nares Lake was connected to the larger Bennett Lake by a short channel, where the tiny Indian community of Carcross was scattered along its shore. Eliza had not seen large lakes in the Klondike. There, the land was sliced by rivers and creeks in the bottom of protective valleys. The lakes made her uneasy. Their endless size and depths left her feeling weak and helpless. Constant wind from the coastal mountain peaks along Lake Bennett blew waves with white caps that pounded and chewed the sandy dunes on the shore. The wind made the waves seem alive, reaching out to capture her. She longed for the broad calmness of the Yukon River dotted with friendly islands where she camped with her Daddy. Sometimes she dreamed of someone she didn't know, an older Indian woman sitting in a boat. The woman would spread her arms wide, saying, "The river same like mother to me." The dream made her lonely and homesick.

The April wind blew relentlessly, tearing at Eliza's long hair as she stood looking across the arid valley filled with sand dunes under the scrub willow and pine. The ice on Nares Lake was covered with a thin layer of snow. It made her more comfortable when the lake was frozen and quiet. At night, it was nearly magical. In some parts the shallow lake had frozen to its muddy bottom; the resulting shifting of ice had caused slight hills and large cracks on its surface. It was a peaceful pale blue in the light from the waning moon. The path straight across the lake to the houses scattered along the shore was a darker shade of blue than the surface. She could imagine it as an open meadow without water underneath. That was where she took her last walk with Patsy.

****

Eliza was proud and amazed to be a close friend to Patsy Jim from Mayo. All the girls wanted to be Patsy's friend. She was called a natural leader by the school's staff, friendly with anyone who didn't cross her. One of the few students who could answer back to teachers and supervisors, Patsy managed to get away with it without too much trouble because she did it in a teasing and clever way, always joking. Nothing seemed to matter to her.

Eliza and Patsy were called the Odd Pair by the staff. Heavy and muscular, Patsy reached her full adult height early in adolescence, with the narrow hips and broad shoulders of many Athapaskan women. Tiny Eliza had to scramble to keep up to her long powerful stride when they walked. Patsy's complexion was much darker than Eliza's and her thick black hair was longer than anyone's. Even if she was punished for it, Patsy found a way to get out of having her hair cut as often as everyone else. She always found some excuse to be gone at hair cutting time. Sometimes she hid and the staff would give up trying to find her. "It's my head and I'll do what I want with it," she said to Eliza more than once, tossing her long braids.

Before she became close to Patsy, Eliza had withdrawn from the confusing, demanding world around her. She anticipated with relief the rare times when she could be alone, able to disappear from anyone's notice. She had quickly learned that the principles of survival were to be fast, quiet, and not to volunteer for anything unless it was absolutely necessary.

For long months, Eliza had endured the taunting voices of three other girls from Dawson. "Hiya Whitey, think you're so great, eh?" they would yell at her when the group was out of sight of the supervisor. Once one of them pushed her against the wall of the dormitory saying, "You don't belong here with us Indians. Why dontcha go home to your snob Whitey father?" Patsy heard the Dawson girls one day when they were bullying Eliza. She walked silently over and stood close in front of them, not saying a word, her hands on her narrow hips, staring. The girls eased their way out of her sight, mumbling. Eliza was speechless. Patsy said, "Come on, Eliza, let's go over to the bridge and see if there's any grayling yet." Eliza loved her from that day. She would do anything for her. A couple of nights later, Patsy invited her to join a trusted group of girls who regularly raided the kitchen for extra food and for the thrill of it. They called themselves The Invaders.

Sometimes Patsy and Eliza told each other stories about their separate homes as they walked through the thick willows beside the lake. They talked about running away and knew other children who had done that, mostly boys. Some of them, standing by the side of the road to Whitehorse, had tried to catch rides home with sympathetic travellers; others had sneaked onto the White Pass freight train when it passed through. Most had been returned to the school, but there was never a search started if they went missing until a week or so went by. The authorities simply waited for the child to appear back home to bring him back. That tactic usually worked. But the winter before last, one boy left at Christmas and the temperature had dropped to 45 below. His body was found the next spring. His arm reached out from underneath a melting snowdrift in a ditch beside the Alaska Highway only a few miles from his home on Kluane Lake. After that, for a few months, the school made more effort to find runaways.

When they had found the dead boy, Patsy said, "He was real stupid, eh? If I run away, I'll make sure that it's good weather."

"Will you take a ride? Maybe on the train?" Eliza asked.

"Nah, the secret is don't trust nobody. Too many snoops. And I'll stay off from the main road. Somebody from the school is sure to come along and make me come back to this damn place. And forget the train. They always look inside them freight cars when they stop. I'll just walk home."

"How'd you know how to find it?" Carcross was 400 miles from Dawson. Mayo wasn't even near Dawson.

"Oh, I'll get there OK," Patsy said, looking in the direction they had all come from. "I'll just *find* home," she said, laughing and waving her arm as if it was around the bend of the road they could see from where they sat.

On one of their long walks, Eliza was fascinated to hear Patsy tell her about what the janitor had done to her. Eliza had learned to stay away from him, but she thought Patsy was strong and safe from him just by being herself. He had caught Patsy three times in the wash house where she couldn't get away, pushed her against the wall and felt her all over, tickling her. Because of her size, Patsy was able to push him away. She went to the principal the second time it happened. She told him she was being rubbed in the wrong places by him when she went to the bathroom. The janitor was called into the office. He laughed, accusing Patsy of lying. He said that Patsy teased him into grabbing her by stealing his cigarettes and running away with them. Patsy was punished for lying. She was made to stay on her bed in their free time for a week and was told to read her Bible. She was watched every minute by students assigned the job because they were in trouble too. The students knew she hadn't lied. She wasn't the only one who hated to go to the bathroom but she was the only one with enough nerve to complain. After that, Patsy used the bush behind the girls' hut instead of the toilet.

Eliza had never told anybody about what Ben the male supervisor had done to her in the shower the first night she came to Chooutla, or all the other things that he had done to her later. On that walk, she told Patsy everything as they sat under the willows, looking out over Nares Lake. "Two years ago, Christmas, when it was quiet, Ben said he wanted to give me a special present," she said. "He stuck it in me, Patsy!"

"That bastard! That *bastard*!" Her face distorted with pain, Patsy put her arm around Eliza's shoulder and pulled her over to her chest.

Eliza's muffled voice whispered. "He grabbed me. I was cleaning up the kitchen. He shoved me into the pantry. Pulled my panties down, ripped them. Right there, he stuck it in me! It hurt, and I was bleeding. It made him mad to see the blood I think. He tried to put it in my mouth after. In my mouth!" She choked with nausea. "That was just...just the first time," she said, coughing and sitting up.

Patsy said nothing, her eyes squeezed shut. Eliza saw tears on her cheek and that made Eliza finally cry. It felt good to really cry, in the daytime, out loud. She had been crying inside, choking, for so long. "He talks to me dirty," Eliza said, sobbing, "In my sleep. Like he did. When he was...he was doing it. I must be dirty like he says. Patsy, do you think I'm just bad?"

Patsy shouted, "You ain't bad! He's the asshole. Don't think that! Me too. Ben did that to me too, twice. That shit bastard! He said if I told anybody, he would say I came into his bedroom at night when he was sleeping." Eliza's stomach churned. He had said he would do the same thing to her. "I punched him the last time, in the eye. I wanted to give him a black eye so he'd get in trouble. But it didn't work. He hit me hard, right here!" Patsy put her hand on her left breast. "He hasn't touched me for a couple of years. But he got me back. He made Marsha give me all the dirty work to do, cleaning the toilets, looking after them damn chickens." She stood up, shaking her fist in the air, and shouted, "I could kill all them fucking chickens! Chop off their heads! Eat 'em all. Make chicken stew out of 'em!"

"Chicken stew?!" Eliza giggled and put her hand over her mouth.

They both started to laugh. "Fried chicken then!" Patsy shouted. They rolled on the ground, threw handfuls of sand in the air, tore branches off the willows and threw them into the lake, laughing hysterically, tears rolling down their cheeks, shouting with each move, "Chicken and chips!" "Drumsticks!" "Chicken sandwiches!" Finally exhausted and dizzy, they lay side by side on the grass, staring at the sky, breathing hard, and smiling.

"Thank god he went away. Good fuckin' riddance," Patsy said.

"Yeah. Thank god he's gone," Eliza said. She felt a little less dirty, a little less alone. If it could happen to Patsy, it could happen to anyone. Maybe she wasn't so bad after all.

The day she heard about Ben leaving, Eliza was working in the laundry room, mending the boys' shirts with a group of girls. Marsha was talking in a quiet, sad tone to the other supervisor while they were having a coffee break. "Did you hear?" she said. "Benny's leaving next month. He asked for a transfer to the school in Portage La Prairie." Eliza closed here eyes and held her breath. Could it be true?

The other woman reached over and put her hand over Marsha's. "Yes," she said, "we just heard the news this morning at breakfast. We'll all miss him. He's such fun, isn't he! Always so cheerful with the children and interested in their games. And just when we're supposed to have a new school next year, out of these army huts. Too bad, Marsha. It looked like you were going to get married, eh?"

"Well, that residential school's near where I come from, you know. I told Benny I would be happy to go Outside too, with him. But he says there aren't any other placements out there just now. He has to go soon because he has a good chance of being promoted to vice-principal there if he goes now. A friend of his is leaving the post and says he'll help Benny get the job."

Eliza had been overwhelmed with such relief that she burst into tears before she could stop herself, right there at the sewing table. She covered her face with the shirt she was sewing. Florence, one of the Dawson girls across the table, noticed her and called, "Hey, Eliza! Crying, eh? Whatcha cryin' for? You that sorry your Benny man's going? You gonna miss him?" She would never have said that if Patsy had been in the room. The other girls at the table knew that Eliza had been singled out by Ben more than once for special duties. They giggled.

Marsha came over to Eliza. She put her arm around her shoulders, saying, "I know just how you feel Eliza. He's a real sweetheart, isn't he?" Eliza pulled away and threw the shirt down. She ran out of the hut, but not before she heard Florence laugh, "Maybe she's jealous, eh, Marsha? Well, he can't love everybody! No sir!"

****

Concentrating on skirting the road as she left Chooutla, Eliza flitted from one tree to another, out of sight. The piles of old snow on the sides of the road had melted with the spring sun during the day. Now with the cold night, the muddy puddles had a frozen surface. She was afraid that they would make a loud crunch if she walked across them. Her shoes were already wet and cold. She had not thought about picking up a pair of rubber boots from the rows of them by the door. Too late now.

Looking over to the staff houses and the boys' hut, Eliza saw that the windows were dark. The month before, Eliza was assigned the chore of working in the men's staff house, changing the beds. She liked it because it was something she could do alone, at her own speed, and it was quiet.

She had just finished making up the bed in the room set aside for the new vice-principal who was expected to arrive that day. She turned to the door to leave. There was Ben, coming through the doorway with a suitcase in one hand. His huge body filled the whole space. He smiled, leaning against the door jamb. "Well, guess who's here - my little Dawson love!" he said. "A welcome home present for the new vice-principal!"

Eliza heard someone scream; she never knew if it was herself. She held her breath, her hand covering her mouth. So the rumours were true: Ben was the new vice-principal. "Let me out of here," she said, panic in her voice. Her heart pounded in her ears. "Or I'll tell Marsha about you."

Ben snorted, "Marsha'd be pretty jealous if you did that. She's just happy to have me back, don't ya know?" When Ben left the year before, Marsha had not followed him to Manitoba as she had hoped she would. The gossip was that Ben had forgotten all about her after he left. He hadn't even written to her.

"You tell her anything about us and you'll really get yerself in trouble, little lassie. With a warning tone, he said, "She'd be real pissed with you." He moved into the room and put down his suitcase. Eliza made an attempt to dart through the door but he easily grabbed her arm. He pulled her roughly towards him. The smell of his sweat nauseated her. She was ten years old again, back in the shower room with him.

"Say," Ben said, "You're getting better looking all the time! Spunky too. I like that in my women." Forcing Eliza to look at him, he said carefully and quietly, "I'm warning ya, if ya tell anyone about us--you 'n' I, that is-- I'll give 'em the names of The Invaders. I know ya do it, stealing from the kitchen, like little rats in the night. And your girlfriend Patsy will get the worst part of it, I can tell ya. She'll get it straight from me. Ya know what I mean, right lassie?" He freed her arm. Turning to leave, he pointed at the bed, "Fix that up good now," he said, chuckling, "I like to be cosy when I'm in me bed."

The vice-principal was always a man, the only man allowed opportunities to be with the older girls. He would drive them in the van, where the rules were more relaxed. By giving them the jobs they liked, he could buy off anyone he wanted. He was in charge of recruiting students to help cook, a favourite chore for the girls, since then they could steal food. More importantly, he was responsible for disciplining any of the students who needed it, boys or girls. He could make daily life miserable for Eliza and Patsy if he wanted to.

If Eliza went to anyone in authority to complain, she knew it would be useless. They would ask for real proof of what he had done to her, like a witness. They would believe Ben before her, just because he was one of them. Ben was especially popular with the staff. The women on staff all thought he was attractive and fun. He could make the day shorter with his good humour and energetic approach to the dullest work of the school, always joking with them, flirting, and pretending to dance with them when he met them in the hallway. "A real charmer," the women said.

Instinctively, Eliza knew that the other girls wouldn't help her either. The girls Ben abused were afraid of him, and most of the others had a crush on him. Eliza's paler skin, pretty face, and small but rounded body made some jealous girls speculate about her being sexually involved with the men in the school. Some of the girls from Dawson had made sure Eliza knew the rumour that was being told about her lately. One of the teachers was giving her extra attention, helping her with her English assignments after class. They said that she was flirting with him. Maybe even doing more than that.

Eliza told Patsy about what Ben had said to her in the staff house. Patsy said without hesitation: "Time to go." They had talked about it endlessly since Christmas, planning every detail as they walked across the ice on Nares lake. Patsy would leave first. Eliza would stay another ten days so that nobody would suspect they had a plan together. Eliza would pretend she didn't know anything about Patsy's leaving. She would act depressed about losing her friend. Then she would follow exactly ten days later. They would meet up in Whitehorse where Patsy had a cousin. They would go together, somehow, north to Mayo and Dawson. Patsy gave her the cousin's name-- Helen Jim--and made her memorize how to find Helen's place in Whitehorse. "When I put Helen's name on a piece of paper and leave it in your Bible, you'll know that I'm leaving that night. Don't say anything, even to me. Rip up the piece of paper and throw it down the toilet." She made it sound like an exciting adventure and they laughed nervously.

It had worked just like Patsy said. Now here Eliza was, leaving exactly ten days after Patsy. A few minutes climb through the trees, and she was on the hill overlooking the school. She looked back for the last time at the army huts that had been her prison. Not even the dogs that were kept in a kennel by the principal's house had been aroused. No one was coming after her. She reflected with a shock that she was on her own. Really alone for the first time in her life. There was no one to tell her what to do. She stood, cold and uncertain for a minute. Maybe she should go back, but if they saw her, she would be punished. Thoughts of Ben waiting for her made her stomach churn. "Help me, Patsy; help me," she whispered to the sky.

Legs stiff with fear, she turned away from the school. She knew she could not do it alone, so she became two people. She could do that sometimes while Ben was hurting her. One Eliza was on the ground, doing the work of trudging along, not feeling anything, while her other self was flying above, watching her go along the path to the road, taking care of her, encouraging her. She thought of this other person as sort of half Patsy and half herself. Patsy stayed with her all that night along the dark and empty road. As she made her way, Eliza gradually became invigorated, elated with the thrill of freedom and adventure. Her two selves became one and she smiled.

****

The day before Eliza left Chooutla, Dave Maclean sat on the uncomfortable wooden bench against the wall outside Father Malcolm's church office. His large hands twisted the grey wool toque he held in his lap. He had been sent a letter in the mail from the Anglican priest to come to the rectory to hear a report about Eliza. Maybe she would be coming home at last.

Dave let himself think about that day five years before when he had stood alone on the river bank watching his little Eliza as she hung onto the railing of the steamer *Klondike,* leaving for the school in Carcross. Until that moment, he had been very certain that he was doing the right thing for both of them. But when the paddlewheeler had turned the bend and he slowly walked away, he thought about the empty cabin he was going home to. He had put his hands in his pockets. The oranges! He had forgotten to give her the two oranges that he promised her as a special surprise! Dismayed, he nearly cried, gazing at the oranges in his hands. He lifted his arms and threw them as far as he could into the middle of the river.

The morning Eliza left, Dave sat unmoving at the empty table in the silent cabin, letting himself grieve for his wife Maggie. Now he would be lonely for Eliza too. Later, he pushed himself up from the table and forced himself to work in the garden, tearing out the dead vegetation, getting it ready for winter. In the afternoon he was hungry and went inside. For a long time, he sat playing with the sandwich he made before he finally began to eat the tasteless food.

Father Malcolm startled Dave into the present. He appeared from his living quarters through the connecting door, an apparition of a oversized raven in his swirling black cassock. A large metal cross hanging from a heavy chain bounced against his waist. He wordlessly opened the office door, waved Dave in, and strode across the room, holding the cross against his belly so it wouldn't hit the desk when he sat down.

"Is it time for Eliza to come home?" Dave asked without hesitation as Father Malcolm settled himself. She had been gone three more years than he thought it would be when he let her go. Dave had never managed to save enough from trapping to pay her way to Dawson on the plane. Now with the new road to Whitehorse and ice bridges or ferries over the rivers, it would be cheaper to bring her back, winter or summer. It was a good year for beaver and he had already saved enough for her trip. He wouldn't need to take the Church's money to finally bring her home.

"I can assure you, as I have before, Mr. Maclean, that the more time Eliza spends at Chooutla, the better it will be for her," Father Malcolm said. His hand reached for his long greying beard and began to stroke it like a cat lying on his chest. "I have to tell you that the vice-principal at the school has requested that she stay over again this summer to assess whether she should stay yet another year. She is not doing as well as she might in the academics and we would like her to have a good start before she leaves for good." With a quick smile and a wave of his hand, "Of course this is entirely up to you," he said. "We don't usually ask for the parents' permission, but then most of the parents can't read our letters to them, as you know."

Stay over this summer. Maybe another year. They needed his permission. Dave recalled what Eliza had said about being at the school in summer, in one of the few notes he had received from her. Looking at the priest directly, he said, "Somebody told me that when they stay at the school in the summer they have to help work in the garden, and sew clothes, and clean the buildings. Is that true?"

Father Malcolm smiled and nodded slightly. He flipped his beard away from his chest as if to give it air. "Yes, Mr. Maclean, to some degree, that's true. We are not a rich church, contrary to some people's belief. The work the older children do is a necessary contribution to the good of everyone, to prepare for the coming year. But remember, she is there to learn how to be a wife and mother as well as to learn to read and write. The ladies there have the time in the summer to teach her essential things like how to sew and to look after the younger children. She is learning those things at the same time as she is helping pay her way, remember."

"I suppose she is learning...things I can't teach her..." Dave turned his cap over and over in his hands.

"That is perfectly true, Mr. Maclean. I'm glad you see it that way. Also remember that she will get special attention during the summer for the subjects she's having difficulty with. There are fewer children then. The teaching staff will have more time for her. They are quite devoted, as you know."

Putting his glasses on, Father Malcolm coughed and said, "Eliza apparently needs to have more individual attention in English than they can give her during the regular school term." He opened a thin file sitting on the desk, sighed, and read in a monotone from the file: "'Eliza has not done well in school because she is afraid to speak up. She has learned to have good manners but she is shy. It seems like she will not embarrass herself'... good heavens," he mumbled, "they've spelled embarrass wrong...'embarrass herself by asking questions and then not being able to understand the answers.' That's what it says here."

Dave offered, "You know, she always had ear trouble. She had lots of ear infections when she was younger. Maybe she can't hear properly."

Father Malcolm looked at Dave over his glasses. "Yes, yes. You told me that before. And as I said then, they would have checked that out long ago, Mr. Maclean. We give them a thorough physical examination as soon as they arrive." He shuffled some papers in the file. "It says here that there is a new vice-principal who came this spring who is especially good at work instruction. He was there before...Ben Shaw I think it is. Yes, that's what it says. I know him. Ben has been away for awhile, in Manitoba I believe. He was very well liked by all the staff and children. He's been promoted. An excellent choice. He'll make sure Eliza has enough experience to help her find work when she leaves."

Father Malcolm dismissed Dave by standing up. "We must think of the good of the children at all times, Mr. Maclean. If you agree, I will tell them you'll allow her to stay over the summer, then."

Dave left without saying anything. He would make sure she came home at the end of the summer. He would go down, bring her back if he had to. He would have enough money for his trip, saved from the summer work he could get in town. He had been asked to help with that new hotel they were building on Third Avenue.

****

The wind died as Eliza got farther from Carcross. When daylight and an early car coming in the distance forced her into the bush, she found a dry spot under a tree. She ate half of the cheese and curled up with her head on her suitcase. She was five miles from Carcross. Before she closed her eyes, she decided she would spend the days sleeping on the driest ground she could find under the trees. She would walk along the road only at night. There was very little traffic. If there was a vehicle at night, she would be able to see the lights before they saw her.

Terrified of bears coming by, Eliza slept fitfully that first day, startled by mysterious intermittent cracking in the trees. At night, when she got up to leave in the moonless dark, she wandered through the bush in the wrong direction looking for the road. She had to make her way around a shallow pond through thick bushes, and it took much of the time before midnight. The marshy ground soaked her shoes and socks. Coming upon a meadow, she looked up into the black sky and recognized a group of stars shaped like the dipper they had in the water pail at home. Her father had shown her how he found his way when there was no moon with the same cluster in the sky, half way to the top of the sky from the horizon. She heard his voice say what he had said then: "Keep it in front of you and you'll find home."

By early dawn, Eliza found the road. She didn't know that she was only a few hundred yards from where she had left the road the day before. Exhausted, she sat on some deadfall trees and ate the last of her bread out of her suitcase. She pushed herself through thick willows to a pond she had walked around and knelt to drink the coffee-coloured water from her cupped hand. She took off her shoes and socks. It was warmer that way and they might get dry. Under the willows at the side of the pond, she slept until the sun in her eyes wakened her. She felt warm for the first time. The rest of the day she spent picking and eating old berries left from the fall. All her food was gone.

The third night Eliza had decided she wouldn't leave the road, and would hide in the ditch if she had to. She plodded along the gravel road, her suitcase banging against her leg with each step that was harder than the last in the mud. The wind made a drizzling rain penetrate her wool clothing so that her skirt clung to her legs. It never seemed that far, the few times the school took them on trips in the van. Her shoes were thick with mud and her skirt had sticky lumps of pitch and pine needles on it. She had slipped down a steep incline to a pond looking for water and a place to rest earlier in the day. She had scratched her left hand badly. It was red and beginning to swell.

Suddenly light flashed on her from behind. A pickup truck curved around the bend. She hadn't heard it over the whistling of the wind in the trees. Leaping away from the road like some frightened animal, she dropped her suitcase and crouched in the ditch. The truck motor stopped. A door slammed. She heard the crunch, crunch, crunch of heavy footsteps on the gravel. She squeezed her eyes shut and put her hands over her ears. In her exhaustion, she prayed that she would disappear.

A stocky male figure waited a few moments at the top of the ditch, peering, his hands on his hips. "What have we got here?" he puzzled aloud. "Mary!" he yelled back to the truck, "Come here and see what you think."

Mary was already coming. When she caught up to him, she said, "Morris, for God's sake, you know as well as I do that's a kid." She called to Eliza through the dark: "Are you OK? Are you hurt?" Mary stepped down the side of the ditch, noisily sliding in the mud and stones. She reached the bundle of wet clothes crouching on the ground and put her hand out to touch Eliza. Eliza jumped up, running blindly a few yards away in the darkness, slipping in the mud. She fell, landing on her bottom. Finally she gave way to despair, sitting on the muddy ground. She covered her face. "Leave me alone," she sobbed. "Just go away. I'm OK."

"Well, you don't look OK to me," Mary laughed. "Looks like another runaway from the school, Morris. Come on, give me a hand with him." She called, "Don't worry, sonny, we won't take you back." She made her way along the ditch toward Eliza, pushing aside the long wet grass, her plump, middle-aged body moving awkwardly.

Eliza was too exhausted to move. "I don't believe you!" she shouted. As a last defense when Mary drew closer, she said, "Just leave me alone. I'm OK. Go away!"

"Hey, this one's got a skirt on. By damn, it's a girl! Morris!" Mary called, "For Christ's sake, get over here. Pronto!"

Stopping within touching distance of Eliza, Mary said sternly, "Look, little gal, I'm too old to stand here in the rain and mud and argue with you. I will not be responsible for you catching pneumonia, and I sure as *hell* don't want to get sick either." She leaned over to look into Eliza's face. With a sigh, she said, "And we won't send you back. I promise you that. Get that suitcase, Morris. Let's get home." Morris retrieved the suitcase from the ditch while Mary dragged frail Eliza onto the roadside by her arm. Struggling to get loose, Eliza sat on the road. Mary lifted her up, and holding her around the waist from behind, she moved her across the road to the truck.

Exasperated, Morris said, "That's it!" He pointed down the road and shouted, "Look whatever-your-name-is, we live at the end of the next road on the right. If you could use a warm meal and a place to sleep, you are welcome. You can walk there if you have to. It's your call. But don't take any more of our time. I'm hungry and I want to get home." Morris threw Eliza's suitcase in the back of the truck on top of a pile of lumber. Eliza stopped struggling and Mary let her go. The couple watched in surprise as Eliza obediently walked around the truck to the passenger side and opened the door. Morris' strict voice had brought back the echo of her father, and she had to go wherever her suitcase went.

With Eliza in the centre, the three rode in silence along a bumpy side road until they reached a log cabin a mile from the main road. A half-grown black and white husky pup raced through the truck's lights to greet them, his tail whirling the measure of his relief and glee. Morris jumped on the brakes to avoid htting the dog and laughed, "Looks like Taku has learned to stay home finally."

Mary got out of the truck and held the door open for Eliza. "You stay out here for awhile," Mary instructed her husband. "She's got to change clothes."

Inside, Eliza washed her hands and face in cold water that Mary had splashed from a bucket into a washpan. Mary noticed Eliza's scratched hand and found a tin of antiseptic for her on the shelf near the stove. She lit the fire wordlessly while Eliza changed her wet skirt and sweater for the damp ones in her suitcase. Mary handed her a cooked potato, and Eliza gratefully munched it, sitting at the home-made wooden table. Slamming two cast-iron frying pans onto the surface of the stove, Mary threw in three generous moose steaks and cooked potatoes. They could hear Morris as he carried lumber from the truck and threw it into the shed.

"Still cold in here yet," Mary said. She disappeared into the back room. "Wrap up in this," she said, throwing Eliza a sleeping bag. Eliza crawled into the sleeping bag and lay on the couch with Taku curled up at her feet. She was warm for the first time in days. By the time Mary had finished cooking, she was asleep.

Morris came into the cabin and placed a box of groceries on the floor by the door. "Did you mean it, not telling the school?" Morris asked quietly when he saw Eliza was asleep.

"Damn right," Mary said over her shoulder from the stove. "You know as well as I do what goes on there. D'you think she's doing this just for fun?"

"Then what're we going to do with her? We don't know where she comes from. Or her name even."

"Well, we'll just have to find that out, won't we." Mary pulled three plates out of the warming oven above the stove and filled them with steaks and potatoes.

"Damn. You meddle too much," Morris said. "We're going to get in trouble, mark my words."

They sat at the table. Mary chewed her steak in silence, thinking. "This steak's tougher than the last one, damn it all," she said absently. "Better get a younger moose next time, old man."

Eliza awoke after midnight. The fire had gone out, and her damp hair was cold against her scalp. At first she thought she was at home in the Dawson cabin with her father, but everything was out of place and it smelled different. She puzzled over where she might be for a moment but then the events of a few hours before came back. She sat up. The couple was asleep. She could hear Morris snoring in the room next to the couch.

Eliza was hungrier than she could ever remember being. In the dark, she felt around the table for something to eat and her hand brushed the plate of moose steak and potatoes that Mary had left on the table for her. She lifted the steak and bit into it. It was cold, but it was the best food she had ever eaten. Taku whimpered at her side, so she gave him a piece of gristle out of her mouth to keep him quiet.

Eliza's eyes became used to the dark, and she somehow found her suitcase and shoes. She gathered the damp clothes Mary had laid by the stove and wrapped the rest of the steak in a blouse. With her clothes over her arm, she pushed open the door as quietly as she could. The rain had stopped. The yard was pale grey in the light of a new moon that appeared and disappeared behind a scattering of dark moving clouds. She stepped down the stairs from the porch with Taku racing ahead of her, his wiggling body and wagging tail displaying his pleasure at seeing a human awake. He ran back to her, sniffed at her ankles, and yelped loudly. Eliza had stepped on one of his paws.

Eliza put her suitcase on the ground to finish packing it and waved her hands at the dog. She spoke as loudly as she dared. "Shut up Taku! Go away! Shoo! Dammit!" He jumped up towards her hands, and she resigned herself to carrying him back into the cabin.

She had reached the wood pile near the steps when she heard Mary's exasperated voice saying from the doorway, "For Christ's sake, girl, don't you know a good thing when you see it? Smarten up. Wherever you live, you won't make it there like that."

"I'll get to Whitehorse. I won't go back to Carcross. I won't."

"So it's Whitehorse is it? Got any relatives I know?"

"I'm just stopping there on my way. Then I'll ask how to find Dawson." Eliza clamped her lips shut. She had said too much.

"Dawson City, eh? Now, that's...let's see...well over 350 miles away. A mighty long walk." By this time, Mary was sitting on the porch steps, huddled in a thick sweater over her long nightgown, lighting a cigarette. She tucked her slippered feet under her nightgown and blew out smoke. "Look, it's not the first time we seen kids run away. If you want the truth, I don't blame you one bit. You should be home with your family. They must miss you too. I know I'd never put my kids in there. I'd miss 'em too much."

"You don't have to. You're not a Indian." Eliza put Taku on the ground near her feet. He chewed on her shoelaces so she picked him up again.

"No?" Mary mused, "Depends on how you look at it I guess." She smiled and spoke with relish. "My father and my mother, they was both half Indian. Dad was from the Alaska coast, near Juneau, and Mum she came from here, Tagish to be exact. Morris is a half-breed mixture too just like me. Neither one of us never got to school at all because we was always in the goddam bush. Seems to me I'm as good an Indian as anybody else."

Eliza sat on the chopping block next to the axe and rubbed the warm soft ears of the husky pup. Mary's warmth and directness made her comfortable. She looked up at the figure sitting on the steps and asked, "So where are your kids if they're not in residential school?"

"Oh, too late for that. All of them is growed up. Most is having babies of their own now. Damn, that time just goes by too fast. We got eight kids, Morris and me, five boys, three girls." She named them all. "Number one died in her crib and number eight he died with whooping cough. November 8, 1931. Six of them in the middle, still alive. Got seven grandchildren now too. All healthy brats." She named them.

Eliza lowered Taku to the ground and put her hands in the pockets of her jacket. She poked the pup with her foot and he rolled over on his back, his paws playing with her foot. They both watched Taku silently. Eliza tried to imagine what it would be like to have five brothers and sisters. It would be nice. She would feel protected. Mary threw her cigarette into a patch of snow by the stairs and said, "Well, kid, tell me your name at least. I'm tired of calling you nothing...make something up if you want."

Eliza took advantage of the offer, "My name's Patsy."

"No last name, I guess, eh?"

"Nope." They both felt Eliza's sudden distrust as an intrusion. A silence fell in the night, something nearly tangible in the air between the steps and the wood pile.

"Well, Patsy-from-Dawson, how do I make you believe that we won't turn you in?" Mary rubbed her chin in mock seriousness. "Maybe this will help: I been thinking about what you could do. My good friends Anna and Donald James live in Carcross, and they said they were headed for Mayo this week, for Easter, before the ice bridges give out. Maybe they could give you a ride at least part the way home, to the road going to Dawson. I could go see them tomorrow and ask them if you want."

"I gotta get to Whitehorse. Somebody's waiting."

"Well, even that's on the way, if you don't want the whole ride. I can tell them you're a niece of mine," Mary offered. Another long pause ended with Mary pulling herself up with a grunt and saying, "Damn it all, I'm too old and too cold to sit here all night, Patsy. Make up your mind. I'm going back to bed."

Eliza stood up, watching Mary go into the cabin. Maybe she would sleep over that night anyway. They would probably give her breakfast too. She picked up her suitcase and went back inside. She undressed and spread her damp clothes by the stove. Mary had started the fire again, and Eliza crawled gratefully into the warm sleeping bag on the couch. Taku jumped up, snuggling against her feet.

When Mary and Morris returned from Carcross the next afternoon, Mary said her friends had decided to go to Dawson first before going on to Mayo. They had a sick cousin there they wanted to see anyway. Mary's eyes nearly closed as she smiled and said, "That way, you can get a ride the whole way." Eliza frowned. Mary said, "Don't worry, they didn't ask me any questions about you being my niece. They got patched-on relatives of their own sometimes."

"But I gotta see somebody in Whitehorse." Maybe they could take Patsy to Mayo too.

"They always stop a couple of days to visit his brother in Whitehorse. The big city, you know. They gotta spend some time seeing everybody. They just take their time when they travel."

Two mornings later, they were eating breakfast, waiting for the James' to arrive. Eliza took a bite of a piece of toast and asked Mary for her last name. "I can write to you when I get home. Daddy can send you something for looking after me."

Mary ripped off the front of an old envelope. She pointed out her name and address and gave it to Eliza. "No need to send anything, Patsy." She shook her index finger at her. "You just promise to help somebody else out some day, somebody who needs it. But I want you to let me know how you make out, so you better write."

Eliza looked up from the paper in her hand and said, "My name is Eliza Maclean, Indian Dave Maclean's girl."

"Oh, really?" Mary raised her eyebrows in mock surprise. "Eliza. Pretty name. Prettier than Patsy I'd say." She looked as if something had just occurred to her: "Then I guess your name is the same as the one on your suitcase!" They both laughed.

"Sorry for lying. Patsy's my best friend," Eliza said.

"I bet she is."

Before Eliza got into the James' truck, Mary hugged her. "Anna says they're staying in Whitehorse for two days," she said. "You can stay with them. Is that enough time for you?"

"Sure is." Eliza smiled. Mary hadn't asked her questions about who it was she was going to see. All she had to do now was find Helen Jim. That should be easy. Then she would only have to talk the James' into taking both of them home. Patsy could even come to Dawson with her. They wouldn't have to worry about finding home. The James' knew where to go to get to Dawson and to Mayo too.

It was crowded in the cab of the pickup truck, so Eliza climbed into the back with the James' three dogs. She wrapped herself up in a blanket and was happy to be out in the fresh air away from the two heavy smokers in the front. That night in Whitehorse, Eliza said to Anna, "I have a cousin here I have to see. Helen Jim. Do you know how I can find her?" She recited the memorized directions from Patsy.

"Don't know her personally, but Donald can sure find her," Anna said, smiling. "He can find just about anybody you can name in Whitehorse."

The next afternoon, Donald dropped Eliza off in front of the door of Helen Jim's place in Whiskey Flats. A tall fat woman leaned around the door and looked with curiosity at Eliza standing on the stairs. Smoke swirled out the door from the cigarette in her hand. Without waiting for Eliza to say anything, she said, "Hi! You must be Eliza. You want Patsy?" When Eliza nodded, she beckoned with her cigarette. "Come on in and sit down. It's good to see you." Eliza went inside and stood by the door. Five men and women were crowded in the middle of the small kitchen. They sat at a table playing cards, reaching around several beer bottles. Three small children played on the floor in the next room.

"Where's Patsy?" Eliza asked.

"You know, Patsy was here. Right up until the day before yesterday," Helen told her. "Too bad. She thought you weren't coming so I got her a ride home to Mayo. I guess you shoulda been here awhile ago, eh?"

There was a hard lump in Eliza's chest. She was alone. She had to find home by herself. "I stayed with somebody on the road for a couple of days," she mumbled.

Helen took her arm, drawing her into the room. "This here's Eliza, Patsy's friend from Carcross," she said. She turned to Eliza and pointed with her thumb toward the card players. "Them's my poker playing buddies from next door. Don't pay no attention. They's harmless."

One of the men said, "Yo!" to her without looking up, waving his cards in the air in greeting.

"Come on in, find a chair, sit down," Helen urged.

"No thanks," Eliza said quietly, turning towards the door, "I better go." They knew enough about her already. It made her uneasy. What if they told the school she was in Whitehorse?

"No, no, come in." Helen tugged at Eliza's sleeve. "Patsy, she left you a note...if I can find it." She beckoned Eliza into the hallway toward the bedroom, and putting her hand on Eliza's shoulder, said, "Don't worry, we're all friends here. Nobody wants to see you go back to Carcross, eh? Really. You can trust us." Helen rescued her purse from a little boy on the floor. "I know that note is in here." She dug into the contents. "Here it is!" she exclaimed in surprise. She handed a tightly folded piece of pink paper to Eliza. "The back of my birthday card," Helen said apologetically.

"Thanks," Eliza said, stuffing the note into her jacket pocket without reading it. She said goodbye to Helen and left the house. Down by the Yukon River she found an old railroad tie to sit on and opened the note. It had two hearts drawn at the top.

> *Dear Eliza, I hope your reading this cuz that means you made it to. I know you will. I stayed as long as I can and just had to go. Write to me in Mayo. I'l be there a long time I hope.*
>
> *love, Patsy*
>
> *PS--you know, you are the most nicest and most bravest person I know*

Eliza looked across the river. Her heart beat wildly. Maybe she *was* brave. She had done something brave already, coming all this way. Maybe she could find home on her own. Maybe even as her own real self, not being part of Patsy.

It was a leisurely journey to Dawson with Anna and Donald. Long overnight stops at the homes of friends and relatives who lived at the ice bridges crossing the rivers at Carmacks, Pelly, and Stewart filled the time with laughter and beer. Eliza knew they had to be visited or it would be an insult. Everyone welcomed Eliza, feeding her as though she were starving, insisting she eat more than she could, but not asking any questions. They somehow knew she didn't want to talk about herself or why she was travelling. When she was comfortable, she boasted about her father. Most of them had heard of Indian Dave Maclean from Dawson.

They arrived in Dawson after supper one night. Donald followed her directions to get to the Maclean cabin as she shouted them from the back of the truck. He stopped, opened the tailgate, and helped her and her suitcase off the truck bed.

Eliza stood in the dark street with her suitcase in her hand and looked out over the Klondike River. She told herself, "I did it. I found home. By myself. I'm back home. In Dawson." She had to say it aloud to be sure that it was true. After wanting to be there so badly, she was frightened and unsure as she approached the lighted window. Maybe he would send her back. She took a few steps, hesitated, and put her suitcase on the ground.

Anna appeared at her side and said, "Let's go, kiddo," picking up her suitcase. Eliza followed her and Anna opened the door without knocking. They stood in the doorway together.

Dave was at the table, reading a newspaper he had spread over his supper plate. He looked up, his eyes narrowed in puzzlement. "Now, Mr. Maclean," Anna said, "I know you won't be pleased with us bringing your daughter home like this." She put Eliza's suitcase down in front of herself. Holding her hand up to ward off any objection, she said, "Before you say anything, I want to talk to you about it first, so please just listen." Eliza turned to her, her eyes wide in amazement. Nobody talked to Daddy like that. Anna said, "I couldn't just take off without saying something, Eliza."

Eliza's mouth was open as she watched Anna stand in the doorway charming her father with non-stop talking. "She is a fine young girl, this daughter of yours. We've been very pleased to have her company, me and my old man. And no doubt she has some pretty good reasons for leaving that Carcross school. As much as I respect the Anglican Church and as much as I am a God-fearing Christian, I don't abide with this taking kids away and putting them in something that is more like a jail than a school. Not that I blame you for it, no sir. Anyways, so we helped her out, and that's that, eh? Not her fault, any of it."

Dave silently turned in his chair. Anna continued, "Eliza has done nothing but talk about you, how proud she is of you, and how much she wants to see you, this whole trip. So if I were you, I'd welcome her back home like you should."

Eliza stood in the doorway and began to cry with exhaustion and confusion, covering her face with her hands. "Please let me stay, Daddy," came as a muffled sound. "I hated it there without you."

Dave pulled his large body up from his chair. "Of course she's welcome back home," he said to Anna. "She's had enough school for both of us I think. Come here, little one." Anna stepped outdoors and closed the door. Eliza ran into her Daddy's arms. She had found home at last.

MARRIED INDIAN WAY

Eliza narrowed her eyes against the summer sun glaring off the Yukon River. In the middle of Walter Thomas' long riverboat, she clutched the seat with both hands. She was afraid to let go to tighten the scarf around her head and she could feel it slipping off. Walter guided the unpainted plywood vessel into a channel that would take them downstream a mile or so from Dawson City to the Indian village of Moosehide. He frowned under his baseball cap, making him look older than his eighteen years. The wind whipped his long black hair around his shoulders. She could see the muscles in his arms stiffen under his shirt. He grasped the motor handle, increasing speed, in complete control.

Eliza had agreed to go with Walter, but now she was beginning to regret it. While she was at the Chooutla Indian residential school 400 miles to the south, she had dreamed of being on the river again as she had been when she was very young. But now it felt dangerous and uncomfortable.

"Don't worry!" Walter shouted over the high-pitched buzz of the motor. "It's safe. Like walking." Eliza's face relaxed and she gave him a quick, cheerless smile. He glanced at her bare legs. At fifteen, Eliza had the body of a woman, but she was smaller than the other girls her age. Seeing Walter watching, Eliza pulled the skirt of her flowered cotton dress down with one hand and tucked it under her leg more securely.

In a few moments they passed the rock slide on the side of the mountain looming over the North End of Dawson City. The massive gash, shaped like the hide of a moose, gave the Indian village its name. A legend said that when an invading party of Indians from the south had camped on the riverbank, the Trondek in the area had danced at the top of the mountain, creating the slide and killing their enemies. Early in the Klondike Gold Rush, before the turn of the century, the Trondek had been forced to settle downriver in Moosehide. The move was meant to keep them away from the chaos of the thousands of Whitemen from the south invading the gold-rich country. A horizontal path, used for fifty years, was clearly visible across the face of the slide.

Walter and Eliza were bringing groceries from town to his mother, Annie. A few families still lived all year in small log cabins at Moosehide, fishing and working traplines. At Christmas Annie would come into Dawson for a few weeks to visit at her sister's, where Walter and two of his brothers stayed. The three younger children were at the Chooutla school in Carcross.

Rounding a slight bend in the river, Walter steered abruptly right towards the landing where three identical riverboats were moored. The motor groaned in protest, coughed, and nearly stopped. Unconcerned, he teased it back to life and, turning at an angle, let the current push them into shore. The village disappeared from sight as they drew closer to the steep river bank. When Walter turned the motor off, they heard several dogs yelping and howling, warning owners of their arrival.

The crunch of gravel scraping the bottom of the boat made Eliza cling to the gunwale. She tried to stand up. "Don't get up yet, eh?" Walter said, stepping past her onto the bow. He grabbed a curled rope and jumped easily out, pulling the boat to shore. "OK. Now it's OK," he said. He held his free hand out to help her, but she stepped over the side without taking it. Water splashed over her shoes. Walter tied the rope to a willow and unloaded two wooden boxes. Picking up the smallest of the boxes, Eliza stumbled up the rough trail ahead of Walter.

"Sure has changed, this place," Eliza said when they reached the top. Two rows of a half dozen identical log cabins with sod roofs overlooked the river. Annie's cabin was third in the front row, counting from the small white Anglican church which stood at one end of the village. A few poplar trees as tall as the church steeple separated the church from the largest building in the community, the two-storey school.

Putting down her box, Eliza nodded towards the school with its boarded windows. "Not many people now, eh?"

"Yeah. School closed last year. So now they got to find places to live in Dawson or send the kids to Carcross."

"Carcross! I hate that place. Better not go to school at all."

"Well, I liked school. But anyway, that's life, eh?" He pointed. "This way to Mom's. Still in the same old place," he chuckled. Eliza reached down for the box she had carried. "Just leave that box. I'll get it later," Walter said.

"It's OK. I can do it." She picked it up.

"Me, I had to quit school, you know," Walter said as they walked. "Wish I could go, but Ma needs the help I guess." Walter had spent a few months in Carcross but his father was killed in Italy during the War. As the eldest son of six children, Annie kept him home to help the family. He worked as a labourer for the City of Dawson and was paid well.

"How come the school closed anyways? Thought that missionary Baptist guy and his wife was here forever."

"You didn't hear?" Walter said.

"Didn't hear what?"

He looked away, grinning, his face reddening. "Well, you know, he was...he was feeling up the kids, eh?"

Eliza stopped walking. She shivered. "That's disgusting!"

"Yeah. My Ma caught him one day behind the school outhouse with his pants down." He laughed in mild disbelief and stopped on the path. "Damned if he didn't have one of the little Charlie boys with him. A boy! Not even a girl, can you believe it? Don't know which one, but maybe..."

"Don't tell me any more about it. I'm not interested," Eliza said. She pushed ahead of him on the trail.

They found Annie behind her cabin, kneeling on the ground. Her stocky body leaned over a moosehide that was draped over a tree stump. She was holding a thick butcher knife with both hands, rhythmically scraping off the dark brown hair. An open fire beside a rough wooden table covered with dishes and food kept a pot of water boiling.

"Ah! He did brought you, Eliza Maclean," Annie smiled, turning to face them. "Real good see you." Her cheery, round face glistened with sweat under her turbaned head. She pulled herself up, put the butcher knife on the table, picked up a towel and wiped her forehead, waving her hand for them to put the boxes on the table. "Sit. Sit down," she said. Eliza sat on a bench beside the table. "Make tea, Walter," Annie said.

"I gotta go to the graveyard," Eliza said, "Daddy wants me to fix up Mommy's grave. He hasn't been down since the king salmon run ended."

"Tea first," Annie said. Walter spilled two spoonfuls of loose tea into the blackened tin teapot, filled it with boiling water, and brought it over to the table where Annie had seated herself across from Eliza. "Maggie Taylor," Annie said, nearly closing her eyes, savouring the name. "Your mama good friend of mine till day she died, you know. She live right over there," she nodded her head towards the far end of the village, "with your dad Dave Maclean and you, little one. White guy, but sure good to her. I sure do miss her. That TB, real bad. Took her, took other my friends. Family too."

Eliza thought of the happy times living in Moosehide with both her mother and father, in that little log cabin at the end of the row, overlooking the river. "I was only seven when Mommy left us," she said. "I wish those days were back again."

Annie said "My, my, we all think that, little girl. Jesus sometime take the best people to be with him. Nice you fix that grave, Eliza, 'member your Mom. Good thing." Eliza and Walter were silent, waiting for Annie to direct the conversation. "Got those cookies I like, Walter?" Annie asked. "Them chocolate kind?"

"Sure thing, Ma." Walter pulled a bag of cookies out of the box, opened it, and pushed it toward his mother. All three took a cookie each. They concentrated on the ritual of pouring the tea, stirring sugar and canned milk into their cups.

"Maggie, she small, like you," Annie said, biting into a cookie. "She sew real good. Real good. Best one 'round for make mukluks, yes sir." She gazed at the river, nodding as if it was displaying scenes from their shared past.

"She showed me how, even before I was six," Eliza said. "We didn't sew any hides at Carcross, though. Just Whiteman clothes. Maybe I forgot how."

"You just come visit me. I show you. You be surprised. Never forget them things. That woman work. Important," Annie said, pointing her cookie at Eliza.

"OK. I can help you tan hides."

"You be good help. Come any time. You got too much Whiteman way. Learn Indian way."

"I want to," Eliza smiled.

"I can bring you down in the boat," Walter said.

Eliza turned to Walter and said, "I know the trail over the slide. I can walk to Moosehide." She put her teacup on the table and stood up. "Think I'll go up to the graveyard now."

"Want me to come with you?" Walter asked, jumping up from his seat on the bench.

"It's OK. Jeez, I been here before, lots of times with Daddy."

"I know that! But Ma said they seen a bear with two cubs around the raspberry bushes back of the school last week. Right, Ma?"

"She probly gone now," Annie said, "But better look out." She picked up the butcher knife to begin scraping the moosehide again.

Eliza hesitated and frowned at Walter. "OK, come with me. Whatever you want."

"Guess seeing a bear is worse than being with me, eh?" Walter laughed beside her. She did not answer. She waited for him to go ahead of her on the short path up the hill to the graveyard.

Eliza stopped at some high bush cranberry growing with bright green berries on the side of the trail and broke off some branches. She said self-consciously, "Daddy told me: 'always leave something alive on Mommy's grave.' This should be OK. Lots of berries even though they aren't ripe yet."

Standing behind Eliza at her mother's grave, Walter watched as she knelt and pulled some sprouting fireweed from the plot. "Please go," she said, "over there," pointing to a nearby poplar tree. Without speaking, he walked away, stretched out under the tree, and pulled his cap over his face. Eliza placed the cranberry branches at the bottom of the two-foot white cross where Maggie's name was barely visible. She hummed one of the hymns they used to sing at church in Carcross. Walter dozed.

"Let's go," Eliza said a little later, kicking his leg gently with her foot.

"Yeah. Lunchtime I guess," he said, smiling up at her under his cap.

"That's all you think of? Food?" she laughed, running down the hill.

****

Through the summer, and before it snowed for good in the fall, Eliza climbed over the slide, visiting with Annie every few days. She helped her with the smaller children who were home from school for the summer and learned to tan hides, smoke fish, and dry moose meat. Sometimes she stayed overnight. After supper they sewed glass beads onto dark smokey moose skins and thin white caribou hide by the light of the kerosene lamp. She was happier than she ever remembered, except when her mother was alive.

On the Discovery Day holiday, August 17, it was a warm sunny day with a clear azure sky. Dawsonites and visitors from all over the Yukon and Alaska were celebrating the beginning of the Klondike Gold Rush over fifty years before by drinking in the bars and dancing in the streets. The Indians were being allowed in the bars for the celebration. Some of them had left Moosehide for town early that morning. It would be a decade later before openly drinking liquor would be legal for them.

"That frost last night must have killed off most of the mosquitoes," Dave said, "A perfect day for the river." Eliza and Dave stopped their boat in Moosehide and along with Walter and Annie, they packed children, food, dishes, blankets, and a gun into the two boats. They went downriver to the mouth of the Thirtymile River and spent the day serenely fishing, picking berries, and taking naps under the golden trees. Annie showed them how to fish "Indian way," making a fish trap from the willows on the shore and placing it in the river. When a whitefish was caught, she let it go, saying in a singing voice, "Don't need you yet. Mussi cho. Thank you."

Later, after their supper of caribou steaks around the campfire, Annie and Dave told stories about the Indian families who used to live around Thirtymile. Annie's husband came from the area, and Eliza's mother grew up there before they moved to Moosehide. "Maggie Taylor, her uncle Jimmy drown here," Annie said. "Never did find him. He fell in over there, across, checking traps. Cold, cold water that day, ice just gone out. Your mother Maggie, she seen him fall in, eh? She holler and holler, but everybody gone out in the bush. She just young, but she take boat, go across fast, fast, but he go under quick. Gone. Everybody look for him for weeks. Nothing."

Dave said, "They say he still walks along the river, waiting to be found. Maggie told me her family saw him once the year after he drowned when they were in their boat headed for Alaska. He was standing under a tree, on the river bank, downriver, close to Eagle. He waved at them to come and get him, but they were too afraid. When the body isn't found, they never rest, she said."

"That right," Annie said. "People they drown, we look for them long time. Long time. They real unhappy, them poor souls."

"Annie, aren't you ever afraid of being on the river?" Eliza asked.

"Afraid? No, child!" She laughed. "The river, she give us food, water. We travel on her, summer, winter. She bring us to place for hunt, trap... she look after us." Eliza shivered when she heard Annie say next in a quiet voice, "The river same like mother to me. We her children. Me, I same like child of the river. River child." Eliza had dreamt of an older Indian woman saying that when she was at the school.

"But it's dangerous too, eh? You gotta be strong, smart." Walter said.

"Only when people forget, don't say thank for good things, don't treat things right, like fish. Got to do right for animals and fish. Then things OK. Bad spirits won't get you then."

"Did Uncle Jimmy do something bad? That's why he drowned?" Eliza asked.

"Dunno, child," Annie said. "Only God know."

Dave said, "You know, for me, the river is like life. It carries us along to the future. The things behind us are in the past. It can be wonderful, smooth, exciting. But it can also be cruel and full of danger. You have to be careful. You have to have courage to live on the river."

"Yeah, Dave Maclean," Annie said. "You right. River is just like life." She was silent for a few moments. "Uh huh, take courage to live", she said, nodding. "Take courage on river too."

"And remember kids, you gotta be smart. Like me." Walter pointed to his head and laughed with everyone.

During the long late summer evenings in Moosehide after her children went back to Chooutla and the boys were in Dawson with her sister, Annie told Eliza stories. The first time she saw a horse, she said, she screamed. "They like big dogs for us, bad dogs. And them Whitemen in town. Look sick, them guys, all pale, some yellow hair even." She laughed, "My Mom she say to my father, 'take them good Indian food, Indian medicine too, from trees. Make them better.' He did! My father, my brothers, they give away plenty moose, caribou ribs too. Take into town. Good stuff. One White guy, he give us rifle for my oldest brother once."

"Did they ever get better, them Whitemen?" Eliza asked.

"Course! Mom, she give medicine root too. Best thing for stomach flu. Plenty flu them days. Them Whitemen never did got black hair, though! Too bad for them!" They laughed.

"Can we pick medicine root?"

"You betcha. Late summer, only time. I learn you names, Han Indian names."

"Can you teach me Indian language? Han language?"

"Nobody use them words no more. Too bad. No use no more."

Eliza never tired of hearing how Annie got married, the Indian way. Annie said she heard about Peter Thomas when she was a little girl. His family lived on the river around Thirtymile and near Eagle, Alaska, a hundred miles away down the Yukon River. They would come up to Dawson once or twice a year and stay at Moosehide.

"My Grandma, she talk to his mother," Annie said. "He a Wolf and us we Crow, so it work out OK." People had to marry into the opposite clan. "That old fashion way," she said. "Nowdays people forget that stuff. Not good, nowdays, no sir, mix up, bad. Better do old way."

Eliza said, "Tell me again about how you got together."

"OK, child. They want us get together. His mama, she send Peter to our fishcamp, tell him help my mother. Oh, he work long. All day he bring wood, clean up camp, even hunt for us. They tell me feed him, bring him tea. He sit beside me at campfire."

"Did he make eyes at you?"

"Make eyes? How that thing?" Annie said. "He never even look at me, no sir. But we know what's up. We know, without talk. In couple weeks, Mama tell me 'go sleep Peter's tent. Cold tonight.' I scared. I take blanket, make bed close to door inside tent. He pretend he sleep."

"And then he pulled off your blanket!"

"Sure did! We fight little bit. We laugh. We forget 'bout sleep alone after that. Married Indian way. Lot more fun."

"But you got married in church, too?" Eliza said, pointing to a photograph in a heavy wooden frame on the wall. Several Indian men and women dressed in their finery were lined up in a stiff row in front of the Moosehide church. Annie and Peter stood on either side of Bishop Bompas.

"Sure thing. When Bishop come round next spring, we do that too. Good have both, you know, Indian way and White way. Twice. Good luck." She picked up the Bible she always had on the table. "Bishop give me this. Church good to me. Learn to read and write from them. Not high tone people like some peoples in Dawson."

"My Daddy never got married in the church. He said he doesn't believe in anything they do. He sure misses Mommy. Talks about her lots. You miss Peter?"

"Oh, my. You bet. Miss him plenty. Good man, my Peter. Good hunter. Always lots for eat, eh? Fun too. Joke lots. Walter same like him, you know." It wasn't the first time Annie had frankly pointed out Walter's good points to her.

"Long time ago girls married animals you said?"

"Yeah. Girls didn't know, though. Thought they was people. Them animals just pretend they men. When they was killed, they turn back to animal. Lynx. Wolf. Like that."

"And you said there was some way you could tell they weren't people, those animals?"

"Them animals, they don't eat human food. Cooked stuff? No sir. Something else too. Sometime they sleep on other side of fire from wife."

"How come they want to marry humans? Doesn't make sense."

"Only in long time ago time, not nowdays. Want woman. Woman help snare rabbits, sew hides, help 'em live. Good in bed too. Even Coast people, trading days down near Whitehorse, they like Yukon woman, marry lot of them. Steal them, too, I hear peoples say."

"But even today, some men are like animals, don't you think?"

Annie laughed. "Not my men. My men good men. All them. Like Walter, he out getting wood right now. Like boy should. Your Daddy, he good too, eh?" She walked over to the stove, brought back the teapot, and poured Eliza more tea.

"Yeah, but Daddy, he's old."

"Old people only good for story, eh?" Annie sat down, laughing.

"No, I mean...you know, old men don't fool around with you."

Annie's lips turned downward. A deep frown appeared between her eyes. "How you mean?" she said, peering at Eliza.

Eliza looked away. "I mean, touch you," she said haltingly. "You know, in the wrong place. Private place."

"That happen to you sometime, child?" Annie's voice shook.

Eliza looked up, her eyes growing wet and large. She lowered her face and covered it with her hands. Her voice barely a whisper, she said, "Yes. One man. He did bad things. In Carcross."

Annie came over to stand beside Eliza's chair. She put her hand behind Eliza's head and gently drew it against her belly. She said, "Cry, little girl. Cry. It good for you."

Eliza's arms encircled Annie's hips and she sobbed. "Am I bad, Annie?"

"No, Eliza, no, no, no!" She stamped her foot. "He make you think like that. He evil. Evil. You good child. Nothin' wrong with you! You stop think like that. No good you think like that."

The cabin door crashed open. Walter's head appeared beside the door above his arms full of chopped wood. He hesitated briefly when he saw Annie and Eliza embracing, then coughed, and tumbled the wood into the woodbox by the door. Turning his back, he pushed the door shut, saying, "Pretty cold these days, eh?" The two women separated. Walter turned and said, "Guess it's maybe the last trip on the river, Ma. Ice floating down today. From now on it's hiking over the slide until she freezes up."

Eliza pulled away from Annie, wiped her eyes, and said to Walter, "You gonna put the boat up for winter now?" without real interest. A few times, she had taken a ride back to Dawson in his boat. She felt more at ease now in the boat. And with Walter.

"Yep. She's going up on shore for a long rest this weekend. Want a ride home? Last chance. Cruise ship SS Thomas leaves in twenty minutes, soon's I have my tea. Moon's full out but it's going behind that mountain before long."

"She go with you," Annie said. "I give her too much things to hike over slide."

Annie rustled around the cabin, putting together a burlap bag full of beaded handicrafts and mukluks the two of them had sewn over the weeks of fall. She tore little pieces of paper from old envelopes, wrote the names of people Eliza would be delivering the crafts to in Dawson, and pinned them onto each piece. "You put money you get for them things in your Daddy's bank. He give Walter half for me. Half for you."

"No, no, Annie. It's not fair. I didn't do much sewing. And I'm no good at it neither."

"What?! You help me all summer! Hard work too. Tan skin. Smoke fish. Dry meat. I need help with kids. I pay you. No argue." She topped the bag with a parcel of dried meat and smoked salmon wrapped in newspaper. "Save some for your Daddy Dave, now," she said, smiling.

Eliza pulled on her rubber boots and jacket. "*Mussi cho,* Annie, thank you. I'll come back soon to visit, over the slide."

"Good. You my daughter now. You learn everything real good." Eliza leaned into the warmth of Annie's arms. "Now you wrap up real good, child. Windy out. Here my winter scarf. Walter, you use them caribou skins, ones with hair on still. Keep Eliza good and warm on way home."

Walter spread caribou skins in the bow of the boat and told Eliza to lie down to keep out of the wind. He lay grey army blankets over her. Tucking them around her body curled against the bow, he held her tight for a few seconds.

"I'm fine. Let's go," she said, pushing his arms away.

"You don't like boys, do you?"

"Boys are suppose to keep their hands to themself."

"Not if they really want a girl, you know," he said, laughing and sitting on his haunches near her. "Specially when there's a full moon, same as tonight, like in the movies." He put his hand on her knee and said, "You know, I really like you. And if we go for each other, we hug and kiss, eh?"

Eliza sat up and pulled her knees to her chest. "I like you OK. You're fun and you're good to me, give me rides, helping me with things. You're like my brother."

"But I don't want to be your brother," Walter said quietly, tugging her hair. "You're too pretty. Too pretty for my sister."

She looked away and said, "I am not. I'm not pretty."

He laughed. "Well, I think so, anyway." He stood up and took a deep breath, stretching. "Well, got to get this old boat going or Dave Maclean'll be down my neck for kidnapping his daughter. Can't afford that."

Eliza tucked herself into the bow again while Walter went to the stern and started the motor. In a short time, they landed in Dawson. "Want me to carry those things home for you?" Walter asked when he had tied up the boat. She nodded. Walter hoisted the bag over his back and they walked along Front Street as a light snow began to fall. Large wet flakes sparkled in the moonlight against the dark false-fronted gold rush buildings.

"Me, I sure like the snow," Walter said, "Makes everything like new, eh? Clean and bright. Might be enough to go tobogaining this weekend, too, up on the Dome."

"Yeah. Wish I had a sled."

"I'll come and get you with mine. OK?"

"OK," she said quietly. All the way to the Maclean cabin in the South end, Walter whistled. Before she opened the door, he handed her the bag, leaned over and kissed her quickly on the lips as if they did it all the time.

"'Night," he said, "See you Saturday. After lunch."

"'Night." Eliza stood and watched him stride confidently away into the dark. She touched her lips. He was the strongest and at the same time the most gentle man she had ever known, except for her father.

****

In the early afternoon two days after Christmas, Dave was sitting at the table when he heard a muffled knock. Steam circled around him from the humidity of the cabin hitting the frigid air as he opened the door. It had been forty-two below that morning. He looked down on a squat bundle of parka trimmed with fur and topped with layers of scarves. A mitt held an envelope up for his view. Taking his pipe out of his mouth, he said cheerfully, "And what's this?"

"Ma says to say Merry Christmas. And here's a card," the voice inside the scarves said.

Dave took the card in his large hand and bent his whiskered face down to peer into two dark eyes above the scarves. He said, "And Merry

Christmas to your family too. Thank you. Step indoors for a minute. Too cold out there." Eliza had left for the day, after Walter had come to pick her up. She said she would be visiting Annie at Annie's sister's, and having supper there later. He could use some company, no matter how small.

"Gotta go. Deliver 'nother one."

"OK," Dave said and reached behind the door. "Here's something for your family." He handed the child a square tin box wrapped in a red ribbon. He had made up several packages of Christmas baking for just such emergencies. He chuckled as he watched the plump creature skip away, not knowing if it were a boy or girl or whose child it was.

Dave opened the Christmas card, and saw his visitor had to be one of the little Thomas children, home for the holiday from the residential school in Carcross. The card was from Annie. In it was a note. "Don't like bother you. You come see me today? To talk bout Eliza," it said.

A half hour later, Dave knocked on the door of Annie's sister's house on Front Street. Annie invited him in, took his parka, and said, "Everybody gone for while. Just us here."

"Something wrong?"

"Tea first." Annie hung his parka up behind the door. "Good Christmas for you?" she smiled and sat down, pouring tea into a cup she had ready on the table near the unopened box of Christmas baking he had given the child.

Dave talked disinterestedly for a minute but then asked, trying to keep the exasperation out of his voice, "Then Eliza's OK?"

"Oh, she good. Just fine. Annie looked closely at him. "You gonna be grandpa some day is all," she said.

Dave hesitated, staring for a second, and then shouted, leaping up from his seat, "What!" His chair fell over behind him.

Annie said calmly, "We talk now 'bout wedding." She pointed to his chair. "Sit."

He picked up the chair and sat down. "Sorry about that," he said with a quick smile. "Wedding? Dammit, they're just kids!"

"Little bit kids, but old 'nough."

"Old enough to get into trouble," Dave muttered. "I'd have to give her permission to get married at her age. And I won't. And that's final." He slammed his hand on the table in emphasis.

"You think plenty 'bout this. We talk first." She opened the tin box of baking and offered it to him. "Please. Eat."

He shifted in his seat and took a cookie absent-mindedly. "She could adopt it out I guess. They just can't get married. That's certain."

"No baby yet, but could be, easy, some day. They like each other plenty."

"So she's not..."

Annie said, "You know, he good man, my Walter. Hard worker. Eliza too. She help me plenty. She Wolf, too, Maggie Taylor a Wolf. Walter a Crow, like me. Important. Young people nowdays forget old way."

"Yeah, I know. And I like Walter. Maybe when she's older..."

"Maybe they have baby before then. Your first grandchild. No good give baby to somebody. You be sorry forever."

"I've got to think. What do the two of them have to say for themselves anyways?"

"Well, Walter ready to marry now. He say they married anyhow, Indian way. But he want make it legal. In church."

"And Eliza?"

"She...well, she say no."

"No? What? No?" Dave shook his head. "What the devil...?"

"You think they marry? You OK for that?"

"I just don't know anything anymore. God, this is stupid. Stupid. Why'd she say no? Did she tell you?"

"She have trouble with man at Chooutla residential school when she there. She say she don't want no man. But she too young to know her mind."

"Trouble with a man in Carcross? You mean...?"

"She ask me to talk to you 'bout that. She never say nothing to nobody 'cept me. But she say she feel dirty, you know...when..."

"Oh my God." Dave's face reddened and he put one hand over his eyes. They sat a long time, not speaking. Finally he said quietly, "It was me who sent her away to that damn school. She ran away from there, came home. That's probably why she did. If I could get my hands on that ba..." He stopped himself. "Did she tell you who it was?"

"No. I no ask. It over now. Over." Annie stood up and threw some wood in the heater in the middle of the room. "That real bad thing," she said as she came back to the table. "Real bad. I pray for her every day. But she still fine fine girl. And my Walter he kind to her. They have good future. Best thing to do, they marry."

"Send her home when she comes back. I'll talk to her."

"You OK on marry then?"

"I don't know. I just don't know," Dave said, shaking his head. He stood up.

"I pray for you both. God and Jesus help us."

Dave took his parka from the door. "Thanks," he said. "Thanks for telling me. I'll think it over good," and left. Tears glistened in his eyes as he closed the door. Must be from the cold, he told himself, wiping his cheek with his mitt.

Eliza opened the door to their cabin four hours later. She stood silently just inside the door without taking off her parka and looked across at Dave sitting at the table.

"Take your things off, little one," he said gently, "We got some talking to do."

She padded across the floor in her mukluks, sat on a chair near Dave, and unzipped her parka, keeping it on. "Daddy," she said, leaning toward him, "I'm scared. Don't make me go away from you. I just want to stay here. We've been apart already a long time."

"And what about Walter?"

"It's finished. I won't see him again. I like him. He's really nice, like you. But I won't get married to him. Can't get married to nobody. Never."

"You don't want to? You sure?"

She nodded. "I just can't. I really thought about this, for a long time, Daddy." She looked away. "Did Annie tell you?" she mumbled, "about the school?" He took a deep breath and nodded and she said in a whisper, "I don't want to live with a man. I hate it. It makes me...it makes me sick." Her eyes filled with tears. "Really, Daddy, don't make me marry him?"

Taking her hand, he said, "You know I wouldn't make you do that. It's up to you of course. You're too young, anyways."

"I keep remembering Annie telling me how her grandma decided who she had to marry, in the olden days, when people got married the Indian way. I know she wants the best for all of us, but I just can't."

"It's only fair to break it off I guess if you don't want to go along with getting married. You going to see him again?"

She nodded. "Just to tell him. I have to tell him, Daddy."

The next Sunday it was milder weather. Walter came by to take Eliza out with his dog team. They were going upriver to hunt on one of the islands where a moose had been sighted. Usually Eliza was thrilled to bounce over the rough river ice behind the excited barking dogs, but this time she worried about what she would say to him. She sat wrapped up in blankets in the back of the sled and Walter's body leaning over her every time he pushed the sled forward suffocated her. They walked the island looking for the moose with no luck, and she couldn't seem to find the right time to say anything. The brief daylight was dying by the time they were hungry so Walter lit a fire in the heater of a trapper's cabin. They stood near it in their parkas. He put his arm around her.

"Look. Ma told me what happened in Carcross," he said. She pulled away from him. He said, "Don't. Please. I understand. It's not your fault. He was a real shit, that guy. I could kill him."

Eliza shivered, her face turned to the floor. "I don't want to talk about it. Forget it."

"You know I'd never hurt you, ever, don't you? I know you don't really like it when we sleep together." He frowned. "But now I know why. So give us a chance, eh?"

She lifted her head. "Your mom wants us to get married. I won't get married to nobody."

"Ma's back in the old Indian ways. I love you. I want to marry you. But we don't have to get married. Only if you want to. We'll just have a good time together, eh? I'll be real gentle for you. You know I will."

"I know. You haven't hurt me. It's not that."

"Give us some time, eh? Just tell me when it's bad. Or good. It can be real good, too, you know. We'll work it out." He poured them each hot tea from a thermos. With his tin cup, he made a toast, winked, and said, "And I know how to make it so there's no babies, too."

"I don't mind a baby. Just don't want no man!" She pulled her parka close and frowned.

Walter laughed, "Well," he said, "I think there was only one baby born that way in the world."

She joined in his laughter. "Walter, you know I really like you. You're good for me. You make everything easier."

"See? That's a good start." He reached out his arm and she came over to him, ignoring for a time the unease she felt.

****

Leaves were just beginning to bud on the barren trees when Eliza felt the baby move inside her. She knew she had to tell her father. She waited until they had finished supper and he had lit his pipe.

"I'm pregnant, Daddy," is all she said. Dave sat in his chair, silent, stunned, looking at the floor. "I have to keep my baby," she said, kneeling beside him and clutching his arm. "Please?"

"Here? In this little cabin? Good God, girl! What're you thinking?" He threw his pipe onto the table and stood up, leaving Eliza crouching near his chair. He clattered the dishes together and dropped them on the counter. Eliza stood up and moved over to sit in his chair.

"I'll look after it real good, you'll see," she said, her fingers playing nervously with his pipe on the table. "I'll get a job. Help you. You'll see, Daddy. We'll be a real family. I want to keep it. I have to. I'll die if I don't."

"How long?"

"Huh?"

"When is it coming?" Dave shouted, his face reddening.

"I'm three, maybe four months."

"We'll just give it up. To a good family."

"No! I won't. I won't! I'll leave. I'll go live with Annie in Moosehide! She's the grandmother."

"What? You talked to her about that already?"

"Yes! She said I could live with her!" She pursed her lips in defiance. "But what I really want is to stay here, with you, Daddy. We'll be just fine. I know we will. I don't want to be near Walter, with his family."

"God! I sure as hell don't want to give away any kid. My grandchild, for Pete's sake. But we gotta think this whole thing over some," Dave said. He took his pipe from Eliza's hand and chewed on the end. Eliza stood up and went over to the counter. She poured water from the kettle into the dishpan and started washing the dishes.

"And what about Walter, the father?" Dave asked after a few minutes. "Haven't seen him around here lately. How come?"

"I won't marry him. I told him no a long time ago. Don't make me!" She slammed a plate into the dishpan.

"What does he have to say? Does he even know?"

Eliza took a deep breath, her face toward the window. "He knows," she lied. "Anyways, he's been going out with that Rosie woman. And I broke up with him. She's older than him, too."

"He's a good man, far as I could see. I suppose he took up with Rosie after you got rid of him? And when was that exactly? You said you'd tell him months ago. Before all this." He waved his arm in the air to indicate the enormity of what was happening.

"No, Daddy."

"No what?"

"No, he started going with her when I was still with him." She swallowed hard at the second lie. Why did he have to know everything anyway?

"What? Thought he had more respect for you than that." He paced the room, his voice becoming louder. "Sure don't sound like him. Still, the way you treated him..." Dave said.

"Daddy let's not fight. We can't do nothing right now. And let's not even think about Walter. He's gone. He's happy with Rosie. Let's just sleep on it. We can talk in the morning." She ran across the room and put her arms around him, the dishcloth still in her hand.

Dave looked down at his little daughter's head against his chest. She was going to be a mother! He put his arms around her. "Right," Dave sighed, "I suppose it's all we can do right now."

"Daddy, we'll be just fine, you'll see," she said.

In September, a baby girl was born. When Dave was allowed to visit Eliza in the hospital, he was shocked. She looked like an exhausted little child, like a stranger, after nearly two days of labour. Always proud of her hair, she curled it nearly every night, and slept with the pins and curlers on her head, making him wince at the thought. Now her thick black hair was flat against her head, the ends straight. Her eyes looked larger than he remembered. She was just a child herself.

Eliza hadn't thought much about what to name the baby. She had played with the idea of calling her Maggie, but Dave wasn't happy with that, so she called her Selena after one of the nurses, because she liked the name. Dave took the tiny Selena in his arms. Her wrinkled red face reminded him of his first days with Eliza when she was a baby. "We'll do better by you, Selena," he said. "You'll stay home and be my own little grandchild. We'll take good care of you, sweetheart."

Eliza reached for Selena and said, "Yes, baby, we'll make sure you are OK. You are my whole life now."

BAND NUMBER 59

"Look at all the homework I have to do!" I shouted through my bedroom doorway. So my grandfather would get the point, I lifted three books where he could see them from his chair at the table. "They're just *mean* to us in grade seven, you know, Pop!" I flung the books onto the bed. "Wish I was back in elementary." The metal springs in the bed squealed as I sat down to change from my school clothes.

Pop looked over his glasses, lowered his newspaper, shuffled the pages together, and folded it. The kettle hummed on the wood stove. He stood and reached for the teapot. "Like some tea, Selena?" he asked. "Water's boiling."

I was calmer now. Pop always said I had his temper - quick to be angry, but even quicker to calm down. I came into the kitchen. "Not for me, Pop." Kneeling down, I tied my running shoes, and looked up at him. "Can I go over to Grandma Thomas' now?" She was teaching me how to sew the soles on the mukluks I was making.

"Your mother's in town," Pop said quietly, spooning loose tea from the tin into the teapot. "She wants to see you." I moved slowly over to the table. "She sent me this," he said, reaching into his shirt pocket. He handed me a slip of tightly folded paper and I sat down to read the note. It was in pencil.

Dear Daddy, I am down from Whrse. At Judys for while. Please let me see Selena.
I miss my baby. love, her mother, Eliza

My mother! I refused to call her that.
Eliza had appeared before in Dawson. Pop said that she had stayed sober the first time she came, as far as he could find out from people that

he asked. So the next time, when I was about seven years old, he let her see me. I remember a tiny woman with a frizzy permanent sitting at the table, her huge belly sticking out from her coat. Her hands kept opening and shutting the clasp on her purse. "Guess what? I'm having twins!" she said. She was proud of it! "What should we name your sisters or brothers, baby? Maybe it's one of each!" She didn't even know that twins are bad luck. Grandma Thomas told me that.

That visit was short. Eliza clung to my arms until they hurt, telling me how much she missed me, and when I struggled to get away, Pop told her to leave. It ended with Pop shouting, "Do you even know who the father is this time?" I cried for hours afterward. Mostly I was ashamed, and afraid that Pop might send me away, make me live with her. Later that year, Pop told me my twin brothers were born. They were taken by the Department of Welfare before they were three and put into foster homes in Whitehorse.

Another time she came to Dawson, when I was about ten, Pop told me she had asked to see me, but he had refused to let her. That time, I saw her downtown. She was coming out of the Northern Commercial store and I watched her from across the street. She was laughing, pointing at a large paper bag that her friend Judy carried against her hip, her dark curly head bobbing. I was disgusted and turned away down another street so they wouldn't see me. I figured the bag that Judy had was full of liquor. Julie Fuller had told me that Eliza was on the Interdicted List. If you were interdicted, Julie said, it meant that you were such a drunk that it was against the law for you to buy booze. Some people called it the Indian List because in the old days, Indians couldn't buy liquor. All it really meant was that you had to pay someone else, a bootlegger like Judy, to get it for you.

Now she was back again bothering us. "Forget it!" I said. I crumpled up the note and threw it in the wood box. "I don't want to see her. Ever."

Pop poured himself a cup of tea and sat down. "Now that you're older, you can decide for yourself if you want to see her or not, I reckon." He stirred sugar into his cup.

"Good. Then I won't." I wanted to talk about anything else. "What about Grandma's? Is it OK?"

"I can understand your not wanting to see her. It's not easy. But maybe you should think about it for a bit. Talk to Grandma Thomas about your mother. Eliza used to spend a lot of time with her in Moosehide when she was just a bit older than you." He picked up the newspaper, folded it twice, and stretched an elastic band around it. He would be giving it to our neighbour.

"No. Why should I tell her that my mother the drunk wants to see me? Eliza makes me sick. And she's staying with that awful Judy, who's nothing but a bootleg half-breed squaw."

The crack of Pop's newspaper slapping on the table shot through the room. "Don't you dare use those words in this house!" His booming voice made my heart pound. "I won't have anyone using that language around me. No one, *no one,* do you hear me, is a half-breed squaw!" Frowning, he stood, swept his hand through his hair, and muttered, "I thought I taught you better than that."

"Sorry, Pop," I said as softly as I could. "That's what Julie called her." As soon as I said Julie's name, I knew I shouldn't have. Pop thought Julie would end up the same as Eliza and he said she had a bad influence over me.

"Eliza's your mother, whether you like it or not!" he shouted. "And she has every right to see you, understand?" He stood up and said, more calmly, "I'm going to tell her to come over tomorrow after school. And you will be here."

I was stunned. "Shit!" I heard myself say without thinking. Pop's hearing wasn't as good as it once was and I hoped he hadn't heard. I picked my jacket off the hook behind the door.

"Any more of that language, young lady, and you won't go anywhere for a week," he said. "Sit down. There's some things I have to say."

I hesitated but shrugged my jacket on. "Aw, Pop. Please let me go." Going to Grandma Thomas' was like going to my second home, and I wanted to be near her right now. I smiled at him. "Come on," I said, "I'm making the mukluks for you, you know."

"You can stop trying to bribe me, little one. It won't work. Sit down." He pointed to the chair across from him, and I did as he asked, trying to look interested. From the strict sound of his voice, I knew I didn't want to hear what he had to say. "This is hard for me to say, Selena, but you have to know some things about your mother." He cleared his throat, blinked, and looked down at the floor, lifting both hands to smoothe his hair. "It's my fault your mother's been a drinker."

"What? That's not true!" I said with a tight little laugh. "What do you have to do with it? It's her choice."

He took both my hands in his and told me that he blamed himself for sending Eliza to the residential school. He should have saved more money to bring her home from there for holidays. He should have gone there to see what it was like. She ran away when she was fifteen, it was so bad. He should have come home from trapping more often to make sure she was looking after me properly. She was too young to know anything about being a mother and he didn't teach her enough. He should have... he should have...he kept on saying how much he blamed himself until I shouted, "Stop that! I won't listen to it! She's grown up. It's her own fault! It's her life!"

Pop let my hands go and lowered his face into his hands. "God I hate to say this!" he said. "But you have to realize...she was...ah...she was...some bastard used her for sex when she was in Chooutla. She never got over that, blames herself. I think she drinks to forget about it."

My insides tightened. I felt like throwing up. Eliza had sex with a man when she was in school! It made her even worse in my eyes. "And what about when she left me to booze it up and I got my hand frozen, eh? That's her fault, my crippled hand. Nobody else's."

"I figure she drinks because she can't forgive herself," he said. "She has a big load to carry."

"Well, I'm not forgiving her neither. Never!"

I saw tears in Pop's eyes. He blinked them away. "I know this is a lot for you to understand. But I think your mother is changing. It's very hard, very hard for her. Maybe she needs our help, you know. Maybe some day we might be able to forgive each other, all of us."

My head was reeling. I couldn't stand it any more. I'd start crying too unless I got out of there. "Let me go to Grandma Thomas' now, Pop," I said quietly. He waved his hand towards the door.

I could hardly breathe as I walked across town. It was as if somebody had their hands around my throat. I could hear my heart pounding in my ears. Eliza must be even dirtier than I thought if she had sex with a man when she was little. And it made me dirty too. I didn't want to think about what Pop had said. I forced myself to walk fast and to think about something else.

Passing Grander's General Store on the way to Front Street I automatically looked for Mrs. Grander on the stairs. I always felt a little afraid passing Grander's. Years before, Mrs. Grander had come after me and Julie when we tried to go in the store, passing her on the stairs. I must have been about eight. I will always be able to hear her yell, shaking her broom at us, "Get out of here! I won't have you dirty Indian kids hanging around my store." Some man on the street laughed.

We had run away down the street, giggling nervously, then turned the corner and stopped out of sight. Julie leaned against a telephone pole, tossing her head toward Grander's store, her mouth twisted in contempt. She shouted, "Stupid bitch! Jeez, as if you have anything we'd wanna steal anyways!" Her laugh was scary, as if she forced it.

I made a face and shouted in support, "Yeah!"

The crisis over, we had wandered down the street shuffling our feet. Julie was ten, nearly two years older than me. She was like a big sister and always answered my questions. "Jules, why did Mrs. Grander call us Indians?" I asked her. People called my mother an Indian but I thought that it was like a swear word--exaggerated, but not true. I never thought that my mother might be a real Indian, like in the comic books. They had feathers. Julie didn't answer me. "She's wrong, isn't she. My Pop's Dave Maclean. He's a White trapper, right? And I'm his granddaughter, so I'm not a Indian, right?"

"Yeah, your Pop's White. Ask him why dontcha?" Julie said, not looking at me, frowning.

"Well, if Pop's White, then I am too. But then why do they call him Indian Dave? Did he just decide to be Indian? Can you do that?"

"I dunno. Everybody's got nicknames, Lena. Anyways," Julie said with a little sigh, like she did when she knew the answer and you didn't, "it's not your grandpop that counts, it's your mom and dad."

All I ever heard Pop say about Eliza was that she was "a drunk gone to Whitehorse", and that my father was Walter Thomas, "an Indian from the Village." I held my breath. A new thought shocked me. If my father was an Indian, maybe I was one too. You had to be one or the other, Indian or White. Maybe I wasn't White after all. All the White people came from Outside the Yukon and had lots of money and cars and good jobs. I wasn't rich enough to be like them.

Julie was ignoring me, gazing at a bunch of boys throwing stones at a black dog in front of the Westminster Hotel. I stepped in front of her and said, "I got a White name too--Maclean, like Pop. That's White, eh?"

She stared down the street. The boys had run out of sight after the dog. "We *all* got White names, Selena. Indians too."

"You're White too, right?" I tugged at her sleeve.

It made Julie feel important, knowing more than me. She glanced sideways at me. "White *status*, Lena. I dunno. It's somethin' about non-status or somethin'. I told ya. Ask your grandpop about this stuff, eh?"

Non what? Non Status. I had heard that name before.

"Gotta go. See ya." Julie waved her hand and ran away.

I remember being mad at her, one of the few times I was. Why didn't she answer my questions? I figured she knew the answers but didn't want to say.

Now I tried to put that day out of my mind. It was a long time ago and it made me feel stupid. What was that word? Naive. That's what Julie had called me the other day. Stupid: that's what it meant. Well, I just wouldn't think about being stupid or even about my mother coming tomorrow. There was too much to think about.

Grandma Thomas was sitting at her kitchen table sewing, her glasses balanced carefully on the end of her flat brown nose. I always wondered how they stayed there without falling. Her head was covered in a red and green cotton kerchief tied in the back. She nodded toward the chair across from her. "Today we do sole," she said, "Hard work. You pay 'tention." We sewed for a half an hour, with Grandma showing me every few minutes how to fold the sole of the boot onto the instep so that it was rounded just right and the stitches wouldn't show. "Mmmm. You do good, my granddaughter. Good sewing!" Grandma Thomas said, patting my hand. "Make fine wife some day!" She smiled, poured me tea, and pushed the sugar bowl towards me.

I loved Grandma Thomas for her kind ways, and for her strictness too. But mostly I loved her because she took me as a part of her family without question. She was my father's mother. I had known that Walter was my father for a long time, even though I couldn't remember anyone telling me. I guessed that everybody thought Eliza and Walter were too young to get married when Eliza had me.

"Eliza's in town," I said. It was out before I knew what I was saying.

"You say Mom. Not 'Eliza'."

"My mother Eliza. Grandma, she wants to see me again." I put my sewing down and looked at her. How would she react?

"Oh? Good. Good, that's good." Grandma nodded, looking absently through her glasses for sinew in the cardboard box that once held chocolates I had given her. "Ah! Here is!" she said, pulling a pale yellow string upwards.

"No, it's not good! Grandma, I...I don't like her. She's bad."

Grandma put the sinew between her strong front teeth, bit it, and pulled, stretching her arm outward. When she reached the end, she wrapped it around both her hands, jerked it with force, and said, "See. I stretch it. Now won't break. Good and strong. You put it in needle. Lick end first. Easier."

I reached for the sinew and tried three times to put it through a large needle without success. With a groan, I tossed the sinew and needle on the table between us and said, "It's my crippled fingers, Grandma. They won't work right. They never do! Ever!" I was close to tears. I clawed at the piece of hide, picked it up and threw it across the table.

"We do tomorrow. Time for supper now anyhow." Grandma picked up the unfinished mukluk. "You tired?"

"No! I'm not tired. I'm mad. Pop says I gotta see Eliza. Everybody thinks they know what's good for me, what I should do, things I don't want to do." I lifted my hand in front of Grandma's face. "She did this to me," I said. "So why should I see her?"

"She your Mom, that's why."

"I don't want her to be my Mom, Grandma."

"While that, she your Mom." Grandma rose stiffly from her chair and started clearing the table. "She good girl once too. Just like you."

"She was never my mother," I muttered. "You are more like my mother should be."

Grandma put our teacups in the sink, turned, and said from across the room, "Eliza help me plenty when I got lots work to do in Moosehide. She start out good, kind person. God know. God and Jesus know what she done." She pointed at me and frowned. "You...not...God," she said.

I had never seen Grandma so angry before. It confused me. "Please... please don't be mad at me." I forced a smile.

Grandma looked at me but did not smile. "Not mad, granddaughter. You see Mom. That all. Maybe you help her, straight out her life. Maybe she need you help her."

Eliza needs me to help her? What a joke! "Just don't be mad at me, OK?"

I knelt to put on my running shoes by the door. Grandma came over to me and bent over. She put her arm around my shoulder, her face close to mine, and said, "You come by tomorrow too? We finish sole tomorrow." I saw the depths of Grandma's love in her wise old eyes. "You tell what happen when Mom visit."

Grandma Thomas wanted me to be somebody I didn't want to be--a good daughter to somebody who had been a rotten mother. "OK, Grandma," I said with a sigh, putting my arms around her soft body. "I don't want to, but for you and Pop I'll do it. I'll see her." I wouldn't let myself think about whether I was lying to her or not.

On the way home, familiar discomfort came back. I didn't belong anywhere. Not Indian, not White. No mother, no father. Who was I? I felt dirty when I thought about my mother having sex. When she was just a kid! Did that mean I was bad too? Maybe it was inherited, the badness. I was uneasy with whatever it was that other people seemed to think I was--good or bad.

I remembered, as I had many times, that evening years ago when I was eight, after Mrs. Grander yelled at us. I had waited until Pop was settled with his pipe across the table from me, the best time to ask him things. I looked at his curly grey beard, and asked, "Pop, am I a Indian?

He said bluntly, "Yes, you are."

"Huh?" I stared at him. My throat tightened and I felt tears coming.

"You're an Indian, Selena. Your mother's a registered status Indian, and so are you. You both have Dawson Band Number 59 because she is your mother and Maggie Taylor was her mother. And when you're twenty-one, you'll get your own Indian status card with your own number." He blew pipe smoke into the air. "I think they're yellow these days, those cards." We both watched the smoke spread across to the stove.

A yellow card? Why would I want a card? And a number? "I'm number 59? Is that your number too--59?" I asked. Please say yes, Pop.

"I don't have a number. I'm White status." There was that word again that Julie used. Status. Pop was different from me. He didn't have a number like I did. And he was different from Eliza too. Maybe because he was a man?

Pop's blue eyes looked straight into mine. He smiled. He shook an index finger at me. "You're only an Indian as long as you don't marry a White man when you're old enough," he said.

I wanted to talk about right now, not that impossible time when I would be old enough to do things. I said, "I'm never going to marry nobody. I'm just going to stay with you. All the rest of my life." I came around behind him and put my arms around his shoulders, my head near his neck, nuzzling him so I could breathe his familiar sweet pipe tobacco smell. His wool shirt tickled my nose and I drew my head back. "Pop?" I said.

"Yeah, little one."

"How come you don't have a number? Are you different than me?"

Pop put his hand up to my arm and squeezed it. "You and I are alike as two peas in a pod, sweetheart. For one thing, we're both stubborn as mules. And we like the same things--going on the river, fishing...eating salmon..." He turned around to look at me. "You're my whole family, so how can we be that different, eh, little one?"

He stood up, sucked on his pipe, frowned, and blew smoke into the room away from us. "Let's seriously consider the facts, my girl. Mmmm. Yes, I guess in some ways we *are* different." He stepped into the middle of the room and pointed his pipe stem at me. "You're a little girl. And I'm a big man. So we have to be different from the start. I'm getting grey hair--and I'm losing it too. And your hair grows long and black as a raven's feathers. To sum it up, you're young and pretty, and I'm just an ugly old S.O.B."

The unease I felt was gone. I ran over to him, putting my arms around his waist and my head onto his stomach. I laughed, "You're not ugly, Pop! You're just teasing. You're the best looking grandpa in Dawson!"

"Well, this handsome man says the water's hot for washing dishes." We did the supper dishes together, with me standing on a chair to put away the plates in the cupboard.

"Time for bed," Pop said as he dumped the water into the slop pail under the counter and folded the dishcloth over the side of the washpan. I forgot the questions that were on my mind for awhile.

****

Our teacher took us grade sevens over to Minto Park to play baseball in the afternoon, something I always liked and was good at. I was the pitcher. But this time I threw so badly that the teacher made me go play on third base. I missed catching two hits, one after the other, and the other kids teased me. All day I thought about Eliza. I tried to convince myself that she would forget to come and see me. She would probably go and get drunk with Judy. When I finally believed my own fantasy, I was angry that she might not care enough to come.

I opened the cabin door carefully and there Eliza was, looking up at me. She sat at the table, on the edge of Pop's chair. I was surprised at how young she looked. And pretty. Mothers were supposed to be old with long grey hair, but Eliza had short black hair surrounding her face in tight curls. She had long dangling silver earrings nearly touching her shoulders, and blue eye shadow like in the movie magazines. She smiled at me, twice, quickly. Her hands were around a teacup, holding it tightly as if she had to keep it from flying away. Her fingernails were painted bright pink.

"Where's Pop?" I asked, still standing in the doorway.

"He's gone out, baby."

Baby. Eliza had called me that the last time she saw me. It made me uncomfortable. "Well, I guess I can see that," I snapped. "Where'd he go? When's he coming back?" That stubborn old man was making it even harder for me, leaving us alone.

"He said he'd come back in an hour." Eliza took her hands from the cup and her pink fingernails opened the worn white purse that was on the table beside the teapot. "Sit down, baby, please. I have something important for you." She searched in the purse and pulled out a small brown envelope. "I thought you would like to have these, Selena. They're the only pictures of my mother."

"Grandma Maggie? Pop said there aren't any pictures of her."

"I took them with me when I went to Whitehorse years ago. Now I want you to have them. Please. Sit down here." Without getting up, Eliza pulled a chair out from the table for me and patted the seat.

"Does Pop know you took them?" I asked, sitting down. Eliza shook her head and handed me the envelope. I pulled out one of the browning photographs. It showed a row of Indian men and women standing in front of the Anglican church in Moosehide, all eyes on the camera, frowning. A woman in the centre in a short white dress and veil stood between a tall White man and a shorter Indian. "Is that Pop and Maggie?" I asked eagerly. Pop had said they weren't married.

"No. That's Grandma Annie Thomas' wedding, and that's Bishop Bompas beside her. He was famous, you know," Eliza said. She got up from her chair and leaned over beside me. "There's your grandmother." She pointed to a short, slim figure in a long dark skirt and white long-sleeved blouse on the far left side of the group, her arms straight by her sides. She was the only person who was smiling, her mouth open as if she had just finished laughing at a joke and her eyes nearly shut.

"She's so pretty!"

"And you look just like her, Selena." Eliza looked closely at me.

I ignored her. "But I can't see Pop," I said.

"That picture was taken just before they met. Mommy was only seventeen. Look at the other one," she said, moving back to her chair and sitting down.

The second photograph was of the same cheerful face, closer to the camera. Maggie was lying in a hospital bed, propped up by pillows, smiling. A young-looking nun in her black and white habit leaned over the bed, her arm behind the pillows holding Maggie. "I was four when that was taken," Eliza said. "Daddy and I were living in Moosehide alone while she was in the hospital. Just like you and him live together now. She died of TB when I was only seven."

"Yeah, I know," I said. "Pop told me." I thought Eliza had something to do with Maggie's dying. Maybe having her had somehow made her sick. I had heard that some mothers died when they had babies.

Eliza closed her eyes and her voice was dreamy. "I can still see her, showing me how to sew, even as young as I was." She looked at me. "I think she knew she wouldn't be around to teach me when I was older, eh? I really missed her. Still do," Eliza said. "Everybody needs their family, whether they are with them or not, don't you think?"

Maybe my mother really did need me like Grandma Thomas said. I didn't know anybody who needed me like I needed them. "Yeah, I guess so," I said.

"Look on the back," Eliza said, turning the photograph over. In pretty handwriting in ink were the words, *Maggie Taylor, Dawson Band No. 34. Dawson City, Y.T., 1939*

"Sister Maria, the nurse in the picture, wrote that. I remember how nice she was to me when I would visit Mommy in the hospital." Eliza pointed to the writing. "Mommy's Band Number was 34. Do you know our Band number, yours and mine?"

"Of course--59. But Pop says mine'll be different when I'm 21."

Eliza put her hand on my wrist. Her long nails tickled. "I want to go down to Moosehide and visit Mommy's grave before winter. Do you think you could come with me?" I pulled myself away from her touch. Her hands smelled like cigarette smoke.

I put the photographs into the envelope. "Thank you very much for the pictures," I said, trying to sound formal. "Pop'll be glad to have them back."

Eliza took a sip of her tea and said with a big smile, "I might be able to go down to Moosehide this weekend, with Judy and her father. They have a boat. Boy, do I ever miss being on the river! We used to be on the river all the time. Want to come with us, baby?"

Go to Moosehide with Judy and Eliza? I couldn't think of anything worse. "I go down with Pop. That's the only way I go."

"We'd love to have you come, baby. Let's have a picnic! I brought stuff from Whitehorse. I made some bread and I bought some nice cheese. I remember how much you liked cheese when you were small, the kind that...."

"No! Did you hear me, Eliza? NO!" I jumped up from the table and flung myself into my bedroom. I sat on the bed, staring at the stumps of fingers on my right hand. How could that drunken woman with her painted nails and long earrings come back now and pretend everything was OK, that we were like any old mother and daughter? Just having her in the cabin made me feel dirty. Her and her sex with a man at school. Dirty Indian!

I shut my eyes tight and shouted from the bedroom, "What about my twin brothers, eh? Where are they? You can't even look after them! Welfare has them. I know about you."

Eliza came to the bedroom door and hesitated. I could see her eyes filling with tears. She shook her head. "I'm so sorry, baby..."

"Go away! Just get out of here! I don't want to go nowhere with you and that ugly half-breed pig Judy." How could I get sucked into Eliza's tricks? She was like a witch, using Grandma Maggie's pictures to get at me.

Eliza came over to the bedroom door, and said, "I've always loved you, baby. Remember that, no matter what happens to all of us. Just like my Mommy loved me." Her voice broke as she said, "I miss you...all the time. I need you."

"Shit!" I threw myself sideways on the bed, turned my back to Eliza, and put a pillow over my head. "Go! Just go!"

When I heard the front door close I came out of the bedroom and sat on Pop's chair. I leaned over the table to reach for the teapot and saw that Eliza had left a five dollar bill on the table. More tricks! A bribe! My throat went tight and I ripped the money into small pieces. I lifted the cookstove lid and let the pieces fall into the fire, shouting, "Just go to hell, you bitch!"

There was the teacup she had used, with sticky red lipstick on the rim. I put it in the washpan, poured water from the kettle over it and scrubbed hard. I told myself that for my whole life I would never call that woman my mother, just Eliza. Better still, I would never even talk about her again. It would be like Eliza died - or like a divorce. Yes! I would divorce Eliza.

If only I was already twenty-one so I could get rid of Eliza's Indian Band number too. Number 59. I promised myself that the first thing I would do on my 21st birthday was to get my name erased forever from that damn Indian Affairs list. I could do that. I could be non-status if I wanted to. That number was the one last thing of Eliza's I had and I would get rid of it.

I picked up the envelope, slipped out the photographs, and touched the face of Grandma Maggie in the hospital bed. It was as if she was looking right at me, comforting me. None of what Eliza did was her fault. She tried hard to be a mother while she could. In a drawer I found some tape and pasted the photographs onto the wallpaper above the table. Pop would see them right away when he came through the door.

FLASHLIGHT TAG

After washing and brushing Selena's hair, Julie laid the brush on the table beside the enamel washpan. The warmth of Selena's shoulders crept into her stomach as she stood close behind the stool. With both her hands she dug her fingers along the sides of Selena's scalp, lifting her long black hair to let it dry a little. Gently she gathered handfuls, playing with its thick texture, and like a teasing puppie's lick, her hands brushed Selena's ears. Selena always said it sent shivers down her spine and across her chest.

"I should cut just a couple a inches off," Julie said, "give it shape, you know, over your ears. And in the back? Maybe bangs too. Keep it off your face." Selena squirmed. Julie's fingers touched her forehead and moved over her cheek, spreading hair down the side of her face. "OK?" Julie asked. She saw Selena close her eyes. She would give in.

Selena had trouble doing her own hair. Three fingers on her right hand had been crippled from frostbite when she was a baby. That was the reason- -according to Julie-- Selena was shy, even though she was the prettiest of all the Indian girls in Dawson City. The other girls were jealous of her clear dark skin, her large eyes, and tidy figure, Julie said. A protective warmth spread through Julie's chest when she thought of making Selena even more beautiful by styling her hair.

Julie thought she herself was too big for a girl, and clumsy too. "When I was born," Julie often said with resignation, "I got all the ugly parts of my White father, even goddam freckles."

"Hey, are you guys playing that game tonight?" Selena asked. Julie knew she was trying to make her think of something else, not the haircut.

"You mean Flashlight Tag? You bet. A bunch of the kids are meeting at my place. You gonna come this time?"

Flashlight Tag was the passion of a gang of teens from the North End of Dawson when the first safe darkness came after the long summer nights, just before school started. Only the Indian kids played. No White kids were told about it. "Them Whites, they're snobs. We couldn't have half as much fun with them along," Julie said. The boys and girls split into two groups. The girls would run to hide, and the boys would search them out. The boys would have to hit the girls with light from a flashlight after they were found and were running away. The girl who was tagged had to kiss the boy who tagged her while everyone watched, teasing them. That night, the girls had planned to reverse the rules without telling the boys. It was bound to be a scream! Julie decided not to tell Selena about the change, in case she decided not to come.

It was unusual for girls from the opposite ends of Dawson City to be friends. The North End, where Julie lived, was for the poor Indians. The South End was where rich Whites, such as government employees, lived. Although Selena was from the South End, her White grandfather wasn't a civil servant, or rich. She wasn't all White either. Selena's mother was half Indian. Her father was full blooded. It made her three-quarters Indian, Julie said. Julie lived with the real Indians in the north end, but she was only half Indian. Julie delighted in ignoring the rules that everyone else seemed to endorse and had been thrilled when Selena and she became friends despite the differences. They had been friends now since grade two, when they were in the same classroom. Both girls knew they would be friends for life.

Selena spent a lot of time with her Grandma Thomas, learning the old Indian ways from her: sewing, tanning hides, smoking fish. Julie wasn't interested in the elders. She said they could only talk about the old days, and how they wished they were still in the bush trapping. "They just aren't in the real world, man. They gotta come into the Twentieth Century," she said. Julie knew Selena didn't know much about the real world either. With a sense of duty, she made sure Selena had fun.

Every time Julie did Selena's hair she announced: "I'm going to vacation school in Whitehorse to be a hairdresser." Everybody called it "vacation" school. It sounded like fun. Julie thought the more she talked about it, the sooner it would happen. She had grown "like a weed," she once said, among eight brothers and sisters, all fighting for attention and food. There was never enough money. Dawson was pretty boring most of the time, too. If she was a hairdresser, she could get out of Dawson for good. She'd make lots of money. She just had to get grade eleven for hairdresser training in Whitehorse. Only two more years.

Selena opened her eyes. Julie moved around in front of her and brushed the hair from Selena's face. She put her hand under her chin. "You know it needs cutting," she said. "You're just afraid to have me do it, right?"

Selena lifted her face and said, "I don't know, Julie..."

Julie looked straight into her eyes. "I been thinking about it for ages. It'd be perfect for you." She leaned on the table, her face close to Selena's. "I brought the right scissors this time. Let me do it, Lena." She shouted, "Please! Please! Please!" making her face bunch together as if in pain. "You told me you don't want your Pop to do it no more." Selena's grandfather had always cut her hair when she was younger, but in those days she didn't care what it looked like.

Selena said slowly, "Oh, all right, Jules. But just trim it, eh?"

Selena closed her eyes again. Julie could hear her shallow breathing while the comb and scissors ate their way through her hair, crunching and snipping. She imagined Selena's heart pounding.

Part way through the cut, panic just barely hidden in her voice, Selena asked, "Where's the mirror? I have to see it." When Julie handed her the mirror, she said, "I can't see any difference."

"Of course you can't. Gimme time will ya? I haven't got to the front yet." Julie took her place behind Selena again. It was strange for Selena not to trust her. "You want me to finish or not?" Julie asked louder than she wanted to. How could she do a good job if she made her feel nervous?

"Yeah. Go ahead. Just don't take too much off, eh, Jules?" Selena pleaded. Lately the two of them seemed to be fighting more, but they always managed to tease each other out of real spats. Julie could tell Selena was going to say something silly by the way she smiled and drew in her breath. "I suppose next time you're gonna want to bleach my hair blonde, right?"

"Ya know, that's not such a bad idea, Lena. Just imagine: Selena the Blonde Bombshell of Dawson City! You might even make your career as a can-can girl. And I'll be your special hairdresser. You can be the lead dancer in the Pearl Harbour." They giggled, remembering breaking into the old boarded-up hotel when they were in elementary school.

"Remember the time we got caught? Wow! Crazy kids or what, eh?" Julie said. It had been the last weekend of the summer. School would be starting in two days. There was already a powdering of new snow on the mountain tops and a cool breeze drifted in from the river. It was their last chance to have some real fun.

Selena said, "Yeah! Jeez, what we used to do! I was always scared in the Pearl Harbour, though. I'd never go inside there alone, like you did sometimes." Julie would not admit to being scared, but she was a little, so she made sure she always had a flashlight with her. The Pearl Harbour was three storeys high, one of the tallest buildings in Dawson, sitting on King Street. The broken windows on the top floor had torn curtains flapping in the wind as if some ghost was inside looking out at them. The windows on the ground floor were boarded up. A covered passageway between the Palace Grand Theatre next door and the hotel had made it easier for people to get a drink at intermission time when there used to be shows at the theatre. The girls would have to go upstairs to get to the passageway, but even with the flashlight, they stayed on the bottom floor. If they listened carefully they could hear the famous Klondike Gold Rush characters whispering to them from above: Klondike Kate, Robert Service, Swiftwater Bill Gates, Arizona Charlie Meadows. Those spirits cast a spell on them, part of daily life in a ghost town.

When no one was looking, Julie and Selena would push through the thick willows at the back of the hotel to get to the window they always used. Julie loosened some boards. She crawled carefully through, avoiding the sharp edges of glass left in the window frame. "Is it OK, Jules?" Selena would call through the window. She said she felt silly doing that, but she always wanted to have Julie in sight when she finally crawled in. Julie would flash the light towards her, guiding her inside.

"Remember how the sun peeked through the boarded windows?" Julie asked.

"Yeah, eery! And it was always cold in there, too, no matter how hot it was outdoors," Selena shivered. It smelled of dust and something they couldn't determine, rich and dark

At the back of the ground floor were a kitchen and a few small empty rooms. The room they headed for was the bar. It took up half of the bottom floor at the front. They held their breath when the flashlight reflected them like ghosts in the mirror stretching the length of the wall behind the carved mahogany bar. Julie loved the brass chandelier hanging from the middle of the pressed-tin ceiling, its fancy twirls holding dead light bulbs hidden amongst the spider webs. She wanted to take it home with her, if only she could reach it. It was the richest thing she had ever seen.

"God! Remember Ruby, Lena?" Julie laughed. Of course she did. They sometimes talked about her in front of the other kids as if she really existed. Julie stopped cutting Selena's hair. She circled her own head with her arm, imitating the nameless smoke-covered painting of the buxom red-head lying nude on a purple chaise longue, her blank face looking out toward the empty bar. Julie had named her Ruby. She held a peacock feather that covered the embarrassing part, but one large breast stood full to the open air, nipple and all.

Along one side of the barroom round tables just big enough for two or three people were thrown in a jumble. Julie turned vinyl-covered armchairs and tin tables upright in the middle of the room. Selena filled a round tray with empty bottles and broken glasses and walked, swaying her hips from one table to the next, carrying the tray on one arm. "What'll it be, Sourdough Sam? The usual?" Selena smiled at Julie sitting in a chair with her legs propped onto the table. Julie snapped her fingers and said, "Bring me one of them bottles, barmaid. And be quick about it."

When they tired of that game, Julie sometimes pulled a yellowed lace curtain off one of the windows in a back room and twisted it around herself. She left a long tail which she twirled suggestively at her side. Coming out from behind the bar, Julie called out, "My name's Klondike Kate, the dancehall queen. Throw me your nuggets, Cheechakos, and I'll dance for you." She would use one of the stools to climb up on the bar. Then she would prance along, singing and dancing as she imagined the Queen of the Klondike did, completely out of tune. Selena would shine the flashlight on her for a spotlight.

Laughing about the days playing in the old hotel, Selena resigned herself to the haircut. Julie took her own courage in hand and pushed on, trimming the back. It was an experiment. Her hair would always grow back in. They sang "I've Gotta Lov-a-ly Buncha Coconuts" and "Down By the Old Mill Stream," songs they had sung in the Pearl Harbour.

The time they got caught was a highlight of their adventures in the hotel. Selena found some old beer bottle caps to throw pretend nuggets at Julie's feet whenever she did something particularly exciting dancing on the bar. She whooped in enthusiasm when Julie kicked first one leg and then the other in the air, her blue jeans flashing under the lace curtain. An upright piano with a few keys missing was pushed against the front door. Selena ran over to it. She pretended to play without touching the keys, but she was soon pounding out a raucous rhythm on the keyboard. Julie could still hear the tinny sound wavering and crashing through the dim barroom.

Without warning, someone was kicking on the outside of the bar door. A man's voice shouted, "Hey you Indian brats, get out of there or I'll call the cops on you!" Julie jumped straight down from the bar, tore off the curtain, and grabbed the flashlight from Selena. They ran back through the kitchen hallway without saying anything to each other. They were out the window and pushing the boards back on the opening before they nearly exploded in laughter.

When they got out to the front of the hotel that day and were walking along the sidewalk, Selena asked Julie, "In the Gold Rush, do you think there were Indian Klondike Kates?" Julie told her there had to be Indian dancehall girls. Indians were all over the place, she said, and they were probably just as good at being dancehall girls as anybody. Now older, they knew it wasn't true. The Indians weren't allowed in town after dark during the Gold Rush and afterward. They were kept downriver in Moosehide and the women could come into town only with a man, during the day.

"I wonder...do you think my mother was a Klondike Kate?" Selena had asked. "I bet she was. They were kinda bad, eh?" Selena had seldom seen her mother. Her grandfather had vaguely said she had done bad things and that was why she was by herself in Whitehorse.

Julie had straightened her out about the history. "Them dancehall girls were way, way back. In the olden days, in the Gold Rush for God's sake, Lena. Your mom's not that old. Even *my* mom isn't that old. You drive me crazy!"

The experiment with Selena's hair worked out perfectly. It was cut so it curled slightly as it hit her shoulders. The sides were shaped around her face, with bangs curving away naturally from a part in the middle. Julie stepped over the pile of hair on the floor and stood in the doorway to Selena's bedroom, smiling with pride while Selena tossed her head one way and then another. Selena patted the new hair-do, holding a hand mirror that reflected the back of her head in the mirror on her bedroom wall. "Jules, I love it! You're a great hairdresser! It makes me look like I have some curl even. Boy, does my head ever feel light! Half of the hair is gone!" Both of them were relieved.

"Let's celebrate! Come tonight and play Flashlight Tag with us!" Julie said, nearly laughing in excitement.

Selena's smile vanished. She put the mirror down. "You know Pop won't let me do that." Julie always said Selena's grandfather was way too strict with her. She said he was an old prude who thought about nothing else but Indians drinking too much. He was worried Selena would end up drinking like her own mother, Julie knew. But it was her job to help Selena enjoy life a little.

"Look," Julie said, "isn't tonight the night you said Pop was going over to play cards next door? He'll be gone until midnight at least, and you'll be home a long time before then. Just leave as soon as it's dark. Bring a flashlight and meet me at my place at 9:30. I won't take no for an answer, Lena."

"I dunno, Jules. Pop might see me."

"Not if you're smart, eh?"

"Is Martin playing?" Selena asked, more interested. Martin was the son of the principal. They had moved up to the Yukon the year before from one of those big cities back East. He was seventeen, tall, and good at everything, even math. All the girls thought his blonde good looks and blue eyes made him the sexiest boy in school. Selena said he was the smartest and most sophisticated boy she had ever seen. He was one of only three kids in Dawson going into grade eleven. "You know," Selena said, "he said hi to me last week when he came back from holidays."

"Well that cinches it. You gotta show off your new hair-do to him. You want to get a head start on the other girls before school starts next week." Selena agreed to try to sneak out. Julie told her she thought she might see Martin. She would let him know about the game, even though it was against the rules to tell Whites.

When it's dark in the Yukon, it's cold. The science teacher said the ground never really warms up, even with the long days of summer because of the permafrost just below the surface. But that night was rare, a warm dark night in late August, with the air still and quiet. The full moon was hidden in the overcast sky, a pale light shining behind the dark clouds. There would be Northern Lights in the early morning when the moon went down. It was the kind of night when no one wants to be inside, the kind of night when everything is anticipation, daring you to do something different.

The only street light in the North End was the one in front of Julie's house. A group of five girls had gathered under the light when Selena arrived. Julie noticed that even though it was warm, Selena was wearing gloves. Her twisted fingers were always sore in the cold, but she wanted to cover them up too. Julie knew the other girls weren't very happy to see Selena. They called her "Goody Two-Shoes" behind her back because she never got into trouble and lived in the South End. But they couldn't say anything about her with Julie there or they'd get punched and they knew it. Julie got them organized. "OK you guys. Everybody got a flashlight? Everybody know the boundaries? You can't go past Church Street south and my house north, and in the other direction, the river and the Dome Road. OK? Everybody meet back here in an hour."

"Where are the boys?" Selena asked.

"We're going to find that out, right?" Julie's sister shouted. Everybody laughed and ran off into the night.

After about ten minutes of prowling around in the lanes and back yards of the North End, Julie and Selena were behind Julie's Uncle Bob's cabin, beside his woodshed. Sweet smoke crept out of the shed, making them hungry. "Maybe we can get inside, snitch some of Uncle Bob's smoked salmon," Julie said. She reached for the door handle but it had a lock on it.

Selena tripped over a cardboard box on the ground. She complained, "This isn't a good place to hide, Jules. I thought we were supposed to hide."

"Different rules tonight, Lena. We're looking for the boys for a change. And guess what? They don't even know the new rules!" Julie laughed gleefully. "They'll just be wandering around looking for us while we're looking for them! Great, eh?"

"God! And do we still have to kiss them?"

Julie opened her eyes wide, deepening her voice, "Yeah." She could feel Selena looking at her hard.

"Jeez, you could've told me," Selena said. "And who're the boys? I don't want to kiss just anybody. Like Tommy. Or--yecchh--George."

Julie wanted to sound logical and older, so she explained it all carefully: "You would have to kiss anybody who caught you anyways, if the rules were the other way around. That's why we changed them tonight. The girls want to be in charge for once. Great, eh? Are the boys in for a surprise!" It was Julie's idea, and she was intoxicated with the power of it.

"I guess I just have to pick good guys to catch, eh?" Selena giggled. Julie was relieved to see Selena finally getting into the spirit of the game. They started walking down the lane. Selena asked, "Is Martin playing?"

"Nope. It's only us guys from the North End who know about it tonight."

"Oh," she said, disappointment in her voice. "How come?"

"Sorry, Lena, but I didn't get to see him." Julie was more comfortable without him. It would mean they couldn't be as crazy as they wanted to be without a White guy along. "Shhh," Julie whispered, "Somebody's coming."

Julie put her arm across Selena's chest and pushed her against the wall of an outhouse. They listened to heavy footsteps crunch in the gravel.

"Gotcha!" Julie flashed her light around as she jumped out into the lane.

"What're you doing?" a man's voice yelled, frightened.

"Oh, shit! It's Uncle Bob! Jeez! Let's get out of here."

"You girls oughta be in bed!" they heard Uncle Bob complain over spurts of giggling and their feet pounding down the lane.

Around the corner, they found skinny little Jimmy sneaking up behind the abandoned truck beside his grandparents' place, flashing his light inside. Julie tagged his rear end with her flashlight before he turned his on her face. Blinking in the light, she told him, "Rules have changed, Jimmy. I got you first." Selena shook her head when Julie told her to kiss Jimmy, so Julie did, although she thought Jimmy was a jerk with his greasy hair and pimples.

"Hey, this is all right!" Jimmy exclaimed. By the time they saw the next boy, his flashlight was put away. He was walking along Princess Street looking for girls. Everybody ran around with silly grins. Boys darted out from behind buildings, yelling to let the girls know where they were, running away, but not fast, hoping to get tagged. The girls could choose whoever they wanted. They owned the whole town. They were invincible.

After awhile, Selena and Julie headed back to Julie's house to meet up with the other girls and to hear what they had done. Selena hadn't done any kissing. Julie had told her not to be so fussy, just pick someone who didn't smell. As they crossed the street in front of the Pearl Harbour, Selena said, "Hey, there's Martin. Going by over there by the old post office. I'm sure it's him. That's his black leather jacket with the white sleeves." He had both hands in his jeans pockets and a couple of books under one arm. Selena said firmly, "I'm going to tag him." Julie was surprised, but Selena tossed her head, swishing her new hair-do around. She said, "Just watch me!" She grabbed the flashlight from Julie and started to run parallel to Martin's route, a block away.

"Watch out, Lena," Julie said in a loud whisper as she ran after her. "He's not playing. Maybe doesn't even know about the game." Julie wanted to say, *he's White*.

Selena stopped and turned. "Yeah, maybe you're right."

"But what the heck, eh? Let's get him anyways!" Julie laughed. Selena should have some fun for a change. They raced around the block to get in front of him. They hid in a doorway, waiting as they heard footsteps coming nearer and nearer on the wooden sidewalk. Selena had to squeeze her mouth shut to keep from laughing out loud.

Julie had never seen Selena so agitated before. When Martin was a few feet away, Selena jumped onto the sidewalk, flashing the light in his face. "Gotcha!" she yelled. She began to giggle, her hand over her mouth.

Martin's books dropped to the sidewalk with a thud. He stood stunned and puzzled in the light. "What's going on here?" he said. "Who's there anyway?" He waved his hands in front of his face as if to push the light away.

Julie said, "New rules. You gotta let her kiss you."

"What the hell are you talking about?" he demanded. "What new rules?" He bent to pick up his books. When he straightened up, they could see his face was red, even in the light of the flashlight. Blonde people blush so easy, Julie thought. He was frowning. "Who're you?" He looked more closely. "Oh, Julie and Selena." He calmed down and said with a smile, "I should've guessed." Selena turned off the flashlight.

The girls stood close beside each other, confused for a few seconds. Somebody had to say something. Julie grabbed Martin's arm and said, "Rules of the game, Martin. Flashlight Tag. Selena tagged you and so she has to kiss you."

"Oh yeah? How do I get to play?" he asked.

"You just have to stand there," Julie said. What an idiot he is, she thought.

"Please, Julie, let's go," Selena pleaded in a small voice, pulling Julie's arm.

"You can't get away with that, Selena," Martin said, coming up to her. "If you won't do it, I will." He reached for her chin and kissed her on the cheek. The girls stood side by side on the sidewalk, shocked, while he sauntered away, smiling. They stared at the back of his black and white leather jacket until it disappeared.

"Wow! Selena! Wow!" Julie turned to her.

Selena's smile made her eyes sparkle. She held her crippled hand against the cheek he had kissed. "I can't believe it!" she said.

It was late. Julie didn't want Selena to get into trouble on this wonderful night. "Jeez! We'd better get home. It's probably eleven," she said.

They began walking toward the South End, when Selena stopped. "You don't have to come with me. I'll be fine," she said.

"Nah. It's OK. I don't have to be home or nothing." Julie always walked Selena home when it was dark.

Selena seemed changed to Julie, more confident than she had ever seen her. She looked older. It wasn't just her hair. "It's OK, just go home. Everything's just great," Selena said, "Thanks for my hair. I just love it," she said quietly. She turned and ran towards home.

Julie wandered towards the North end. The thrill of the night was gone. She kicked at the gravel on the street, angry with Martin for changing the rules.

Martin never showed any more attention to Selena. He hardly spoke to her again. Before the end of October, he was sent away to a boarding school in Vancouver. The girls heard that his mother had said she didn't like the "bad influence" that Dawson kids had on her son.

For Julie and Selena, the fun of being dancehall girls and playing Flashlight Tag faded with that fall. They were too old for games, they said.

RIVER CHILD

Six in the morning. A finger of sunshine touched the wall behind my bed long ago. The sun reaches us early in the day, summer or winter, because our cabin faces south. I like it here, under Crocus Bluff. It's quiet, hidden away from everything, and close to where the Klondike joins the Yukon River.

The sweet smell of frying bacon drifts across the room. The old man has nothing to do all day but he still has the habit of getting up early. I wait until I hear, "Selena! Breakfast on the table! Come and get it, grandchild!" I turn over and stretch between the warm blankets. Pop knows I don't have to go to work today, or tomorrow. Two whole days off in a row from my waitress job at the Westminster. The job is hard for me. I'm too shy with some of the customers who like to joke. They make me feel childish and stupid. Walking all day is hard on my feet too. I want to buy some heavier shoes, but any I see in the catalogue are too ugly and also expensive. We need the money for other things.

It's important for Pop to do things properly, on schedule, he keeps telling me. He'll be upset if I don't get up for breakfast. I still fear him a little, even though I'm way over sixteen. I force my feet to the floor, wrap my long wool cardigan around my shoulders, and come into the kitchen.

From Pop's broad back as he bends over the stove and scrapes the frying pan, I hear, "Just look at that sun out there! It's going to be another great day. You oughta go to Moosehide. Check the fishwheel again." He's already thinking up things to keep me busy.

"Maybe," I say without enthusiasm. I can't decide right now what I want to do for the whole day. I make the toast and pour coffee. He's so ancient. How can he be interested in everything around him? He's so full of energy especially at this hour in the morning. I want only the least amount of effort to start the day.

"Trappin' too many whitefish. Throw them back when you go," he says, slapping two plates with bacon and fried eggs on the table. "All this sun will be good for the garden, but we could use a little rain by the weekend. Nothing like a good solid rain, especially for the potatoes." He plops himself in his big chair. "I fiddled with that starter on the boat motor yesterday. You shouldn't have any more problems with it today."

The wrinkles around Pop's eyes make him seem permanently cheerful. He smiles at me as if he is going to ask me a question, but first his hand reaches up to flatten a thin wave of white hair. It's a habit he has before he starts to eat. He takes a bite of toast and picks up his fork. Blue eyes peek at me as he proudly announces: "Yesterday Alex Johnson said that you were the best waitress the Westminster ever had."

"Really?" I ask with some interest. Pop's pride warms me inside when we are together, but I'm embarrassed when he boasts about me with other people. I can't be everything he thinks I am.

I watch Pop take his toast and wipe the egg yolk off his plate. As usual, he is finished breakfast and I'm just starting. He pushes his plate aside and says seriously, "Alex said that you could have a job with him any time you wanted." I smile at this. Alex Johnson's hotel, the Occidental, is right next door to the Westminster. Everyone knows that they're long-time rivals for customers and staff.

But I remember what I've been told. "Yeah, well, I wouldn't work for old man Johnson on a bet," I say, "Julie says he pinches the girls' bums when nobody's looking. He only picks on us Native girls, you know." Pop is always lecturing me about the evils of letting men touch me. He should realize that sometimes it's the man's fault too, like with Alex Johnson's "roving hands" as Julie calls them.

Pop frowns. Right away I'm sorry I said anything. "He'll only pinch them that let him," he says. He frowns and gets up from the table with his plate. He doesn't like Julie. What he says next he's said so many times I'm able to mouth the words behind his back: "Mark my words, that Julie will go the same way as your mother did, drinking herself to death in Whitehorse." Julie has always been a real good friend, since I was a little girl. They aren't the same kind of people at all.

It's better if I change the subject. "Oh, I forgot to tell you what happened to one of my worst customers yesterday. You know Tom, that guy who's with that bunch of kids who're always sitting with an empty coffee cup and no money, killing time? Well, he was fooling around with one of those little plastic pouches of ketchup. You know the kind. I brought some home last week. Well, he has it in both hands, aims it across the table at me. Squeezes the bag, trying to break it and hit me with the ketchup, right? Guess what happens? It pops open and hits him right in the face! His hands were just covered too! Oh, did we laugh, all of us! His face was as red as the ketchup!"

Pop laughs his loudest, and says, "Serves him right, eh?"

By the time I finish breakfast Pop is out in his garden, kneeling between the rows of vegetables, pulling weeds. While I wash the dishes I see him through the window, green puffs of weeds flying through the air from his strong hands. I wonder if he knows how much he means to me. We never talk about things like that.

Not many girls I know have a room to themselves like I have. I keep it neat. I make my bed every morning. I love this room, my own little part of our cabin. No one is allowed to come in it without my permission. It doesn't have much furniture except my single bed, an old wooden chair, and a small chest of drawers. There's no room for anything else. Above the drawers there's a cracked mirror that I found. I painted everything I could in bright yellow and orange, my favourite colours. The walls are rough logs, but I've decorated them everywhere with pictures of Elvis Presley and Jackie Kennedy cut from magazines.

On my days off, I give myself the luxury of standing in front of the mirror, twisting my hair in new styles. I like how thick it is, how black. Pop says I've inherited a slim face and a long, straight nose from the Macleans. Julie says my face is exotic, with my dark complexion and eyes, and that the other Native girls are jealous of my looks. I don't know about that. I'm short and tiny and wish I was bigger. But I am secretly proud of my rounded hips and slim waist. I show off with wide belts whenever I can.

Yesterday a bunch of boys whistled at me. I always pretend not to notice them. Something warm stirs inside me, but their whistling scares me. Julie laughs at me. She says that when I'm older, I won't mind male attention any more. Julie's not that much older than me, but she likes to make sure that I know how much more experienced she is.

With a crash, the brush I'm using to style my hair slips and falls to the floor. I reach down, clenching my right fist in anger. The thumb and two first fingers are shortened and permanently twisted inward. The nails are bumpy. They're ugly, half the size of the others. I keep them away from sight as much as possible. Sometimes it takes people a long time to realize that there is anything wrong with my hand.

My mother Eliza lied about what happened, trying to make everyone believe I was born that way. I was born when she was only sixteen. She was already a mess by that time, I'm sure. The truth is that when I was three months old, she left me in our unheated cabin at forty below while she partied. My hand and feet froze so they didn't grow right. I hate to say that she's my mother. I call her by her first name, Eliza, not mom or mommy. Some mother! She'd rather party with her slob friends than look after me.

Sometimes when I'm awake at night and can't sleep, I make myself think about what must have happened that night. I'm in the bedroom. Pop is gone, out on his trapline on the Thirtymile River, waiting until it's warmer so he can come home. Eliza is out somewhere drinking. The fire in our airtight heater is in the front room. It burns out and it's cold for four hours before Eliza remembers to come home. She's drunk as usual. She lights the fire again and passes out beside me in the bed without undressing. I have long ago stopped crying. Pop has told me that I was probably in deep hypothermia. The cold makes you go to sleep. Sometimes you never wake up. Both my feet are white with frostbite; my lips are blue. My frozen diaper sticks to my skin, thick frost from my breath gathers around my face on the pillow. My right hand is partly uncovered, exposed to the air, my left arm tucked inside the icy blanket against my body. Sometimes I make myself sleep like that, with my hands exactly where they were then, while I think about it, trying to figure out why it had to happen to me.

Pop never talked about it when I was younger, but other people did. Some people love to tell the worst on others. It makes them feel better about themselves I guess. When Pop came home two days later, he noticed my hand and feet right away. They were swollen and red, blistered, like with burns. He knew it was frostbite. A neighbour told me that he ran with me in his arms to the doctor, swearing at the top of his voice, without stopping even to untie his dog team. Pop says I screamed for weeks in pain. My constant crying made Eliza angry, but for awhile, she stayed home. Probably scared of getting charged with something.

Pop told me the doctor threatened Eliza with a charge of child neglect. The doctor left the Yukon a few weeks later, so nothing was done. My mother told her friends she had to take some kind of pill when she was pregnant. She said it caused deformities. Not many people believed that story because they had seen me when I was still all right I guess. But the story of the pills became part of the gossip in Dawson, until people didn't care what was true and what wasn't. I walked much later than most kids, with a kind of limp. I've always had problems with walking any distance. The bottoms of my feet get sore.

I finish my hair. I am restless. Angry. I have to get out of here, get rid of this energy. I'll go to Moosehide after all. It's in a place downriver that gets more sunshine than Dawson, just a few minutes in the boat. When I'm there, I feel the happiness the olden day people had in their little log cabins with sod roofs.

I make a lunch of sandwiches from Pop's homemade bread to take with me. When I close the door, I can see his straw hat bouncing along between the tall rows of peas in the garden. "I'll be in Moosehide," I call and he nods and waves a hand in the air in approval. Even without seeing his face, I know he's smiling.

On my way to Front Street where our small aluminum boat is docked, I meet a couple I know. I'm not often able to talk anyone into coming with me on the river, but I keep trying. "It's a great day to be on the river. Come with me." I say to them.

The girl laughs. "Too early, man!" she says. "We haven't even been to bed yet. Hey, we were at that party at George's place last night." She tries to make me jealous. "You don't know what you missed--a real good one--wow! Dope and everything!" Pop won't let me out to anything like that and she knows it.

Her boyfriend says, "What's there to do down there in the daytime anyways?" Some kids go to Moosehide at night to get out of town and drink without worrying about the cops finding them. "Ain't nothin' in Moosehide. Just a lot of old junk and empty cabins." He pulls the girl by her arm, "Come on, let's get home. I gotta sleep." I turn to go and hear him say, "Jeeze, you'd think she lived on the river or something."

Pop is right about the motor. It starts easily. It's a warm, windless day. I am glad for the breeze from the boat's speed. Now I'm happy to be alone. Energy sweeps through my body as I skim over the surface of the tan-coloured water. The river looks muddy, Pop told me, because the White River empties into the Yukon south of Dawson. It's fed by glaciers in the St. Elias Mountains hundred of miles away to the southwest and the Yukon River picks up silt from the White. South of the White, the Yukon River is clear blue-green. Some day I'll take a boat down the river from Whitehorse to Dawson and see it for myself. I'd like to try a canoe, maybe a kayak, tent along the way.

The orange government ferry carrying two tourist campers on their way to Alaska is headed for the west bank. I bounce through its wake, waving to the captain, Julie's father, and then cut over close to the steep cliff between Dawson and Moosehide. The safest currents are there.

While I am going downstream for the few minutes it takes to get to the old village, I feel as if I'm in a different world, a place where I'm older, in control. I hear the echo of Grandma Thomas talking to me one time when I stayed with her in Moosehide. "Me, I'm child of the river," she said. "That river, she give me everything I need. Just like mother to me. You treat river right, it help you live." I think I know how she feels. I'm a child of the river, too.

On the riverbank in front of Moosehide, I tie the boat to our wooden fishwheel that floats close to the rocky shore. Pop says it's the laziest and simplest kind of fishing he's ever seen. A paddlewheel about ten feet high grinds and squeals in a regular rhythm, turned by the power of the stream. The fish aren't frightened by the splashing because they can't see it in the muddy water. The wheel picks them up, drops them in a trough fed by river water, where they stay, alive, until we want them. Couldn't have anything easier.

I throw a half dozen silvery whitefish back and clean three red king salmon that are caught in the pool. Leaving them in the cold water, I climb the river bank and spread a blanket in the grass above the fishwheel. As I doze in the morning sun, I listen to the screams of gulls. They fly inland all the way from the Alaskan coast, following the Yukon River. Once in awhile they are interrupted by the hollow plunking talk of ravens and I wonder what they are saying to each other. Maybe they are thanking me for the fish guts I have left for them as they dive close by me to eat. Pop says it's not true, but I like to think that as long as I can hear the birds, there won't be any bears attracted by the smell of the fish. He said sometime I should see huge grizzlies, as he has, eating fish right beside the gulls that are puttering around, waiting for leftovers.

After awhile, I wander through the fireweed behind the deserted log cabins. Some of the magenta stalks waving in the breeze are taller than I am. Stories the old people have told me about when they lived here come back. They talk about the fun they had, the dances and the feasts, before they moved into Dawson. It was a freer life, they say, living off the land according to the seasons and the wildlife, not working for Whites, and away from cops telling you what to do. I pick up some beer bottles scattered on the ground around an old campfire, left from some kids' party, and throw them in the garbage barrel near the little white Anglican church. Maybe the kids still feel some of that freedom here.

I have the key to Grandma Thomas' cabin and I always check it when I'm in Moosehide. I can stay there whenever I want. It will be mine some day, Grandma says. I push open the door to the one room. The three windows are boarded up but enough light comes through the door for me to see that the things I left the last time I stayed are still there. My sleeping bag is rolled up on the mattress at the foot of the wooden bedframe. The tin dishes are on two shelves over the counter holding the dishpan and water pail. People leave Grandma's place alone, even though they could easily break in the wooden door with a good kick.

I wander around a couple of the other cabins, peering in through broken windows. On one, the door hangs lopsided with only one hinge. I lift it, push up, and go inside. A pale green foam mattress is in one corner. There are paper bags and a couple of empty liquor bottles thrown on the floor. It smells of urine.

I know the raspberries behind the school house must be ripe so I find a glass jar in one of the cabins. I fill it with Pop's favourite berries in no time. He'll make some jam this weekend. I climb the short hill to the graveyard behind the village and eat my sandwich sitting in the tall grass watching the birds fight over fish guts. My eyes are alert for any sign of a bear in the raspberries. I mentally make plans about where I will go if I see a black patch in the bush on the right, the left, or behind me. You don't do anything foolish like running away. You react smarter if you figure it out before you see them. Pop has taught me to be prepared before things happen.

The last thing I always do before I leave is to visit Grandma Maggie's grave marked by a small white cross. I could find it even in the dark. I kneel down, pull a few weeds, and sprinkle some raspberries on her grave like Pop taught me when I was small. Grandma Maggie's family was from the Thirtymile River, downriver. They built a cabin at Moosehide, but they spent more time in the bush than there. As with many families, they moved around the country all the time, following the moose, the caribou, the fish, depending on the season. The Taylors got all their food by hunting and fishing and they trapped animals to make almost all of their clothes.

For a long time, we had no photos of my grandmother, but I had a clear picture of her in my mind. To me, she was a tiny, pretty woman with a motherly smile. Her shiny black hair was tied back with a pale blue ribbon, and she had kindly dark eyes. She wore a light brown moosehide dress with colourful beadwork on the shoulders and chest and fringes along the sleeves. The mukluks on her feet were trimmed in dark red beaver fur.

Pop and I had a favourite ritual about going to bed when I was young that kept Maggie alive in our minds. I crawled under the covers and Pop would sit on the side of the bed and say, "Want me to tell you a story about Maggie and me?"

I would sometimes start with, "What was that name, Pop, that you call the Indians?" I knew that my part in the familiar storytelling was to prompt the right response.

"Nomads, you call 'em. Families would travel all over, no matter what the weather was like, walking in the summer, or in a boat made of skins. Dogs helped them. They would carry things on their backs."

"In the winter they had a dog team to pull them, right?"

"Right, dogs with a tobaggan made of skins. We all had dog teams. I had eleven good strong huskies that pulled us everywhere. Winter was easier than summer to get around."

"And your lead dog was Skookum!"

"Right you are, little one! He was Grandma Maggie's special dog, big and strong, could go for days in the bush. She taught me how to make the dogs listen, and lots of other things. I am very grateful to her. She knew how to survive in the bush without anybody's help if she had to, and then she taught me."

"How come we don't have dogs now, Pop?"

Pop would sigh and look sad. "I miss them for sure. But they cost a lot nowadays, and they have to be kept out of town, and the price of fur is down...but I sure do miss them."

One night I was tired of hearing about the Indians. They weren't part of my life. I was White. "You said all that stuff before. I know Grandma Maggie's a Indian. Not me." I looked sideways at him to see if that made him angry.

Pop was quiet for awhile. Then he said, "But you and your mother are both Indians because of her."

"You're not a Indian."

"I know it's pretty confusing, isn't it?" he laughed. He took a breath, and said carefully, "Grandma Maggie stayed being an Indian even though she lived with me, a White man. It's because I didn't marry her. I told you that before. If you married a White man, you wouldn't be Indian any more."

So it could change then. Good.

"Grandma Maggie wasn't your wife? Then how did you get my Mommy?"

Pop chuckled and poked me in the stomach. "Well, sometimes that's possible, you know, to have a baby without being married. If you love each other a lot, like we did." That was a surprise.

Pop always went into the kitchen after our story. He would come back with milk and a cookie for me. Careful not to spill any milk in the bed, I sat up straight, two hands wrapped around the glass. "How can you tell who's who?" I asked. I really wanted to ask about my friend Julie, if she was Indian like me, but Pop didn't like talking about the Fullers. He always looked disappointed if I said I had been playing with Julie.

"You're sure full of questions tonight, aren't you? You mean you are wondering who's Indian and who's not?" I nodded. Pop chewed on the mouth part of his cold pipe and I heard the little gurgle coming from the other end it. He took it out of his mouth and said, "Well, Indian Affairs keeps a Band List. That's what registered means. Your name is on the register. On the list. You know, just like at school when the teacher takes attendance. Indian Affairs gives you a number on the list so everybody can tell who's who."

I was on that government list. So everybody could tell who I was. Indian.

I bit into my cookie with a crunch. How could I ask about Julie without saying her name? I swallowed the last of my milk, and asked, "Pop, what's non-sta...non-stat-us? Somebody told me that word today, and I heard it before too."

"That's when you have a White father and an Indian mother who got married. Like Julie Fuller. She doesn't have a Band number." I looked at him. Funny how he always guessed what I really wanted to know. Non-status. No number. Not Indian. Not White. Half and half? Julie must know that she doesn't have a number and that I have one: number 59, Pop said. But that meant that I was different from my Pop and my best friend too. They weren't Indians and I was.

I put the empty glass beside the bed, and snuggled up under his arm, my head against his chest. My ear felt the vibrations of his deep voice. "There are lots and lots of good things about being Indian, you know," he said. "You should be proud of it. Grandma Maggie and I made a darn good living out in the bush when lots of people were starving to death Outside during the Depression. That was because of what Grandma Maggie and people like her knew about the land and the animals. And they knew it from their ancestors who survived in the wild for thousands and thousands of years before any Whiteman came. They were a lot smarter than some of those Whitemen who came up North in the Gold Rush, I can tell you. Lots of them died because they didn't know a darn thing about living up here in the Yukon and were too stupid to ask."

Pop pointed his pipe at me. "Listen to me close, now, eh?" He sounded stern. "How important you are depends only on how you live with other people. Nothing else. It's got nothing to do with the colour of your skin or how much money you have. Or if you have a number or not. You remember that always. Promise."

"OK. I'll remember." I had enough serious talk. I slid down under the covers. "Now tell me the story about when you and Grandma Maggie just about freezed to death." It was one of Pop's favourites and it would keep him in the bedroom until I was asleep.

****

I always feel a little let-down having to come back to Dawson from Moosehide. The mid-afternoon sun flashes off the surface of the water and hurts my half-closed eyes. Today will make the skin on my face and arms even darker. Black like the rest of the Indian kids.

On the river's edge in Dawson, I tie the boat to a thick willow leaning over the water's edge, I throw the fish into a burlap bag and toss them over my back. I'm strong but I've got my mother's small body. The weight is more than I'm used to, and I stumble a little as I climb the sloping river bank to Front Street. The salmon aren't running as much as they were at the beginning of summer. I'll only be able to sell one of them. We'll need the other one for ourselves and there will be one left for Grandma Thomas. I'll wait to bring her the salmon and go to the Westminster first. I hope I can sell the biggest one to them to get rid of the weight, but they may not want it.

On Front Street, I walk by the row of nine identical log houses owned by the Indian Agency where the status Indians live. They huddle close to each other, as if to protect themselves from the rest of the town. There is a metal number attached squarely in the middle of each unpainted door. No one else in Dawson has numbers on their doors. Some have added a small porch to keep out the cold. Windows on either side of the door look out on the Yukon River where only a few of the Indians still travel for fishing.

A gang of skinny dogs scavenges in scattered garbage, chasing each other. Three of them break away from the pack and trot up behind me, smelling the fish. I kick some stones at them but they keep following me.

A pickup truck going too fast passes me as I make my way down the gravel street. I lift my free hand, automatically waving at the three Smith boys in the cab. One waves a beer bottle at me in a salute, not looking back as they go by. The powdery dust rises in billows behind the truck. I breathe it in and feel the dust cover my hands and face.

The Westminster wants the biggest salmon in the bag so I lighten my load for five dollars. I stop at the Northern Commercial to buy a can of butter for supper. We'll have the rich fresh salmon and new potatoes from the garden, with butter, my favourite supper.

****

A simple thing like my leaving the house can be so complicated for Pop and me. During the day, he wants me to go out; at night, he wants me home. When we finish washing the supper dishes, I try to sound casual as I walk toward the door, carrying the salmon in the burlap bag. "I'll take that fish to Grandma Thomas now, Pop," I say. I avoid his eyes. They follow me whenever he's worried. I am relieved that he hasn't said anything about my going this time. I know he heaves a sigh after the door closes behind me. He's thinking if only I'd been a boy. It'd be so much easier. I heard him saying that to somebody when he thought I wasn't listening.

Pop needs to trust me. I know no matter who you are, there's trouble to be had if you look for it. Sometimes even when you don't look it's there. The girls in town do all right, just getting pregnant pretty young. Pop doesn't see that the boys are in more trouble than the girls. I know some boys who have disappeared into booze, sometimes freezing to death, passed out in a snowbank in the winter, or they kill themselves, shooting their heads off. The girls don't do that. I've tried to stay away from problems, but it's not easy. Everybody my age drinks and smokes pot too. Pop has said God help me if I so much as come home smelling of beer. I wonder if he would beat me to try and kill the devil in me. He's already said that. But he doesn't have to hit me. I'm more afraid of his yelling at me than his beating me. I think he's trying to change whatever it is he thinks he did wrong with my mother, to do it better this time, with me.

I'm headed for Julie Fuller's place in the North End. It's known as Cherry Hill, always said with a snicker. It was only last year that I realized what that meant. It disgusted me that people would say such things about the Fuller family even though Julie's sisters are pretty wild. Her mother and father drink too much, too, but my Jules is not like them. The stories

I hear from other people about what goes on in Julie's house are never mentioned between Julie and me. Pop told me a long time ago not to go there, but my friendship with her is important to me. It's sometimes even stronger than the fear of facing his temper. Julie and I talk a lot about one day leaving Dawson together. We're going to have a better life than this, in Whitehorse, or even Outside.

It's always a problem getting anybody to come to the door at Julie's. I have to pound on it with my fist. The latch inside finally bounces off from my effort and the door opens. It's a dark room, but in the summer it's light enough to see, with the long daylight, even after supper. The little three-year-old girl of one of Julie's older sisters gazes up at me. She's wearing a dirty undershirt and no pants. She recognizes me and smiles, raising her arms: "Seena."

I look closely to see how dirty she is before I touch her. Sometimes she has nits in her hair. Today, her black feet and hands turn me off. I manage to get safely past her little body standing there and turn towards her. "Go get Julie," I kneel down and push her gently, insisting, "get Auntie."

The girl stumbles over bedclothes on the floor, farther into the warm darkness, singing, "Auntie, auntie." In the back, a deep female voice says that she'll get Julie, and someone climbs the ladder that goes to the upstairs. I've never been up there. I come here often, but I am uneasy, and I don't like to stay long. Julie's brother Paul shot himself to death in the back bedroom.

I push aside a jumble of clothes, carpenter's tools, and cooking pots on the bench near the door. I put the salmon on the floor under the bench, and sit down. The stench of the closed room sweeps into my lungs as I sit waiting. It's a suffocating smell, a combination of beer and urine maybe. It's much worse in the winter, when it's mixed with the sour smell of wet wool socks drying near the stove and the contents of the slop-pail rotting under the makeshift sink. Once in awhile someone cleans up and the smell is less, but it's always there, a part of the house. The smell makes me feel hopeless and reminds me somehow of my mother. That smell is one of the things keeping me from going to the teenage drinking parties that I know go on all the time. Drinking causes the dirt. I'll never live like that.

My eyes grow used to the gloom. I spot two bodies on a mattress on the floor across the room from me. A naked leg stretches out from under a torn red blanket. From its bulk, I see that it must be Julie's mother, Mary Ann. The other body stirs. A man groans as his arm finds its way around Mary Ann's hips under the cover. I sit as still as I can. I hate coming here.

"Julie! I'm waiting for you!" I yell into the distance.

The man rolls over and sits up at the sound of my voice. His green plaid shirt is open, showing masses of black hair on his chest. He gropes in the shirt pockets, his long hair drooping over his shoulders. He doesn't find anything. He looks blankly across at me and asks, "Hey, Beautiful. Got a cigarette?"

I'm not as hidden as I thought I was. "Don't smoke," I say. I look away and down to the floor.

He's the Whiteman from Mayo that I noticed in the cafe last week. A couple of girls in the cafe had giggled about how good looking he was. His fingers surprise me. They are like a woman's, long and beautiful as they roam through his loose black hair and over his shoulder and finally scratch his chest. He coughs loudly and mutters to himself, "Oh, man, what a head I got. Should stick to pot."

Pushing Mary Ann gently aside, he searches for cigarettes. The blanket falls away from her, exposing her large brown buttocks. He slowly stands up, wavering, and I can see he is naked below his shirt. Turning away from me, he gropes for his pants and pulls them on. His hand discovers cigarettes and matches in one of his pants' pockets. He lights a cigarette, stepping across Mary Ann who is still asleep, and walks towards me. I can smell his sweat.

"You're Sheila, right?" He mumbles through the cigarette in his mouth.

"Selena." As soon as I say it, I regret saying anything. I'm torn now between a strong urge to run away, and being strangely curious about the tall man coming towards me.

"Selena. Right on." He takes the cigarette out of his mouth and smiles. "Pretty name for a pretty girl." He pulls a metal stool over in front of me, balancing it on the uneven floor, sits, and reaches down for a half-empty bottle of whiskey near Mary Ann's head. He points the bottle toward me, "How 'bout a drink, Selena?" I shake my head. Noticing Mary Ann's bare legs and bum, he laughs, and leaning dangerously over, he draws the blanket over her. "Man," he asks, "ever seen anything like that? Wowwweee!"

I sit still, somehow paralyzed. I should get out of here. He's standing up, leaning closer to me. I should go. He's over me. His hair touches my forehead. The cigarette smoke hurts my eyes. His body smells. Sweat and booze. I can feel his heat. His long fingers go around my waist. They give a hurting squeeze as he leans his head into mine.

It takes all my strength to push him away. I am standing on the road in front of Julie's. I've run out of the house. I don't see him. He isn't there, but I feel that man's hands on me, strong, crawling around my waist, upward, upward to my breasts. I can't stop him. Horror pushes me, filling my body with energy, and I run. It feels like he is trying to stop me with his hands. Even as I run away, he pulls me back. I struggle away from him toward the river.

My feet hurt as if I've run on needles. Breathing hard, I throw myself into the long grass on the river bank. I'm nauseated and my head pounds. I put my hands up to my face and I can smell old fish and Julie's house. There's dust on my face. I crawl to the river's edge, kneel, and wash in the icy water. I lean back and sink down into the comfort of the cool grass, letting the setting sun seep into my skin. I makes me feel clean. When I close my eyes, all I can see is red with little floating purple circles slowly coming toward me and disappearing somewhere behind my head. One side of my head is throbbing. It becomes gradually less as I let myself concentrate on the purple shapes instead. When the throbbing ends, I doze.

A car horn bleeps and I wake with a start. A mosquito buzzes close to my ear. The sun has set behind the mountains across the river and the air is chilly. It must be close to ten o'clock or later. I feel my puffy face. My eyes will be red. Pop will know something has happened when I go home. What will I say to him? Damn it all. I stumble to the river and splash my face again with its comforting cold.

Why don't I grow up? Julie lives in that house, and she's fine. She'll be mad at me. Maybe even embarrassed. I'll have to go back there and explain it somehow. A wave of frustration sweeps over me. I've left Grandma Thomas' salmon on the floor under the bench. The Fullers will keep it and I won't be able to get it back for her.

The whole day has changed now. It started out with promise: a day off work, a trip to Moosehide. I thought I would enjoy every minute of it. I climb the river bank, counting each step. Why didn't I shove that disgusting man away? Why did I just sit there? I didn't even tell him off. Why did I let him get near me with his strangely beautiful hands?

"Hey, Lena, over here!" I hear Julie's call and see her waving both hands high in the air a block away. She is with two tall men. She leaves them and runs up the street to me, laughing. "Hey, silly. I been looking for you all over. They said you came to the house. Where'd you go anyways?" Julie is chewing gum and snapping it with her teeth in a fast rhythm, not missing a beat while she talks. Before I can answer, she says, "Never mind. Listen." She nods her head toward the men standing at the corner. "Them guys, they want to take us to that street dance tonight. Great, eh?"

Julie's plain freckled face gleams with excitement. Something warm grows in my chest whenever I see her happy. She says, "They're from Mayo. One's that White guy I told you about--Freddie, and the other's his friend, Richard. Whadya say, huh?" She pulls my sleeve, her short brown hair bouncing with energy.

She always looks so good when she's smiling. I smile back at her and say, "Oh, Jules, you know I can't go to the dance. Pop says I'm not old enough yet."

She raises her hand and gestures as if throwing something away, "Well to hell with *him*!" From her exaggerated movements I realize that she's been drinking, or maybe smoking pot. "Anyways Lena, it's just a street dance. Anybody can go. Little kids can go for Christ's sake. There's no booze. You don't even dance unless you go inside that roped-off part. Come on, you can at least go and take a look, eh, whadya say?"

"I dunno..."

Julie puts one hand up beside her mouth and says in a loud persuasive whisper into my ear, "Lena, for God's sake, Freddie's got just *tons* of money. He's down from working in Inuvik. They just want a good time, man. Dancing, nothing else. C'mon and dance with us."

"OK. I'll come with you for a while. But I'm on my way home." She has always been able to talk me into doing just about anything.

"Wow! Great! Let's dance!" She snaps her fingers to an Elvis tune, singing the words she knows. We start walking toward the men and she turns to me and says, "You know what? Richard asked about you. He was at my house this morning and said he saw you there. Called you Sheila, he said."

My stomach lurches. We are close enough so that I see that it really is him, that dark-haired man I saw at Julie's. He has changed his clothes and tied his hair behind in a pony-tail.

I turn to her meaning to say, "Jules, I can't..." But it's too late to argue with her. She'll never listen. I have to go by the dance on my way home anyway. Freddie and Richard are on either side of us, laughing. Freddie takes Julie's hand, and I stay close to her, silent, not looking at Richard. I can smell pot.

We all walk quickly toward the Downtown Hotel where the street is blocked off. Before I know it we are in the crowd watching the dancers.

Freddie pays our way into the dancing area and Julie pulls me towards her and cheers as I begin to dance with her. It's easy to follow. No one holds anyone, we just stand in one spot, moving our bodies in time to the loud music coming through the speakers from records being played inside the bar. Everyone is laughing and excited.

"Oh, wow, I bet Moosehide dances were never like this!" Julie calls to me through the noise. I laugh at her. She always teases me about liking to be in Moosehide. My hands are over my head and I'm twirling around. I feel sexy even in my old jeans. When I stop turning, Julie is a few feet away, looking up at Freddie as she dances. Richard is standing in front of me. He's the best looking man in the crowd. What the heck, I tell myself, it's only a dance. Stop being a wet blanket. What's there to be afraid of?

Richard and I dance facing each other. The beat pulses in my chest. It's as if the music is coming from inside of me. I watch his tall body swaying to the rhythm, expertly responding to every other beat with his feet and hands. Then he comes close and takes my right hand, the one that's deformed. He doesn't seem to notice that it's bunched together and that he has to cover it with those long graceful fingers of his to twirl me around. I can feel his strength as he turns me again and again, until I am dizzy and nearly fall over. He stops, grabs me around the waist. We both laugh. I twist away from him to the music, feeling admired as his eyes follow my moves. He snaps his fingers in time to the beat.

A little later he shares a coke with me. We stand and watch the crowd. The music is slow. He puts both his arms around my waist, pulling me to him. I lean my head against his chest. My arms go under his and around to his back. His strong back muscles slowly move under my hands. The smell of his sweat and cigarette smoke reminds me of him in Julie's house. I let myself remember his leaning over me, his touching me then, only this time it is perfectly all right. What might have happened if I had let his hands caress me then? I close my eyes with a thrill as he puts his hand under my chin and kisses my forehead. Before long, a deep voice comes from his chest, "Hey, sexy, let's split this place."

I pull back from him, stumbling on the gravel. "What? Where to?"

"Let's go back to Julie's. We can have some privacy there. Toke up a little, eh?" He gestures as if he is smoking a roach. He takes my good hand in one of his and beckons Freddie and Julie to come over. He says some things to Julie that I don't hear over the loud music. She nods and then I can't see them any more and Richard is pulling me through the crowd.

THE WAY UP IS WORK

Deserted buildings form a small canyon on either side of Dave Maclean as he tugs his wooden cart along the street. He passes Klondike history: Bonanza Hotel, Old Post Office, and Madame Tremblay's Store, their clapboard walls bleached greyer year by year with sun and rain. Unusual humidity this July paints shaded walls with a silver-green skin of lichen. At street level, the windows are covered with plywood; the upper windows, dark and brooding, look down on him.

A saw and axe rattle in the empty cart, protesting the ruts in the street left by the last hard rainfall. Lining one side of the dusty street is a precarious sidewalk made of wooden planks. Dave ignores it. He walks with determination in the middle of the street, heading towards the Midnight Dome Road. He is preparing for the long winter ahead, anxious to have enough wood. No matter how warm summer can get in the Yukon, winter is never far from his mind.

Walking King Street for the first time forty-five years before, Dave felt as if he was in a cowboy movie. When yellowed curtains on broken windows allowed a little sunshine into hollow rooms, he would gaze inside the Western theatrical sets past the dust sparkling in the shafts of light. Sometimes he climbed inside. There, he would pick his way through the broken grey furniture, smelling the musty darkness, aromas left by long ago lives. Now the sights and smells are in his bones and he journeys unaware that Klondike ghosts are his companions.

Dave's tall body leans into his task, broad shoulders bent forward. His head, with its thin covering of white, bobs in rhythm with his steps. Against his throat, his unruly beard is nearly stifling. He is reminded of pulling the plough through the fields of his uncle's farm in Saskatchewan, where he was sent as a young boy after his father died. This work is easier. The prairie is a remote landscape to him now, relived only in abstraction, in books and atlases, more a thought than a homeland. The Yukon's pyramid mountains and deep valleys have replaced the horizontal lines as his connection with the earth. Still, Dave likes to get to the very top of the Dome behind Dawson when he can. He breathes easier when he is out of the Yukon River valley and the blue-green mountains are pushed out of the way by the big sky.

Exactly how many winters are between him and his family in Saskatchewan? He has lost track. Over fifty. Now his whole family is his granddaughter, Selena, sixteen years old. They live in the log cabin he built near the Klondike River. He has managed to look after them both with handyman jobs around town, supplemented by his skill at gardening and hunting. This summer Selena is working as a waitress in the Westminster Cafe and it's good to have the extra money, but something grips his stomach when he thinks about how she may not need him much longer now that she is becoming independent. Another life will be gone from him, following his wife and his daughter.

Dave starts the ascent of the steeply rising Dome Road at the end of King Street. Dawsonites know the Midnight Dome for raucous all-night celebrations around bonfires on June 21, the longest day of the year, when the sun dips only momentarily below the distant horizon. The American tourists who come through Dawson City every summer are rewarded for the ambitious drive up the Dome with a view of both the expansive Yukon and Klondike River basins. Tailing piles from gold dredges worm their way up the creeks, and snow-topped mountains mark Alaska in the western distance.

With surprising energy for his sixty-five years, Dave climbs the steep gravel road looking for deadfall wood that might be dry enough to burn. Over the summer he routinely follows the same path a dozen times. As long as he's able to walk he will have his own wood. He hopes it isn't as cold this winter as last. For six weeks starting from New Year's Day, it reached 45 degrees below zero or colder every day; it was something no one wanted to see again. The Indians say this winter will be warmer. *Well, that's a safe bet,* Dave chuckles to himself, *since it was the coldest winter on record it's bound to be warmer this winter.* As much as he respects the intuitive Indian knowledge of the seasons and the bush, his logical brain takes over in the end.

With his practised trapper's eyes, Dave spends as much time reading the ground for animal prints and leavings as he does looking for wood. On his last climb, he found himself passing by good chunks of dry birch, the best wood for heat. He had let himself think about his trapping days. This time he reprimands himself. He doesn't want to take any wood from the welfare supply again this winter. Last winter he had to borrow a cord from the government because he miscalculated the extent of the cold. It took three months of small amounts of cash to pay them back, and it meant he couldn't buy new boots for Selena. The welfare man said that Dave didn't owe anything. But he knows that taking the wood might be the first step in the short downward slide toward complete dependence on the government. He would have nothing to do with that.

The afternoon sun beats Dave's neck to a bright red. Sweat runs down his back, attracting mosquitoes. His Scottish ancestry has allowed neither his skin nor his mind to adapt to a climate that is perfect for biting insects. With a loud clap, Dave swats the mosquito that has landed precisely on the hottest part of his neck, and uses some of the language that made him the subject of many evenings' stories around the campfire: "Damned country! Not fit for human shit!" He never swears when a woman or a child is present, and although Selena has heard some of the stories about him, she has never heard the language, or so Dave thinks. He keeps that part of himself for the bush. He is acutely aware that he is living the old bush life more in thought than in reality as time passes.

Ahead, blue smoke curls around spruce and poplar trees in the windless heat, and the sweet smell of burning birch directs Dave's thoughts to new graves lying open, waiting. The City crew is thawing the permanently frozen ground in one of the graveyards with fires, digging inch by inch. The ultimate destinations of Dawson's winter dead are prepared in the summer; it is cheaper and easier than paying someone to scratch through permafrost in the winter cold. For all of Dave's lifetime, there have been more dead inhabitants on the Dome than alive below in Dawson City. Some people joke about digging up the permanently frozen bodies who made Klondike history and displaying them for the tourists in some kind of large freezer.

No one knows how the City crews are able to figure out how many will die the next winter. Do the gravediggers make bets on who will go that year and who will not? They were short of a winter grave only once that Dave remembers, the time a friend of his found Home Brew Anderson frozen solid in his cabin on Bonanza Creek. It was complicated enough, not having a grave, but his arm was flung above his head and no one had the courage to saw it off so he could fit into the coffin. Someone's garage became a temporary morgue while they kept Home Brew for a month before his grave was prepared and the arm yielded enough to pull it decently down to his side.

These last years, Dave never manages to get much farther up the Dome than the graveyards. Coming down, when the cart becomes too much to pull one more inch, he tires at the same spot, an opening in the trees that reveals the squared streets of Dawson. Carefully seating himself on top of the gathered wood in the cart, he leans, elbows on knees. This respite and the trip down the hill are the reward for his work. His eyes wander to the new school being built and the hole where the Gold Pan Motel burned down last winter. In the bush in front of him his favourite patches of brilliant magenta fireweed are interspersed with wild roses of several shades of pink, dying in the summer warmth. A brief breeze rustles the grass and soothes his neck, taking away some of the dizziness he was beginning to feel. The sweet scent of wood smoke and wild roses clears his head.

Pensive now, Dave allows himself the luxury of philosophy. *It's like life,* he muses, *the way up is a lot of work, the way down is pleasure. But you can't get on the easy path down without climbing up first.* It strikes him that a lot of people expect life to be all downhill and flowers. He knows it to be mostly uphill.

His peace is interrupted by the sharp laughter and excited calls of four youths running up the hill. It's the Miller boys with two girls. From the way they try to straighten themselves up when they see him, Dave knows they are up to no good. They carry a small paper bag, the focus of great attention and care. He hears ill-disguised laughter behind him after they pass. *If that's a bottle, I sure as shit hope the cops aren't around,* he thinks. He frowns at the thought. If this had happened when he was younger, he would have reprimanded them, maybe even told someone in authority. But the Yukon has taught him as much tolerance as he will ever have. Lately he surprises himself that he can go against things he once strictly lived by, even in dealing with his own family. Someone said to him once that relationships between grandparents and grandchildren were somehow better and easier than between children and parents, and he had to agree.

Uncomfortable thoughts of Selena's mother creep into his mind. A few years ago, Eliza would have been in that bunch that just went by. He had seen her a few times, when she didn't know he did, carrying on like that, even when she was pregnant with Selena at sixteen. With discomfort, he remembers the times he found Selena alone as a tiny baby and how angry he was with Eliza. Now he reminds himself that Eliza was too young herself, not ready to be a parent, just a teenager. Maybe he should have been more understanding of her then.

"Why don't you interdict the mother?" the doctor had said to him when he treated Selena's frostbite on her hand and feet that horrible time she was left alone in the unheated cabin. "You can put anyone on the Interdicted List by simply signing the papers, you know. The JP can put them on the List any Monday morning. And they don't even have to appear in court."

Shocked, Dave had yelled at the doctor, "She's only sixteen, for Christ's sake! Not supposed to drink anyway for another five bloody years!" He waved his arm in the general direction of the RCMP station. His voice louder than he wished, he said "Cops don't even pick her up now for drinking, like they oughta!" and left, slamming the door.

When Selena was three, Eliza had left Dawson, taking his only grandchild with her. Dave had to travel to Whitehorse to search for Selena and bring her back. He told Eliza never to set foot in Dawson again, but she did come, asking to visit.

Dave tried to stop Eliza's drinking by putting her on the Interdicted List when she was old enough. It was supposed to keep her out of the bars and the liquor store. Indians were only recently allowed to buy liquor, so it was called the Indian List. When he went to the RCMP station to sign the papers, Corporal Bruce warned him, "You know, this may not do you any good. We put lots of people on the List. Nearly every Indian in town is on it. But there's too much bootlegging going on. We can't keep up with it." The thought of having to write intimate evidence about his own daughter in those public papers infuriated him, but Dave was desperate. He filled out the papers anyway.

The Justice of the Peace, Harvey Snideman, was every bit as bad a drinker as Eliza, the butt of jokes around town for his inability to hold his liquor. The RCMP privately admitted to friends that the JP's reputation was "spotty." But they had no choice. They had to tolerate his drinking, hoping that he was not too embarrassing to the higher ups in the Court. They kept looking for someone to replace him, but no one else would take on the JP's job. Snideman was the only person they knew who wouldn't quit because of the public scrutiny and complaints that came with the job.

Snideman was also the postmaster, so Dave had to see him whenever he went to pick up his mail three times a week. There he was, standing behind the high counter, looking important. Dave imagined Snideman reading the court papers about Eliza, then sitting in the bar with his cronies while they laughed at Dave's family and his inability to raise his daughter properly.

Sitting on his cart, Dave picks out the City Office building where court is held every Monday morning. It was the most humiliating day of Dave's life, going to court, openly admitting that his daughter was a drunk. Dave's face still burns and his throat constricts with the thought of that day.

He had come early, climbing the steep stairs to the City Council chambers. He sat squarely in the middle of the three rows of chairs facing the desk and windows in the over-heated room. He wanted to be the first to arrive so he didn't have to face anyone. Snideman stood in front of the desk, his back to the room, separating papers, joking with Corporal Bruce who was both court clerk and prosecutor. Snideman unbuttoned his red flannel plaid shirt, raised his arms, took it off, and threw it over the back of his chair, saying, "This damn thing is too hot." The rolls of fat around his waist popped out below his undershirt as he bent over to draw on the black court robe. He shoved the sleeves up, sat down behind the desk and began to read the papers the Corporal put in front of him. The long hair on his stubby forearms was black.

Corporal Bruce led five Indians into the room and told them to sit on chairs in the row in front of Dave. Dave heard a few others arrive. They stood at the back of the room, but he didn't turn around. Everyone was whispering. There was some stifled nervous laughter.

Snideman pushed his glasses far enough down on his reddened nose to look over them at the short parade of hungover humanity in front of him. He glanced at the familiar faces and looked bored.

"Order in the court!" the Corporal yelled louder than necessary as he jumped stiffly to attention behind a table placed beside the JP's desk. Everyone shuffled to stand up, except Snideman. "I declare this court open. His Worship Justice of the Peace Harvey Snideman presiding," the Corporal said with military authority.

Snideman said, "You may be seated," to his audience. Dave had never been ordered to stand or sit, treated as if he were an animal being trained before. It reminded him of church, which he did not attend except for important funerals.

Each case was preceded by the passing around of many long papers and a brief description in legal tones from Corporal Bruce of what the offender had done, sprinkled with a lot of "Your Worship's." No one defended themselves against the charges and everyone pleaded guilty. No witnesses were called to prove whether the charges were true or not. A serious charge of breaking and entering with intent to assault against one of the men was adjourned for Magistrate's Court the next month and Snideman told him he should look into finding a lawyer. Snideman's round, sweating face frowned his disgust when he sentenced the others to fines or jail for traffic or drinking violations.

Sideman gave one woman who had been caught drinking in public on the riverbank a lecture about looking after her kids. He shook his head, pointing his short fat finger at her, and saying, "I don't want to have to send you to jail in Whitehorse again for neglect of your kids, Mary. But I will, next time I see you in here. You gotta stop your drinkin', eh? Stay home with those five kids of yours. God knows there's plenty for you to do for them. Should keep you out of trouble. What you got to say for yourself?"

"Nothin'," Mary mumbled, looking at the floor, her hands clutched together and twitching behind her back.

"Right. Forty dollars plus costs this time, Mary. Got the money?" Seeing Mary shake her head, he added, "OK. Two weeks to pay, eh? In default, one week." The Corporal leaned over his table and scribbled the sentence on his list. Mary sped out of the room with two other women, mumbling.

They had left Dave for last on the court docket. Dave knew a half dozen young men had stayed on at the back of the room to see why he was in court. They would be speculating that he had finally punched someone. He sensed their disappointment when the Corporal called Dave's name and said, "The matter for the Interdiction Ordinance, Your Worship." Still, they didn't leave.

Corporal Bruce waved for Dave to move forward. Shuffling to the space in front of the desk, Dave bumped into a wooden chair that scraped on the floor. He was made to take off his cap and swear on the Bible that what he had said in the papers on the desk in front of Snideman was "the truth, the whole truth, and nothing but the truth, so help me God." Dave's body wavered. He didn't know where to place his feet or his hands. He clutched his cap in one hand and held the Bible in the other until the Corporal came over, took the Bible away from him, and stood back behind his table.

Dave looked down at Snideman's balding head. The skin below the thinning grey hair was remarkably red. Snideman looked up from the papers, adjusted his glasses to see over them, and asked, not unkindly, "And what makes you think this is the right thing to do, Dave?"

"Well," he said lamely, "she drinks too much. Maybe this'll stop her."

Snideman indicated the front row of chairs with his hand. "Did you see all them people in front of me this morning?" Of course he had seen them. Snideman waited for an answer, so Dave nodded. "All of them interdicted," Snideman snorted. "All of 'em." Was he trying to talk Dave out of putting her on the List?

"Maybe so," muttered Dave, "gotta try something." He looked past the Corporal through the window behind. He heard voices of people who were walking on the street below, unaware.

"Shouldn't never've allowed Indians into the bars in '51. Just a lot of wasted court time and paperwork," Snideman sighed. "OK, if that's what you think'll work. For the record, Eliza Maclean is on the Interdicted List."

Corporal Bruce leaned over and wrote Eliza's name in a book. "Band Number?" he asked.

"Fifty-nine. Dawson Band," Dave said. He had never married her status mother, Maggie Taylor, another embarrassment for him.

Snideman signed two long sheets of paper and passed them over to the Corporal without looking at Dave. He said, "You may go."

Dave left the court relieved that he had not had to say much in public about what was in the papers. But by the time he reached home, he was in a rage. He was disgusted with Snideman, the RCMP, the whole court system, but mostly with himself. He told no one about the experience and it was of little interest to the people who had witnessed it. They had seen too many others interdicted.

As predicted, putting Eliza on the List had not stopped her access to liquor at all. Instead, it had made her furious with him. It would cost her more to drink bootleg liquor and she was avoided by some people not on the List who used to drink freely with her. They could be charged for supplying her.

Dave watches the two couples with the brown paper bag disappear up the Dome Road. Now, at last, Eliza lives in Whitehorse and mostly leaves them alone. She likes Whitehorse because the bars there don't know she is interdicted.

Well, thank God Selena isn't with them kids, anyway. The mosquitoes find Dave's sweating neck again and a blackfly buzzes irritatingly around his head. It stirs him to take his long legs down the gravel descent. He is satisfied with the push of the full cart downhill and the heavy tugging needed along Seventh Avenue. He nods once or twice to acquaintances who offer automatic greetings as they pass. He stops in front of his cabin and one hand digs into the breast pocket of his shirt, searching for the key. It has disappeared from where he has put it. He looks up to see Selena walking quickly away.

"Selena!" *Damn and blast, I know I put that key in this pocket. Bloody country, never used to have to lock my door.*

"Selena! Come back. Time to eat." He knows Selena has heard him. He sees her hesitate, her trim body always reminding him of Eliza at her age. She hurries back to within his hearing, puts her hand beside her mouth, and calls, "Not hungry!"

Dave insists upon meals at certain times, and it's nearly time for supper. If you don't keep regular schedules, you turn into no better than an animal, eating when you're hungry, sleeping when you're tired. But maybe he should let her go on her way, seeing it was her day off work. Except that he needs that bloody key. The key sparks his temper.

Watching him, Selena smiles and shakes her head with affection. The familiar blaze spreads over Dave's face above his beard. She wanders over to him, saying, "OK, Pop, what's wrong?"

He frowns and says sourly, "The key. I've lost my goddam key." He stands, legs apart, his hands bulging the breast pockets of his shirt with their fruitless search.

"Look in your back pants pocket?" Selena asks. Lately he has put the key there because he might lose it when he bends over to pick up wood. He has forgotten that he changed the routine. The key is there. He snorts in temporary embarrassment. But it's only Selena who has seen his forgetfulness.

"I guess I'm really hungry after all. Why don't you start supper? I'll get the wood in," Selena says as she pulls the cart off the street and begins to throw the wood beside the cabin wall.

It is Saturday. On Saturday nights Dave sometimes invites the soft-spoken and patient Jan Erickson in the cabin across the lane for supper. Lacking other immediate neighbours, they socialize. The two men play cribbage, drinking Jan's home brew that he keeps cold in the crawl-space under his kitchen floor. Their friendship is the result of a long and cautious acquaintance. They are seen by others as true opposites. Dave's figure towers over the slim, fine-boned Jan. Dave ignores his own wild beard, while Jan is clean-shaven. Loud and spontaneous, easily roused to anger, but as easily calmed down, Dave's temperament contrasts with Jan's. He is more brooding.

Jan has never spent much time in the bush, always working for someone else in the placer gold mines up Bonanza and Hunker Creeks. Secretly, Dave sees Jan's dependence on wages earned from others as an inferior way of life, and it spurs him on to help him. Jan is always grateful for Dave's knowledge and strength as they gather wood or hunt together for moose in the fall. In return, Dave borrows an old truck and other equipment from Jan when he needs it. It is a strange and fragile relationship, but each knows the value of being good neighbours in the North and their regular habits fit well together in mutual assistance.

Jan sits in his usual chair across the table from Dave while Selena serves them king salmon steaks. The two men sip the pungent brew Jan is famous for. After supper, they settle into their chairs and prepare to play cribbage while Selena clears the table. She goes to her room a few feet from the kitchen table to read a movie magazine. The two men will tell and re-tell old stories and the rhythm of Jan's lilting Nordic accent will blend with the soft music from Selena's radio. The sweet smell of Dave's pipe tobacco will drift into her bedroom, and the men's voices will grow softer and more intermittent as the night wears on. Selena will finally turn her radio off and go to sleep to the gentle rise and fall of their different voices. The familiar stories will become part of her dreams.

Dave's memories of his prairie life have ripened in his older years. When he hears reports about Saskatchewan on the radio, he discusses the price of wheat and the damage hail and drought can do to a good crop. Jan breaks in with tales about fishing in the cold Swedish fjords. Those sentimental evenings are both comforting and painful for them. They drink more of the brew than they should, melancholy about distant choices they have made. Neither of them could have returned home with the fortune or the honour they had sought when they came to the North. Now it is many years too late.

"Ya hear about old Snideman?" Jan asks Dave. Both of the men are years older than Snideman, but anyone over forty is given the adjective *old*.

Dave grunts, "Nope, but I wouldn't be surprised...your first deal." He shoves the deck of cards across the table.

Jan shuffles the worn cards. He takes his time dealing them while Dave sticks the red plastic pins in the board. Jan throws his cards into the crib and turns the seven of hearts over on the deck after taking a swig from his bottle of brew. He is waiting for exactly the right time to start his story. "Now what the heck can I do with a seven of hearts?" Jan mumbles to no one in particular. Dave never quite knows when Jan makes comments about his cards if what he says should be trusted. Was he simply being too open about his hand, or trying to mislead him? Knowing how to fool a card player is a more important skill than deceiving a lover, which Dave knows Jan has done. He listens seriously to Jan about his cards only when they are playing for money, but it still doesn't help him win much.

In an unusually talkative mood, Jan smiles and begins his story. "Well, last night, old Snideman gets into that blue Ford pick-up of his--after sitting all night in the Occidental bar as usual you know. He puts her in gear..." He lifts a card out of his hand and looks at it just long enough to get Dave's ear, "And drives *in reverse* down Third Avenue!" He throws the card down.

"What?!"

Jan, louder with enthusiasm, his Nordic accent deepening, says, "What happens, but he hits the telephone pole, yah, in front of the fire hall, by Jesus!" The fire hall is half a block down the street on the opposite side from the hotel. Jan looks up from his cards, his eyes sparkling with humour. "He must've thought he was going straight ahead, yah? Or--I dunno--maybe he passed out with his foot on the gas or somethin'?"

"That stupid old bastard," Dave says with a humourless snort. He counts: "Fifteen two, fifteen four, and there ain't no more." He piles his cards together and, more for something to say than anything, he comments, "Well, he must've lived, or I woulda heard."

"Yah," Jan agreed, "he's alive today, worse luck, but the rear end of his truck's a goner. Tailgate bent and brake lights on one side totally smashed." His smile reaches his eyes as he pegs his points into the board. He's winning as usual.

"Serves him damn right," Dave says, irritated, throwing down an empty crib.

It's not like Dave to be frustrated with losing at cards. He likes the company and cares very little about who wins. "Most likely serves him right, yah," Jan agrees. His interest in the story rises with Dave's anger and he fills in the details he has heard. "That new Constable whatshisname was supposed to be coming to pick him up as usual. Somebody phoned the cops from the bar to watch out for him, to take him home like they always do, eh? I guess they got busy down at the cop shop. He got there just a few minutes too late. Saw it all."

"I bet you anything the RCMP don't charge him. They oughta, you know." Dave adds wryly, "Maybe the old bugger'll lay low for awhile and we can be safe walking around town for the next week."

"Don't think so, what I hear. Snideman's all over town telling it like a joke on himself. Even says he got a ride home with the cops after. Your deal."

"No shit!" Dave frowns as he restlessly shuffles and deals the cards. He looks at his hand, awkwardly moving the order of his cards several times without seeing them, his slippered feet rustling below the table. Dave knows that Jan wants him to enjoy this joke on Snideman. He doesn't often pass gossip along. He had probably rehearsed it in his mind, how he would tell it to Dave, while they were eating supper. But they are getting onto dangerous ground.

Dave roughly throws down two cards for the crib, and says, "And he's the guy who puts all the Indians on the Indian List. You'd think he'd be ashamed to sit in court next Monday." When they first started keeping company, Dave and Jan had come uncomfortably close to arguments about Indians. It is difficult to avoid the controversy that Indians provoke in Dawson amongst Whites, but the two of them, without discussing it, have somehow agreed to avoid the subject for the sake of their friendship.

Jan says nothing. He once told Dave that he doesn't have anything personally to do with Indians anymore. Jan never lived with the Indian women he knew earlier in his life. He had slept with them when he had to, he said, but that's as far as it went. Dave believes that secretly Jan feels a little superior to him because of it. Dave overheard Jan say once that some Whitemen were idiots to live with Indian females and their little half-breeds, sometimes even to marry the mother. Dave sensed that Jan had waited to begin visiting him until he was certain that Eliza wouldn't return to Dawson from Whitehorse.

As he has done many times, Dave tries to force the memory of his humiliation in front of Snideman out of his mind. He opens another brew and suggests they play poker, which he knows will take more concentration. He plays automatically, solemnly. The vision of his daughter as a child moves around the small kitchen where she used to help him, standing on a chair to reach the plates for supper. Little Eliza. He loved her so much then, just as he loves his beautiful grandchild Selena. It was right at this table that Selena had courageously sewn him a pair of mukluks with her awkward twisted fingers. He watches himself play cards while his child and then his grandchild play and laugh beside him. He can feel their little arms around his shoulders giving him a hug.

He had wanted to say so much more to both of them: how he would always be grateful to his lover and companion, Maggie; what amazing knowledge she had; how he loved her sense of humour; that they had had a life rich in security and love. Maybe he could get it all out before Selena grew up so much that she didn't care. Or before he would get too old to remember it all. Maybe knowing something good about the past would help Selena to be different from her mother somehow, give her self-respect. He didn't pass along even that much to his own daughter. Eliza had been away in that damn residential school too long and he suspected she hated him for it. If only he hadn't been stupid enough to be pressured to send her off when she was too young to be away. No wonder she's a drunk. If only he had been home earlier that night when Eliza left Selena freezing in the cabin. If only putting her on the List had worked. It was his own fault, all of it. If only...if only...the old failures and accusations will not leave him this night.

His frustration turns to anger directed at Snideman. "Nobody has the guts to do anything about that asshole Snideman," he says long after Jan's story is over. "Even worse, the few officials in Dawson who might do something about him just protect the precious bastard from anybody who might complain. Who is he, God or something?" Jan doesn't say anything.

At midnight, while he is clearing the empty bottles from the table, Dave announces: "I'm going to write to somebody in RCMP Headquarters in Whitehorse about Snideman."

"What?! What good is that going to do?" Jan looks up at his friend, smiling, and shakes his head. Dave could see him thinking, *Silly old fool.*

"Not sure. But maybe they'll get somebody else to be JP."

"So what good will that do you, eh? You don't have nothing to do with the court. All you do is collect your mail from the asshole."

Dave wonders briefly if Jan has never heard about the time he went to court. He knows Jan wouldn't understand even if he tried to explain what he had done. Jan would think that Dave was stupid to believe the List would work. He takes the high ground: "So why does it have to be good only for me? Someone out there is going to get hurt bad by Snideman some day. He's dangerous!"

"Keep your nose out of it is my advice," Jan says solemnly.

Jan's composure hardens Dave. He sits down, emphasizing his words by slapping the table, "Harvey Snideman shouldn't get away with it. He should be charged, dammit! You and I would be, eh? Or any old Indian would. And for doing much less."

"Well, you're sort of right there," Jan says reluctantly. "He shouldn't be the JP, now that's for sure, but I don't know how much anybody can do about that." Jan sits quietly for a moment and says, "Anyway, what's your proof? All you know is what I told you."

Dave is getting louder. "Proof? Lots of people have been condemned on less proof than that in his courtroom. You said the cop saw it all last night. Somebody else must have seen him too. Who was it told you...?"

With a cold laugh, Jan interrupts, "Oh, saving the world are you! Well, don't involve me in it." Jan gathers the cards and puts them into the package. They sit, each with his own thoughts while Jan slowly places the plastic pegs in the back of the crib board, secures them with the metal cover, turns the board over and puts the card pack on top. He stands up and places the board and cards carefully on the window sill above the table. Moving over beside Dave's chair, he leans over and takes him firmly by the upper arm. He says, "Keep out of it, Dave. You don't know what'll come of it. What about the new constable? Want to get him in trouble too, before he's been here a month, yah?"

Jan's grasp on his arm is insulting, and Dave pulls away from him. His anger quickens. "Shit on the new constable! What about all those people in court, eh? RCMP picks them up, throws them in the can every weekend to sober up." His hand flies out. "All of them Indians! All up for drinking, for doing the same thing we all do, White or Indian. Then on Monday Snideman fines them money they can't afford or sends them away and then wonders why the kids go bad. Think that's fair? You think that's *justice*?"

Moving to the door, Jan buttons his jacket, his hands shaking. He says, "Well as far as I'm concerned, in my fifty-odd years in the Yukon, I haven't seen an Indian who can handle his liquor yet. They're all the same. Nobody forces them to drink in the first place, by damn."

Dave rages, jumping up from the table: "You asshole! Get out of my house! I will not have you talking about my wife and my family in my house like that! I always knew that's what you thought of them. Get out, you fucking racist bastard, Goddam it!" He slams the two chairs at once in place under the table, breaking the leg of one. Jan exits through the door.

Selena calls hesitatingly from her bedroom, "Pop, isn't it time to go to bed?" Startled by her voice, Dave goes over to her bedroom door to reassure his little girl. "It's OK, sweetheart," he says from Selena's doorway. "Just a little tiff. Go back to sleep. Nothing to worry about." By calming Selena, his anger dissipates and he regrets the outburst against Jan. He pulls the broken chair away from the table. He'll fix that in the morning, after he writes his letter to the RCMP.

Dave glances through the window. Across the lane he sees Jan in his cabin, the grey twilight of summer midnight filling his tidy room. He is sitting in his old wooden rocking chair, his jacket still on. Dave can nearly hear the familiar creaking of the chair punctuating the room. Maybe he should go over and apologize. He is dismayed to see Jan roughly rub his cheek near his eye. *Tears? The silly old fool.* He watches Jan force himself to get up, turn on the light, and then draw the curtain across the window between them.

It'll probably take Jan a few days to calm down. Dave tells himself that next weekend he'll ask to borrow Jan's truck to get both of them some wood. Maybe they can go up the Dempster Highway for a change, see if there are any moose yet.

Dave sighs. *This neighbour of mine is a lot of work. Uphill all the way.* He turns out the lights.

JUST LIKE A FULLER

There was one neon sign in Dawson City. It flashed on and off, on and off. In the morning summer sun, it was dull red: *Get it at Stewart's. Get it at Stewart's.* Frank Stewart switched it on only when the store was open, winter or summer. He turned and looked around the shelves with a sigh. Better do the tinned vegetables today. The week before, he had decided he was getting too old to do everything himself and had let it be known that he was looking for help. He needed someone to clean up after hours and shift things around from the back to the front as room slowly appeared on the shelves. He hated those jobs. They had nothing to do with people.

Stewart was the last living grandson of the original Stewart who had built the general store on Third Avenue during the Klondike Gold Rush. His wife had died ten years before. He lived alone above the store, leading a life of set routine, inherited from his father and grandfather. True to the flashing neon slogan, Stewart took a special joy in finding just the right item to satisfy his customers. Stewart's was famous for supplying anything needed for Northern survival, and it was available in any season. If he couldn't find what the customer wanted in the store's main inventory, he would silently disappear to the back for a time, coming back with exactly what was looked for, or a good substitute.

There were special items in Stewart's three warehouses across the lane that newer stores in the Yukon had long ago given up on or had run out of: rubbers that were shaped to cover mukluks in the wet weather, babiche, powdered red dye for finishing hand made snowshoes, dog harnesses, hand-held ice augers. Stewart stayed in business because of this traditional inventory, and the fact that he was always willing to extend lengthy credit to Dawsonites. His core of customers hadn't shopped elsewhere for years. Stewart wanted to make sure that they shopped at his store not because of what they owed, but because of the service he provided. He wisely kept his prices below that of the Alaska-owned Northern Commercial down the street and around the corner.

Stewart unlocked the front door and peered through the window. There was that young Fuller girl, shuffling toward the store along the wooden sidewalk. Probably coming to buy something for her mother. Her parents wouldn't be in until they could pay something on their bill, at the end of the month. When the kids asked for a tin of tobacco, he would say, as a kind of ritual, "Tell your father to come for that himself next time," but it never worked. He knew they would steal the tobacco from their parents at home anyway.

Climbing the three steps, Julie Fuller pretended to be interested in a car driving by. She pushed opened the unstable door and it squealed. She would oil that damn door if she got the job. She noticed the two youngest Roberts boys picking over the brightly coloured pieces of candy near the door, arguing over a choice of caramels or ju-jubes. Stewart stood behind the counter, both hands held close to his face, lighting a cigarette, his eyes on the boys.

Yesterday, the Roberts boys had teased Julie about the hated freckles sprinkled across her broad, flat nose. She hurried to the back of the store, gazed absently in the dim light at the packages of cookies, and showed unusual interest in the baking goods. Baking powder, baking soda, icing sugar. Why didn't those kids get lost? When the front door crashed shut behind the boys, she seized the five-pound bag of flour her mother had asked for and carried it to the front of the store. The ornate silver-coloured register rang as Stewart vigorously pushed two keys down, threw some change into the open drawer, and slammed it shut. Leaning over the counter, Julie hung onto the flour as if it were going to slide away and pushed it carefully over to Stewart. His grey head disappeared under the counter, looking for a paper bag. She spoke to the cigarette smoke left drifting in the air: "I don't suppose you could use some help in the store?" Her voice seemed awfully small.

"Who you got in mind?" Stewart's muffled voice came from under the counter. Julie heard him shuffling the scattered pile of paper bags, looking for the right size.

"Me?"

Stewart straightened and rubbed his back with one hand. With the other, he slapped a used brown paper bag on the counter. Julie stuffed the flour in it, not looking at him. He turned to a taped and torn shoe box on the shelf behind him, digging through it for the pad of bills that had

"Caleb Fuller" written on the front. Even for cash, the details of all but the smallest sales in the store were carefully handwritten by Stewart on invoices, signed, and the original copy given to the customer.

Stewart kept his eyes on the Caleb Fuller bill pad. He flipped through several yellow pages, folded them carefully to the back, and placed a curled piece of carbon paper between the new white and yellow copies. Taking a pencil from his breast pocket, he licked the business end of it, and began to write the date. He had never thought of taking on a female in the store, let alone a young girl, least of all one of the Fullers. Whenever he saw any of the Fuller girls he remembered that a few years ago, his son had told him that one of the Fuller girls had confessed to a teacher that she had been raped by her father. Not just once, either. Everyone seemed to know about it, but no one in authority was moved to do anything until somebody visiting the family from Outside complained to the police. After a short investigation, the girl was put in a foster home in Whitehorse, and Caleb was warned by the RCMP, but no charges were laid. The word *incest* was never used by anyone; it seemed too drastic a word. Stewart hadn't been able to look Caleb Fuller in the face since then.

Stewart said, "Need somebody to do men's work. Lifting. Carrying. Cleaning." He handed Julie the white copy of the bill.

All in a rush, Julie said, "I'm sixteen. I'm a hard worker. Good as a man. You can ask Mr. or Mrs. Miller. I work for them lots. Heavy chores sometimes too." They had told her to use them as a reference. Since she was eleven, Julie had earned money around town by chopping wood, hauling garbage or water, weeding gardens, doing laundry, babysitting, shovelling snow, and whatever else her teachers found for her to do.

Including the two toddlers of Caleb's older daughters, thirteen Fullers survived within the white-grey peeling walls of a battered two-storey frame building in the North End, on what was known as Cherry Hill. Ordering her chaotic life, the comfortable regularity of routine and cleanliness at school had given Julie some security. In return for this stability, she had responded with lively interest and intelligence. Her teachers were pleased to find a Fuller child who could read at the proper age and was not withdrawn. They encouraged her with extra praise and assistance. One teacher used to take her home for lunch and even give her a bath or wash her clothes now and then when she was younger. A survivor, Julie had recognized at a young age where to find support.

Stewart peered at the Fuller kid through his cigarette smoke. This one was not at all pretty. Mary Ann Fuller's dark Indian colouring was tinted to a pale brown by Caleb's white skin. She had Caleb's thin downward lips, high forehead, and narrowly-spaced eyes. Looked strong enough, though. That Fuller build, the masculine bones. A pain shot up Stewart's back from the left hip. The arthritis acting up again. Must be from the lifting he did yesterday, taking all that garbage up to the dump. He did need help in the store. He'd better get on it quick before he ended up in bed with his back and having to ask his son to work. He was sick and tired of the local bums he'd had to deal with in the past. Maybe he could train her properly; she seemed eager enough to learn. Someone who really wanted the job was what he needed, someone who would stay past the first pay cheque. No doubt she could use the money, being a Fuller.

Years ago, Stewart went looking for Caleb Fuller to do some staking for asbestos claims over on the South Fork of the Fortymile River. He had glimpsed inside the Fuller house while he waited for one of the boys to find Caleb inside. In the front room (an extended kitchen, it couldn't really be called a living room) he had seen some of the debris of their failing lives. Near the wood stove were food-encrusted pots, broken dishes, empty liquor bottles, and caribou bones. On the floor there was a collection of torn blankets, grey clothing, worn comic books, and the dog's dish full of half-eaten fish heads. Rumour was that Caleb hadn't left another one of his daughters alone for long after the one girl was taken away to Whitehorse. He didn't need those kind of people around the store.

"Come back tomorrow." Stewart said.

"I got it?!" He was startled to see Julie's smile spread to her eyes, giving her solemn face life and sparkle.

Coughing, Stewart frowned. He stubbed out his cigarette in the overflowing tin ashtray sitting by the cash register. "I'm not saying that," he said. "I'll think it over. You think it over too. Minimum wage. Three hours a day. Only for the summer." He hoped that would discourage her. Then he wouldn't have to make a decision about it.

That afternoon, a local bachelor in need of some cash came into the store looking for work. Stewart hired him. After an hour, the man asked for a package of cigarillos on his pay. He joined two men already sitting on the broken kitchen chairs around the massive wood stove made from two oil barrels, one above the other, that dominated the back of the store. The space was a warm gathering spot in all seasons for regular male customers who drank Stewart's bad coffee and shared the latest news. Loud jokes and stories floated most afternoons through the smell of wood and cigarette smoke while Stewart bustled busily in the background.

Stewart's new employee was still sitting around the barrel stove an hour after he started his break. He was smoking those smelly cigarillos, telling lies to the others about his past, instead of hauling in the freight that had arrived that morning and sat in the back alley in the rain. Stewart gave him five dollars and told him to shove off. The man would no doubt be back again in a few days, sitting around the stove.

There was no one else in the whole town that Stewart could hire who was reliable, so Julie got the job. Besides, he could pay her less than a grown man. When she came in the store her first day of work, he warned her, "I'm only taking you on trial for a week. No fooling around. No kids in the store. That goes double for your brother Bobbie." He had caught the nine-year-old shoplifting more than once.

"Sure thing, Frank." Julie startled him, using his first name.

"And don't call me Frank. Stewart's fine."

"Right you are, Mr Stewart." Mr Stewart. That was worse.

Somehow after the second day, Julie forgot the part about using Stewart's first name. She acquired the habit of bouncing through the door, cheerfully calling, "Hi, Frank, how's she goin'?" He gave up attempting to change her after two more unsuccessful tries. It was part of her energetic character. And he needed her energy.

Stewart had to admit she learned quickly. He had shown her around only once and she remembered where all but the smallest items were. The main room held the groceries and in the centre of this room stood two short rows of shelves filled with cans and packages. Against the walls more shelves reached to the ceiling, stuffed with dry foods that were sometimes of doubtful freshness because of their longevity. Eggs were kept in a special spot in the back which always had the right temperature, winter or summer. The one freezer held a few blackish steaks and roasts for those who ran out of the moose meat or caribou most families ate. Vegetables (imported from Outside and wrapped in plastic bags) consisted only of potatoes, carrots, and cooking onions. In the summer, the vegetable selection was supplemented with cabbages grown in Dawson.

A dusky room on the side was choked with a profusion of hardware and dry goods. Ancient shelves overflowed, jammed to the ceiling with an assortment of boots, toques, baby clothes, carpentry tools, hinges, ropes of several varieties, dish cloths, stainless steel knives, enamel camping dishes, cast iron frying pans, gold pans, ink for fountain pens, candles, yards of canvas, and a hundred other items. A thin film of wood smoke and road dust gave everything a grey tone.

Instinctively Julie knew there was an unspoken rule in Stewart's: she was barred from sitting with the men who frequented the circle around the barrel stove. But her curiosity kept her hovering nearby when the talk stirred her interest. She knew she probably picked up more information that way anyway. Her initial fear of Stewart disappeared as she heard the respect the other men had for him. "By a long shot, the only honest storekeeper in Dawson," they said. She learned that he had financed dozens of local people to prospect for just about anything in the mountains and creeks of the Klondike. "The best person in Dawson by far to work for in the bush--always pays on time." "Leaves you alone to do your work." "Grub's good too."

Julie boasted to her father, "Frank's a millionaire, you know. He's grubstaked hundreds of prospectors. And he owns all those claims, 'cause they didn't pay him back." Almost all of the mineral claims Stewart had an interest in had turned out to be useless, and he let them lapse. With others, he was never paid for the grubstake, but even Stewart's friends didn't know that.

"Did ya know that Frank owns Clinton Creek?" Julie announced one day at home. Her excitement was tinged with worry. "Jeez, I sure hope he doesn't close up the store and retire. What'll I do without that job?" Caleb just snorted in disbelief but the next day he heard downtown that Stewart's investment in local prospectors had finally been rewarded. He had sold his claims to the Cassiar Asbestos Corporation for a new mine at Clinton Creek, west of Dawson near the Alaska border. Caleb had worked for Stewart staking those claims for $15 a day and grub.

The Clinton Creek income could have meant a comfortable retirement for Stewart. But since his beloved Bella passed on, he was reconciled to staying on in the store until he joined her. They had planned to buy a camper and drive to Florida for the winters, imitating in reverse the American tourists they saw coming North every summer. That was a long ago dream of Bella's. Without her, he wouldn't think of travelling. He was more or less content with his life. The thought of being without his daily routine of opening and closing the store, and the delight he took in being able to find just what a customer needed, kept him from thinking seriously about retiring.

On the weekends and holidays, Stewart visited his only son and his grandchildren. The son had decided to break the line of storekeepers and owned a garage down the street. He was a good mechanic, but the garage was close to being broke most of the time. Stewart had helped the business out a few times. He wanted to leave his family something when he died so that his son could do what he wanted, not be tied to a failing business. The Clinton claims were his legacy.

When the barrel stove gang heard that Stewart had hired Julie, they wanted to hear some complaint from him to add to the Fuller legends. Embarrassed to be seen defending a Fuller kid as his helper, especially one who called him by his first name, Stewart was careful not to discuss Julie with anyone, not even his son. He would make a non-committal grump in his throat when anyone asked, "How's your new partner, Stewart? She rob you blind yet?" They eventually grew tired of his lack of response.

His new employee satisfied Stewart. She always came to work on time, never objected to the chores he gave her, and worked harder than any man he had ever hired. She would take the initiative to help customers find what they needed, and they didn't seem to mind her being around. He had worried that she might be too forward, as she was with him, but she seemed just friendly enough with customers--most of the time. He rewarded her with extra hours of work. Stewart stopped worrying about her being alone in the store after they were closed. He went upstairs for supper, trusting her to lock up for him after she swept the floor and made sure the stove had enough wood for the night. He soon gave up going downstairs after she left to check if she had done everything right and that nothing was stolen.

With Julie there when he went to the bank on Fridays, Stewart left the store open instead of locking up and taping a handwritten sign in the door window: *Back in 15 mins.* While he was gone, if the sales were not too complicated, she looked after the customers.

Before he went to the bank, Stewart counted out the same amount of change to be left in the cash register as he had done for years. "Just going to the bank," he called from the door to Julie as usual before lunch one Friday.

"OK, Frank. Want me to bring in those cases of canned fruit?"

"Sure. Good idea."

There was no one sitting around the barrel stove when Julie went out the back door toward the warehouse. She strode across the alley behind the store and returned with a case of canned peaches to put on the shelf. Dropping the peaches to the floor, she heard the front door squeal. Stewart had told her not to oil the hinges of the front door because then you could tell when someone came in if you were in the back. She emerged at the front in time to recognize the skinny form of her brother Bobbie through the glass of the open front door. He was hurrying down the steps. Two weeks before, she had found Bobbie in the store when Stewart was at the bank. She had bought him his favourite chocolate bar, an O Henry, and chased him away, telling him not to come back.

In one smooth movement, she slipped through the door, grabbed Bobbie by the sleeve with one hand, and dug her other hand into his jacket pocket. There it was, an O Henry, the yellow paper torn open, and a bite taken out of it. In the other pocket, she found a handful of coloured bubble gum balls. Bobbie stood still, looking up at her, chewing, pinkish saliva dribbling from the side of his mouth.

"Damn you, you little bugger!" She shook him angrily. "You wanna get me fired?" She shoved the opened chocolate bar at his chest. His hand automatically grabbed it and he smiled, a large wad of wet half-chewed bubble gum with bits of coloured candy in it showing between his teeth.

Her strength was no match for the thin boy. He tripped as she pushed him down the stairs but he regained a foothold on the sidewalk. Julie yelled at him, "Don't you ever come here again! That's the last time I buy you anything."

Julie pulled the door closed and replaced the unused bubble gum from Bobbie's pocket in its box on the counter. She opened the cash register, paid for the theft, and gave herself change for money she had in her jeans. Just as she slammed the drawer shut and put the change in her jeans pocket, Stewart returned.

"Did Arnie come in with that list for the camp?" Stewart asked.

"Nope. Not yet. Nobody was in while you were gone."

Stewart had heard the clang of the cash register drawer and thought he had seen her put something in her jeans pocket. He lit a cigarette to occupy the time while he went behind the counter, left the cigarette in his mouth, and pushed the No Sale button down on the cash register. He squinted his eyes against the cigarette smoke as he counted the money in the drawer. Fifty cents more than when he had left. He added some one- and five- dollar bills that he had brought from the bank. Maybe he hadn't counted the money right; but that would be unusual. Puzzled, he counted it all again. There should be less money, not more, if she had taken anything. Still the same--fifty cents too much. She said nobody had come in. Maybe he hadn't left the right amount in the drawer. But he had always left the same amount, for years. He slammed the drawer shut.

Bring in some of those cans of tobacco from the back, would you?" was all he said.

Stewart thought about little else that evening after supper, even going downstairs to count the money and look over the yellow invoices once again, with the same result. He was unhappy with himself for doing that; it wasn't in his nature to be suspicious, and over such a small amount. What bothered him most was that she said that no one had come into the store, when somebody must have. He had told himself a long time ago that it was a lot less trouble for him if he could trust people, but could he turn his trust on or off just because it was easier? He had convinced himself after Julie came to work for him that he should stop worrying about the minor shoplifting he knew went on all the time. Julie would know the kids they had to watch out for and he wouldn't have to try to remember who was who and which ones were trouble or not. She seemed to be responsible enough. Just last week, he heard her telling those Roberts boys off when they were hanging around the back of the store. It was a long time since he had had to remind Julie to keep that little brother of hers away from the store.

When Stewart went back upstairs, he poured a drink of scotch to help himself think about something else. Maybe she forgot that someone came in and bought a small item. Or maybe he was just getting senile in his old age, fussing over small problems. He crawled into bed. A bloody fifty cents wasn't going to keep him awake all night.

At the Fuller house that evening, Julie cornered Bobbie upstairs and hit him hard on the face. "You try to steal anything again and I'll tell Frank, you little bastard!" She shook him roughly by the shoulders. "You just stay out of our store, hear me?" He nodded in silent agreement, holding a hand on his cheek, his red face streaming with tears and his lips pursed tightly. The blow had made him bite the inside of his mouth, but he wouldn't give her the satisfaction of crying out loud.

While making coffee the next morning, it occurred to Stewart that Julie might have bought something for herself. Of course! She very seldom bought anything and until now, she had always told him when she did. She was careful to show him that she paid for anything she wanted, and bought things only when he was in the store so he could see. Maybe she was feeling more at home, and didn't think she had to report everything to him that she did. Maybe this time she simply didn't tell him she had bought herself something. He was happy to finally put it out of his mind.

The next Friday, with Stewart at the bank, Julie locked the front door when she had to go to the back of the store. Stewart wouldn't like that, but she didn't want to be responsible again for someone else's shoplifting. If somebody wanted to come in, they'd just have to wait.

Standing on a stool to take down a carton of corn flakes, Julie noticed a movement over to the left, just out of sight. She carefully stepped down from the stool and around behind the shelves, hidden from view. Waiting. Bobbie suddenly darted in the direction of the large sliding back door. Julie watched him struggle with opening the heavy steel latch with one hand. In his other hand were a cellophane bag of candies and an O Henry bar. The little bastard must have sneaked into the store earlier and then hid.

Julie's feet pounded the floor getting across the room to him. She wanted him to see her. He turned his head to look back as the door slid open with a metal crunch. His narrow eyes gazed intensely at her, a twisted smile on his face. Not moving, his whole skinny body was stiffly alert, challenging her to do something. He said flatly, "Go ahead. Rat on me. You're not supposed to let me in the store. I'll just tell Stewart you let me come in lots of times and you even give me free stuff." He escaped through the open door.

Bobbie would do what he said. Julie didn't want to guess if Frank would believe him or not. There was enough truth in his story to be dangerous. He had come in the store before, although Frank had told her not to let him in. She would be responsible. The crazy part was that Frank would probably not even miss the candy Bobbie had now. She was the one who kept a close eye on the merchandise in the store and seemed to have an instinct for missing items. But she sensed that the amount of Stewart's tolerance had a limit. He would likely blame her for Bobbie's stealing and maybe he would suspect her of stealing too. At least, he would be angry that she hadn't told him about other things that Bobbie stole and she paid for.

Julie was beaten. Her legs went limp and there was something heavy in her chest. How long would Frank go on trusting her in the store, if he knew? How long before he would fire her just because the two of them were a nuisance? Why should Frank put up with the Fullers anyway? She sat on a box and gave way to tears of frustration. She didn't concern herself with how Bobbie might have sneaked into the store, or how to prevent his stealing again, or what she was going to do with him when she got home. With a terrible certainty she realized that whatever she did, wherever she went, something of the Fuller family would always be there with her, a little demon Bobbie following her around, pulling her down.

That night before she left, Julie sneaked the money for the stolen candy into the cash register. She wouldn't talk to Frank. It would be easier to quit working than to tell him about Bobbie and take the risk of being fired.

The next morning Julie didn't show up for work. Stewart waited for the inevitable question one of the men around the barrel stove asked: "So where's your helper today, Stewart?" His grunt was the only reply he was willing to give.

"Quit, did she?"

The barrel stove gang nodded knowingly to each other. "Just like a Fuller", one of them said, and laughed.

"Nope. Sick." Stewart announced laconically.

"Sick? Thought I saw her this morning with that Maclean girl down by the river."

"Hhummph." They knew it was hopeless to try to get any more reaction from Stewart.

Stewart closed the store that night and instead of heading up the stairs for supper, he left by the back door. He approached the Fuller house with a determined walk and stood briefly in front of the door. What the hell was he doing there? He was an old fool. What was he going to say?

He stared at the door. The surface was inconsistently patched with thin boards and canvas covering the cracks made by frustrated visitors kicking to gain attention. Shades of pale green paint peeked through the dirt where children's initials had been scratched into the thick surface. The door was never quite closed, and Stewart's knocking pushed it open. A strong sour smell wafted through the doorway.

"Hullo in there! Anybody home?" he called and peered into the dusky interior. Stewart was shoved roughly against the door jam as Bobbie's wiry body fled through the door. Recovering from the encounter, Stewart called again, trying a forced hint of anger. "Julie? Are you home?" He pounded on the open door.

"Yo! Frank." Julie said quietly, behind him, outdoors.

He turned, frowned, and said, "Well, what've you got to say for yourself?"

"Nothin'." She leaned against the wall and narrowed her eyes as if to see more clearly what his reaction would be.

"Nothing?" Now he was genuinely angry. He had never in his life chased down the store help to come to work. "Well, you might begin by telling me what you plan to do about your job. Are you coming to work tomorrow or what?"

"Nah. I guess I quit."

Stewart's stomach lurched. "Quit. Just like that? Quit?" He could only repeat the word to fill the space that was in front of them. He needed to be more formal. It would help to control his growing anger. She was just a kid. Just a Fuller. "Would you at least have the courtesy to tell me why?" he asked, folding his arms in front of his chest and staring at her.

"Tired a workin' I guess," she mumbled and put both hands in her jacket pockets, gazing over his shoulder at nothing, putting on a bored and disinterested look, avoiding his eyes. A crooked smile teased her lips as she chewed the inside of her cheeks.

Stewart made himself loud and severe: "You're old enough to show more responsibility. A job's a serious thing. Don't you care about your reputation? You were doing great. You wanta spoil it all now?" She didn't answer so Stewart added, "Eh?" and felt silly.

"Just need a holiday I guess."

Stewart stopped himself from saying, What a lot of crap. When did a young energetic kid like her need a holiday in the summer? I get it, he thought, she's acting. A scene with his fourteen-year old son came back to him as they stood awkwardly in silence. He had lied once to Stewart about where he had spent the night. The boy had talked like that, as if he were above caring about it. He knew his son was terrified, and vulnerable. The words he had said then came back to Stewart. "Dammit!" he shouted, "Stop it, right now!" He had memorized his role and made himself sound menacing, shouting, "You know what I hate most? It's your goddam lying. I know you're not telling me the truth. I'm not sure why you think you have to lie, but I can tell you I'm not at all sucked into this silly game you're playing." He stepped away from the doorway, waving his hand in an exasperated gesture of dismissal.

Julie looked at him and said, "Bobbie's the only one playing games around here."

Surprising himself, Stewart said, "Look, has this got anything to do with that damned little brother of yours?" Julie said nothing, shuffling one foot in the dirt. Stewart said, "That was him I saw leaving the store out the back way yesterday, right? What've you got to do with him? Did you let him in?"

"You think I'd do that, don't you? Shit on you, man," she said coldly and moved to go inside the house.

He caught her arm. She stopped. "No," he said, "No. You wouldn't let him in. Does he sneak in, then? And what about the bits of extra money in the till at night? You paying his way?" he asked quietly and dropped his grasp. She nodded sullenly. They stood silently for a moment and Stewart said at last, with a wry smile of conspiracy, "You know, we just might be able to stop him if we work together on this."

"What d'ya mean? What can we do about it?"

He did not reply, and turned to go. Then he spun around and pointed his finger at her: "Whatever your reasons are for being such an idiot, you show up tomorrow or you're fired!" and walked briskly away.

"Hey, man, I thought I just quit!" Julie called to Stewart's determined back receding down the street, and smiled.

The next morning, out of habit, Julie woke up at the usual time to get up for work. She lay on the bed puzzling out her immediate future until a new thought suddenly came to her mind, something she would never have imagined in her life before: maybe Frank needed her. Why would he come around to get her otherwise? He said she had been doing great. Only her teachers had ever said that to her before.

The door to the store protested as Julie pushed it open. Stewart glanced up at her from behind the cash register and said loudly for everyone to hear, "Glad you're feeling better, Julie. Take that garbage out to the alley before the City truck gets here, will ya?"

Two of the barrel stove gang eyed Julie closely as she squeezed past them to get to the back of the store. She hung up her jacket and called over their heads, "Sure thing, Frank."

FOSTERING FAMILIES

"Jeez, Molly, is there really nothing else we can do?" Michael was louder than he intended to be on the phone with his supervisor. Not a great idea. He puffed twice on his cigarette, blowing the smoke across his desk as if to blot out his question. Maybe she'd think he had to be loud, because of the distance, the notoriously bad phone lines to Dawson.

Still, it was absurd. The Department of Welfare was asking an old age pensioner living in a rundown log cabin in Dawson City to look after two grandchildren he'd never even seen before. It was Molly's idea. Easy for her to say, over 300 miles away in Whitehorse. Her Master's of Social Work degree--from England, no less--was the only one in the fledgling Department. It carried a lot of weight when decisions were made, even if she knew next to nothing about life north of the capital.

Molly let a long breath escape. A slight smile twitched Michael's lips. The "detached interest" she kept reminding Michael to use was slipping away from her. It didn't take much. Her clipped accent pierced Michael's ear. "You know the Department's recent policy on fostering these children." *These children* meant Indians. "We must put them first with the family if at all possible."

He imagined Molly Murphy on the other end of the line: an unremarkable face with too much makeup, topped by a rounded mass of artificially blonde hair. Rumour had it that the hair was a wig, needed because she over-bleached her own. She was only a few years older than Michael. Her short plump figure would be sitting on the edge of her seat, her ankles dutifully crossed, knees a little apart. She looked far from Michael's picture of a English social worker. He could faintly hear her long red fingernails clicking a rhythm on the desk in front of her. Or was it just static on his phone?

"We talked about this before, Mike. Surely you remember?" Mike! She had never realized that she was the only person who continued to shorten Michael's name. To him, a Mike was a tough guy with a beard and lots of long curly black hair. He pictured a Mike encased in leather on a motorcycle, SEX dripping from his every move, the exact opposite of himself. He was short, skinny, with thin blonde hair.

"I remember the policy," Michael said, hoping he sounded neutral. Then, despite his resolve to be more co-operative, he added, "But you know how I feel about it."

Molly ignored his bait. She said, "I remember you said a fortnight ago that Dave Maclean's done a fine job with the granddaughter. What's that name? It's here in the file somewhere...oh, here it is: Selena. Selena Maclean. Looks like grandpop's had her for absolutely eons, with no assistance. No problems with that situation, right?"

"No problems. But there could be, if we push it. Are you sure there isn't a foster home down there? Dave looked after Selena's mother when she was small, too. His wife died before the War."

"He sounds like a splendid placement to me, Mike. Mom's a loss down here. Has been for years. I think she's in jail from what we hear."

One of the principles Michael operated under was that social workers were obligated to keep in touch with the parents of children in their care. He believed they ought to support them to get their kids back, help them to make a family again. He recognized another myth that had long ago been shattered for him, but said anyway, "You aren't in touch with her?"

"Can't find her any more it seems." In the way that only Brits could, Molly tried the coldly chummy, rather nasal approach. "Just ask Gramps if he'll do it, m'dear. Let him make the decision, arright?"

"Let me have a look at the file a sec." Michael opened the Child Protection file Molly had mailed him marked *MACLEAN, Eliza, C/P,* and glanced through the record. Twin boys, John and Jake. Born in Whitehorse, 1957. Nine years old. Four different foster homes for John and three for Jake since first apprehended from Eliza at three years old. Now both foster homes were breaking down again. One family was moving out of the Yukon. The other foster mother was pregnant and needed the extra bedroom.

"Looks like they could be problem kids from the file," Michael said, "moved a lot, energetic at that age. A handful for Dave."

More arm twisting from Molly: "Believe me, we have no other choice, as much as we would like to have." She waited. No response, so she continued, "You've told me hundreds of times there aren't fostering possibilities in Dawson, right? And all of ours down here are full. We simply have to repatriate kids to their home towns if we can. Frees up space here for us. Brings families back together, Mike." Michael wanted to say that their home town was Whitehorse; that's where they were born. But he didn't. Silence as they both paused. Molly finally said, "This girl, Selena, shouldn't she take some responsibility for them, do you think--help out, like? She's...what? How old?"

"Seventeen." Old enough to work. Old enough to quit school and look after kid brothers.

"See if Gramps can take even one of the tikes, luv, and it'll work out fine, I'm sure."

"Well, Dave'll take both if he takes one." His attempt at sounding less argumentative became muttering.

"Eh? What's that Mike? This bloody line's acting up again today."

Michael said without enthusiasm, "He'd probably take both. Won't want to split them up. Anyway, maybe he could use the money." If he mentioned the payment now, maybe that decision would be out of the way. The unwritten Whitehorse policy seemed to be to try to convince relatives to take foster children without payment. He didn't even discuss money for fostering; he always issued it as payment for what he saw as a valuable service to the Department.

"Mmmm...yes, well, that's lovely if he takes both. Try and see if he'll take them with a little help for food, eh? Don't force him, but...you know... however much he can handle. You'll be able to judge. Maybe check out his bank account if he asks for payment." Michael was embarrassed when he had to get clients to sign over permission to look at their bank accounts. He often accepted their word rather than doing the hated paperwork.

"Uh, Mike, can you let us know by Monday next?" Molly was eager to get on to better things.

Consciously Michael kept her on the line. He felt the power shift to himself. "Just tell me why they won't build a group home," he said. One more stab at that old argument. They rarely saw a foster family accept a child permanently. Some foster families were not that healthy despite careful enquiries and studies. Group homes were like a small orphanage, with paid professional staff, a new idea in the Yukon. "Maybe we need to revive the idea of some kind of small institution. Something like residential schools, only smaller, more intimate. More like a family, without the sticky personal problems of a real family. Gives the kids continuity. And it's more efficient and probably cheaper for us if nothing else," Michael said.

"Well," Molly laughed that shallow laugh of hers in recognition of the repeated request, "we're working very hard on that one, believe me, m'dear. Even showed around some blueprints the other day. Costs a lot more, you know. But Territorial Council election's coming up in the fall, luv. Maybe something'll happen after that. New blood and all that. Ta ta now." She hung up.

"Damn it," Michael said aloud. He pushed back his chair and went into his residence adjoining the office. In the kitchen, he poured himself a fresh cup of coffee and looked out the window. He had to learn to be more diplomatic with her. Maybe he hadn't inherited the famous Dutch genes for compromise and discipline. After all, it must take some guts to be a social work supervisor. It wasn't a job he would take on. If her husband wasn't an RCMP officer transferred to the Yukon, she would have been working down south in a big city no doubt. It would be harder coming here from a foreign country, too. Friends told him that Molly still felt the stinging stares and comments from the Whitehorse staff when she arrived from England in her bright blue mini-skirt. The style was unheard of in the isolated Yukon. But determined to bring civilization and British fashion to the colonies, she continued to wear the revealing skirts, in a profession known for conformity. Michael smiled thinking about it. He admired her for that.

Back in the office, he reached for the ashtray and put out his third cigarette of the morning. It smouldered accusingly. Lately he had been counting the cigarettes, trying to shame himself into quitting. He felt worse as the tally grew. Well, it was a good thing he smoked only cigarettes, forgoing the numerous opportunities to smoke pot since coming to Dawson. He wasn't in the bar every night like some of the government crowd either.

If she could be here, Oma would say to him, "Smells like some rotten sewer in here! Bad like Opa's storage shed. You should do that out behind the barn, by the manure pile." The thoughts creep up on him, as if she was standing there behind him, sniffing loudly, tightening her apron around her large middle the way she would do when she wanted to emphasize her point.

Michael had no memory of his parents, the De Bruins. The only child of their young marriage, he was three years old in the spring of 1943, in Holland. His parents were both killed when the Allies mistakenly bombed parts of Rotterdam and the surrounding countryside, destroying their house. His De Bruin grandparents--Oma and Opa--owned the next farm down the road. That's where he lived afterwards, along with his two unmarried uncles. When he was older, asking about his parents, and why he wasn't killed too, Opa told him: "Seems you wandered outdoors. Probably you wanted to see the planes. A miracle that you were saved from those stupid Limeys!" Opa cursed the English for killing his only son whenever he found an excuse. It left Michael confused about who the real enemy was. You couldn't trust anyone, Opa said.

Michael ran his hands through his hair. Was it getting thinner already? He was too young to be balding, not quite 28. He'd have to get to Whitehorse soon for a haircut unless he wanted to risk the questionable skills of the town's part-time barber or someone's well-meaning wife. The Personnel Director in the government made it clear when he was hired that his long hair and beard had to go if he wanted the job. "...even if it is the style these days Outside," Molly had said with some sympathy. Resenting the personal imposition, he cut his hair, shaved off his five-year-old beard, and settled for a thin moustache. It was still an uncomfortable surprise to see his younger, naked face in the mirror. He was exposed now, his inner thoughts and secret habits revealed to the world. Sometimes he sensed the town watching his every move, judging him on how well he did his work, reminding him of his responsibilities, discussing what he was doing with the position of power he had in Dawson's hierarchy. "You can't do a thing here that the whole damn town doesn't know about," he had been told more than once. Living in Dawson made him feel sometimes as if Oma had made him do something he didn't want to do and she was there, again, watching him from the kitchen window.

But he had to admit that life in Dawson City was a trip. A trip and a half! He didn't have time to feel lonely. He was never bored, never missed TV. He laughed a lot. The work was an exciting challenge, and he had more of a social life than he had ever had in his life. Entertainment was a night dancing to the juke box, gossiping in one of the four bars, a home-cooked dinner, or a curling bonspiel. Nearly all the professionals were young and single. For the first time in his life, he belonged to a large group. They accepted him as one of the crowd without making any demands on him. There were parties for any old reason, sometimes just because there hadn't been one for two weekends running. Evenings and weekends, when he wasn't out on an emergency call, or travelling to Mayo and Pelly Crossing, he was at some shindig with the teachers or the nurses or the RCMP or the bank boys--or often all of them at once.

He was too busy to think, and on weekends often too drunk to care about anything. He fell into bed in the early morning, relieved to sleep dreamlessly, sometimes with one of the nurses. It had been a long time since he had dreamed about the hard black leather belt hanging behind the kitchen door on the farm, the one Oma used to strap him with.

Back to reality. Paperwork. He dug out several forms from the filing cabinet. The boys were nine. He remembered being nine. That was the year he had a favourite soft white rabbit in the pens near the outhouse. He secretly named him Flopje. When no one was looking, he would take Flopje out of his cage, stroke his ears and back, looking into those trusting pink eyes. He would hum a tune to him. He fed him extra greens, stolen from the garden. On Christmas Day, Michael couldn't find Flopje in the pen. He ran to Opa, and was told they had eaten Flopje in the stew the night before. He vomited in the manure pile. They thought he had the flu.

Michael sat down to copy the Maclean names and birthdates into new foster child files. Were they non-status? In between? Neither white nor Indian. Half breeds. Can't even call them Metis in the Yukon; not a French mixture. There was the Maclean name on the Indian Affairs list, so they were status. Registered. On the list with a band number. Number 59. Like the numbers tattooed on Jewish arms. Worse, in a way. Invisible numbers. Hidden hatred. And the Indian people couldn't emigrate to get away. No safe America or even Israel for them. As a youngster, he had daydreamed that there was no young family called De Bruin in Holland, that his parents were really Jewish and were taken off to a concentration camp in Germany. It sounded logical. He let himself think that the De Bruins needed help on their farm so they took him in, pretending he was their grandchild.

"No one seems to understand how demeaning numbering of people is, labelling them like the Jews were in Germany," Michael said once at a dinner party at the teacherage. He was proud of having said it, although two of the teachers protested the comparison. Maybe they would remember him saying it, some day when there were no longer any band numbers for Indians in Canada. He stopped himself short of talking about Indian reservations being exactly like the homelands where blacks were forced to live in South Africa.

"Canada's the safest and the richest place on earth, next to America," Oma had said when she announced to the uncles in 1952 that she and Opa would be emigrating from Holland to British Columbia and taking Michael. They wanted to escape the post-war poverty, build a new life, Opa said. They sold half the farm and left the uncles to work the rest. Oma and Opa worked every day as farm labourers in the berry fields in Richmond and in the cattle barns in the Lower Mainland. Michael spent three years--all his weekends and holidays--working alongside them, raking manure, carrying water, picking berries, until they saved enough for a down payment on a small farm in Langley.

Michael's eyes soon wandered from the files. The sounds outside the window meant Dawson City was coming slowly to life at noon. It was July, so even the morning wave of children going to school had ended with summer holidays. Mornings weren't at all like his pre-dawn rising to milk the cows in Langley or his early morning shelving library books to pay for his room and board at university. Soon after he started the social work job, he learned not to do any home visits until late morning at the earliest if he wanted to catch someone between waking up and going out. His apartment and office were in the same building, with only a door in between. He could comfortably go from breakfast to work with just a few steps. He relished the quiet mornings in the office, knowing he would seldom be interrupted by visitors, and that he could work at his own speed.

"Hi Michael!" His half-time secretary's curly red hair popped around the corner of his office door. "Hey, it looks like I'll have to spend my coffee break washing your dishes again, eh?" Kay laughed, pointing to the sink in the kitchen. She disappeared into her office.

Laying a stack of files on Kay's desk, he smiled and said, "No washing dishes until you're finished these. I got all caught up, and, man, I'm famished." He went into the kitchen.

"Slave driver!" she called through the connecting door. "Just look at that great outdoors! What sunshine!" She bounced her wide hips into her chair. "Warmer even than yesterday. Too bad we have to be in the office, eh? Days like this in Dawson should be automatic holidays, don't you think?"

He found an old sandwich in the fridge and came back into the office. "Right on! And it should also be a holiday when it's forty below and dark at lunchtime or when it rains, which I love...you know, I think that's how the Indians used to live, just taking each day as it comes and then deciding what to do with it. Maybe we could learn something from them. I'll send a memo to Molly about that."

"Oh, you silly boy! It's a good thing you're away from that university and into the real world learning some lessons from us more mature types. You'd make us all into a bunch of hippies if you had your way." Kay smiled, picked up a letter to be typed, skimming it without interest.

Kay's habit of chatting before getting down to work was a ritual that had given Michael valuable information about the town's workings. When Kay had let him know most of the latest gossip, Michael said to her: "Well, I have news too. Guess what they're doing now." *They* always meant the Whitehorse office. Kay looked up, and he said, "They want Dave Maclean to take on two more kids, his grandsons."

"You mean Eliza's twins? From Whitehorse?" Kay frowned. "That poor man. As if he doesn't have his hands full already. I remember when Eliza ran off and left him with Selena. When was that? You know, Selena was only a couple years old. He's looked after her ever since."

Michael didn't say that he knew Kay wasn't living in Dawson at the time that Eliza left. Sometimes the town's myths got mixed up with reality and time sort of shifted together. It's accepted, especially if you lived in Dawson for a decade or more like Kay and her husband. Longevity, not truth, gave you credibility.

"I guess Selena got that summer job waitressing at the Westminster Cafe," Kay said.

"Yeah, and if Dave agrees to take the two kids, the pressure will be on her to quit school and keep her job in the fall to help with money to look after them." Would a seventeen-year-old girl help look after two boys, brothers she didn't even know? She might resent it, become angry, maybe run away. They were asking her to sacrifice her future, like they had asked him to do when he was her age. Oma had told him they needed him to quit school to work full time on the Langley farm. That's when he ran away. The police found him at a friend's house. He adamantly refused to return. He said he would run away again if they made him go back. When he told the social worker about the beatings and the long days of work, he was placed in a foster home in Vancouver. He was relieved that he never saw his grandparents again.

"I'm going to visit Dave this afternoon," Michael said. "Man, can you beat it? For all the taxpayer's money we spend, we still can't offer a good foster home to two little boys."

"Well it might not be so bad. He's certainly experienced at being a dad. And Selena can help. She's old enough." Michael's lips squeezed together. Kay asked, "Have you been arguing with Molly again?"

"Sometimes these family placements aren't as good as they look, Kay. Worse than foster homes that do it only for money and pay the kid no attention," Michael said coldly and turned into the kitchen. He barely heard Kay's mild response. His foster parents, Mr. and Mrs. Scott, had tried cheerfully to make him feel welcome in their home, but they were involved in their own two little boys who were half his age. He was used as an unpaid baby-sitter for them after school and on weekends. The Scotts were simply happy that Michael was no trouble. He counted the years and then the months when he would be free of them.

They had all spoken Dutch at his grandparents' home and he found English difficult at school. He was over a year older than others in his grade because of it. But he studied hard. When he turned nineteen, because he was a foster child, the government said they would pay his tuition and clothes if he went on to university. He dropped out for two years in the middle of his degree, but returned to complete it, paying his own way, and earning a Bachelor of Arts with majors in English and History.

At first when he was with the Scotts, Michael used the English translation of his name, Michael Brown. Then when he registered for first year at the University of BC, he used his foster parents' name. Later he had his surname legally changed to theirs. They were flattered, but Michael did it because Scott was a good solid Canadian name that anybody could have. It helped him to be like everyone else and to disappear.

****

Michael walked across town to the South End to see the Macleans in their cabin overlooking the Klondike River. He wanted to give himself time to clear his mind and to become as neutral as possible about this placement. The sunshine helped, but his mind wandered to an uncomfortable dinner party he had been to in Whitehorse the month before. It was with the social work crowd, who were out to say goodbye to a departing colleague at the Monte Carlo, a favourite haunt of civil servants. Michael found himself sitting across from Molly saying, "I wanted to talk with you about that family we are working with in Mayo. I have a problem with placing the girl with her aunt."

"What's your problem, Mike?" Molly asked.

"For one thing, like I told you, I have my doubts about the uncle. I've heard he likes the teenage girls a bit too much."

"And as I told you, you'll have to get proof, not just hearsay. You know that."

"Anyway, apart from that, speaking generally, don't you think we kind of take advantage of Indian people when we put kids with their extended families?"

"Whatever do you mean, Mike?" she asked, taking a sip of her wine and looking hard at him over the menu.

"You have to admit it's less work for us, not having to find foster homes. And it's cheaper. I notice we don't always pay full foster home rates to the families. A lot of them can't cope with the added expense. It helps the Department more than the family sometimes." Molly did not respond. "Don't you think that the relatives who are the most willing to go that extra mile for their families--the aunties and grannies--are kind of, well, used by us?"

"There's always social assistance if they need financial help."

"Sure, but not everyone is comfortable with taking SA. Doesn't it also get the Native Brotherhood off our backs? They object to Indians being placed in White homes, right?"

"We don't think politically like you do apparently. We are trying to think of the best interests of the child." A blank space dropped into the middle of the hum of conversation around them.

"Hey, has anyone else seen *Midnight Rider*?" Molly's secretary beamed cheerfully. "I got to see it last week on our holiday in Vancouver. Wow! The most groovy movie I've ever seen!" General approval greeted this.

Molly looked around the table and called, "Who's for dessert later? The chocolate cake is divine here, nearly as good as me mum's."

Later, they were putting on coats by the door when Molly pulled Michael aside. She smiled without warmth and said in a low tone, "Let's leave work at the office after this, eh Mike? A dinner party isn't quite the right place for debating cases and philosophy. Not very good for morale, m'dear." He started to protest. Molly stopped smiling. "Maybe you don't realize it, luv, being out in the hinterland up there, but we like to think of our office as one big family. Maybe not always an extremely happy family, but we try to support each other as best we can." She said, "You sounded frightfully disloyal." She frowned and turned away.

Michael's cheeks burned. "So when can we talk about these things, then? I'm not able to discuss my work with anyone in Dawson if we want confidentiality, and you and I never seem to have the time to talk in any depth when I'm here."

They left the restaurant together and started down the street. He was grateful for the cool air. Molly sounded serious when she turned to him after waving good-night to the others, and said, "Right then, chum, I'll get up to Dawson soon and we can have a great philosophical night of it over a couple of beers. Sound good to you?"

"Sounds great, Molly. Look forward to it," he remembered saying to her that night.

Driving back to Dawson the next day, he looked back on Molly's offer to come to Dawson. She had never come to see him in the two years he had been there. He was generally happy with that arrangement; it allowed him more independence. Still, there were times when the isolation made him uneasy. He was frustrated with the decisions he was called upon to make alone in Dawson, without advice. He had taken Molly's silence on many questions as her approval, but sometimes he felt adrift without direction. They gave him no training before he started, just throwing him into the office, handing him a stack of filing cards with clients' names and types of cases on them. He had to figure them out on his own. "Applied pragmatism," he would answer when someone asked him what his method of social work was.

He recalled a friend in the Whitehorse office saying, "Molly has convinced the Director that they should replace the untrained social workers like us with people who have Master's degrees. Looks like our days are numbered, man." Was Molly setting him up for failure by not letting him in on what everyone else seemed to know, giving her an excuse to fire him? Maybe she wanted to come up to Dawson to find things she didn't like, ammunition for the great cause of replacing him. Be fair, he said to himself. She was very busy. She seemed frank and open most of the time. He chastised himself for feeling paranoid. He needed to learn to trust people more. That kind of thinking wasn't solving any of the immediate problems of the Maclean boys.

Dave Maclean's small cabin had a tin roof and traces of dark brown paint on the thick log walls. At the back, a meat cache shaped like a miniature cabin itself on raised legs was not used any more because of kids stealing things that they didn't eat or even want. It stood beside a greenhouse made of glass with pots of petunias, pansies, and nasturtiums in vivid colours hanging from the eaves. Michael had heard that Dave was teased about growing the flowers, not a usual masculine activity in Dawson. But everyone admired Dave's green thumb. Other Dawson gardeners relied on his advice, especially when attempting to save their own crops in mid-August. He seemed to know exactly the right time to harvest, just before the inevitable frost.

Approaching the fence, Michael marvelled at Dave's talent. Precisely straight rows of onions, cabbages, potatoes, broccoli, turnips, and carrots grew in various shades of green between weedless paths just wide enough to walk on. Red and green stalks of rhubarb with huge tropical leaves nearly hid the windows on one side of the cabin. Long hours of warm daylight, rich river-bottom soil, and Dave's magic touch combined to fill his root cellar with hardy vegetables that would last most of the winter. He would sell or give away what he couldn't use.

Dave's wide back bent over a patch of brownish leaves. He waved a handful of weeds in greeting, stood up, and came over to lean on the fence. "Thought I'd try celery this year," he said, "but it's none too good. Have to see if there's a better kind in the catalogue next year. I hear there's an experimental farm at the university in Fairbanks that grows it fine."

"Think it might be just the heat coming so suddenly after our cold spring?" Michael startled himself with his knowledge of gardening remembered from his childhood. The De Bruin farm in Langley grew everything from grapes to sweet potatoes. But it was an easy task to grow things there compared to the struggle in the Yukon where gardening really had to be in your soul to deal with the short growing season and the demanding climate.

"Could be the heat," Dave said, "but some kind of bug got into it too. Maybe came in with the seeds. Don't want to use any of them damn pesticides neither. I'll just wait and see what happens next year. Them bugs can't survive our winter, I'm sure."

Without asking if Michael could use it, Dave handed two heads of early lettuce and some long red stalks of rhubarb over the fence as if it was the reason he came by. He already had a refrigerator full of the products of other people's gardens, and he wasn't much of a cook, but Michael knew it would be an insult not to take the gift. He would pass it on to one of the clients who could use extra food.

"You're here on business," Dave stated, his hands streaking dirt across the front of his overalls.

"Afraid so." Michael had tried to be casual, to make it easier.

"Eliza? She OK?"

"Well, still the same..."

Michael was interrupted by a harsh laugh. Dave seldom talked about his daughter except when necessary. He told Michael once that she was "the curse of my life."

"It's the twins, Dave," Michael said quickly. "Both of their foster homes have given them up. John's is moving out to Edmonton, and the other mother's expecting a baby and can't keep Jake." Michael wondered if he sounded like he was apologizing for the foster homes. He stopped himself from making a comment about commitment.

"You want us to take them for the rest of the summer?"

"Well, to be honest, it may be longer than the summer. I'll try to find some other place for them here or in Whitehorse, but we don't have a lot of foster homes right now."

"Well, don't think we can do it for more than this summer, Michael. Just not enough room. Two young boys..."

"Can we try just the summer, then?"

Dave picked up a spade and turned over the moist black soil near the fence. Thinking aloud, he said, "Not going to be easy. Guess I can put the wall tent up in the back yard. I'll sleep there. Need another bed. Maybe Jan has one."

"Maybe I should look somewhere else."

"Where else?" Dave echoed Michael's thoughts. He said, "I can't see them anywheres else in Dawson, do you? And it'd be damned embarrassing, having my own flesh and blood in a stranger's house down the street somewheres."

"But if it's just too much for you..."

"Be able to make out OK for awhile, the summer. Be good for Selena. Keep her busy."

"Dave, I just had a thought: maybe we should discuss this with Selena first too. Should I come around tonight?"

"Well, I don't know if that's necessary. I'll just tell her. Not much we can do about it, eh?"

"No, please don't tell her just yet. I really would like to know that she has some say in this. It means responsibility for her, too, you know."

"Anything you say."

When Michael arrived back at the Maclean's cabin that evening, Selena opened the door with an excited smile and, leaning out, called over his shoulder to a girl passing by, "My twin brothers are coming! Both of them! Neat, eh?"

"Crazy, man! Right on!" the girl called back, "When?"

"Pretty soon!" Selena said.

Irritated that Dave hadn't waited for him to discuss it with Selena, Michael said, "Hold on, Selena, I'm just here to talk it over. It hasn't been decided yet."

Selena's dimples played on her cheeks and her face lit up with energy. Her eyes sparkled. "Oh, sure, I know that," she said, tossing her pony tail. "But Pop said it's OK," giving notice that she wouldn't be recognizing any other authority in the matter. She promptly sat on a chair, arms straight, her hands grasping the edges of the seat to hold herself down. She tried to suppress a smile and a dimple appeared on her left cheek. She will be a real charmer some day, Michael thought.

"Tea's made. Have some?" Dave asked, bringing the pot and a cup over to the table. He gestured with his thumb at Selena. "She's real excited about this. Together like a family at last, I guess. Must say I look forward to having some masculine company for a change."

"Slow down, Dave." Michael said. "We need to know a lot more before a final decision is made. What are the sleeping arrangements? Did you get a bed from Jan?"

Dave cleared his throat. "The boys, the twins, they can have my bedroom," he said, "and I'll just sleep on the couch like I always do in the winter, anyways, to tend the fire. I know your bosses won't think too much of that, but it's been fine for the two of us, so with the boys, it shouldn't make any difference."

"We were only talking about your having them for the summer," Michael reminded him. "You know, I'm not so concerned about the physical space as I am about your age and Selena's involvement in their care." Michael tried to sound detached, professional, like Molly.

Offended, Dave said, "My age? Nothin' wrong with me yet. Heart's good. Legs are too, so's I can run after them. They're what, nine?" Dave asked. "Seems to me they pretty much look after themselves at that age, eh? Just need some food and some rules. Keep 'em out of trouble."

"They could be a handful for you, you know. They haven't had a great life so far. Might be trouble."

"Time they got a better life, then, is my guess. Couldn't be worse than them foster homes that don't want 'em," Dave said with a grunt.

Michael turned to Selena, "What do you think, Selena? How do you see yourself with the boys?"

"Well," she said, counting off her prepared answers on her fingers, "Pop said I'll have to help around the cabin more. Cooking, washing clothes.

Stuff like that. But John and Jake can help Pop too, with the wood and--let's see--the garden and all that dirty stuff. I don't like doing the wood and I hate weeding!" She laughed. "They can have all the boys' jobs."

"We got no choice, Mr. Scott," Dave said with pretended formality. "The lady of the house has spoken."

"Well, I'll take all I've heard into consideration of course," Michael said. "I'll let you know soon."

As Michael was leaving, the Macleans stood in the doorway. Selena put her hand on Dave's arm, looked up at him, and said, "Now I can be the older sister and a mom too, right?" She giggled with anticipation.

The next morning, Michael called Molly. He had written a list of all the reasons he believed the placement of the twins with the Macleans was not a good idea. He read it to her: Dave was too old, the house was too small, Selena was not mature enough, they would need financial help, and the boys might have a lot of social problems that Dave wasn't prepared for.

"But what about love, Mike? Is there enough love, do you think, for us to trust the family with these boys?" Molly asks.

Michael was mystified. "Love? Well, ah, yeah..." Enough love? Can we trust? "They both...they both seem to want the kids all right."

"And do you think they believe that their own future as a family is safe? Not threatened by the boys being there?"

Michael hesitated. "Seem to...well, actually, I'd say they think it might be better for them all, to tell the truth."

"That's lovely, Mike! Quick work. Nice and tidy. In the family. I'll bring them up myself on Monday's plane."

Michael listened to Molly promising to have a long talk with him about "the latest philosophy in social work practice" that she had read about in her professional journal. She would have to stay two nights to wait for the next plane back to Whitehorse so there would be plenty of time. She would bring him a pineapple she had seen in the grocery store.

Puzzled, Michael hung up the phone. Something was telling him he was supposed to feel good. It had all worked out. But for the rest of the day, he was dispirited. Molly was pleased; Dave was hopeful; Selena was positively delirious; even Kay was happy. He should be positive, like everyone else. He hadn't thought much about what he was doing with people's lives up till now. The words crept into his consciousness with a shock: foster homes. Foster families. Fostering families. Making families. Was he really capable of doing that? And doing it wisely? What about this love and trust bit that Molly hit him with out of the blue? Maybe he was letting his own past affect his decisions too much.

In bed later, Michael punched his pillow into a ball under his neck. Why couldn't they provide something better--a real family--for the kids like the Macleans? He turned out the light, staring into the dark. Finally he forced his eyes to close. Maybe the tumbled-together life in the Maclean family would turn out all right after all, with his support. He could only hope so. That was what most of his job consisted of, it seemed: lots of hope. He was beginning to think he could work miracles, play God, change families, revolutionize the world while he was at it. *Watch out, man. That's a power trip. Relax.* A lot of people seemed to think he was too serious, too involved in his clients. Maybe there was something he needed to learn here, like take every day as it comes and let the future take care of itself.

That night, for the first time in years, Michael dreamed in Dutch. He was singing a child's song to Flopje, his rabbit, as they ran through the strawberry field in Langley. He found himself with Flopje in his arms and flying above Oma's house, looking down on the gardens. He woke himself up laughing, his heart racing.

A PROPER PLACE

Through the lingering winter months of the coldest climate in North America, Michael Scott had learned to pander to the needs of the mechanical monster assigned to him as the Northern Area Social Worker based in Dawson City. He gingerly kept his foot on the gas pedal of the red Pontiac station wagon until it started its familiar grinding and spitting and then settled into a steady off-beat chugging rhythm. It was like some behemoth aroused from a contented sleep.

Mid-morning sunlight was breaking up pink clouds clustered on the Klondike valley hills. The colours of spring were finally coming to Dawson City in mid-March and the weather was distinctly warmer at twenty-five below. In Mayo the month before, at forty-five below, Michael had been shocked to find that an orange on the seat beside him was frozen as solid as a baseball. It had been there for only three hours with the heater blowing its cool air. He left the orange on the seat for three weeks to remind him of how fragile his body could be in a Yukon winter.

Slipping his foot off the gas pedal, Michael rubbed his bare hands together trying to warm them and gazed at the opaque windshield covered completely in last night's frost. In this warmer weather, the car's interior might warm up enough to melt it while he made a couple of phone calls, saving him the trouble of scraping it off. He pulled on his fur mitts, got out, and slammed the heavy door. Walking around the corner of the yellow one-storey building housing the office and his apartment, he muttered, "Maybe next winter they'll give me a new vehicle." If he said it often enough, like a mantra, it might happen. Sometimes to get to sleep he listed ways he could sabotage the Pontiac, forcing it to die so they would have to replace it.

In January, he had driven only a few miles out of town when the car became sluggish and groaned to a stop. Checking the oil, he saw it was nearly empty, and he noticed a pool of it accumulating on the road. The motor had come close to seizing up because the labourer at the Territorial garage compound had forgotten to tighten the plug of the drain hole after changing the oil. Later he wished he had taken the opportunity to kill the red beast by driving it to its death. When he complained to the Whitehorse office about the poor work, he was told that there was nothing they could do about the labourer. They admitted he wasn't too bright, but he had the distinction of being the brother of Dawson's Territorial Councillor. There were five children to consider. They needed to be fed. Michael was advised to ask next time about getting the district highway foreman (who Michael knew never left his desk) to do the work. Another small town conundrum for him to solve. His BA in History and English hadn't prepared him for such far-reaching dilemmas.

Although the roads were gravel and a challenge at any time of year, Michael enjoyed driving and relaxed after the first few minutes, away from any concerns except travelling. During those quiet times, he often thought back to his childhood on his grandparents' farm in Holland. In the freezing seclusion of the station wagon, he still smelt the pungent sweetness of the hayfields and imagined the heat that made him exhausted and thirsty as he tied the dry stalks together with twine. He threw the bundles onto the horse-drawn cart and the cruel hay scratched his bare arms and legs like needles, so that he had long scabs. At night in bed he would pick them when the blood dried. Sometimes that pain kept his mind busy and he didn't cry from the frequent beatings his grandmother gave him for being lazy or for not listening.

He was eleven in 1951 when he had his first exciting driving lessons on the second hand tractor that replaced the cart. The first time his uncle tried starting the tractor he had trouble, and he snarled, "*Godverdomme* piece of junk! Made by *klootzak* Jews in the war!" Young Michael was surprised to think that Jews made the tractors. And why did his uncle swear at them? The Germans had been the enemy, not the Jews. It was confusing.

His grandparents emigrated to British Columbia in the year after the tractor was bought, taking him with them. One of the first things Michael really understood in the cumbersome English language was a long series of films called "Canada at War." His grade seven class was made to sit in the gymnasium every Friday afternoon for weeks to watch them. He learned that the Nazis made Jews work in forced labour camps and realized that maybe that's where the tractor had come from. He found out that there were many Jewish families hidden from the Germans in Holland during the War, some in the town close by his grandparents' farm. Passionately, he read *The Diary of Anne Frank* three times, twice in Dutch, and then slowly in English. The Holocaust fascinated him. He memorized the names of all the concentration camps he could find. Maybe Oma and Opa weren't his real grandparents. Maybe he was Jewish, and his true parents were still alive in Europe somewhere, trying to find him, not killed in the war as his grandparents said. He promised himself that one day he would go back and find them.

Michael glanced back at the station wagon to see that it was still running before he opened his office door. Overheated air hit his ruddy face as a high insistent buzz announced recess for the school next door. That meant there would be fifteen minutes of children's wild voices in the playground, followed again by morning silence.

Sooner or later, every one of the 500 souls remaining in the Klondike ghost town had to pass by Michael's office in the centre of town. They would go along the wooden sidewalk lining the gravel street to the post office, the school, and the mining recorder. In the other direction, they walked toward the Yukon River to the liquor store, the grocery store, the gas pumps, and four hotels. After two winters he knew everyone - more people than he had known in his entire twenty-eight years. If needed, he was able to recall who was related to whom, where they lived and worked, and the consensus on their character, true or not. Nobody did much that wasn't known to everyone else. And if they were foolish enough to try to hide what they did, there was some kind of kharma that made it even more certain that everyone would know. There were times when he felt exposed, even spied upon.

Within a week of his coming to the job as the "Welfare Man", everyone he met already knew his name. They even knew that he had first arrived in Dawson to work on the gold dredge several miles out on Hunker Creek. He was reputed to be a hard worker on the dredge, seldom joining the rest of the crew in stretching their coffee breaks. Proud of being conscientious, he knew he had learned to work hard from his grandparents. If he had stopped to rest on the farm, Oma would yell at him from the house, "*Machiel! Luilak*! Lazy dog. Stupid lazy dog! Get to work!"

The dredge crew had spent their one day off in the bar at the Downtown Hotel, two short blocks away from Michael's present house and office. He had laughed at the name when he first saw it. To him, "Downtown" meant the busy junction of Granville and Georgia Streets in Vancouver. But like the title "City" in Dawson City, the town's ironies had come to mean something more than a joke to him. Most newcomers --*cheechakos*--who continued to laugh or complain about the idiosyncracies of Dawson didn't stay long. If they stayed, their perspectives inevitably changed. Surviving one winter in the Yukon meant being eligible to be a novice sourdough rather than a cheechako. That meant there was a degree of respect involved, and a sense of belonging. True Dawsonites could complain about the muddy streets, the weather, the cost of living, the lack of services, but only amongst themselves.

Cradling the phone between his shoulder and ear, Michael dialed the City office. He lit a cigarette and looked out through the Venetian blinds onto the dead morning street while the phone rang at the other end. He could see white exhaust drifting by the window. The car had not stalled.

"City office," a gruff voice said. Bob Kerr was the City manager.

"Hi, Bob? It's Michael. The Welfare Michael?" There were two Michaels in town, and neither one of them liked to be called Mike.

"Oh, yeah. How's things?"

"Nice day, eh? Good to see the sun again. Just hope it doesn't melt the ice before the bonspiel." In Bob's spare time he was the president of the curling club and was skip of the team Michael was on.

"Yeah, but March, you can never tell...unpredictable...what can I do you for?" Bob asked.

"It's about the Jimmy boys. Thought you might have some work for them to do in the curling rink, you know, to pay for their fun the other day?"

The week before, the two young cousins had crawled into the curling rink through an unlocked window. They broke open the pop machine and took a half dozen bottles. One of the boys had readily admitted to the RCMP later that they had also spent some time trying to throw the heavy curling rocks at each other. They had given up when a rock hit one of the walls, splitting the plywood with a loud noise. A few minutes later the boys were caught by the treasurer of the curling club when she went inside to clean up after the weekend's bonspiel. She had peered out the open window and found Joe and George Jimmy leaning against the wall beneath her, drinking the stolen pop in the spring sunshine. The curling club had the boys charged with the breaking in and theft.

Bob snorted. "Just what kind of work did you have in mind?"

"I thought maybe we could get them to fix that wall." Michael wanted to show the judge that the boys had done something about restitution. They would be going to Juvenile Court in two weeks.

"Sorry, Michael. No can do. I won't have those Indian kids in the rink for any reason. That wall's going to cost us a pretty penny, and this year the club's budget's already shot to hell."

"What if I supervised them after school? They seem to be pretty good kids, really."

Not on your life. Look, I gotta go. Got a meeting with the Mayor in ten minutes and I'm not ready, and I gotta get over to the rink this morning to make some more ice for our bonspiel." Michael heard Bob's voice soften. "Say, Michael," Bob said, "why don't you come around Friday for supper? Donna's making her specialty, a roast beef with Yorkshire pudding." Michael thought, *he needs me on that team.* "There'll just be us," Bob Said. "We'll talk about it then, OK?"

On Friday evening, Michael sat on Bob's couch and took a cup of coffee from a tray Bob was offering him after their supper. He looked up to Bob's balding grey head above horn-rimmed glasses and ventured, "About those Jimmy boys, Bob. I found some old carpentry tools in my store room. I could save the club some money if I got them to fix up that wall."

"Are you kidding? No thanks! Some carpenters, the three of *you*!" Bob laughed. "Here, have some of this cream. It's real; we got it in Whitehorse day before yesterday. Have some rye. Or try that orange liqueur. It's the wife's favourite. Get it for her every Christmas. Birthday too." Loud enough for Donna to hear in the kitchen, he added, "Otherwise, you never know what the old lady might do to me. Cut me off or something." Donna joined in his laughter over the sound of dishes being piled together.

Michael waved his free hand in a negative gesture over the liquor. He waited for Bob to settle into his chair. "Bob, seriously," he said, "those kids are going to court because your club wants to charge them. I know Judge Wilson will ask me what they've done to pay you back." The lines on Bob's forehead twisted together as he raised his eyebrows. "Besides, it's good for them to do the work, don't you think?" Michael persisted. "Sets an example for the other kids who think they've gotten away with it. I'm pretty good with a saw and hammer. It's just a patchwork job."

His arms spread along the arms of his chair, Bob sat with coffee mug in one hand and rye glass in the other. He twisted his large body awkwardly and became conciliatory. "Michael, I'd really like to help you out, you know that, eh? Must be hard on you in court. I can understand your problem. But...OK--first of all, they probably won't show up, eh? Then if they do come, they'll just wreck the place again. Scratch them rocks or even steal them." Michael formed a mental protest. He would supervise them better than that.

Taking a sip of his coffee, and then of his drink, Bob looked directly at Michael as if to make a very serious pronouncement. "Curling rocks are damned expensive. Those ones we got cost us a bloody fortune. We had to order them all the way from Scotland twenty years ago. Can you imagine the shipping costs today? Not on your life. I can't allow them kids in there again. End of discussion."

Michael breathed in deeply and suppressed a protesting response. If his university friends could see him now, Michael thought, they would laugh at the seriousness with which he and Bob were taking this mundane conversation. He remembered how he used to love to discuss points of principle and philosophy when he was out socially. He missed the clever give and take, the cheerful thrusts and jabs. He learned much about the world and himself in those challenging discussions, more than his university courses had given him.

Donna entered the livingroom and poured herself a drink in a tiny liqueur glass. It was time for a change of mood. Michael offered them each a cigarette, lit one, and searched his mind for something to say. "Hey, did you notice I got my garage finally? Big surprise when I got home from Mayo this week," he said. Michael warmed up to his current favourite story to tell at dinner parties. The government carpenter, up from Whitehorse, built it while he was away. The winter before, Michael had to walk across town at 45 below three times in one week to check on a couple of kids that the RCMP said had been left alone. The Pontiac wouldn't start because students going through his unfenced yard thought it was a perfect joke to unplug the block heater. After weeks of phone calls, memos, budgets, estimates, and an inch-thick file of paper sent to Whitehorse, they agreed to construct an unheated garage behind his building. They wouldn't give him a fence.

"Yeah, noticed that the other day," Bob smiled and shook his head. "Finally, eh?" The Territorial Government--YTG--was always fair game for verbal punishment amongst the City workers.

"Yeah, finally," Michael said. "They forgot just one thing. They didn't measure the length of the damn car. If it's inside, I can't close the door!"

"What?! No kidding! Hah!" Bob shouted. Donna joined in the gleeful laughter.

"I called the carpenter in Whitehorse and he said he'd fix it, add a couple of feet to the walls, but he says it's a big job. Can you imagine, stretching the garage? He won't be back until next fall, either. Who knows if they'll ever get around to it."

Bob said, "Yeah, that's like building a whole new garage, for Christ's sake. Needs paint, too. That'll have to wait. More taxpayer's money down the drain. We'd never get away with that shit at the City, you know. We'd have to answer to our neighbours for it, not like YTG, long gone 300 miles away to Whitehorse."

"Well, now you won't have to sweep the snow off every time you use the car anyway," Donna said with a smile, seeing the best side of things as usual, "at least, not the whole car, just the part sticking out." They laughed again. "And maybe the kids will find it's just too much trouble to unplug it next winter if they have to sneak into the garage."

"That's a very attractive necklace you have, Donna," Michael said, drawing attention to the silver chain with turquoise stones she was wearing. The colours contrasted with her dark hair and the chunkiness emphasized her trim figure.

"Oh, thanks, Michael." She touched the necklace. "I just love it. Bought them for my sisters, too. It's made by the Navajo Indians in a little pueblo we visited on our Christmas holiday in New Mexico."

Bob said, "There's a family we go visit down there, in Albuquerque. They come up every coupla years, tourists. Ya know, they said the Navajos are in the same boat as Indians here. Drinking. Stealing. On Welfare. It must be something in their blood or their genes or somethin', don't you think?" When Michael didn't reply, he summed up, "Well, you'd know all about that anyway, eh?"

Donna sipped her liqueur and said, "Tsk. Bobby. Sweetheart. This isn't the proper place to make Michael talk shop. His job's hard enough as it is." Michael smiled inwardly as he saw Bob flinch at the "Bobby". Not many people heard him called that. Donna turned to Michael, sincerely worried, "Really, how do you do it day in and day out, Michael, working with them?" She meant it kindly, and didn't expect a reply. He tried to smile.

Enough time had passed so that he could politely leave and Michael stood up with gratitude. As he passed by the kitchen door, he called, "Thanks for the wonderful meal as usual, Donna."

She turned from washing dishes, came to the door where Michael was putting his boots on, and asked, "Finish your business with Bob?"

It wasn't worth being direct and honest about his feelings. Hoping he sounded disinterested, Michael said, "Looks that way." As uncomfortable as he was, he needed to have good relations with Bob in this small town. He was learning to pick his battles and wondered if that was a sign of maturity, or of simple survival.

Donna wiped her hands on a towel, saying, "Well, bye for now, then," and disappeared to look for more dishes.

Bob came to the back door while Michael was putting on his jacket and said, "Just want to tell you something, Michael," amiably reaching for Michael's shoulder. "I'm not in any way prejudiced, of course, but those people..." he waved the glass of whiskey in the general direction of Front Street. "Down there. They're all alike, ya know." His voice became nostalgic. "Years ago, when I first came here, I really respected them, eh? Those days they were out trapping and living in the bush. Tough life, but it was the place for them, where they should be. I admired them, doing that. Respected them. But, honestly, seeing them day after day hanging around the liquor store and the bars like they do nowadays, well, you have to conclude they're just lazy and drunk like people say, eh?"

Michael's chest tightened in the effort to keep quiet. He said, "I'd better go. It's late, Bob. Donna wants to get to bed I'm sure." He opened the door.

"Mind you," Bob said, leaning on the door frame, "I feel real sorry for the kids. Not their fault. Left alone and hungry like they are half the time, it's no wonder they do what they do. I wouldn't say I'm in any way against the kids."

One last chance. "Well, maybe that's why we should try to help them..." Stop it, man. The revolution does not start here.

Bob offered his hand to Michael for a friendly shake, laughed good naturedly, and said, "Michael, Michael, Michael..." Michael moved away without shaking Bob's hand and Bob said confidentially, "You know, Michael, just between the two of us...it's not my place to tell you what's right or wrong or nothing, but just between us, now..." Bob's voice was quietly determined, "we gotta stick together, us Whites, ya know? I've lived here for twenty-three years, and believe me life can get pretty damned complicated in a small town. It's not easy. And you need all the support you can get in that job of yours."

Fascinated with how far Bob might go in the conversation, Michael spurred him on. "What do you mean, Bob?" he asked.

"Well, believe you me, you start mixing up too much with Indians and you'll end up with nothing but trouble for your efforts. Look at old Dave Maclean, a good example of what can happen, looking after Eliza's kid while she's drunk in Whitehorse. They're parasites. D'ya get what I mean? D'ya know your proper place in this town is what I'm asking." Michael's eyes spread open in disbelief. Bob said with a grin, "Well, anyways, let's sleep on it. 'Night." Michael stepped outdoors and Bob closed the door.

Closing the Kerr's picket gate behind him, Michael said aloud, "Asshole!" He kicked an empty pop bottle. It clattered along the sidewalk in front of him. Did he know his proper place in this town, Bob had asked, as if Bob had the right to decide propriety for anyone. Was his proper place with his grandparents who had worked him like a slave when his parents died? Or maybe it was in the foster home that he was put into when he ran away, where he was ignored like a piece of furniture. Did kids like the Jimmys have a proper place to be? He stooped to pick up the bottle, and without thinking, threw it into Bob's garden, harder than he anticipated. It shattered against the wall of the house, depleting any satisfaction from the act. He hurried away, hoping they hadn't heard anything. His shoulders slumped. He wasn't much better than Bob. Maybe only the Bob Kerrs of this world had a proper place to be and he should join them.

****

Driving along Fifth Avenue the next Monday, Michael's hand rose now and then automatically from the steering wheel, waving to anyone walking by who looked up. He noticed the two Jimmy boys huddled together, their skinny bodies making them seem younger than their twelve years. They were leaning against the wooden fence in front of the post office. Mischievous dark eyes flashing, their nearly identical round faces were topped with straight short black hair and red wool toques Michael recognized from Stewart's Store. They were throwing snowballs at the wheels of cars going by and giggling. They waved vigorously at Michael. He chose to think it was a friendly wave, and not triumphant. He still had to find some way of making them pay back the curling club.

The short, wiry figure of Wilma Woods stumbled out of the post office door and past the boys. She waved her hand at Michael in a signal to stop the car. He started to drive by, pretending not to see her, but seconds later he felt guilty and jumped on the brakes, making it necessary to back up.

Wilma knocked on the driver's window and ungracefully leaned in when Michael opened it. "Wafare, you gotta give me money. My kids gotta eat."

"Where's Andy, Wilma? I heard he was working on that City project."

"My old man, he run out on me. Again. He's with that bitch Florence. You should do somethin' 'bout that. You gotta go, get him back from that woman." She flung her arm up and nearly fell over from the effort.

"Didn't he get paid yet?" Michael asked, forced into what had become their ritual exchange over the past weeks.

Indignant, Wilma hung onto the heavy car door with both hands and said, "Course he did. Spent it on Florence like I told you before."

"Didn't he give you some money from his cheque?"

"Never give me money." Her dark eyes narrowed.

"Come on now, Wilma. That doesn't sound like him. I know he must've."

"OK, but not much. Not 'nough. Anyways, it's at the store. Just left it there. Never give me money."

"You mean he gave it to the store so you can get food, eh?"

She ignored the question. "You gotta go. Get him outa Florence's. Bring him home. Where he should be, with his kids."

"How about a ride home? Who's looking after the kids?"

"Mom's there. Hey! You know I look after my kids good. If my old man stopped drinking and fuckin' around, I wouldn't drink neither. You can't say I don't look after my kids, Wafare." Through the open window, she punched Michael's shoulder in friendly emphasis.

"Did I say that, Wilma? I've never had any trouble with you. Now come on. We'll go home. Maybe Andy's there already."

Wilma giggled. "OK Blondie. Just this once."

So now it's Blondie...Welfare Man, Wafare, Scotty, Mike. How many names he has had in his short life. None of them has stuck. Maybe he started the trend when he changed his name from the Dutch De Bruin to Brown when he got away from his grandparents. Then he legally changed it to his foster parents' name, Scott. When he first started in the welfare office, most of his clients called him Mr. Scott. But now no one used his last name unless they were trying to impress him, and it didn't. The importance of names struck him, how they were a way to get close to people or to push them away, and how they could even change a person's identity simply by their use, as he had done. Maybe they were more than a convenience for labelling.

Wilma wandered around the long station wagon, using the hood for balance. Michael leaned across the seat, opened the heavy passenger door for her, and she slid in. The stench of liquor and unwashed clothes made him stop rolling up his window. Without prompting, Wilma repeated something she had said many times to him: "S'not my fault I drink. It's Andy's. If he only stay away from Florence, everything'd be jus' fine. Hunky dory." She stared out the window at some new world where everything was hunky dory.

Michael believed most of what she claimed. That was the trouble. Each side of the stories he heard was plausible. No one seemed truly at fault. Everyone and everything was understandable and probably forgivable in the end.

Along Front Street on the way to her house, Wilma turned and said, "Jimmy and George. I hear they's in trouble..."

"What'd you hear?"

"You know. Broke in the curling rink. Wrecked the place. Stupid kids. You know, they's cousins. My nephews. Both them.

"What do you think should happen to them, Wilma?"

She slapped the seat between them and said, "You gotta strap 'em. Good strapping, just like me when I was kid. That's what you do." She said with her lips tight, "Use good hard belt."

Michael shivered at the thought. Opa had a heavy leather strip that he used for sharpening his straight razor. It was like an extension of Oma's arm, he saw her with it so often. The arm lifted and came swiftly down. The leather cracked against his bare legs and the searing pain was almost a relief from the terror of waiting, the yelling. Bruises remained for days every time and they made him wear long pants to school so no one would see. The hardest thing was the time he ran crying into the barn to Opa after one of Oma's beatings, when Opa got angry and told him to get back to work. He never turned to Opa again.

"No good kids," Wilma was saying. "Gonna get in real trouble some day. You gotta do somethin'."

Michael asked, his voice louder with frustration more than he liked, "Well, what about you guys doing something? What about Mabel and Johnny, your sister and brother? Isn't there something your family can do?"

She laughed wryly and shook her head. "We try. We try everything. Up to you now." She added darkly, "Jus' bad, those kid."

"What about making them do some work - pay for the damage?"

"Yeah. Good idea. You find them jobs, they pay back. Good idea."

"Can't you and Mabel and Johnny figure something out for them to do? Pay them for work?" Michael wondered why he was pursuing the impossible.

She sighed helplessly, "Nah. No money. Told you that. No money for nothin'. 'Sides, them kids your job now. Up to you."

They reached Wilma's house in the North End in silence. She struggled with opening the door and rolled out, diminished even more as she stood beside the station wagon. "Thanks, Blondie, you're all right," she giggled through the open door. "You can give me ride anytime." Michael sighed. She slammed the door and wandered in a crooked line homeward, her original request for money forgotten.

Three youthful Indian men sauntered over to the Pontiac as Michael watched Wilma go into her house. Billy Anderson opened the passenger door, and, sliding into the seat, said, "Michael, my man! How's she going?" The other two men leaned against the hood, hands dug into jacket pockets at their waists, looking away, cigarettes in their mouths. Billy turned his slim, handsome face toward Michael and asked, "Still want some grayling?" Spring grayling were beginning to run under the ice. Billy had promised to show him an open spot at Flat Creek about 30 miles away on the highway south where he said you could "throw a line in the water, no bait, one throw, and just hook 'em in the back."

The thought was pleasant. "Sure, Billy. Saturday tomorrow. OK?"

"Yep."

"We can use Johnny's pick-up?"

"Needs gas."

"Oh, sure. Should've thought of that. Here's my contribution." Michael gave Billy a ten dollar bill. He took it silently, closely watched by the other two as he folded it neatly and put it in his pants pocket. For a moment, Michael wondered if the money would be spent on gas or beer. He had paid for things before that hadn't materialized, and a few times he had loaned money he'd never seen again. His judgement was getting keener on who to trust. Everyone said that Billy was reliable, drunk or sober. The others might talk him into spending the money on beer, but Michael knew that Billy would supply the gas anyway, borrowed from some other source that would eventually have to be repaid in some way, maybe with the fish they would catch, through the intertwining economics of village life.

"Don't bring your twin brother, though," Billy smiled. "One of you cheechakos is enough to handle." They laughed. The day before, Billy had been sitting on the stairs at the front of the Northern Commercial store when Michael went in. They nodded at each other. Michael came out, and a minute later, had to go back for something he forgot. As he came out again, Billy jerked his thumb at Michael and remarked to his friends: "Hmmm. Must be twins, eh?"

Billy continued smiling at his joke, looking out the front window, and stroked his chin covered with a thin black Van Dyke beard that dramatically accented his good looks. Michael waited. Billy wanted to say something important.

"Them kids, Joe and George Jimmy?" Billy said. "My cousins."

"Oh?" Everyone was cousins to everyone else it seemed. If Michael drew family trees some day to get them straight in his mind, it would be a complicated diagram.

"Yeah. Feel bad about them, breakin' in like that."

"Yeah, I guess a lot of people do."

"White man's club, that curling. Makes it hard for all of us, they do that. Not proper."

"No Indians in curling?" Michael had never seen any Indians in the curling club.

"Not our game, I guess. Pretty dumb game when you think about it, eh? Sweeping ice with a broom? Only a Whiteman could think that one up." They laughed and lit cigarettes. Billy said, "Hey, I got some money. Sold firewood the other day. How much you think to fix up that wall? Fifty bucks?"

"Well, now, you shouldn't do that, I don't think, Billy. You could pay the curling club, but then the boys will just get away with it."

"Me pay Whiteman's club? No way Jose! I figure maybe make them kids work. They work for me, cutting wood. I make 'em sweat, pay 'em--maybe two bucks an hour, good money. The kids pay you, you pay Bob Kerr at the curling club." He paused. "OK by you?"

Michael smiled. Billy's eyes shone; it was an emotional speech for him. "OK. It's a deal," Michael said.

They sat silently for a few minutes considering the possibilities of Billy's scheme and watched the two men on the hood of the car shift their bodies to find a more comfortable lean. When the length of the contemplative silence of all of them reached a certain point, Michael looked into the afternoon shadows on the spring snow and I said, "Well, I'd better go and do some work or they'll fire me. See ya."

"Yup. See ya in the morning." Billy slammed the passenger door, leaned down, and saluted through the window with two fingers to his forehead. He walked away and the other two paced silently behind him, hands in their jacket pockets.

There was no reason to set a time for starting the next day or to know who else might go fishing. Michael knew that he would be given the opportunity to enjoy sleeping in, and to get ready. If he wasn't ready, it would be of no concern to anyone if they waited while he made breakfast and packed a lunch. If the weather was poor, Billy might not even show up, assuming that Michael would know why. Michael's social life in Vancouver was in direct contrast, regimented by telephones and bus schedules and time commitments that were always confirmed and then met, no matter how inconvenient or unnecessary. Which way was more considerate, he wondered.

Michael looked forward to tomorrow's drive along the Klondike valley. Spruce-covered hills on both sides of the river would be perceptively greener, a sure sign of spring. The cliff along the road would be covered with sparkling snow melting in the new sun and the cool wind through the open windows would be refreshing on their faces. They would cast their fishing lines into the creek standing on the road beside the pick-up. Later there would be a campfire off the road, hidden in the trees. They would have a grayling supper, a few beers. In Billy's silent competent company Michael would listen to the breeze and the occasional car driving by. It was a proper place to be.

UNHEEDED RULES

John stood in front of me by the kitchen table, bouncing on one foot and then the other. Jake joined him, and their voices rang in chorus as they tugged at my arms: "Please, Selena, please, please...can we go sliding, huh? It's boring here...Sunday, no school...it's only 20 below."

Our grandfather wouldn't allow my ten-year-old twin brothers to go alone. I couldn't resist the excitement of their cheerful faces, with their dark eyes shining under scruffy black bangs. I laughed, "Sure! Why not?" and rubbed Jake's cowlick to try to keep it down. I was as happy as they were to escape the confines of the cabin after days of being indoors because of extreme cold. Amid warnings of caution from Pop and frantic searches for lost mitts, we dressed and left, pulling the wooden toboggan.

We had a quiet life in our log cabin in the South End of Dawson. My twin brothers had been with my grandfather and me for nearly two years since they had been brought home to us from foster care in Whitehorse. We were crowded in the little cabin, and not rich in things, but we were comfortable with each other. Pop was a loving grandfather to all of us. The boys brought Pop and me gifts of energy and laughter that had rarely been a part of our lives before they came.

It was February, and the cold winter sun cut through pastel clouds to the south in a golden burst that was both sunrise and sunset. Twilight would lighten the Klondike valley for only a few afternoon hours. It was as if the sun reminded us she was there, only to leave, hiding behind a screen of mountains, painting a tranquil landscape of pink, blue, grey, and white.

We chattered and teased each other walking across town to the steep hill below the Dome Road everyone used for tobogganing. The sliding trail had three treacherous twists where the trees loomed wonderfully close. At the bottom was Eighth Avenue and if you were going fast enough, you could cross the street and continue on down another short hill. Anyone driving a car in the area learned to stay on Sixth Avenue, out of the way of the children as they burst out of the bush onto the street, screaming in joy and terror. The Dawson tradition of sliding on that hill was so strong that the driver would be blamed for any accident.

Our noses and cheeks were already bitten red by cold by the time we arrived at the top of the hill. The sun peeked through sparkling snow clustered on the trees, giving us a sense of warmth on a windless day. A faint wet smell of tree sap filled our lungs, a sure sign of spring to come. We had been pulling up the hill and sliding down for over an hour when I yelled gratefully, "Last run!" The tops of the white and black hills were a deep pinkish gold. It would be dark soon and then suddenly much colder. John, Jake, and I flung ourselves down the hill, clutching each other, careening and screaming wildly, snow and scarves scattering in the wind.

We hit Seventh Avenue and over Jake's shoulder I glimpsed a streak of red to the left. Jake pulled the toboggan sharply to the right. We tumbled onto the road in a blind jumble of snow, bodies spilling across the road directly in front of a large red car that slid in jerks toward us, desperately trying to stop. It came to a halt just inches from John's leg. I lay against the snow bank.

A man jumped out of the driver's door. "Good God, is anyone hurt?" he shouted over the roof of the car. It was Michael Scott, the social worker. Afraid and agitated, I yelled back at him from the ground: "No thanks to you! What are you doing driving on Seventh? You could've killed us!"

Michael swept across the road in two or three strides, leaned over me and said, "Oh, man, I'm so sorry. Are you hurt anywhere, Selena?" He helped me to stand with his arm around my waist.

"Where are the boys?" I asked him frantically.

"Over there." He pointed to the front of the car where John and Jake were hysterically describing the spill to each other in explosions of laughter, swinging their arms and pointing. When I saw that they were fine, I gave way to their hilarity, laughing with them, tears of relief running down my face.

Michael's blue eyes peered at me and he asked me again, "Can you stand up OK? Are you sure?" I caught my breath and nodded. He still held me up by one of my arms. "Man, I feel awful about this, Selena. I am so sorry. I should have gone along Sixth."

"It's OK. I'm fine," I said and moved away, brushing the snow off my parka with my mitts. He looked so worried that I did a little dance to show him I could move everything, and he laughed in relief, brushing back his light hair with one hand.

"Let me drive you guys home at least," he said. "It's getting dark."

I pointed. "We've got the toboggan..."

John called from in front of the car, "Can we go over to Ted's till supper? Huh, Selena?"

"Take the toboggan home first. And be home by five!" They never seemed to run out of energy. I waved them off. Four hours of week-old CBC television programs called the Northern Package were broadcast through a local transmitter in the post office building three times a week and Ted Barlow had a TV. He was very popular amongst the boys his age because of it.

"I'll take the ride," I said. "I'm cold." I got into the passenger seat.

Michael started the car and pointed to my left cheek. "Let's do something for that scratch. I've got some salve at home." I began to say no, but spurred on by the drama of the last few minutes, I agreed. I had never been inside a government employee's house in all of my eighteen years. Except for the old business families of Dawson, civil servants were the most important people in town. The rest of us were just poor Indians.

When we got to Michael's house, I was disappointed to see the ordinary furniture and worn carpet. Books and records were strewn around the living room. Michael showed me the bathroom and made me wash the scratch while he found some salve to put on it. We were soon comfortably sipping hot chocolate in his kitchen, gossiping and laughing about local characters. He had just received one of the new Beatles records, and played *Hey, Jude* for me, the first time I had heard it. "...Take a sad song and make it better..." That song still tugs at me. I relate it only to that day.

Michael said, "You know, I talk to your grandfather a lot, but I'm interested in how things are for you with the boys. I was worried they might be a drag for you when we put them there."

"We're getting along great! Sometimes they're a headache. They tell me I'm not their mother when things get tough, but Pop puts them back in line," I laughed.

"Did you quit school for them? You were going into grade twelve, too."

"No. I just like working. The money helps a lot." It made me feel grown up and important to be working full time in the winter at the Westminster Hotel. Not many of the other native girls had responsible jobs like that, year-round. "Besides, what difference does graduating mean to me?" I said.

"I'll probably just stay here, marry some local native guy and have a dozen kids like everybody else. I like kids."

"You're sure it's not hard on you, working and the kids?"

"No, not one bit. They're good kids, and it hasn't been hard, except for money. Like everybody, eh? Anyways, I'm a short-order cook now instead of waitressing. Not as hard on my feet, and it's more money, even without tips. Besides, I don't have to deal with customers I don't like. Some of them are pretty awful." I had never said so much about myself in a long time.

"What local native guy?" he asked.

"What?"

"What local native guy are you going to marry? Steve?" I expected teasing in his voice, but he was serious.

"Far out!" I giggled. "Steve and I, we've gone out a bit. He takes me to the dances, but I don't dance much. My feet always hurt."

"But you don't have to get married yet."

The excitement of the afternoon made me feel brave and witty with him, which was unusual for me. "Lots of us Dawson girls are married by eighteen," I said, "But I don't have to get married. I can always shack up with somebody, eh? It's the Sixties thing to do, man."

He frowned. "You shouldn't take it so lightly, wasting your life on dead ends like that, living with someone or getting married too young, having a bunch of kids. Your life's worth more than that. I think you have a lot to offer. You should maybe think about going back to school, like your friend Julie Fuller did." Julie went to Whitehorse where she trained as a hairdresser, and was working in a shop there.

That really annoyed me. Julie and I had planned to go to Whitehorse together. But I'd never be able to learn to type or to do anything with my hands like she could. I had deformed fingers on my right hand from frostbite.

I heard myself saying sharply, "Man, do you ever stop being a social worker?" and got up to leave. He came over to the door with me, and held my parka silently while I struggled with putting on my boots. I looked up at him and said coldly, "Don't worry about driving me home."

"Selena, I'm sorry. Believe me, I'm not saying these things because of my job. I...I'm interested in *you.*" He held out my parka for me to put on, then gently turned me around to face him and awkwardly took me in his arms in a hug. His slim body was surprisingly strong. My annoyance turned to shock. Then I was puzzled and delighted at the same time, as we slowly separated. I smiled my surprise self-consciously, not knowing what to do next.

Michael stepped away, embarrassed. He looked up to the ceiling and ran his hand through his blonde hair in a habit that I would learn to love, and said, "Wow!" He nervously plunged his hands into his pants pockets as if to keep them out of the way and looked at me. "I'm sorry, Selena. I shouldn't have done that. Man, this is so hard!" He blurted out, "Would you...ah...would you go out with me?" Then with a sigh, he said, "I'm sorry, I didn't mean to say that." He changed his mind: "No, I did mean to say that. Would you...I don't know, what do people do in Dawson who go out besides drink in the bars?"

"You could come to supper at our place." It seemed to come from someone else.

"Really? Right on. That'd be great!"

But everyone said he was supposed to be engaged to some girl in Vancouver. "And what about your girlfriend Outside?" I asked bluntly.

"Oh, yeah. Right. Thought you heard. Sandra and I split before Christmas. She didn't want to come up north. Found herself another guy." He laughed nervously, "Man, can you believe it? Leaving this fine specimen to freeze all alone up here?"

"Oh. Right on. I mean...sorry." We both laughed awkwardly, relieved.

He took control of the situation and looked serious. "OK, so when can I come? Tomorrow?"

"OK. Six o'clock."

I opened the door and flew home feeling as if I were still sliding down the hill, my breath taken away, my heart pounding.

****

The way I measured the coming of spring was by how low the sun shone each day on the Dome behind Dawson. The light slowly progressed from snow-covered tree to tree and finally hit the line across the middle, the Dome Road. Sunshine crept farther into the cabin each day, until one late morning it startled me by shining into my eyes while I was in my ordinary spot washing dishes or putting on my boots or reading at the table, not paying attention. Early spring penetrated our calm winter darkness with light and life, just as I was confronted that incidental February day with Michael coming into my life.

It was the beginning of a wonderful time of shared warmth and new love as the snow disappeared. We revelled in simply being together, sorting out each other's likes and dislikes, doing many ordinary things. The next weeks became precious mementos of our love: gathering wood for Grandma Thomas, walking on the frozen Klondike River, painting his kitchen, going with my brothers and Pop fishing for grayling through the ice on the river.

Soon I was staying overnight at Michael's, leaving in the morning dark. Pop never said anything about what time I came home. After years of his strict rules, he had become more relaxed with me as I took more responsibility for the boys and the household. I think he was secretly happy for me, although he never directly commented about us being together. I think he looked at it as a natural thing to have happen. Pop liked Michael and they had a good friendship from Michael's visits as a social worker when they talked politics, gardening, fishing.

Michael sincerely loved me. After the first time we slept together, he walked me home and deliberately took my crooked right hand in both of his. I pulled it away, but he insisted, and kissing each distorted finger in turn, he said, "I love your wonderful eyes; I love your pretty hair; I love your whole body."

Lying beside him in bed, I listened to Michael tell me about when he was a little boy in Holland, brought up by his grandparents because his mom and dad were killed during the War. He had such a sad life. They lived on a farm, and his grandparents made him work in the fields all the time, even when he was very young. His grandmother beat him a lot. He told me, "I used to daydream that I was Jewish, that my real parents were in a concentration camp and I had somehow escaped and the De Bruins had taken me in so I could work for them."

"A Jew? You mean, like the ones the Germans killed? Why would you want to do that?" I had never met a Jew.

"It was the only way I could survive living with them I guess."

They came to Canada when Michael was twelve, and then he had to work even harder to help them pay to buy a farm in B.C.

I said, "Is Scott a Dutch name? Sounds like English."

He surprised me even more then, when he laughed and said, "I've had a few different names in my life. I started out with my Dutch family name, De Bruin, but changed it to the English translation, Brown, when I got away from them. Then I changed it legally to Scott, my foster parents' name. I wanted to get as far away as I could from the De Bruins." When he said he ran away from them and was in a foster home until he finished high school, I was really shocked. I never thought a social worker would start life that way. He was so brave!

"Say something in Dutch. I've never heard it," I said, putting my arms around him. He sang me a song that he said he used to sing to his pet rabbit in Holland when he was a boy. It was like a lullaby. He caressed my cheek and hair.

"I feel so lucky to be with my Pop, even more so now, hearing about your grandparents," I said. I told Michael about when I was eight years old. I had run home crying from school one day. Some boys were chasing me and calling me a smelly Indian. "Pop told me over and over that the kind of person I was depended on how I lived, that it didn't matter what anybody called me or what colour my skin is. So I guess it doesn't matter what you call yourself either, my sweet Michael De Bruin, Brown, Scott. Take my name if you want it. Michael Maclean. Sounds good."

"Right. 'What's in a name? A rose by any other name...'" he smiled.

"I heard that in school."

"Shakespeare. Romeo and Juliet. Star-crossed lovers, like you and me, eh?" We laughed at the comparison.

Julie Fuller wrote to me from Whitehorse and said, "So you're finally a rebel, eh? Mom told me you nabbed that cute social worker. I can just hear the gossip! Crazy, man!"

Michael and I preferred to be by ourselves, or with my family, so we hadn't seen much of anyone else outside of work. While we were making plans for Easter, Michael said that Kay, his secretary, had invited him for Easter Sunday dinner. Did I want to come with him? I hesitated, knowing that I'd never be invited by myself to the mining recorder's home. "Dinner at Kay's place? You're joking, man! I can't go."

"Why not?"

"Come on. Natives and White civil servants don't have dinner together in Dawson. You know that."

"Come on, yourself! It'll be fun. Don't be shy," he teased me.

"Anyways, she didn't ask me to come too. You go ahead by yourself."

"I've gone there before with a friend who wasn't officially invited. They have always welcomed the extra company. They don't stand on ceremony. C'mon Lena..."

He talked me into it. I wanted to believe in myself and be strong. It would be a test of my new-found confidence. That night I dressed very carefully, putting my hair up in a mature style, with a special beaded hair clip that Michael had given me.

When she opened the door, it was obvious to me that Kay was surprised and not happy that I was with Michael. She hesitated in the doorway. "Oh," she said, "Selena. Hi." She recovered and, pointing to her husband, said "Selena, you know my husband, Fred. Shirley's here too, Michael. You know her, don't you Selena?" It felt weird to have to be introduced. Everybody knew everybody else in my part of town.

Shirley was the new Public Health Nurse who had moved to Dawson the month before, from Old Crow. She and Michael were already on easy terms, working together. I knew instantly that Kay was match-making, and I was sure that Shirley knew it too. Michael didn't seem to notice any strangeness. Shirley turned out to be friendly and fun, and Kay's good nature bubbled through the awkward silences that were part of most of the evening. I thought I noticed a gleam of humour in Shirley's eyes a couple of times when she looked at me. I didn't know if she was laughing at the situation, or at me.

Sensing that there was something in the air that needed fixing, Fred took charge of entertaining us with Dawson stories. "Kay, remember that party we were at, Christmas before last, at the teacherage?" Fred called into the kitchen where Kay was making the salad.

"You mean the Ann and her Mukluks story?" she called back.

"Kay's got all my stories titled," he laughed. "She even has numbers to different versions!" His stories were the best part of a terrible evening for me. I felt exposed, awkward, and very young. This wasn't my world, and never could be. All of them knew I shouldn't be there. My crooked fingers were obvious to everyone when I spilled peanuts on the carpet, trying to crack the shells. By the end of the evening, I was blaming Michael for bringing me and making me embarrassed. Why had he insisted I come? I tried to put the thought out of my mind that maybe he was using me to prove to the world that he wasn't prejudiced against Indians, that he was just showing me off.

Walking to his place, Michael told me that the next week he would be going to Old Crow for five days. He was excited about seeing the isolated Indian village north of the Arctic Circle for the first time.

"And Shirley's going with you?" I asked. Shirley had mentioned something about going back to Old Crow at dinner.

"Well, there's only the one plane to Old Crow next week," he laughed.

"I thought she worked here now."

"You heard her. She said they asked her to go up and help them with giving some measles shots to all the kids or something. It'll be good to have someone there with me who knows everyone."

"Where're you staying when you're there?"

"Shirley says we can both stay in the nursing station. They have extra rooms for visitors."

Jealousy and the embarrassment of the evening shot through my chest with a sharp pain. Before I could stop myself, I stopped walking and shouted, "Go to Hell with your Public Health Nurse for all I care!"

He put his arm around me and tried to tease me out of it, but when I pulled away, he let me go. "Why don't you trust me, Selena? What do you want me to do to prove that I'm not interested in Shirley?"

"Trust you? Why should I?" I asked. "You must have known that Kay wanted you and Shirley to get together. It was obvious the minute we came to the door she didn't want any dirty Indian kid in her house. Especially coming there with you. And then you and Shirley talked all night about things I don't know nothing about."

"We work together, for God's sake. Do you want me not to talk to anyone else but you?" He stopped walking and took a deep breath. "Damn it all, Selena, now you've got me feeding into this silliness. I should know better."

"You should know better, eh? Who are you? You my father or something? I guess I'm just not good enough or old enough for you and your bloody sophisticated friends. High society people."

"Lena, Lena..."

Driven by anger at all the Whites I had ever known, I yelled, "Maybe we should just forget the whole damn thing!" I turned away and ran back towards home in tears. But he didn't come after me like I so much wanted him to, to comfort me and tell me they didn't matter, none of them.

While I lay in bed, I told myself that I was a joke of a native girl, completely out of place. Me with my crippled hand, sitting in the living room of a Federal civil servant, the girl friend of a Territorial Government employee who was too old and too educated for me. My cheeks burned and I quietly cried most of the night, not letting Pop hear me, burying my head in my pillow. I was afraid Michael would be so mad at me that he'd remember that I said we should forget it and take it seriously. Before I fell asleep, I planned how to say to him how sorry I was.

Michael knocked on our door early the next morning. His reddened eyes looked as bad as I felt. We both said we were sorry at the same time, and I laughed in relief. He asked, "Can we go for a walk?"

We went along our favourite route, across the frozen Klondike and up Bonanza Creek, silently. Finally he said, "I've decided to change my trip to Old Crow. I won't go when Shirley's there. I can tell the Whitehorse office I'm too busy here and go up later in the month."

"You'd do that for me?"

"Of course." He took off my right-hand mitten and held my twisted hand tightly in his pocket as we walked. We stopped to sit on a favourite log looking over the river. The spring sunshine sprinkled diamonds on the snow.

"Lena, I've been awake most of the night", he said, "sitting up in bed, listening to music. I tried to figure out my real reasons for wanting to be with you. I asked myself: am I just on the rebound from Sandra? Am I being a starry-eyed romantic about native people? Am I going too far, in love with the idea of an exotic Northern girl? And the worst one: am I taking advantage of you? You're so young."

"You're too hard on yourself, Michael. Sweetheart, it was just a silly argument. My fault. I'm so jealous! It's all over now."

"Well, I can tell you that by this morning I was just as stumped as when I started. I have no answers. This morning all I can say is that I don't care about the reasons. I just love you. I want to be with you. That's all I know. I love you, Lena." He had never said that before. He put his arm around me and kissed me. His breath warmed my face and neck.

I was silent. No one except Pop had ever said they loved me. When Pop said it, it made me feel warm and protected. But with Michael, it made me feel strange, as if I were being asked to go some place that was new and frightening. I felt alone, and anxious.

After awhile, Michael asked, "And how do you feel?"

It came out all at once: "Michael, I do love you too. I want to be with you all the time. But I'm scared. Last night at Kay's, it was just awful for me." He didn't say anything, and I asked, "How can we be together if people don't want us to be? I just hate it. I feel like...like we're breaking some rule. Some law or something that everybody else knows about but us."

He shouted, "Oh, who gives a shit about them?!" He jumped up, facing me directly. "For Christ's sake, man, it's not like either one of us is married or something. Think of the people we know who are doing that, eh?" he laughed and reached to touch my cheek.

I moved my head away. I could think more clearly without his touching me. "Don't you see? This is worse than that somehow, worse even than sleeping around with somebody's wife or husband. Adultery's OK in Dawson, as long as no one does it openly. It's like what we are doing is something more, for God's sake, something even worse than a love affair." I stood up.

He smiled and shook his head, not looking at me, as if I were a child. It made me more frustrated and I became louder: "You don't understand it, do you?! I'm eighteen, an illegitimate Indian kid, living in a puny old log cabin with my grandfather." I took a breath, seeing myself as I thought Kay did. "I'm looking after my brothers because our mother is drunk half the time, eh? And who are you? You're a Whiteman, you've been to university, you're a social worker, nearly ten years older than me...for God's sake." My voice wavered. For the first time, I saw how different we were.

"Don't let them make it so heavy for you, Selena honey," he laughed, putting his arm around my shoulders and gently shaking me. "They're just not worth it, man. Believe me they're not. You're worth a ton of them." He was too calm. There was something destructive out there, silently waiting to hurt us, and he refused to see it.

"You know what I felt last night?" I had to make him see it. "I felt like Kay and Fred were saying *Who does she think she is?* every time they looked at me. Shirley was laughing too."

"They're no better--I'm no better--than anyone else, and neither are you. You have to believe that or they'll destroy you. They'll kill your soul, honey. Remember what you told me Pop said. Who you are depends on how you live, no matter what anyone calls you or the colour of your skin. It's not up to them to run our lives, it's up to you and me."

That afternoon ended as many others did, with us in each others' arms in bed asleep without anything concluded except our love for each other. We tried to be honest about everything, but for long weeks Michael and I never talked about the problems people were having with our being together. He was never again invited to Kay's. He said that she had changed at work, that she didn't talk much any more. Making it a joke, he said he liked the quiet office.

A couple of weeks after Easter, Reverend Masters, the Anglican minister, called me into his church office when I passed by. I was surprised, because our family never went to church. I sat in a stiff wooden chair while

I listened to him. He was a single young man who liked to think he was popular. I guess he saw himself as worldly and practical. "Don't be foolish, Selena," he said. "You know how many Dawson girls have been left alone with kids to look after. The father decides to leave town and go back to where he came from Outside. The girls get no support and end up working at crappy jobs to feed the kids."

"Michael wouldn't do that."

"Don't you believe it. What happens when he gets tired of you, or goes to another job? You're only eighteen, with your whole life ahead of you. Don't ruin it."

I was so angry I began to cry. I jumped up and heard him calling after me, "You're too young to know what you want. Give yourself a chance." Maybe he was right, I thought as I ran home. Maybe I was being used. After all, Michael had said he thought about that too.

My brother Jake told me years later that Masters came to see Pop one day to ask him to get me to stop seeing Michael. He told Pop that I was hurting Michael's career and that I could stop it if I wanted to. He made out that I was the one who was controlling the relationship, seducing Michael, and jeopardizing his job. Jake told me that Pop listened politely, stood up, opened the door, and in a calm voice laced with all the cursing that he was famous for, told the minister to leave, and in no uncertain terms where to go and how to get there.

If I wasn't with Michael, and especially when he would travel around the area for a week or two each month working, I began to have trouble sleeping. It wasn't simply that I missed his body snuggled against mine. When I was beginning to fall asleep my ears rang as if a strong wind was passing. My head was squeezed tight, and I felt as if I was choking and falling downward into black nothingness. I struggled until finally I woke with a start, gasping for air. That would happen three or four times before I could get to sleep for a few hours. I was losing weight and exhausted at work. I was terrified that I was going crazy. I thought maybe I was having some kind of fit.

If I did sleep, I would have the same dream over and over: I was swimming across the Yukon River, which was full of huge chunks of ice floating downriver like at spring breakup. I had to get to Michael, who was across the river, calling me. I was swimming hard to get across the river as the force of it pulled me swiftly downstream. Each time, I woke up, breathing hard, before I reached him.

When I was younger my Indian grandmother was always my comfort. Grandma Thomas' soft arms would hold me securely to her breasts and she would tell me everything would pass some day, and it did. After work one day, I wandered along Front Street towards the cluster of red-brown Indian houses and walked past the first two. I opened the door to Number Three. I didn't have to knock on Grandma's door. She lived alone except for occasional visits of family from out of town.

"Grandma, you home?" I called as I entered.

"Always home to you, grandchild," came her voice from the kitchen.

Everyone called all the elder Indian women Grandma, but Annie Thomas really was *my* grandmother, my father's mother. As I grew up, I'd gotten the name of my father from hints and stories I'd listened in on. Pop confirmed it one day. He was Walter Thomas, the Dawson Band chief, married, with a family of five children. The fact that I was his daughter was never openly acknowledged, but I was secretly glad that my father was the chief, and that his children were my half-brothers and sisters. It made me someone special and I knew that Grandma Thomas loved me like her other grandchildren, sometimes even more, I liked to think.

Grandma's warm smile welcomed me from where she sat in her usual place at the kitchen table, her dark eyes looking up at me through her glasses. She was short and plump and dressed in a flowered cotton housedress and an apron. Her long grey braided hair was pinned in circles like a crown around her head. "You been a long time come visit," she said.

"It's the job at the Westminster. And Michael too. Keeps me busy I guess." I put my arm around her soft shoulders in a hug and sat down across the table from her where she was beading onto a piece of moosehide. The table, pushed against the wall, was covered with an oil cloth of her favourite pattern, bright red roses. It was worn pale at the end where she sat most of the day. The small boxes, paper bags, and tins full of her sewing needs were close by, sitting between two vases full of plastic flowers kept from a relative's wedding or funeral. On all the walls were framed pictures of Jesus and bright plaques with prayers for special days and special people. Notices from the Indian Women's Auxiliary were pinned to the back of the door. Grandma was the President.

I didn't like Grandma's talking about the church, so I usually tried to get her to talk about the old days downriver at Moosehide instead. It was easy to draw her attention to details about the days when everybody made their living from the bush and the river, about who was related to whom, and stories about the dances they used to have at Moosehide. Everybody was happy there, she said. She told me once that being in Moosehide, together, away from the Whites, made the Indians strong. She said we lost a lot by moving into town.

The smell of sweet woodsmoke drifted from the coffee-brown, tanned moosehide as Grandma meticulously picked up tiny green beads along a needle with her index finger. The work would take her days. The beadwork would be the instep for some Whiteman's fancy mukluks, the warmest thing to wear in the winter, selling for $25.

"I was at Moosehide on the weekend," I said. She didn't respond, so I asked, "Want tea, Grandma?"

"Mmmm. Kettle's full." I added another stick to the wood stove and placed the heavy steel kettle where it would boil fastest.

I envied the way she sewed leaves around a dark pink five-petalled flower. I was reluctant to sew because of my twisted right hand, but her encouragement made me persevere at it and many long cold winter evenings were spent at Grandma's table silently sipping tea, the colourful work warmly enveloping the two of us. For a long time now I had sold my beaded necklaces in one of the gift shops for tourists. We were both proud of me for that.

After a long pause which indicated that Grandma was not interested in talking about Moosehide, she said, "You like job?" She meant: "better than school?"

"Sure. Sometimes it's a drag, but we need the money."

She was upset with my quitting school. "You make money. More school, more money. Too young for kids, working."

"Maybe. Tea's ready." We added teaspoons of sugar to the hot tea and sat drinking it from cups with a red rose pattern. I had given them to her for Christmas a few years before. Grandma saved the cups to use only for my visits or when Reverend Masters came to see her on church holidays.

We were quiet for a long time, each with our own thoughts, the old concerned with the young, and the young feeling the concern and the peace of it. This precious woman was always there whenever I and so many others needed her strength. Our problems didn't need to be spoken of directly in words, and that too was a comfort.

In the centre of the wall across from the table was a large browning photograph of Peter, her husband who had died before I was born, in the War in Italy. His unsmiling face looked stiff and uncomfortable above his dark uniform, but his lively eyes shone confidently through the years. I broke the lengthy silence. "Grandma, were you ever scared of men?" The question startled us both. Was I afraid of Michael?

"What men?" she asked. Grandma was giving herself time to think about her answer. She smiled to herself, searching for the right spool of thread in her sewing box, avoiding my eyes.

"You know what I mean," I giggled.

Finding the thread she wanted, she chuckled and threaded her needle, her eyes peering into the middle-distance through her glasses. She let her breath out slowly and said, "I guess girls all scared. I'm real scared when I marry. You save yourself. Need good man. For marry. That all." The ritual of the simple question and the simple answer somehow comforted me.

I told her about my dream with Michael on the other side of the river. "What does it mean?" I asked.

"God only want you to make decision," she said.

"About staying with Michael? You think I should leave him?"

"God say: you make up your mind."

"Well, I know I want to stay with him." But did Michael want the same thing?

"Michael a good man for you. But you sure you want him? Some people sure make hard time for you." She had heard things, then. I suspected that the minister and others had tried to pressure her to break us up. She always stood with me, quietly giving me strength and the rare freedom to decide things for myself. But she would not openly make her own opinion known to me. She had taught me that influencing others' decisions was not the Indian way. She must show respect for my intelligence and for my ability to determine my own future or I would never learn to be a full human being.

"Yes, they are making it hard. Very hard," I admitted. I saw fear in her eyes for me. I jumped up. "Don't worry, though. We are very happy. Gotta go now. Thanks for tea."

I kissed her on the cheek, a tradition in our visits, and I heard her say in my ear, "You make me think about hard things. That good. Come soon 'gain." I nodded and smiled as I closed the door.

****

Michael and I went as often as we could to Moosehide to be away from town, sometimes taking the twins or Pop with us, sometimes staying over in Grandma Thomas' cabin by ourselves. It was good to get away from all the prying eyes and the gossip in town. In mid-summer we tended Pop's fishwheel as I had done for many years since I was old enough to lift the enormous king salmon out of the water. We cleaned them and I sold the fish we didn't give away in town. Later in the summer, once the salmon had stopped running, we picked berries or simply enjoyed a meal over the campfire and soaked in the golden autumn light.

In late September, Michael and I sat huddled by our campfire on the stony beach at Moosehide. Our warm jackets and the bright fire kept us slowly sipping our last cups of tea. We were both reluctant to leave, knowing that the days left for travel on the river were few. I always felt a sense of renewal and comfort being on the river.

Michael broke into the silence, saying, "Selena, I've got to tell you something. I didn't want it to spoil our day, so I didn't tell you before this." I looked across the fire at him, trying to read how serious he was. "They've asked me to go to Whitehorse for supervision. I just found out yesterday."

No problem. Just another trip. I was relieved. "When do you go?"

"Monday."

"That's pretty soon. Don't they usually give you more warning?" Maybe it was more serious than I thought. He didn't answer. "You going for long? Does it sound like there's a problem?" I asked.

"Yeah. There's a big problem." My heart sank.

"John, my friend in the Whitehorse office, phoned me yesterday. He says that our new director, that guy from Edmonton, has boasted all over the place that he's going to replace all the social workers who don't have social work training. He wants us all to have Master's degrees in social work. Just like him."

"And you don't have social work training at all..."

"That's right. The bastard's already been phoning social work students at the universities to see if they're interested in coming to the Yukon. Can you imagine the gall? Man, I don't stand any chance at all with my shitty little BA in English and History. A couple of my friends in Whitehorse with BA's are really upset. I guess I'm not the only one he wants to get rid of."

"Oh, no!" I stared at him, watching his eyes narrow in frustration as he poked hard at the embers. I said quietly, "Man, that's heavy. What'll you do if you lose your job?" What if he leaves me?

"Well, first of all, they're not going to get rid of me without a fight." His voice got louder. "I've worked for them for nearly four years, and I think I've done a good job. At least they've never complained, so it's their fault if they don't like what I've done. They've never properly trained me. Or supervised me." Jeering, he said, "And they're so far behind the times here that the social workers don't even belong to a union. Threatening your job because someone more qualified happens to appear...they shouldn't be able to do that...it's just not fair. It has implications for everyone." He threw the stick he was holding into the fire and make sparks fly into the air.

"But what will you do if you lose your job?" I repeated. I wanted to ask: Will you leave Dawson? My insides were churning. I was worried for Michael but also sick with the thought of the possibility of his leaving.

"Let's not think about anything like that just yet," he said, frowning. "First I'll go to Whitehorse and listen to the bullshit. Then I'll know exactly what I'm up against." He reached for my twisted hand and put it to his lips in a familiar motion. He stood up and said, "If they don't want me to work for them, then I sure as hell don't want to work for them either. The bastards can't treat me like...like a sack of bad potatoes. They just can't do this to us."

He could always work at something else. It was no big deal. He looked up at the sky where the light was disappearing. "Right now, though, we got to clear out of here before it gets any darker. Have we got everything?" I kneeled at the wooden box we always used and added our cups to the other things.

I looked up at him and said, "You said they can't do this to us. What could they do to us? Do you think it's because we're together?"

"Honey, I meant that they can't do this to us social workers without Master's degrees." He looked closely at me. "I don't think it has anything to do with you, Selena, or us. They haven't mentioned it."

"Oh." I was relieved to think that what we were enduring in Dawson wasn't important to his bosses in Whitehorse. So we didn't matter after all, Michael and I.

Without thinking about it, I said: "I want to stay here tonight, Michael."

"Selena, damn it all, we can't do that tonight. You know I have to get to work tomorrow, early, to get ready for Whitehorse, eh?" He headed down the riverbank towards the boat, carrying the food box.

I followed him. "No, Michael, I mean I want to stay here. By myself. I have to. I just can't go back yet."

"For Christ's sake, Selena." He threw blankets on top of the box in the boat.

"I'll be fine in Grandma's cabin", I said. "I've stayed here alone before lots of times. You know that. I'll take those blankets and walk back over the slide tomorrow."

"OK, then. If you really have to," he said, his voice short. He looked closely at me, and said, "I really thought you might want to stay over with me, eh? With my leaving on Monday?"

Usually that would have changed my mind, but I had to be alone for awhile, to sort out what was happening to me and what I wanted to do. "Just tell Pop for me, OK?" I leaned over and gave him a quick kiss on the cheek.

Michael got into the boat and started the motor. He moved it into the deeper water in the middle of the river and turned upstream. I watched his silhouette against the shining water, a man waving absently without looking. I tried to call him back, but the boat motor was too loud for him to hear. I was terribly alone.

That night, I sat by the fire for hours, my back against the cold wind from the river, trying to sort out my feelings, thinking about Michael leaving Dawson. I wanted him to assure me that he wouldn't leave me. For a long time I had hoped that he might even ask me to marry him or even to go somewhere else with him, some place where no one knew us, to live together. Instead, he was thinking only about the fight he was going to have with the government, not about us. Was he taking advantage of me like Reverend Masters had said?

There was a big open hole in my stomach. I was exposed and helpless. He was in control. I was amazed to realize that he frightened me. I thought back to what Grandma Thomas had said: God only wanted me to decide, she said. Me. It was my decision, not his, whatever I did. I had to believe that.

After a long time, I lit the fire in the cabin's heater and crawled into bed with my clothes on. It was hard getting warm enough to sleep, but once I was warm, I fell asleep without dreaming, exhausted physically and mentally.

Three days later, Michael returned from his trip to Whitehorse. He came by my place to pick me up and I climbed into his camper van. I looked at him anxiously. "The bastards have told me to transfer to Whitehorse or be fired," he said, his lips pinched. He looked straight ahead, missing Billy Anderson who waved at him from the sidewalk as we drove along Fifth Avenue.

"Transfer? To Whitehorse!"

"Yeah. Whitehorse. They claim they want me to be with my colleagues. Molly says I need 'professional supervision and training that you can get only in Whitehorse,'" he said, exaggerating his supervisor's British accent and tone of voice. "They made it sound like they were doing me a favour. After four bloody years of working here. If I've been doing such a lousey job for four years, why not train me before this?"

"What did you tell them?"

He was suddenly calmer. "I told them I was staying in Dawson and that they could fire me before I would go."

So he was going to stay with me! "What about us? Did they say anything?"

He hesitated. "Yes, they did," he said, and looked at me.

"Well, what?"

"Well, for one thing, before the meeting with Molly, my good friend John said I should stop seeing you because you're too young. I'm robbing the cradle, he says." His laugh was cold.

"I thought he understood."

"Yeah, he understood all right," he said with a cruel chuckle. "John said to me, 'You have nothing in common except sex. You should end the whole thing, and the sooner the better for your reputation,'" Michael said calmly, factually.

It sounded to me as if he agreed with John. "Do you believe that?"

"Don't be ridiculous. Stop trying to read things into everything."

I had to hear the worst. "Did anyone else say something, more official?"

"Yeah." He hesitated, took a breath, and the words tumbled out: "Molly said the director wants me to stop seeing you. They both say I'm being a fool and that I'm taking advantage of your age. In their words, I'm being 'unethical and unprofessional'."

I sat stunned. He continued in a tired voice, "I asked them if I was doing anything criminal. No. You're old enough so I can't get charged for sleeping with you. But you're considered a client because the boys are children in our care and are living with you." He chuckled without humour, "I guess I'm not supposed to be sleeping with foster parents."

"Michael, Michael..." I reached over and put my hand on his shoulder. He felt distant, hard, even dangerous. "Please stop the van?" I asked him. He kept on driving.

"Shit!" he said, and jumped on the brakes, grinding the gears to slow down for a man walking across in front of us. The man turned and raised his fist at us. Michael did not react, and said, "I see it all more clearly now. Our being together is the real reason for this so-called transfer to Whitehorse. I guess I should consider myself lucky not to be fired on the spot. They've probably been plotting down there for a long time, since I started going with you. It'll just be easier to get rid of me if I'm in the Whitehorse office, under their noses."

A dog ran across Front Street. He barely missed hitting it. "Michael, stop the van. Now. Please!" I said. I could hear the fear in my voice. He stopped by the ferry landing. We sat in glum silence, looking at the Yukon River but not seeing it, trying to sort out all the bad news, to find something to say to comfort each other, but not finding it. He didn't reach for me. I said, "Let's get out of town. This place is a drag. I'm sick of it all. Let's take the ferry."

The Sixty Mile Highway is called the Top of the World Highway because you can see for hundreds of miles in all directions, west towards Alaska, north and east up the Dempster Highway, south along the Yukon River. We parked at the look-out. Moosehide was a little patch of bright green in a clearing downriver amongst the dark spruce with the huge rock slide separating it from Dawson's neatly squared streets. The poplar trees were tinged at the higher levels with yellow. Winter was coming early.

We ate a cold meal from the things he had in the camper and watched the dark blue clouds turn bright pink and gold with the setting sun. "Things always look a little more in perspective up here, somehow," Michael said. We drove farther along, then off the road. That night we made love longer and more fiercely than ever before.

On the way home after midnight, we were both silent, as if we were hypnotized, staring into the blackness of the autumn night. I kept hearing Grandma's voice saying I had to decide. I realized I wanted to stay with Michael, wherever it was. How good it would be to leave all these problems behind us and start again, maybe even in Whitehorse! We could get married some day too. Without looking at him, I said, as if I had memorized it, "Michael, I want to live with you. Dawson or Whitehorse, it doesn't matter. Why don't you take the job in Whitehorse? We could be together there, with strangers, nobody to bother us. If your job gets bad in the office, there's lots more work there. For both of us. I want to be with you every day. Wherever it is. I love you."

He didn't say anything. I plunged on, careless with exhaustion. "If you don't want to live with me, I've decided..." I took a deep breath, "I've decided then we'd better not see each other. It's too painful this way."

Stop saying this! What was I doing? I wanted him to get rid of my pain, to console me, not to listen to what I was saying.

I jumped as he slammed his fist on the steering wheel and burst out, "Fuck! Why bring that up right now? We're both wiped out. Man, I'm in problems up to my ears with this transfer bullshit, trying to decide what to do. I'm too confused to think about us or anything else right now. Jesus Christ!"

We stopped with a jerk at the ferry landing and he turned the lights of the van off and on again fiercely to signal the ferry. We waited in uncomfortable silence for it to come. His lips tight against his teeth, he said, "Let's talk about it some other time, OK?" when we got onto the ferry. We drove through town without speaking and he let me out of the van at my place with a curt, "Good night, Selena." No promise of when we would see each other again.

Through the next two days, I waited to hear from him. He didn't come into the cafe while I was working like he usually did. I was torn apart with the temptation of going to his place and with worry over what was happening to him. I told myself I was more determined than ever to face him with a decision: either we were to live together, married or not, or nothing. That might force him to do it. I waited, frightened to confront him and our future.

Pop handed me a note that was waiting for me when I came home from work on the second day:

My dear Lena,

I am so sorry that I haven't had the courage to come to see you before this. I've been thinking a lot about us, and trying to sort out what we should do. Can you meet me at my place? Please come.

Michael

I raced across town. When he opened the door, he pulled me towards him and against his chest. He said, "I wish...I wish I could give you the answer you want, Lena..." I looked up at him. He looked into my eyes, sadly. My stomach cringed. He let go of me and walked across the room. I didn't move from the doorway and watched while he reached for a cigarette burning in the ashtray and sat on the couch, his eyes on the cigarette. His voice changed, became impersonal, as if he was talking to one of his clients. "I really think we have to spend some time apart. It'll give us both a chance to find out what we want." It wasn't a question. There would be no discussion. He had made up his mind.

I walked into the room and sat beside him on the couch. "I do know what I want, Michael. I told you. Trust me. I love you." I knew the risk I was taking. I could lose him altogether by pushing too hard. Was I ready to lose him? But I had to have an answer from this man who was now somehow a stranger, so far from me.

"It's too terrible a time to know anything for sure, Lena. I think you were right last Easter when you said that there are rules that everyone else seems to know that we haven't paid any attention to. We can put up a fight, but what do we lose, even if we win? We'd end up hating each other." He ground his cigarette into the ashtray. "Right now my fight is with Whitehorse, not here, with this damned town."

"Let me fight along with you."

"Selena, you're so young. I really don't want to mess up your life. Let's just go our own ways for awhile." It was like something the minister or his social work friends had said.

I sat, vaguely hoping that if I was there long enough, the Michael I knew would come back. I wanted everything to stop and start over again. He finally stood up, took my hand and led me to the door. I knew then it was over. He offered to drive me home, and I shook my head, no. I walked, my legs wooden with the effort, seeing nothing. In my mind were the words of *Hey, Jude*: "take a sad song and make it better..." I guess we weren't meant to make it better. I would have gone anywhere with him, without question or condition. But he didn't ask me. They took him away from me, because we loved too well, too soon. Against the rules.

SONG OF THE WHITE CARIBOU

I was thirteen when Grandma Thomas first asked me to close up her cabin in Moosehide for the winter. How proud I was! She said, "Me, I'm too old to do that work no more. Time you do it. That cabin, Selena. She yours when I'm gone. Now's time you need find out how you look after it."

Over the next six years, it was my fall tradition to close up the cabin for her and to sleep overnight. It was my last goodbye to the summer. Secure in the dark one-room cabin with the windows boarded up, ancient musty smells brought back memories of being there as a little girl when I slept in the same bed, next to Grandma's soft warm body.

The last time I did that work for Grandma was just before my nineteenth birthday. A rare warm contentment stayed with me throughout the afternoon. I climbed the familiar hill behind the dozen empty log cabins, to the graveyard, pushing my way through tall dry September grass and dead fireweed. Fluffy white seeds floated through the air in my wake. I picked the last of the pungent highbush cranberries near the trail, my fingers turning blood-red with their wet pulp. Stories Grandma told me came back about the women of the village picking those cranberries in the days before they moved into Dawson. It was looked on as an excuse for women to get together, get away from the daily routine, talk about things. She told me about her auntie who was mauled by a bear because she didn't stay with the group, but went off on her own. "Good and safe with all together," she said, "No good by self. Got to talk, make noise." To warn any bears to stay away and because I felt so happy, I sang all the Elvis Presley songs I could think of and the old gold rush songs Julie Fuller and I used to sing, in my loudest voice. I ended with Christmas carols when I ran out of other songs.

In the late afternoon, I climbed farther up the hill and entered the broken white fence surrounding the graveyard. My other grandma, Maggie Taylor, was buried there amongst her family. My grandfather never failed to visit her grave every time we were in Moosehide, nor to place fresh wildflowers alongside the faded plastic roses he had left there years before at the base of the small white wooden cross. On my knees, I cleaned away the golden poplar leaves and straightened the painted white stones marking her ground. I scattered a few of the cranberries I had picked. I felt a little foolish saying aloud, "For winter, Maggie, from Pop." He told me to always leave something living on her grave, to keep her memory alive.

I came back to the cabin tired and hungry and put the plastic pail of berries safely inside. My favourite meal waited, cold salmon and potato salad. I ate it outdoors beside a campfire, the sweet smell of birch smoke warm and comforting. The mountainsides were splashes of brilliant gold across the black-green stands of spruce. The poplar, birch, and cottonwood had turned with the first frosts in mid-August. The days since then had been warm and sunny, but seemed warmer than they were with the sun reflected from the glowing trees. Our short Northern fall would soon be over. The mountains swallowing the sun made the temperature fall quickly in the late afternoon shade. The air became crisp, with a strong breeze, warning of many cold nights to come.

Some time in the night, I awoke to the wind howling around the corners of the cabin. I had already boarded up the windows but I knew every inch of the room and didn't need the oil lamp. I felt my way to the door, opened it, and peered out. I was surprised to see thick wet snowflakes flying past the doorway in the wind. The sky had been clear with a sliver of dying moon rising above the trees behind the village when I went to sleep. Now, dense clouds hung low everywhere.

In the snow accumulating on the ground, crossing close by the front of the cabin, were the fresh tracks of a large caribou.

Caribou! Grandma said there hadn't been caribou near Moosehide since most of the people left to live in Dawson soon after she was married, many years ago. Excited, I threw on my shoes and jacket. Maybe I could see it. Grandma would love to know about it. I closed the door behind me. I was amazed how easy it was to see the cloven hoof prints in the snow. The wind was blowing my hair over my face and into my eyes but I was able to follow the tracks leading away. They crossed in front of the church, curving around behind the boarded-up school. From the corner of the school building, I gazed into the spruce trees behind.

Standing majestically under the branches of the largest spruce was a bull caribou with a full spread of antlers. He was white! Light radiated from him, making the lower branches of the tree lit as from a campfire below. He stared straight at me and I knew he could see me, although I was in the shadows. Grandma told me caribou aren't skittish with people and are curious about anything around them when they feel safe. I sucked in my breath and tried not to move, hoping he wouldn't run away.

His eyes held me perfectly still. I could hear my heart drumming. A quiet humming sound began to keep rhythm with my beating heart. I couldn't tell if it came from him or from inside me. I felt like laughing aloud. Wanting to throw my arms around this wonderful creature, I took a step toward him. He scratched the ground with his hoof, lowering his head in warning. The humming stopped. He turned away from me, lifted his head and ran gracefully over the rough ground into the bush. His dignified back was perfectly level.

The light disappeared with him. I wanted to follow, to hear his song again, and quickly reached the large spruce tree. I stood under it in the gloom, with snow blowing around me. I knew the white caribou wouldn't come back. Looking down, I saw what looked like an "S" scratched in the snow by his hoof.

Exhilarated, I ran back to the cabin, laughing aloud. When I got there, I looked for the caribou tracks, but they were gone. I guessed they were covered by the snow which was now coming down in streaks. I had no sense of how long I had been gone, but there were inches of snow drifted against the cabin door. The fire in the heater was nearly out, so I stoked it with wood and went back to bed. Although I was stimulated and completely awake, within minutes I was in a deep dreamless sleep which lasted until morning.

When I woke, there was no sound of wind. I opened the door and was shocked. There was no snow on the ground. It was too cold for the heavy snowfall I had seen in the early morning to have melted. I raced back to the tree behind the school where I saw the caribou and looked for signs of him, wanting to see if there really was an "S" scratched on the ground. There was nothing.

I finished closing the cabin and, carrying the pail of cranberries, crossed Moosehide Creek and climbed the narrow trail leading to the slide. Part of the trail clung on top of a bluff called Lover's Leap. I rested there for a few minutes after the long steep climb, idly picking out the familiar little islands in the river far below, my mind on the night's strange events.

I could think of nothing else but the white caribou. I couldn't believe it was merely an animal. It was something more. Was it a dream? A vision? Was the "S" on the ground only an accident, or was it meant to be the first letter of my name? I vaguely remembered Grandma telling stories about animals and dreams, but I couldn't determine what my experience might mean. I was anxious to see her, to tell her what I had seen, and to get some answers.

Hearing a rustle over the breeze, I turned. Through the aspen trees I saw two slight figures, my brothers Jake and John, bobbing along the trail. "Hey, you guys!" I called and waved. "I'm over here!" They came up to me, and I said, "Was Pop worried?" I patted the ground. "Sit down and enjoy the view."

I looked up and saw Jake frowning. "Selena, something bad," he said. "We gotta tell you." He kept standing and coughed. He was just becoming aware of his voice changing.

"Oh God! What is it?" I was suddenly deflated and frightened. "Is it Pop?"

"No. Grandma Thomas," John said. "She's in the hospital. Pop says it's a heart attack."

I don't remember any part of the hike back over the slide from there. We ran straight through town to the hospital. My legs were like wood and my feet were pin-pricks of pain. A nurse met us at the door and said, "We've chartered a float plane to Whitehorse. Matron is with her. They should be taking off any minute. You might be able to catch them at the dock if you hurry."

John said, "Give the nurse the cranberries, Selena, it'll be easier." I shook my head. I had to keep anything connected to Moosehide close to me.

We ran along Front Street toward the float plane dock until we heard the scream of a single-engine plane taking off. "There she is!" I pointed to the bright yellow Beaver struggling upward against the valley wall. We stopped on the river bank and watched it circle and then head south. My throat tightened. Grandma Thomas had never been in the air before. I had teased her, said she was too stubborn because she never wanted to fly to Whitehorse, even when it would be easier for everyone than travelling in a car. We had laughed and she said, "Me, I'm not going up there in no tin coffin. No sir, when I die, God want me to go in wooden box, not tin."

Pop was waiting for us at home. I handed him the pail of cranberries, saying, "I looked after Grandma Maggie." He smiled and nodded, but said nothing as he put the pail on the table. He took me in his comforting arms and I leaned my head against his chest. For the first time that terrible day, the tears came.

Without thinking, I blurted out, "What if the plane crashes?" He drew me away from his chest to protest, concern for me sweeping over his face. I hung my head, "I know. That's stupid to say, isn't it? But she'll hate it. She'll be afraid she's in a tin coffin."

Pop said, "I think they'll give her something to make her sleepy, little one." It would take almost three hours for the Beaver to reach Whitehorse. Every minute seemed like an hour. When Pop finally went next door and phoned the Whitehorse hospital, there was no change. She was stable, and sleeping.

I couldn't sit any longer after he called the hospital. "I'm going to Walter's," I said, and stood up. The boys and Pop watched me closing the door. We all knew Grandma's son Walter was my real father, but we never visited each other. I had to know if they had any news. When I got to his place, there was a large padlock on the door. Their neighbour called over to me and said they had left for Whitehorse.

Within an hour, I was leaving too. Julie was going back to her job in Whitehorse after being home for a holiday. She had heard about Grandma and she came by our place to see if I wanted to get a ride with her cousin Wally who was taking her. Pop put together a large bag of sandwiches and apples for us. For once, he did not give us dire warnings about keeping safe.

We travelled through an endless late fall night, black with no moon and no snow to reflect light. It was raining heavily, and the dirt road was slick with mud. Wally drove slower in the old pickup than the few vehicles on the road. Every time someone passed or met us, liquid brown flew at us, covering the truck, making it impossible to see for a few seconds. Handfuls of gravel crashed against our side, a sneer from faster drivers. Every once in awhile, we were startled when a rock hit the windshield like a gunshot. Some left a quarter-inch star that would become a spidery crack creeping across the view in the days ahead. Between rain showers, Wally got out and threw cans of water from the ditch on the windshield to wash away the fine clay mud clinging stubbornly to the glass.

In the monotonous darkness I thought about the white caribou. I kept rehearsing how to tell Julie: "I've got something really fantastic to tell you..." Some of the joy from the night before came back, reliving those moments in my thoughts. I wanted to share it with her, but somehow we found it easier to talk about ordinary practical things, planning what we would do in Whitehorse. There would be time later.

We pulled into the campground at Fox Lake and tried to sleep, leaning against each other in the crowded cab. Later in the morning we went on into Whitehorse and they dropped me off at the hospital. They made me repeat the address of Julie's apartment and we made plans to meet there at noon.

I had never been inside the Whitehorse Hospital before and I was confused about where I should go. It was so huge. Everybody else seemed to be confidently marching somewhere without hesitation. I stopped a young White woman in a uniform and said, "Sorry to bother you. Where's the place they put people with heart attacks?"

She pointed down the hall to the stairway and said, "Medical ward. Upstairs of course, where it's always been," making me feel stupid. When I got there, I saw a nurse behind a counter and the Thomas family spilling into the hallway from one of the rooms. The nurse frowned, but with a tired sigh, she said she would ask them if I could see Grandma.

Walter immediately came out of the room toward me and put his arm around my shoulder. He smiled and said, "I'm so glad you're here. She's been asking for you." We had never spoken directly to each other before. I said nothing. He confused me, talking to me so easily, as if we were used to each other.

Walter's wife Rosie and the other people quietly melted away, and I found myself next to the bed, alone with Grandma and Walter. There was a heavy smell of some kind of medicine. Walter stood at the foot of the bed, watching us, and then moved to the chair on the other side of the bed. Grandma slowly opened her eyes and reached for my hand. "So good you come. All that way. I just happy." She smiled and closed her eyes. Her hand, cool and like silky paper, fell away from mine.

I didn't know if I should talk to Walter, or what to say. After long silent minutes, I made a motion to leave. He surprised me by lifting his hand and saying, "Wait. She'll wake up. She wants to say something to you. She said that before."

The nurse came into the room to write something in the chart at the foot of the bed, and it woke Grandma. She looked at me, taking my hand again. She asked, "You going tell me something?"

"I do want to tell you something, Grandma. Are you OK? You aren't too tired?"

"Tell me, grandchild. Not much time."

I glanced across at Walter. He smiled and nodded assurance.

"I saw a white caribou in Moosehide...he sang to me..." I began.

Grandma made small grunts of recognition in her throat through my story. When I finished, she said matter-of-factly, "He found you. Good. I send him."

Dizzines from lack of sleep and the strangeness of the place swept over me. I wasn't really there. I was watching from somewhere else, intensely aware only of everything between the two of us. I even forgot Walter was there. "You sent him?"

"'Member, Selena. Told you 'bout him long time ago. Long time ago, when you just small."

My throat was dry and I swallowed hard. "I think I do. What does it mean, him coming to me?" I asked in a voice that wasn't mine.

"No meaning, grandchild. He just yours now." Slowly shaking her head, she whispered, "Never forget who you are. You Indian." She closed her eyes and clearly said, "You Indian, Eliza, same like us." I shivered. She called me by my mother's name!

Grandma looked like she was asleep again. I sat by the bed, dazed, leaning my head on the mattress. After a few minutes, Walter's arms around my shoulders lifted me up. Rosie was standing at the doorway waiting to come in. Walter said kindly, "You should go now, get some rest." He gave me a piece of paper. "Phone this number and ask for the Medical Ward later this afternoon. Ask for me. I'll let you know how she is."

I mumbled thanks and stumbled out of the hospital. I knew it was the last time I would see Grandma Thomas alive. I was cold and numb with grief, searching for Julie's place. At last I found it and she answered the buzzer. "How is she?" she said, opening the door, her face pale with concern.

"She's dying, Julie. I won't see her again." I walked into the room.

"How do you know? Did the doctor say so?"

"No, Jules. She told me in her own way."

"Well, maybe she's wrong, Lena."

"No, she's not!" She didn't understand and it made me angry. "You know she's always right about things like that."

"OK, OK, Lena, whatever you say. Just don't give up hope, eh?" She said she would find me something to eat and threw on her jacket. "Gotta get something from downtown. Nothing here. Take it easy, eh? Just crawl into bed. That's what you need more than anything."

I drew the blind and curtains in Julie's bedroom. Huddling under the blankets in the darkened room, I closed my eyes, but couldn't sleep. The humming of the white caribou drifted through my mind. When he came to me, he was singing, making me happy. Grandma was close to dying, thinking of me, sending me the caribou. Along with her Moosehide cabin, he was her last gift to me. What was it she told me? *Never forget you are Indian.* Is that what the caribou meant? But she said there was no meaning. *He just yours now.*

Maybe I could choose to do whatever I wanted with the cabin and with the white caribou. The responsibility frightened me. I didn't want to be an adult. I wanted to be a child again, looked after and comforted. Grandma always said the river would take care of you like a mother if you treated it right. She said she was like a child of the river. I drifted off to sleep with visions of taking our boat downstream to Thirtymile with Grandma Thomas and Grandma Maggie on a bright sunny day. We laughed and told stories, we three women who had never been together at one time, but who were joined in spirit on the river.

Julie woke me, rushing through the bedroom door with hamburgers and chips in a bag. She pulled up the blind and I blinked with the light. "I got tea going in the kitchen," she said.

"Thanks, Jules. You really are good to me." I said quietly, "Julie, I want to be home. Can you get me a ride?"

"What about Grandma?"

"I've said good-bye to her. And the Thomas family are all there. I just want to get home."

Julie came over to the bed and gave me a hug and a hamburger. She said she would be back in a minute and I could hear her phoning people to see if any of her numerous cousins were going home to Dawson. She she came back with tea and the news that she had found me a ride.

I phoned the hospital and Walter told me Grandma had passed away a half hour before I called. With a start, I knew it happened when I was falling asleep, thinking of us going to Thirtymile on the river.

"We'll have the service at St. Paul's next weekend," he said, "then down to Moosehide. I'll see you then." He chuckled sadly when he said her last words were her last joke. She had complained about the thin porridge they had brought her that morning. She wouldn't eat it. He said she told the nurse: "Whiteman food no good. Tell them give me dry meat; then I be OK," she had said in mock anger, smiling.

After nearly nine gloomy hours on the road, we arived back in Dawson long after midnight. I gratefully crawled into bed and sleep overtook me immediately. Late the next morning Pop woke me, gently shaking my arm and saying, "There's someone here to see you." For a few moments I was bewildered with sleep. Then grief overwhelmed me remembering the day before. I shuffled to the kitchen, not knowing what to expect, and was puzzled to see the backs of two women sitting at the table. Pop had served them tea.

In my confusion, it wasn't until one of them turned around and spoke that I realized who they were. The bigger woman stood up, came over to me, and put her arm around my shoulder. It was Rosie. "Walter and I want you to come to Grandma's funeral as part of our family," she said. I looked at the other woman, her sister, who was sitting, smiling and nodding.

"Pop?" I turned to him.

Pop said, "We've talked about it, Selena. This is your family, too. Grandma Thomas wanted it this way for years. And so do I." I stood there, amazed and comforted. I had lost Grandma, but had found her family. Walter and Rosie included me with their own children in all the plans for the funeral at the Anglican church in Dawson and the burial in Moosehide.

Julie came from Whitehorse for the weekend of Grandma's funeral. She started right away to talk about my moving to Whitehorse, saying she wanted us to share her apartment. I told her there were too many things going on to think about anything just then.

At her funeral, I said good-bye to Grandma Thomas feeling terribly alone, although Walter's family was kind to me even in their own grief and Julie, Pop, and my brothers stayed close by me the whole time. They gave me my jacket against the cold, took my arm, led me in the right direction, said the right things.

The last of the people were leaving in boats late in the afternoon when Julie came up to me and said, "Lena, come with me. I've got something for you."

"Pop's waiting to take me back to town, Jules."

"Just come for a minute," she said. We walked behind the church where we had often sat on some old logs piled there. Julie said, "Come and stay with me in Whitehorse, Lena. You can get a better job and everything. Better than this old dump. It's a drag."

"No. I'm going to stay in Dawson. I want to be near my family."

"Well, no surprise I guess. The invite's always there. You know that, eh?"

I smiled and nodded, "Yeah, I know that. You're still my best friend, Jules, even so far away." I wanted to tell her then about the caribou, but I needed more time to do it.

Julie pulled a small liquor bottle out of her purse and I shook my head. She said, "Hey, just one sip, eh? It'll do you good and make this a whole lot easier. It's vodka. You can't even taste it." Without thinking, for the first time in my life, I reached over and took the bottle. It's harmless, everybody drinks, even Pop, I told myself. She had mixed it with orange juice and the first taste was surprisingly like breakfast. With the second sip, warmth spread from somewhere in the centre of my body. A pleasant faintness crept into me, selecting and comforting all my aches. I closed my eyes, swollen and hurting from too many tears, and my body drifted into the dusk.

"See you later at your place," Julie said quietly and gave me a hug. I sat for a few minutes, breathing the old wood and listening to the wind rustling through the grass. I wanted only to be alone with memories of Grandma and the caribou.

I found Pop waiting by our boat, looking anxious. "Sorry, Pop. Had to talk to somebody," I said. I climbed in, and desolation overwhelmed me. I was leaving Grandma there in Moosehide. Nothing would ever be the same again. I had to tell someone about the caribou, connect again with it. It was all I had of Grandma now. Pop untied the boat and stepped in. Before he could start the motor, I said, "Pop, I have to tell you about something fantastic!"

"What is it, child?"

"Something happened to me here last week when I stayed in the cabin," I said. "I saw a white caribou! Standing over there behind the school, in the middle of the night. He was singing to me. And there was snow, all over the ground. It was gone when I got up." My story sounded shallow, not enough to describe my feelings then and when I talked with Grandma.

Pop said, "Yeah? I've heard of albinos. But are you sure it was a caribou? Not many of them around here for years." He didn't sound interested.

"Maybe it was a dream," I said, deflated. I couldn't finish what I had to say, that Grandma said she had sent him to me. It was impossible to explain it, even to Pop. I didn't understand it myself, so how could he understand? I knew then I wanted to keep the caribou for myself. I shivered and zipped up my jacket. "We'd better go," I said, "Rosie's expecting us at the supper."

Pop started the motor. I sat facing him and gazed past him toward the shore. He steered the boat into the deeper water and we headed upstream. The log cabins grew smaller. I blinked and frowned. There was something large and white in the shadow of the trees behind Grandma's cabin. Then it was gone.

BIG BETTY'S REVENGE

Dawsonites were always eager to talk about their own history and to embellish everyone else's, whether it was good or bad, true or not true. Michael felt vulnerable when he was being talked about himself, but it held some fascination for him to listen to the intimate stories of the town's families. He longed for the support and comfort of a close family, but he saw himself as removed from deep emotional attachments. His own difficulties as an abused child made Michael's understanding of the workings of healthy family relationships mostly intellectual. Being too involved personally led to problems. They were distracting and often dangerous. He believed his attitude was an asset for social work and made him a better professional.

Mabel Miller was one of only a few people Michael Scott had heard about but had not yet met in person during his four years as the town's social worker. They said that Mabel stayed up all night and slept all day. No one seemed to know why. She seldom talked to anyone who encountered her walking alone at night through the dark streets of Dawson City.

When he returned to Dawson from a trip to Whitehorse early in August, Michael finally met the town's recluse. He was asked to bring a parcel to her from her daughter. Curious to learn more about the Millers, he took the opportunity. He waited until late in the afternoon to deliver the parcel, not wanting to catch Mabel asleep. He pushed open the gate in front of the little frame house and passed through a flowerless yard. After he knocked twice, he saw curtains stir in the window next to the door. The lock shuffled. The door slowly opened.

A tiny, rounded figure with clipped grey hair peered out from behind the door. Mabel wore a white sweater and grey slacks. In one hand she held horn-rimmed glasses attached to a chain around her neck. Michael smiled inwardly. She was far from the darkly mysterious woman whom he had anticipated would be wearing a red silk dressing gown, holding a cigarette in one hand and a martini in the other.

"Oh, the parcel from May," Mabel said with a cheerful smile before he could say anything. "I was expecting it." She took the box from his hands. "Thanks so much for taking the time to do this." Inside the room, the telephone rang. "Excuse me just a moment, OK?" She reached over to a phone on the wall, keeping the parcel under her other arm. "Hello? Oh, May! Isn't that funny that you called. The parcel just arrived. Yes, just now. Michael Scott brought it." She looked at him when she said his name, smiling. Michael was not surprised that she knew who he was.

Michael made a motion to leave, but Mabel waved her hand, shaking her head to stop him. "I'll call you a little later, May. Michael's still here. Yes, I'll tell Dad hello. Bye."

Hanging up the receiver, Mabel placed her glasses carefully on her face and asked, "Why don't you come in and have a cup of tea? I've just made a pot." She sounded as if she meant it, so he stepped into the narrow living room. Dark curtains were drawn against the oblique summer sun, making the room cool. Mabel disappeared into the kitchen at the back. He sat down on a couch scattered with dark blue embroidered cushions. There was a teapot covered by a hand-made tea cosy on the coffee table. A half-empty pale blue teacup and saucer sat beside it. "I have always wanted to talk to you, Michael," Mabel called from the kitchen. Michael's curiosity stirred. What would Mabel Miller have to talk to him about?

Mabel brought a cup and saucer, sat down in the chair across the table from Michael, and poured his tea. She said without any preliminary niceties, "What they are doing to you is atrocious! There are a lot of people in this town who think you shouldn't have to leave your job, Michael. You are by far the best social worker we've had." She sat back, frowning, and looked intensely at him through her glasses.

Michael's face warmed. He was relieved the room was dark enough to cover his discomfort. So even Mabel knew he was fighting the Department of Welfare over his position. They had given him one month to transfer to Whitehorse or leave, claiming he needed supervision and "the support of colleagues". Certain that he had done a good job, he was proud of the position of respect and power he had held. The thought of not doing the work any more was confusing, debilitating. The rare news of a government worker's job being threatened had spread quickly. Some of Michael's friends who belonged to unions had said they felt the government was being unfair, possibly even making an unlawful order by transferring him.

With friends urging him on, he had decided to fight the decision. But the talk in town made him feel exposed, even ashamed.

"I have told them that...ah...I would resign. For October first," he said. "I guess they are still thinking about what to do with that bit of news. Sounds like they'd like me long gone before that if they can get it."

"Really! They can't just wait it out? Doesn't sound the least bit fair."

"Well, someone from our office in Whitehorse said it's because they've already hired someone. She's waiting Outside to come to Dawson, I hear. Fresh new graduate. Master's of Social Work."

"Do you really believe it's because of your qualifications, after all your years working here? You've stayed the longest of any social workers we've had. I'd suspect it's more because of Selena, wouldn't you? Some damn so-called respectable individuals here--and you know who I'm talking about--they have no business whatsoever butting in on you two."

Michael said nothing. His chest tightened. His relationship with the Indian girl ten years younger than he had been the subject of the town's speculation for most of the time they had been together. He had thought a place like Dawson, with its lurid gold rush history, would have been more tolerant of unusual couples.

"Of course no one here ever has the nerve to stand up to anything Whitehorse does to us," Mabel continued with undisguised scorn. "They just take whatever is dished out to us. You can't expect any support from Dawsonites, dealing with Whitehorse." She paused. "You're still...um... with her now, I presume?"

Selena was a part of his life he was hoping to leave behind. She had asked him-- no, forced him--to decide about living together. The prospect of that commitment had made him take stock. They had had a wonderful time together, and he had been very comfortable with her and her family. But before long he began to see that she was too young, too emotionally dependent. He felt stifled sometimes. He didn't want to be his lover's mentor forever. In darker moments, he admitted to himself that the town's disapproval of their relationship had made him very uncomfortable. The exposure had pushed him to break up with her. They were ready to split and the town made sure they did.

"No, we aren't together now," Michael said. He took a sip of tea. It was difficult to swallow. He remembered seeing Selena with a group of youngsters, giggling on the riverbank a few weeks after they broke up. He presumed that they were sharing a bottle and that she would become a sordid carbon copy of nearly every other Indian kid in Dawson, a replica of her own mother. Over his years as a social worker he had seen enough of alcoholism and despair. It disgusted him. He was helpless to change it. He felt his own drinking was moderate, and the possibility of it invading his life the way he had seen it with others hit him as if he were being physically assaulted. He had turned from the scene on the river bank with deep sadness, but relieved that he was well out of an addictions trap.

"Oh, I'm so sorry!" Mabel chided herself. "This is none of my business whatsoever. I thought I was showing you some support, and here I am, only making you uncomfortable. What a silly old woman I am. I *am* sorry." She reached over. Touching his hand, she said, "Tell me, what are your plans now?"

"Well, I'm not sure." Her interest and support gave him confidence. "But I have to see this through. There are people in Whitehorse who are urging me to stay and fight, on principle, for them as well as myself. I'm not the only one they are after in the Department. I love the North and being outdoors. I'll stay this summer and look for work if I have to. I might even stay next winter if things turn out OK."

"You know, I was just talking to a friend about a job May mentioned. It's in Whitehorse..." For someone who wasn't supposed to be involved in the community, she surprised him with her knowledge of what was happening around her. Perhaps he and others had misjudged her isolation.

Once he relaxed, Michael found Mabel's frankness refreshing and sometimes quite humorous, but he soon recognized a bitterness similar to his own underlying her remarks about Dawson. Several times she made comments such as, "You don't know how bad this town can be to someone a little different" and "It's really not a friendly town underneath." Although he did have some support in Dawson with friends, he was inclined to agree with her. She intrigued him when she said with an ironic smile, "You know, a lot of our so-called respectable citizens have pretty dark histories themselves."

When Michael stood up to leave she startled him by saying abruptly, "Just one word of advice. You probably don't need it now, but it's this. Never fall in love in Dawson. It'll kill you like it has me. And you'll never be able to get away." Leaving the Miller's house, he was saddened. Why had such an open, friendly person isolated herself from everyone?

A few days later, he casually asked a friend who had lived in Dawson many years about Mabel. Michael was shocked when the friend said she had been "one of the girls" for a short time in a brothel in Whitehorse. It was during the Second World War while the American Army was building the Alaska Highway. Shortly after arriving from Outside, she had, fortunately for her, met and married Don Miller, one of Dawson's most eligible bachelors at the time. He had been the owner and only mechanic of one of the two garages in Dawson. He had a thriving business. But after a few years, he was in debt and was forced to sell out to his rival. Michael's friend said, "Don drank more and more after he married Mabel. Most people seemed to blame her for it. They say she blew all his money. She was never happy with anything he did. Don pretends to ignore the stories about her. Well, you've seen him, eh? He spends most of his time sitting in the Downtown bar talking about better days or fixing friends' cars in their back yard."

Michael said, "Well, there's more than a few families like that here. They don't all turn into recluses like Mabel."

The friend suggested, "You know, I think Mabel probably figured she could gain respect by being the good wife and mother. Then the town would forget her past. But she was never accepted into the social life of Dawson. Her history is still talked about. It doesn't help that she's hidden herself away. Makes for a kind of vicious circle for herself."

****

Months later, the insistent scream of a fire siren rising and falling felt like tangible waves against his skin, rousing Michael from a sound sleep. Groggily fumbling for the flashlight he kept by the bed he shone it at the clock: 2:30. Pulling his arm back under the sleeping bag, he curled into a fetal position for warmth. It was the darkest and coldest time of winter, two days before the new decade of the 1970s.

It had been 45 degrees below zero when Michael gratefully crawled into his goose down sleeping bag only two hours before. The room was already beginning to lose its heat. He had thrown a mixture of green and dry wood into the sheet metal air-tight heater that was the central feature of the room. Dismissed from his social work position, he had lost his comfortable government housing in September. He rented this old one-room log cabin on the Dome Road with an eager sense of the romance of roughing it in the bush with no plumbing or electricity. The cabin offered a full view of the town, but for days now the windows were patterned with thick ice making it impossible to see through them. If he was interested in whatever the fire siren was announcing, he would have to open the door, letting in more cold.

For a minute Michael stayed in bed with his eyes closed, debating whether he should get up and look out the door to see if he could locate the fire. Fires were a source of the town's entertainment. They were even more exciting and dangerous in the dead of winter. Three or four old buildings were destroyed every year and the supply seemed limitless in the old ghost town.

Spurred on now by curiosity and the increasingly cold room, he pulled himself up, wrapping his sleeping bag around the woolen underwear covering his thin body. *Need more fat to keep warm,* he thought for the hundredth time. The bare wooden floor of the cabin was always cold, so he slept with wool socks on. He kept his boots conveniently by the bed and slipped into them. Thumping across the uneven floor, he opened the stubborn door. White clouds immediately billowed over him as humidity in the cabin met the frigid outdoor air. A pulsing orange glow lit most of the centre of town below him. Ice fog clinging in the valley like a huge crystal dome exaggerated the size of the blaze. He hastily slammed the door. He couldn't determine which street it was on. Almost against his will, he was drawn to investigate further. For two years, he had been active in the volunteer fire department, a young men's exclusive social club. Now he didn't have a telephone, so he had been ignored on the fire call-out list and wasn't told about the social events they held.

Now fully awake, he dressed himself as quickly as he could: another pair of underwear, more socks, wool pants, light nylon wind pants, flannel shirt, two wool sweaters and a knitted cap. He chose his moosehide mukluks instead of his heavy boots; they would be warmer and easier to walk in. He threw some wood in the heater, zipped up his down-filled parka, flung the hood of the parka over his head, draped a scarf around the hood, and tied the scarf backwards to cover the lower part of his face. Outdoors, he pulled the fur trim on the hood of his parka closer around his face to keep out the windchill from a slight breeze and pulled on heavy mitts. His moustache began to turn white with frost from his breath before he was out of sight of his cabin.

As he had several times in the last month, Michael automatically calculated the amount of time he would have to stay in Dawson City. He was ready to go. One more month. Then he'd be long gone. Vancouver. Warmth. Sunshine. Rain. All the elements needed for life. This cold dark country wasn't meant for human habitation. He felt stuck. Even the mountains surrounding the Klondike valley hemmed him in. He was bored with the sedentary life he was leading without work in the weeks since breaking up with Selena and his fight with the government. He had promised someone a ride to Vancouver in his old camper van which was sitting frozen in a friend's yard. His passenger could leave only at the end of January, because of his job. Now Michael was beginning to regret the offer. If only he didn't need the extra help with gas money and the company driving the Alaska Highway alone in winter.

Without running, Michael moved at a quick pace. Running could mean frozen lungs if he gulped air. He went down King Street, crossing Seventh Avenue, Sixth, Fifth. There was a building burning near Fourth Avenue and York. A crowd was gathering. Bright flames were shooting straight up in the air and there was a constant roaring sound, as if the fire had burnt a tunnel through the intense cold and ice fog. When he stopped only a few yards away from the flames, he could still feel no heat.

A man came up behind him and muttered, "Damned if it ain't Big Betty's." An oldtimer, one of his clients when he first arrived in Dawson, had told him the history of Big Betty's. It had begun as a modest hotel called the Aurora. For awhile it was a boarding house for older single men, re-named the Lone Spruce Tree. Over the following two decades, the building housed various madames with their girls. During the Second World War, a large gregarious woman with black hair called Big Betty kept three girls to entertain her clientele in the rooms upstairs. She was found draped across a bed, blood flowing from her mouth and chest, her dark hair across her face. It was said she had been stabbed to death by one of her girls. Because of that notoriety, or because she was the most popular of the owners, Big Betty's name survived, and the house remained known as Big Betty's Place. The names of the other businesses that had been in the building were long forgotten. The front door of the two-storey building had been nailed shut, the lower row of windows boarded for a quarter of a century.

As he stood by one of the small groups of people, Michael heard them discussing the possibility of the fire consuming the old buildings on either side. Their breath made white clouds in front of their faces as they spoke. Most of the sightseers were shuffling their feet, plunging mittened hands into deep pockets to keep warm. All of them kept their parka hoods up. Some had also wrapped scarves around their heads, leaving only their eyes visible, like turtles with heads drawn into their shells. It was difficult to determine who the anonymous bodies milling around were, even whether they were men or women.

"That you, Michael?" someone called into the hood of his parka. It was a firefighter with a blackened face peering at him. The man was covered in a long black rubber coat over his parka. It had icicles hanging like glass knives from the bottom. He had crackled as he walked over to Michael.

"Yeah. Some fire, eh?" Michael yelled over the fire's constant roar.

"Grab this hose. Play it on the left there, eh? I gotta get warm in the truck." Michael joined two firemen who had turned to saving the adjacent buildings and aimed the hose at a slant to avoid the fine spray of water flying back. It could become ice on his face in seconds. The pressure in the hose was hard to control with his mitts on, but he briefly turned and pointed the hose upward on the fire. He was rewarded with steam gushing from open windows on the second floor. From the intense heat inside, the windows' glass had exploded with with loud crashes. One wall crumbled. It fell inward on the burning heap, amid the crack of breaking timbers and the muffled cries of dismay and excitement from the watching crowd. Like a volcano, above the building was a seething cauldron of steam mixed with heavy black-grey smoke. The thick boiling mixture made a stench that would stay in the clothes and minds of the watching crowd for days. Brilliant light from the fire was absorbed by the ice-fog. An eerie orange-yellow canopy glowed for a hundred feet above and around the collapsing building. Windows of the dark buildings surrounding the fire sparkled orange reflections and the two remaining walls of Big Betty's glittered as water nearly instantly froze on them.

Awkward with the pressure in the heavy hose, Michael stepped over a menacing stream of slush on the hard-packed snow. He moved closer to the building. He knew if he didn't avoid the threatening rivulets his mukluks would soak up water like blotting paper. Wet feet at that temperature would mean frostbite in a matter of minutes.

It was the usual crowd that came out to Dawson fires. Michael was able to attach names to some of the voices in the excited crowd by their tone. He recognized the Blamer: *Do you think it was that Fuller kid started it, the dense one?*...the Problem-Solver: *It couldn't be electrical, Betty's hasn't been connected for 25 years or more*...the Promoter: *Well, there goes another piece of our history; pretty soon there won't be anything left for the tourists*... the Cautious Optimist: *at least there is no wind*...and the inevitable Jokers, spurred on by the thrill of the fire: *we could do with a little warmth at this temperature*; *hot time in the old town tonight, eh?*

The firefighter came back to relieve Michael of his hose, turned the pressure down, and leaned the hose over some loose boards, pointing it toward the fire. With his head, he indicated a woman's dark blue parka with white fur trim. He said in a low voice, "See that woman over there, next the telephone pole? That's Mabel, Don Miller's wife. Ever seen her before?" Michael nodded slightly. The man continued, "You never see her, you know. Except at fires. And only the ones at night. Weird, eh?"

Big Betty's fire was the first time Michael had seen Mabel again since his visit to deliver her parcel in August. He walked over to the dark figure standing alone and greeted her with a few comments about the fire and the cold. She seemed grateful for being recognized, and smiled cheerfully. Suddenly exhausted, Michael pushed back his sleeve to see what time it was. He had forgotten his watch. When he asked Mabel for the time, he was amazed to discover it was 5:00 a.m. He had been gone for two and a half hours.

"My damn cabin will be frozen up. Better go."

Mabel said eagerly, "Come by tomorrow for a drink with us? It's New Year's Eve, but we'll be home--afternoon, evening, doesn't matter when."

"Right on." Michael turned to go, waving a mittened hand toward Mabel. Invitations to socialize, once too numerous, were now rare. He never refused a dinner or a drink these days. He had no regular contact with the government employees he had once considered friends, now that he wasn't working with them. He knew for them he was "out of sight, out of mind." It was as if he had some disease they might catch. He tried not to be bitter, but he was battling shadows. Some of the ostracizing was because of his relationship with Selena, maybe, but no one had the courage to tell him so. He thought sometimes that he was getting what everyone called cabin fever, a destructively negative view because of the dark and the cold. Well, he told himself, he was finally leaving Dawson and all its gossip. He wasn't going to worry about what people were thinking of him at this late stage. Tomorrow would be the last day of the year and of the decade. Time to think ahead, not back.

Leaving Big Betty's smouldering remains, Michael climbed the hill, re-lit his fire, and slept until close to noon. He awoke with the cold nipping his ears and nose, the acrid smell of smoke in his hair and moustache. In spite of his disturbed sleep the night before, he felt rested and excited. The fire was still a strange and vivid experience in his mind, a change of pace from his dull existence.

The sun was barely above the hills to the south as Michael finished his breakfast of a jam sandwich and coffee. While there was still light enough in the short day, he decided to return to Big Betty's Place to take some photographs. He had begun to take photographs of the old buildings and the people he knew, making prints to show friends Outside. Experimenting with photography made him feel artistic and he found it technically interesting as well. He was teaching himself to take slides, trying more challenging techniques to take them in the winter's extreme cold and darkness.

On the days when he felt productive, he was most ambivalent about leaving Dawson. Losing the social work job and breaking off with Selena had left him time to follow new interests. Although there were fewer people in his life, he had more time for them, and more time for reading, for contemplation. Those were the good days. If only it wasn't so damned cold, he might stay on. Still, he had to leave. If he didn't he might go really crazy, or become as isolated as Mabel Miller.

Michael re-traced his route of the night before down the Dome Road. The ice-fog had dissipated and a slight breeze from the river bit his exposed cheeks when he stopped in front of what was left of Big Betty's. Two walls and the roof had collapsed completely into a black pile of rubble. The remaining walls were like huge gravestones marking the death of the whorehouse. Winter had overtaken much of the heat of the fire but he noticed wisps of steam curling upward from the centre of the debris. In a few weeks, the fire department would knock down the remaining walls and burn it all. That really would be the end of Big Betty's.

Michael took several shots of the false fronts on structures bordering the blackened gap that had been Big Betty's. They gave a deceptively tall, rectangular presentation, hiding their twisted log construction behind. The grey clapboard buildings tilted drunkenly, an uneven protection of ice on their walls shining dully in the midwinter light. Barely visible letters testified to their former uses. ARDWARE could be deciphered on one, and FRES FLOWER on the other. Half of one wall of the hardware store was muralled with a black abstract design by the fire. Looking inside, Michael saw the wooden floors were a precarious terrain, tossed and ripped apart as alternately melting and freezing permafrost over half a century had shifted the ground under weak foundations.

Fat icicles that would hang gauntly from the house for weeks streamed like tears from Betty's remaining windows. They would survive even the attacks of children attempting to break them to use as swords. He angled his camera to catch the glittering ice. He saw icicles only when they were left from a fire. He was fascinated by the effects of extreme cold in the semi-arid climate. Unless a building had a poorly insulated roof, the intense dry cold did not allow the snow to melt enough to make icicles. Only briefly in spring did they appear, and those were quickly gone with the returning warmth of the sun. Contrary to the southern myths of northern winters, there was very little snow and what there was had a fine sugary texture most of the winter, impossible to pack into a snowball it was so dry.

Keeping the camera inside his parka against his chest between shots protected it from seizing in the cold. Michael knew he could take only a few photographs before the cold would have its way. Working quickly, he held his breath as he fixed the camera settings. The lens would fog over if his breath hit it. In a few minutes he was satisfied with what he had done and walked down the street to find a hot cup of coffee in the Westminster Café. He was optimistic about the 70s, and feeling somewhat daring, even a little rebellious. He would go from the Westminster to have a New Year's drink with the Millers. It cheered him, receiving her invitation. No one else he knew had ever been invited to the Millers. It made him special.

Miss Bingham was holding forth, surrounded by four men at the communal round table in the corner of the Westminster Café when Michael arrived. Her slight figure was dwarfed by the male parkas thrown over backs of chairs. Her thin-boned face was topped by permanented curly grey hair and her eyes were difficult to see behind thick black-rimmed glasses. She had been a teacher at the Robert Service School for two years and her enthusiasm for history had helped her decide to retire in Dawson the year before. She prided herself on knowing more than almost anyone else about the history of the Klondike Gold Rush.

Even as a teacher, Miss Bingham was one of those women who had never stopped her energetic pace in life long enough to learn the rules. Her ignorance about the importance of social niceties was well known. Other women knew instinctively they were not supposed to sit at the round table unless they were with their husbands, and husbands rarely brought their wives to that male enclave if they could avoid it. But she paid no attention to the custom. She didn't want to be provocative, but simply assumed her rights without thinking about the social consequences. Feared because of her education, she was not confronted by anyone about the normal thing to do. Most Dawson women agreed with their men that she was an uncomfortable aberration to be avoided. A few younger women thought of her as some kind of revolutionary and egged her on without too obviously supporting her in her causes. She was relatively new to Dawson and therefore of no real consequence to the social infrastructure. As just another odd character passing through, she would eventually move on and be forgotten.

"It's true!" Michael heard Miss Bingham's sharp voice insist. She tipped evaporated milk into her coffee, looked up at Michael and repeated her monologue for this new audience. "I was just saying, Michael, that Big Betty was killed on December 30th, the same day as the fire. That's exactly 25 years ago yesterday." She thought for a moment, and said, "You know, I'm not even sure why I remember that date." She lowered her voice to a mysterious tone. "It just seemed to come to me like a voice in my ear while I was watching the fire. It's like she's getting her revenge, burning the place on the anniversary of her death, don't you think? Weird, eh?" She looked around the table for confirmation, but the men were silent. Michael surmised they knew more about Big Betty and her girls than they cared to talk about in public.

"She's a little late if she's after revenge, I'd say," Michael commented to general laughter and the uneasiness surrounding the table lifted briefly. He sat down and reached for the cup of coffee the waitress had brought him without being asked.

Watching with ironic interest, Michael had always kept his distance from Miss Bingham, at the same time empathizing with her. He knew the Yukon's mythical tolerance for eccentrics was a thin covering over the solid bedrock of social convention. He too felt on the fringe of things sometimes, not quite fitting and not quite knowing why. At the same time, he didn't want to be a misfit completely, like her. Or Mabel.

Sideways looks and grunting replies to her questions did not slow Miss Bingham down when she was on an important mission. "What do you remember about Big Betty from your family, Fred?" she asked one of the men at the table. Fred Grant had closed the liquor store early for the New Year holiday and was enjoying some company before heading to his daughter's house for supper. He was born in Dawson and therefore was treated with reverence, an archive of accurate information about the past and notable opinions about the present and future.

Fred didn't look as if he was eager to help Miss Bingham. "Well, I can't rightly say. I don't recall Mother and Dad saying much about her. She was murdered by one of her girls in the mid-40's as I recollect. Stabbed to death. Winter of '43 or '44. Around there. During the War, anyways." He looked around, and added with a smile, "I was a youngster, couldn't care less about anything but my girlfriend Josie and my Ford pickup. Put both together and it was even more interesting."

Once the supportive laughter died down, Miss Bingham pounced on Fred's addition to her puzzle. "See? It was winter. Likely Christmas, 1944. Exactly twenty-five years ago. I'm sure I'm right. Wish there was some way to find out. Just the kind of thing to bug you in the middle of the night, eh?" The men's lifted eyebrows and barely smothered smiles around the table didn't quite agree that her problem was a major obstacle to their rest. Miss Bingham persisted: "But what about the woman who stabbed her, Fred? Don't you remember hearing anything as a kid? Even her name?"

"Too many girls in those years to remember all their names! Anyways, the murderess took off, probably to Alaska. We never heard of her again. Easy to get lost in those days I guess." He leaned back in his chair and called for another round of coffee for the table although it wasn't needed.

Miss Bingham countered, "I'd think it would be pretty hard to get lost, Fred. There wasn't even a road between here and Whitehorse. She would have had to fly. Couldn't get far with a dog team."

"Michael," Fred said, "Aren't you off to Whitehorse pretty soon? Why don't you look it up wherever it is the records are kept?"

"What a great idea!" Miss Bingham said.

Why not pitch in? Nothing better to do. He said, "Well, yeah. I've got to get to Whitehorse when it warms up, fix up my van for the trip Outside." Everyone enthusiastically endorsed the plan to have Michael research the facts. It would get Miss Bingham off their backs.

Before the group broke up, Miss Bingham asked the waitress for a large piece of cardboard and a pen to set up a betting pool for the exact date and time of Big Betty's murder. It would be confirmed by a death certificate or something else legal found by Michael. For $2 a try, the one closest to her time of death would win the pool. There was always a pool for something or other in the Westminster Café to make life more interesting, and Michael placed a couple of bets on the board. The waitress had collected $34 by the time the Westminster closed at five o'clock, in time for everyone to go next door to the bar for the New Year's party. While the café was closing, Michael wished the group a happy New Year and then walked the three blocks over to the Miller house.

"I'm sorry, Don's not here," Mabel said at the door. Michael hesitated. She sounded preoccupied.

"Well, happy New Year, then," Michael said and turned to leave.

"No, no, come in, Michael. Sorry. I asked him to be sure to be here, but he's over at the Downtown." A grimace passed across her face, "As usual, I'm afraid."

Mabel closed the door behind him and Michael removed his parka and boots. He noticed a bottle of rye and some ginger ale ready on the livingroom table.

They exchanged opinions about how long the cold spell was going to last while Mabel poured them each a drink. Her restlessness worried him. Maybe she didn't like him to be there without Don in the house. But she didn't mind last summer. Of course then it wasn't a holiday or in the evening. Maybe she was just angry at Don. "Well, here's to the 70s", Michael said, lifting his glass. "Hope the new decade brings us all the things we really want." Maybe she needed to have him alone for some reason. He hoped it wasn't sex she was after. She would embarrass both of them because he simply wasn't interested. What if Don came home drunk and found him there, drinking with his wife? Who knows how volatile he might be. He would just finish his drink and go home.

Michael watched from the kitchen doorway as Mabel put together some crackers and cheese on a tray. To make conversation, he started to tell her about the betting pool at the Westminster. "That old fool Bingham," Mabel interrupted, throwing a knife into the sink with a crash. "She can never leave things alone, can she? What difference does it make to her when Big Betty was killed, or who did it? It's none of her business. She's a stranger here." She picked up the tray and swept past Michael into the livingroom.

He would try to keep the conversation neutral and then get out of there. "I guess the Klondike history intrigues her, that's all," he said. "Nothing much else for her here now. I've gotten enthusiastic about it myself, the last while." He told her about his interest in photography and the way he had to keep his camera inside his parka because of the cold. They moved into the livingroom. "I'm really excited about showing the slides to people in Vancouver. They've never seen anything like a ghost town. With real ghosts," he laughed without humour.

Mabel's face brightened. "Want to see some pictures of old Dawson buildings, ones that are gone now? I took them when I first came. A lot have burned since then. I thought I was quite the photographer." Without waiting for a reply, she opened the door to a cupboard, pulled out a photograph album and sat beside him on the couch, opening the album on her lap. The black and white photos were of buildings and people that had disappeared many years before. Sprinkling her stories with ironic comments about some of the old Dawson families, Mabel talked with animation about Dawson characters he had heard a little about, both famous and infamous. Before too long, they were laughing, chatting, and drinking. Michael began to relax and enjoy himself as the grey winter afternoon quickly faded to dark.

At the back of the album were some loose photos. Mabel picked them up and held them against her chest. "These are of Big Betty's place," she said. "Do you know anything about her?" Her cheeks were flushed and her eyes were large behind her glasses as she searched his face.

He said he knew very little about Betty. He was fascinated more with Mabel's enthusiasm than with Betty's story, much of which he had already heard.

Michael recalled that the last of the "houses" in Dawson had been officially closed as late as 1954, many years after those in southern Canada. "She would have been driven out of town in other places," Mabel said, "but maybe because of our wild history, Dawsonites tolerated prostitution. It wasn't like today. I suppose people felt that 'the girls' were part of our being on the northern frontier with men outnumbering women ten to one. It was a good business from all accounts, here and in other places in the Yukon."

Lifting a photo, Mabel said, "Look at this one. That's Harry Labiche on the far left. You probably know he owned most of Dawson at one time. That's his wife sitting beside him." Michael reached for the photograph of a crowded dinner party with a waiter dressed in a black bow tie leaning over the couple Mabel pointed out.

"Her parties were by invitation only, mind you. RSVP and the whole bit," Mabel said. "Even the wives of businessmen and government officials came. Wouldn't miss it. They all dressed up as if it was still the Gold Rush. Drank champagne. Expensive china. Silver plate. Betty was known for her generosity, gave extravagant gifts to everyone."

Warming to her story, Mabel said, "Big Betty had a friend in Keno who was also in the business. They had an agreement about the girls. Betty would send hers over when they got a little stale here. She changed the girls right at the end of the year, and while the old ones and new ones were still in Dawson, she would throw one of her fancy dinner parties for the upper crust of Dawson, to introduce the new girls to the town. Betty brought in three new girls from Outside every year and sent the old ones over to Keno Hill."

Keno Hill was the silver mine north of Mayo. Michael had been to Keno on working trips and knew that the RCMP still regularly questioned a couple of waitresses working there about their spare-time activities. Just like the old days, they made their real money from the miners.

Mabel continued, "The parties she threw helped her to keep in business without too much trouble. Even the Dawson wives wouldn't have much to complain about if they went to her parties. They didn't have to go if they were too prudish, but most of them were curious. And if you were invited, it meant you were recognized as part of the elite of Dawson I guess."

In the middle of one photo a buxom woman with long dark curly hair, taller than the people seated near her, was laughing and lifting her glass of champagne to the camera. "There she is. Big Betty," Mabel said. "She had auburn hair, not black like some people say. Dyed it of course."

"Fascinating! How did you get these pictures? They should be in the museum."

"Oh, heavens no! Almost everybody in Dawson keeps historic things. That bunch at the museum would probably lose them or sell them off to the tourists." She closed the album. "Anyway, these were given to me by my sister and belong to me. Not to anyone else," she said firmly, taking the album over to the cupboard.

"Your sister? How did she get them? Was she in Dawson too?"

He saw Mabel hesitate and her back stiffen as she knelt down to put the album away. "I've said too much already. I haven't shown these to anyone before. It's been twenty-five years."

Michael took a breath and heard himself say, "Twenty-five years? Almost to the day since Big Betty's murder..."

"I shouldn't have said anything. I must be drunk," Mabel said with a small laugh, shaking her head. She shoved the album to the back of the shelf.

"You know more than you're saying, I think," Michael guessed softly, watching her closely. She stood up, turned around, and looked at him. He asked, "Do you want to talk to me about something?" He leaned forward, intensely curious.

"No," she said quietly, shaking her head. She took in a deep breath and blinked, looking past Michael to some hidden scene. Firmly, she said, "Yes. Yes, I do. It's been too long. For all these last months I've thought of nothing else." She sat next to Michael on the couch, looked at him, and said with no emotion in her voice: "My older sister Frances murdered Big Betty."

Michael's heart skipped and he stopped himself from speaking. They sat quietly for a few seconds. He asked gently, "Then she...ah...worked... for her?"

Mabel took a sip of her drink, and said, "Yes. She was in Whitehorse when they were building the Alaska Highway. Then she came to Dawson. To Betty's place."

"And you were..." Michael hesitated, "...in the Yukon?"

"In San Francisco, where we lived." Mabel stood and walked across the room. She said, her voice terse, "I was in secretarial school. Then I worked in a munitions factory. It was the War, lots of jobs, good money. Even for women."

"Quite a trip for your sister, coming this far North." Mable hadn't moved from standing and it made Michael a little nervous, looking up at her.

"She left San Francisco after a big fight with our father over money she owed him. They never did get along. I was the only one she kept in touch with at all. She was mostly in Seattle, and I guess she heard about the Yukon there."

"Another adventurous black sheep...lots of them in the North," Michael smiled.

Mabel looked at him briefly and said, "Yes. She was certainly a black sheep." She walked over and switched on a lamp near the couch. The action made her more animated and with relief in her voice, she said, "I wrote to her a few times, to a Dawson box number she gave us, and she replied--at first. Then I didn't hear from her for months, but none of my letters were returned, so I figured she was getting them. I was very worried. I took out my savings and came up from California to find her."

"Man, that was so brave of you in those days!"

She sat down across from Michael and said, "My mother thought I was insane and tried to talk me out of it. But it was a crazy time, that summer of the War. People were doing impulsive things all over the place. And I guess I wanted some of the adventure and excitement I thought Franny was having, too."

"But how did you look for her, in a strange place?"

Mabel spoke carefully, almost formally. "Well, on the White Pass boat going up the West Coast to Skagway I asked about her from the Dawson passengers. No one seemed to have heard her name. I found out later Franny didn't use her real name, and she changed it two or three times.

Damn her, you know she even called herself Mabel for awhile. Some people in Dawson think I was a working girl too because of her I'm sure."

"Oh, I really doubt that." Michael's voice sounded false even to himself.

"People here will say anything about anybody. You must know that by now?" She looked at him directly.

Michael hoped his face was neutral as he helped himself to a piece of cheese and avoided her eyes.

"Anyway," Mabel said with a short irritated sigh, "the day after I arrived in Whitehorse, Don--who is now my husband, Don Miller--came to see me at the Regina Hotel. He was trying to find her too. He had been collecting Franny's mail in Dawson and he opened anything looking important. That's how he knew I was coming; he'd read my letter to her."

"Pretty presumptuous of him, opening her mail."

Mabel hesitated and said, "Don and Franny were...they had been planning to get married in the New Year, but they kept it a secret."

"Married? But how come it was a secret?"

"Franny insisted on it. I guess Betty fired any of the girls who got too involved with anyone outside the house, even with innocent friendships. Bad for business, she said. And Franny wanted the money she'd earn until they married. It was just a few weeks."

"Oh, of course." Michael gave her what he hoped was a reassuring nod to keep her talking and tried not to be too obvious about his curiosity. "Funny that she would disappear with her marriage coming up..."

Mabel put her drink on the table and took off her glasses. She rubbed her eyes. "I told you. She killed Betty. She had to leave. Don said that after Betty's end-of-the-year party--as they had planned--Franny told Betty she was quitting to marry Don. Betty was furious. She insisted Franny owed her a thousand dollars for the loss of business for her Keno friend, who was expecting her to move over there. Betty said she had to go over to Keno as they had agreed when she was hired, or pay Betty the money. Well, my sister was pretty broke as usual."

"Couldn't Don give her the money for Betty?"

"Everything happened so fast, he didn't even know about the money until it was all over. Franny always was headstrong, and she just blew her top I guess. Betty and Franny had a big fight and in the early morning, Franny took a knife from the kitchen, sneaked in and murdered Betty in her sleep. Shoved the knife right into her heart. She ran to Don, and he arranged for a charter flight for her to go to Whitehorse with a pilot who was a friend of his. There wasn't a highway to Whitehorse then, and people flew all the time. There were always lots of small planes for rent, willing to go anywhere anytime. Don wanted to leave with her, but she insisted that it would be safer if he stayed and she would keep in touch with him."

"What about the pilot? Didn't he know?"

"Don never told him the truth of course, just said Franny had to meet someone in Whitehorse right away. The pilot was sworn to secrecy about the whole deal. There were all kinds of mysterious things happening during the War, even up here. The Japanese were near the Alaskan Coast. You know, that's why the Alaska Highway was built. And everybody thought everybody else was a spy with secret messages to carry. Most people were willing to go the extra mile in what they thought was defence of the country, and keep their mouths shut about anything a little shady. Don paid the pilot a hefty sum, and he flew her out before daylight, which even then was against the law and was really dangerous."

"Wow! And no one has heard from her since?"

"Nobody knows where she went from Whitehorse to this day. Sometimes I think Don might know, but I don't have any proof at all. I think she must be over in Alaska somewhere, but who knows. Could be in Australia. She had a friend there."

Mabel poured them each another drink, and slumped in her chair. Her voice was dull, vacant: "Twenty-five years ago, before she left Dawson... she gave those photographs to Don to mail to me in California. She's in two of them. You wouldn't have noticed her. She looks pretty ordinary, like me."

Michael's mind was churning with questions. "What about the RCMP? They should've been able to find her. You couldn't just disappear in the Territory in those days. Everybody knew everybody else."

"Well, of course, neither Don nor I were going to the RCMP to find her. And I guess they didn't care too much about a couple of prostitutes fighting. Don said they didn't seem to worry about talking to her or even the other girls in the first few days when they should have. They talked to Don, but they never even talked to me when I came. They had probably closed the file by then and they may not have even known we were sisters. She wasn't going by the right name."

"And then you and Don..."

"Don married me six weeks after we met, the next time he came up to Whitehorse. On the rebound, I thought then. But now sometimes I think it was to protect Franny. I promised Don I would never tell anyone about her. We were the only two who knew what really happened and if he married me, he could control what I might say. And I was desperate. No job or money, no friends or family. And I guess I was in love, too. Oh, yes, he was a real charmer in his younger days." She smiled, paused, looked down at her hands. Tears welled up in her eyes, "I think I actually still do love him, you know. Otherwise I wouldn't stay in this town."

Mabel wiped her eyes. "Damn. I didn't mean to cry." She Mabel stood up and said with bitterness, "Well, we've been paying for Franny's stupidity ever since. Paying for keeping silent about what she did. Over and over."

"How do you mean, paying for it? Blackmail?"

"No. Paying, you know--emotionally. It has eaten us both up. He still loves her, you know. He talks about her all the time when he's drunk, but only to me. Sometimes at New Year's, like tonight, he makes me put an extra plate on the table at supper for her if he's drunk enough. He sits there, talking about her, how wonderful and beautiful she was, the good times they had, how blue was her favourite colour...he doesn't call me down, or beat me, or anything like that. But this is worse." She shivered, and drew her sweater closer around her chest. "I hope he doesn't want supper tonight." She looked at Michael and frowned. "Do you know he even wanted to call our daughter Frances? But I couldn't do that." She reached for a tissue and blew her nose. "May doesn't know any of this. If it weren't for her and our grandchild, I'd be ready to die tomorrow."

The struggle of the Millers' life together moved Michael. It was a twisted symbiosis, never quite concluded, each one tearing the scabs off the other's wounds, the painful silence about Frances hanging morbidly over them. He walked across to her and lightly squeezed her shoulder.

Mabel leaned away from him and began putting the dishes they had used on the tray. "I just had to tell someone," she said. "Especially after watching Big Betty's burn down. I wanted there to be some kind of conclusion, even if it was only telling someone the truth after all these years. I had to get Franny and Big Betty out of my life. Clear away their... their evil presence, get them out of my nightmares. They have invaded my sleep and my life." She stood up with the tray. "I hate her, you know, Big Betty. And Franny too. It's as if...as if...Big Betty has been getting some kind of revenge for her murder, and Franny, too, for my marrying Don. Making my marriage a turmoil. Twenty-five years of turmoil. It's Big Betty's revenge. She's taking it out on me." She walked into the kitchen.

Michael felt as if something was crawling on the back of his neck. He said quietly, "Oh, man, that's heavy, really heavy." He came to the kitchen doorway and sipped the last of his drink from his glass while Mabel placed dishes into the sink.

"But telling someone, that should make it end, don't you think?" Mabel said, looking at him sadly. "It might purge the ghosts."

"Yes, of course. I think it should help get it out of your mind at least."

"Thanks for listening. I hope you didn't mind me talking like this too much? It's why I invited you over. I didn't even tell Don you were coming for a drink so we could be alone."

Then she had lied to him earlier about Don when she said she had told him to be home that evening. It made him uncomfortable. Michael forced a smile and said, "Of course I don't mind. What a terrible burden you've had all these years! It must be agonizing for you. I'm happy if I've helped you in some small way." He placed his glass on the counter. "And it is a fascinating story, one I won't soon forget. I'm curious, though. Why did you choose to tell me instead of someone else?"

"Well," Mabel took his glass, put it in the sink with the other dishes, and said, "I guess it's because you're a social worker I deliberately chose you. You must be used to people's skeletons in their closets, all that sort of thing? And you have to keep things confidential, right?"

Michael should have seen it coming. His position had made him something of a listening post, especially for women. Nearly everyone had something they wanted to confess and his ethics kept him from gossiping about what he knew. At first the confidences had made him feel useful and important, even powerful. But it frustrated him when advice he gave wasn't acted upon. He felt his interest and energy were wasted, abused, that people really didn't want to change, just to get things off their chests at his expense.

A desire to leave overcame him, leave Mabel's house, leave Dawson. He'd get the trip to Whitehorse over and then be gone. Soon. "Dammit," he said, "you know, I said I'd look up the records about Betty and how she died when I go to Whitehorse in a couple of weeks. For that bloody betting pool at the Westminster. Maybe Frances' name--or even Don's-- will be in the records."

She looked straight at him and said quietly, "But Michael, you don't have to do it, you know. It's only Miss Bingham's stupid idea."

It wouldn't be possible to ignore Miss Bingham or the round table crowd. He wanted to keep his word with them, if only for the sake of his reputation for being reliable. Well, he'd figure out something.

"Besides," Mabel added, "you're leaving the Yukon. What difference does it make to you, breaking a silly promise, telling a white lie to people you'll probably never see again?"

"Not much, I guess." But it did.

Mabel smiled, "Promise me you won't tell anyone about my sister and Don? I don't know what Don would do to me if he knew I said anything and especially since I showed you the pictures. He can get awfully mean and it scares me."

Was she implying Don might hit her? She had said he never did that. But what else had she lied about? "Of course I won't say anything about what you told me," Michael said. He thought aloud, "After I come back from Whitehorse I suppose I can just..."

Mabel walked past him, out of the kitchen. The visit was over. "Anyway," she interrupted, "I don't know if anyone would even believe you if you told them about Franny. You're just an Outsider, here for a job, for a short time. You're like all the others. You'll leave and probably never come back." Her voice was like a slap to Michael's face, cold, biting. "Isn't that right?" she asked.

She had chosen to talk to him not because he was Michael Scott, a reliable, sympathetic, compassionate person. But because of his job. Because he had been a social worker. And besides, he was leaving town. In her eyes, he was a safe bet. He wouldn't cause her any problems in the future. He just wouldn't be around. She had put him in a position with other people where he might have to lie, just because he was good enough to provide a listening ear. And she was leaving it to him to figure out how to deal with it.

Michael silently drew on his boots and zipped up his parka. He had been involved in her fear and sorrow, had felt her pain. But she was indifferent to his feelings. He felt trapped, manipulated by this woman. And easily forgotten. Once again he had been trapped into becoming too close to someone. It was as if she had bought his sympathy with a few drinks and a little charm. Was he just someone to be used to gain her own ends? Like a client to her, like one of the johns in Betty's house?

Mabel opened the door for him and he looked coldly at her. Hoping to hurt her, he said, "You know, Mabel Miller, I think you chose to tell me for another reason. I think it was because we two really have something in common. We're both social outcasts. It doesn't really matter who I am as a person, or that you have asked me to not say anything, does it? I'm expendable. But, lady, so are you. Happy 1970." He slammed the door.

Anger made possibilities whirl in his head as he walked quickly away. Maybe the whole sordid story was in Mabel's imagination, some crazy hallucination her boring life created to compensate for her rotten marriage and her isolation. Maybe she had some sick obsession with the idea of prostitution. Maybe there was no sister at all. His head began to swim. He was being ridiculous.

Several gunshots cracked the frigid air. Someone celebrating the turn of the year. He trudged, exhausted and miserable, up the Dome Road to his cabin. He had always hated New Year's Eve with its phony cheer.

****

In the Westminster, the cardboard sheet on the wall with Miss Bingham's betting pool on it had the words "Big Betty's Bet" at the top in large red letters. It had attracted over $100, and was threatening to spill over to another sheet until someone decided the cutoff date for bets was the day Michael left for Whitehorse. Miss Bingham reminded Michael twice before he left about his promise to look up any papers to do with Betty's death.

When Michael arrived back at the Westminster Café two weeks after New Year's, Miss Bingham followed close behind. Two of the men who were the heaviest bettors on the board had seated themselves at the round table in anticipation. "Heard you were back," said one of them to Michael as he sat down. The waitress came over to the table, curious. She had put $6 into the pool herself.

Before Michael could say anything, Miss Bingham sat down in a rush and announced to the group: "Listen to this: there were no records in Whitehorse proving anything!" Michael had told her this while they were walking toward the café together. It was not true.

"Hmmm. Guess we'll have to bet on something else then," one of the men offered.

"Yup. No point in giving it all back," the other bettor echoed to general agreement around the table.

From her face, Michael saw the news Miss Bingham had proclaimed did not have the impact she hoped. She pinched her lips together and shook her head in disbelief. With the same effort at clarity she had used for so many years in the grade two classroom, she said, "I really don't think you people realize the seriousness of this. Michael said he looked for everything: a court record of a charge of murder, a story in the *Dawson Daily News*. She would probably be sent Outside for burial, so there wouldn't be a funeral. But there have to be records, permits. I gave him a list of every relevant record I could think of. I even asked him to check for three years before and three years after Christmas 1944. Nothing. Not a scratch on a paper about Big Betty or her girl, whatever her name was."

"Papers must be lost, eh?" Fred Grant asked with frustrating logic.

Miss Bingham said, "I won't accept that idea for a moment. It's obvious not any of you have bothered to do historical research about the Gold Rush or the years afterward as I have. It would be the first time in history, if the papers were lost," she asserted. "As you should know, Fred, Dawson's records were always kept in impeccable order, and were transferred safely to Whitehorse when it became the capital. I have always found anything I was ever looking for."

The men took Miss Bingham at her word, pausing to absorb this. She was a teacher, even if a bit fanatic. She felt their rising interest and added, "And get this: a friend of mine in Whitehorse says she did some research on two men who froze to death in the same week that I believe Betty died-- death certificates, burial certificates, everything in perfect order. Even their names in the paper. So why not for Betty?"

A few people were gathering around the table. Michael's breath was shallow. He felt as if he were naked in public. Ignoring Miss Bingham's new twist to the mystery and her tenacity, Michael said, "Well, I guess that's over. What should we bet on next? Be awhile before the river breaks up."

"You sure you did your homework, there, Michael?" One man teased.

"Yeah, you gotta please the teacher or you won't get a gold star," another muttered under his breath.

Michael smiled weakly at the reproaches and left the table with relief, waving his hand at the group. "See ya."

Over the next few days, several theories emerged at nearly every gathering and the story grew with each telling. Maybe somebody didn't want anyone to know about her murder; maybe somebody wanted to make her disappear from the records to save his reputation, somebody who was a witness; maybe the editor of the *Daily News* was one of her customers and hushed up the story. Michael wished the town had television to entertain themselves with so they wouldn't want to spend their time rehashing Big Betty's past. He felt oppressed by the constant chatter and wanted more than ever to leave Dawson. Everyone agreed that in those days, prostitutes didn't count enough for records and permits to be insisted upon. But still...maybe it wasn't a murder by one of her girls, maybe it was someone else, someone prominent who could cover up the story...or maybe she didn't really die, just disappeared out of town because of some bad deal she had made, and somebody made up a story for her, somebody she was blackmailing.

Although no one would admit to actually being on the premises of Big Betty's Place for any reason, some older Dawsonites confirmed seeing Big Betty when she was in Dawson--walking home, or in a bar--in all her fullness. Some even had a few stories about her gala parties that others had gone to. The consensus was she was murdered, probably stabbed, but as important as it should have been at the time, no one seemed to be able to remember the date of her death or who exactly was her murderer. The mystery sent a shiver down more than one spine in Dawson. Did she exist only as one of Dawson's phantoms, another myth among the many in the Klondike or was she real?

The day before he was to leave Dawson, Michael checked his mail for the last time. He was anxious to get his slides back from processing in Vancouver in case he had to re-take some of them before he left. Along with the small package of slides in his mail box, there was a card. He opened it and glanced at gaudy red and pink roses on the front. "Thanks for everything" was written inside, in a female hand. No signature. It must be from Mabel. Well, he deserved thanks. He had done more than enough for her. He had taken pride in never being involved even in a small cover-up before, and was still uncomfortable with the deception. He had been used. His integrity had been tarnished, and he had even exposed himself publically by lying.

Michael crumpled the card and envelope and threw them in the waste basket. He didn't see the elaborate letter "F" on the back of the envelope.

CHRISTMAS IN THE FLATS

The key to the door of Eliza Maclean's trailer in Whiskey Flats slipped out of her fumbling hand. "Damn!" she said. She leaned over and put down her shopping bag. Scratching with her hand through the wet snow, she found the key and glanced up at her daughter. Selena moved away, clutching a cardboard box in her arms, her lips pursed and her eyes on the unstable wooden step. Eliza put the key into the lock and turned it. She asked, "What's wrong, baby?" As if she didn't know. There was no reply, and she opened the door. The poor kid was kicked out of an apartment she was sharing with her friend Julie. They were both cold and hungry. Well, she could solve that at least. Her smile and voice were more timid than she hoped when she said, "Come on in. Put those things over by the couch." She pulled a string attached to the naked bulb hanging from the ceiling.

Selena stepped into the front room. "Pretty small, eh?" she said with a grimace, glancing around. She put the box on the floor and brought the shopping bag inside.

Eliza's heart was pounding in her ears but she said, "We'll be just fine! Lots of room here for just us two." She laughed too loudly. "We're both the same size--nice and small, eh? We'll fit just right in my little place." She sat on a chair and removed her boots with a grunt. She would show Selena enough hospitality to convince her to stay more than the one night. "I have enough welfare left this month to keep the both of us going over Christmas. Don't you worry about a thing." Eliza stood up and said with more confidence than she felt, "Always room for my baby when she's in Whitehorse, any time."

Eliza's two-room trailer was one of those aluminum boxes with rounded edges that had been pulled behind pick-up trucks coming up the Alaska Highway after the Second World War. It had once been painted yellow and had a round porthole beside the one door. It was like a refrigerator in the winter and a sauna in the summer. A lumpy couch that could have originally been any colour sat under the front window. It faced a tall brown heater that separated the cooking area from the couch. The air smelled of fuel oil.

"I'm just so happy to finally have my beautiful grown-up daughter staying with me. A wonderful Christmas present," Eliza said. She smiled with pleasure and put her arm around Selena's waist. She never tired of looking at Selena's face, a younger version of herself, only prettier, with big eyes. Selena was darker, but then she had more Indian in her than Eliza. It was hard to believe that she was all of twenty-three already.

Selena pulled away. Eliza said, "Just keep your jacket on till it's warmer in here. I'll turn up this old heater. It's supposed to get warmer out after tonight anyway."

"I'm only staying tonight, *Eliza.*"

Drawing in her breath sharply, Eliza bent down to raise the thermostat on the heater. She was silent, moving stiffly across the room to the two-burner camp stove. She lit the gas under a pot of moose stew. Using a dipper hanging on the side of an open pail of water on the counter, she filled the tea kettle in three careful moves. She put it on the second burner and lit it.

"Open up one of those beers for yourself, here, under the counter," Eliza said, pointing without turning around. She added quietly, "It'll get warmer in here with the cooking, you'll see." She stirred the stew with a shaky hand. Selena ignored the invitation, throwing her box and bag in the one empty corner by the couch. She stood awkwardly by the heater, lit a cigarette, and blew smoke towards Eliza.

Eliza said, "I been living here for...well, for just ages." She clattered through a metal box of silverware in the cupboard. "People come and go around me, but me, I just stay." She found two soup spoons and mugs and put them on the table. "It's real cheap here. No rent, do you believe? And the guys pretty much leave me alone." She heard courage returning to her voice. "I got some good friends, too. We help each other out all the time. I even got a phone I can use, over at Gus's, and that's where I get my electricity from. Pretty good, eh?" She didn't expect an answer.

The Flats was a community of scarce but shared resources. A loosely strung extension cord joined Eliza's trailer to Gus's cabin where the electricity metre was. She paid Gus for her share, calculating it according to how many favours he owed her. He was happy with whatever contribution Eliza made and accepted her estimate as accurate without question. Eliza was a tidy housekeeper, and cleaned Gus's cabin whenever she thought it was getting too rough for his health. Other times, she cooked for him or brought him some of her own meal. Gus often said, so that she could hear him: "It's always good to see Eliza. She's like a little chickadee." And then he would add: "She looks like a little bird too!" and he would laugh a toothless cackle, his small hand scratching his unshaven cheek.

Selena punched her cigarette out in an ashtray on the table and roamed around the room. On a shelf near the front window, Eliza's only vase held a cluster of pink plastic roses that a boyfriend had once given her for her birthday. Stuffed into them was a red and white Canadian maple leaf flag. Selena picked it out of the flowers. "Got that the other day," Eliza said. "Pretty, eh? Nice bright red. We'll show them damned Americans coming up North, invading the Yukon. Bunch of Viet Nam draft dodgers, that's all we get nowadays. Think we're Alaska or something." Eliza realized she was repeating things she had said earlier when they were in the bar. But she was a true-blue Canadian Indian. The land belonged to her and her people. Some day everybody would know that, even the Americans.

"Man, do I need a shower! Where's the bathroom?" Selena asked, walking over to the murky bedroom at the back. She pushed aside a curtain of dark green cotton printed with bouquets of indeterminant orange and yellow blossoms.

"Sorry, baby. No bathroom inside," Eliza said. "I get my water from the stand-pipe behind me or from the one at Gus's." She unhooked a washpan from its nail above the sink and filled it with warm water from the kettle. Placing it on the red checkered oilcloth covering the table, she brought Selena soap and a towel. Selena gingerly took off her jacket and placed it over the back of a chair. She tested the water with a finger before washing her hands and face.

When Selena had finished, Eliza washed her own hands in the water and dumped it into the sink. It splashed loudly into the empty five gallon slop-pail underneath. Eliza reached under the sink and added a gurgle of bleach to the pail. She used the slop-pail for peeing emergencies. Along with her neighbours, she crossed the railway tracks and emptied the slop into the river at night so no one would see her and complain about it to the City. In the winter, there was a distinctly greyish-yellow colour to the ice on the Yukon River near the Flats. Whenever Eliza seriously needed to go, she used an outhouse shared with three others, carrying her own roll of toilet paper under her arm. She was the only one who cleaned the outhouse and threw lye down the hole.

The stew bubbled. Eliza dished it into two thick bowls. "Eat up while it's hot, baby," she said. Selena was too quiet. Eliza needed to fill the space with chatter and said, "That standpipe we use is covered by cardboard and blankets so it won't freeze in the winter, but you know, damn it all, it always does freeze up after 30 below. And you should see the ice! Dangerous! But when we get real froze up, Gus gets his barrel filled up by the City delivery. There's three of us. We pay him something or give him some food to use it."

"How come you don't just have your own barrel? Seems to me it'd be easier," Selena said without enthusiasm,

Eliza warmed to Selena's interest in her domestic arrangements. "City won't deliver to some of us down here. Says we're unsanitary. Bah! The bastards want to get rid of us I guess. But they won't get me out. Not on your life."

"Got some bread or something, Eliza?" Selena asked.

"Oh! Nearly forgot!" Eliza jumped up and came back with a plate of bannock. She said, "Have some of this. Just made it yesterday. You used to like bannock even when you were real small, specially when I put raisins in it." She buttered a piece and said, "D'you remember that? You were here before, right in this trailer, when you were three, baby. Just after your birthday. Over twenty years ago! Boy, does time fly!"

Selena's eyes widened and she put down her spoon. "I was in Whitehorse when I was small? Pop never told me that."

"No?" Eliza thought for a moment and said quietly, "No, I guess your grandfather wouldn't want to talk to you about that. He's too embarrassed to talk about me. My own father. But I brought you here when I came up to Whitehorse, baby. Then Daddy came a couple weeks later and took you back down to Dawson." She waved her spoon in the air frivolously and laughed self-consciously, "His only daughter, gone to hell in Whitehorse, eh?"

The kettle squealed. Eliza got up to make tea with the boiling water, and said with her back to Selena, almost in a whisper, "I'll never forgive him for taking you. That was worse than him sending me off to that damned residential school for five years. He never gave me a chance with you. Whatever he did or said was always the law. Meddling old Whiteman."

Selena began darkly, "You were probably too..." and stopped herself. She put a spoonful of stew in her mouth.

Eliza came back to the table. Too late to stop herself, she raised her eyebrows as if to say, "What?" She knew Selena meant *too drunk*.

Selena said, "Good stew." She dipped a piece of bannock in the bowl.

Eliza was grateful for the reprieve. She hated fighting and wanted nothing more than to keep out of trouble. "Yeah," she said. "Can't beat moosemeat, eh? Bought it from a friend of Gus's this fall."

Seldom angry herself, Eliza would leave wherever she was if people were fighting. She liked living alone for that reason. Less complicated, she said. She had had her share of turmoil in her younger days, wild drinking binges, not remembering what happened the night before, even ending up in jail once or twice overnight for punching another woman over some man she didn't really want anyway. Her twin boys, seven years younger than Selena, were taken away from her by Welfare and were in Dawson with their grandfather, like Selena had been until lately. But Eliza was happier now that she stayed away from all that heavy boozing. She knew when to stop, not like before. Maybe it was just getting older that helped her to drink less. A friend said to her once that she was probably just "sick and tired of being sick and tired." She figured that was how it was.

"I loved you to bits, my sweet little baby. Still do, of course!" Eliza said. She had so much to say to her! "I just hated to see you go to Dawson. But my uncle Harry was here...he wasn't too good for you to be around sometimes."

"Did you have these tiles on the floor then?"

A pleased smile crossed Eliza's face. The conversation was turning easier. "Haven't changed a darn thing since I moved in. Why?" She poured tea into their mugs.

"I think I remember the tiles. The black and white squares."

"Yeah? Well, you played on this floor a lot. You had some blocks and I'd let Uncle Harry help you build things on the floor. Only when he was sober of course. I remember you..."

"Maybe that's what it is," Selena interrupted. She took her mug of tea and moved to the couch. "I'm beat," she said, laying down. "Let's just get some sleep," she said, putting the mug on the floor beside the couch. "I have to leave here early tomorrow." She punched the one cushion into shape under her head and closed her eyes.

In the back room Eliza dug out an old sleeping bag from a cardboard box under the bed and spread it over Selena. "Maybe take off your jeans, baby, you'll be warm enough now," Eliza said. "I'd let you sleep in the bedroom, but it's warmer out here." Selena obeyed, leaving on her socks and underwear.

Enough was said about the past for now. It could wait. While they were in the bar that afternoon, Eliza had glanced at Selena's right hand a few times, when she thought Selena didn't notice, at the hand with the three crippled fingers. That frostbite when she was a tiny baby made her fingers grow wrong. Things like that were better left alone for now.

For an hour before she slept that night, Eliza tossed in bed. She gave up trying to sleep and sat up, chain-smoking. Selena was drinking too much. Maybe it was like some people said. Problem drinking was inherited. Selena should cut down on her drinking, just like Eliza had finally, after the twins were taken away. That was the last blow, the bottom of the barrel, losing her boys. Eliza had gone to an AA group and stayed completely sober for a year after that. Now she knew she was able to stop when she wanted to, and not get in trouble with it. They didn't have anything like a Sprucewood Treatment Centre in those days. Cold turkey, no help, that's how she quit the heavy binges.

Eliza would have to think of some way to convince Selena to go to Sprucewood. Yes, that's what she had to do. She had to save her daughter. What if Selena did some of the stupid things that she had done herself? She would have to talk to her when things were more settled between them. Eliza promised herself that in the morning she would talk Selena into staying with her longer. Maybe she would be given the chance to make up for some of that lost time with her, show her she really did love her. She could teach her a lot of things. They'd be like sisters, they were so close in age.

It would be hard for both of them to talk about, but maybe Selena would even understand about the frostbite some day. Some wonderful day. Eliza hated herself for so many years over what she did to her baby, but she was just a child herself then. Sixteen. No wonder she left her baby in the cabin, went off to a party and forgot to get home in time. It was Christmas; she deserved a good party. It wasn't her fault that it was so damn cold. That old broken-down heater never did hold enough wood in the real cold; even Daddy complained about it. Daddy was supposed to come home from trapping by Christmas and he didn't. She knew it was wrong that night, not to go back home and check, but she kept on partying, driving any cares out of her head. She had passed out in the back room of the party house, and when she woke up, no one would give her a ride home. Their vehicles wouldn't start, they said. She didn't want to walk across the whole town at forty below. Her parka was too thin for that kind of weather, but that's what she finally did. Selena had looked fine when she crawled into bed with her. "Merry Christmas, baby," Eliza had said to her. Every Christmas since then, she had tried to forget. She hated Christmas.

The next morning Eliza sat at the table sewing beads for two hours before she saw Selena moving under the sleeping bag. When Selena rubbed her eyes and groaned, Eliza poured her a mug of coffee. She stirred canned milk and sugar into it, and brought it over to the couch. "Just use the slop pail if you want to pee," she said.

Eliza switched on the bright green transistor radio sitting on the table and went into the bedroom while a lively fiddle tune bounced across the room. CBC Radio was her constant companion. She was always up on the latest local news and even knew what was happening most of the time in places like Ottawa and the States. She knew all the announcers. One of them was a cousin, so they were just like family down there at the station. She phoned them from Gus's whenever she needed the latest weather forecast or had to send messages on Outpost Message Time. She made requests of cowboy music for distant friends, like Patsy Jim in Mayo, who had been in the Chooutla residential school in Carcross with her. Patsy liked the railroad tunes, especially "Movin' On." She said it reminded her of running away from Carcross. The White Pass and Yukon Route railroad brought them to the school when they were little girls. It was the only time either of them had been on a train.

"Look at this, baby," Eliza said, coming out of the bedroom with a piece of orange, green, and white beadwork in the shape of a five-petalled flower and leaves sewn onto a circle of felt. It would later be attached onto a long strand of beads to make a necklace. "Pretty, eh? Mommy showed me how to do necklaces like this before we moved into town from Mooseside. Before she died." Eliza sat down at the table. Her voice turned dreamy and she said, "She died when I was only seven. TB. Like lots of the Indians in those days." She smiled at Selena and waved a hand in the air as if to push something away. "Anyways, you know all that old history, eh? We talked about it that time I seen you in Dawson."

"Yeah." Selena yawned, sipped coffee, and shifted uncomfortably on the couch. "Got any cigs? I ran out."

Eliza brought her a package of cigarettes and an ashtray. "Remember that time I came to Dawson, gave you Mommy's pictures? You still got them I hope?"

Selena looked dully up at her, taking the cigarettes. "Pop's got them."

Going back to the table, Eliza said, "Sure wish you could've knew Mommy. She showed me lotsa good things, even sick in bed like she was. You woulda loved her like I did, I know." Her face brightened and she said, "You know, I can sell these necklaces downtown for two dollars each. Gold Rush Jewellery over on Second buys them from me anytime. Anytime! They sell them for four-fifty sometimes. Depends on how much beadwork. They're real popular. Even the tourists buy them. I sell them in the bar too. Make more money there."

Selena sighed and said, "Yeah. I used to make them in Dawson. Sold some at Grander's store."

"Baby! That's great!" A picture of Selena with her twisted fingers trying to put tiny glass beads on a needle flashed through her mind. Her throat tightened and she swallowed hard. To clear her mind, she stood up. Flinging one arm wide as if she wanted to include the whole world, she said, "Why don't we just make our living here, sewing away every day? To hell with being a waitress or a barmaid, eh? And we could work all year round!" she laughed, slapping her hand on the table in emphasis and sitting back down.

"Sure thing," Selena said indifferently. She finished her coffee. "And be sure to starve to death while you're at it. Stop dreaming. You can't make a living off selling beadwork for Christ's sake. And tanning's too tough a job for somebody by themselves. I tried it once." Eliza saw Selena leaning over a wash tub of cold greyish water in Daddy's yard, twisting a heavy slippery moosehide with her weak hands. She should have been there, helping her.

Dreams were better than the memories, the regrets. "Well, you know... this time of year, late fall, I just wish somebody'd give me a moose hide again," Eliza said, her voice almost musical. "I'd even pay to get it tanned. The money's in mukluks. The price is getting better and I can sell them any old time, not only winter. You can get twenty-five or thirty bucks a pair now, did you know that?" Her small hands touched her feet and moved in delicate dance-like motions around her ankle. "Beaver with long guard hairs and lots of beadwork. That's what they like."

Selena came over to the table, lifted a cellophane packet of pale blue beads, and rubbed it between her fingers. "After breakfast, baby, show me how you can sew." Eliza smiled. They were good for each other.

Somehow Eliza got her daughter sitting at the table after she cleared away the dishes from breakfast. She threw a pile of old *Whitehorse Stars* and the Eaton's Christmas catalogue onto the couch from the table and threaded a needle for Selena, poking it into a red pincushion, a stuffed cloth tomato. With legs spread wide under her skirt and her head bobbing, Eliza dug into the wicker sewing basket she kept under the table. It held her best beads and coloured felt ordered in from Winnipeg. "Look at these. Aren't they beautiful? The latest thing," she said. She opened her hand and showed Selena cellophane packets of tiny gold- silver- and copper-coloured beads.

Selena picked up the copper ones and opened the packet. She spilled some onto a piece of felt and pushed them around with a finger. "Never seen anything like this before. They are pretty."

"Make the strand for this necklace, eh?" Eliza urged, handing her the threaded needle. "The orange and green will go real nice with the copper. Should be able to get three dollars for this one."

They smoked and sewed without speaking for a few minutes. Eliza hummed to tunes on the radio. Suddenly she stopped sewing, pointing to the radio. "Listen to that! Patsy's favourite!" She sang, her voice high and wavering, "There's a big eight wheeler comin' down the track, means my true lovin' baby ain't comin' back...I'm movin' on. Oh, I wish I could sing! Boy do I love that Hank Snow!" she laughed. "He's Canadian, you know, Hank. Imagine him, famous even in Nashville, for Pete's sake. You have to be damn good to do that."

To gather the copper beads, Selena reached with her needle to the small pile on the felt. Unused to the fine movement needed, the three deformed fingers on her right hand curled of their own accord. She pricked herself badly, jumped up, and spilled Eliza's mug of coffee over the table. "Shit!" she shouted. She shook her hand and sucked on one finger. "My goddam fingers! Too fucking stiff!"

Eliza grasped the overturned mug and sped over to the dishpan in the sink. She grabbed the dishcloth and rushed back to the table, saying in a singsong voice, "No problem, baby. Here, I'll get it..." and she began to wipe the oil cloth.

"It's not the fucking coffee that's the problem!" Selena said. She held her right hand in front of Eliza's face and shook it. "It's my damn hand! The hand you left me with!"

As if she were slapped, Eliza sat down hard in her chair, one hand over her mouth, the other automatically wiping up the spilled coffee with the dishcloth. Her eyes darted from Selena to the table and back again like a frightened rabbit looking for escape.

Her face contorted, Selena yelled, "That's what you gave me for Christmas, Eliza! Some mother! Look at it! Look at my hand, will you?" She waved her twisted hand in front of Eliza's face and with an angry sweep of her hand, she brushed the half-finished beadwork off the table. It scattered on the floor. "You went out and got drunk with your shit friends, remember? I hope it was a good party. Was it worth it, worth leaving me in that cabin at forty below to freeze to death?" She strode over to the couch, threw herself onto it, and said in a whisper, "Sometimes I wish I *had* died then."

"No, baby! Please. No. Don't ever say that. Don't say you wish you were dead. It's bad luck. Real bad." Eliza held the dish cloth tightly in her lap, leaned over, and picked the beadwork up from the floor. "Let's not fight, eh?" She sat with the beadwork in one hand and the dish cloth in the other, staring across the room at Selena.

Selena glared. "You even lied about it, didn't you? Said it was some medicine you took when you were pregnant. People in Dawson just loved to tell me that. Boy did they ever! But they knew what really happened, didn't they? And so do we." Her voice was cold, dangerous.

Eliza's eyes closed. Her stomach was hard and her chest was full of pain. She squeezed the soaking dish cloth against her chest. "Please, baby, please," she whispered, opening her eyes. "Please don't say that. I was only sixteen when I had you. Didn't know nothing..."

"Keep your fucking excuses and your beadwork and your stupid trailer! I'm gone, man!" Selena grabbed her purse and jacket from the couch and pulled on her boots. She threw open the door.

"Please stay, baby. It's too cold out there. We don't have to talk about anything. Just one more night." Eliza was still sitting there, begging Selena to stay after the door slammed shut, shaking the whole trailer. She slowly put the dish cloth and the beadwork on the table. Her face was ashen. Under her stained cotton blouse, her breast was cold and wet.

Two days later, Selena was back. A pickup truck dropped her off in the Flats while Eliza was away. Eliza kept the door unlocked even when she was gone, hoping Selena would come. Exhausted from two nights of drinking and sex, Selena fell asleep on the couch. Eliza said nothing when she found her. Eliza saw her through a bad trip on LSD one night a week later, and she knew that Selena was mixing whatever she could get together for a better high. For days or a week at a time Selena would be gone, sleeping wherever she could with men she met in the bars. Eliza knew from her own experience that Selena's memory of much of that time would be lost to her. She kept track of her through friends, and waited for Selena to crash.

It was a mid-December night a few weeks later when Eliza woke, startled. Someone was pounding on her door. Julie Fuller, Selena's old room-mate, pushed open the door. Eliza had nailed up an old blanket to keep the cold out and Julie pushed it aside, stepped in, and called, "Eliza, you here? Wake up! It's Lena. She's in the hospital." Eliza came out of the back room and listened, stony-faced and wide awake. Selena had been badly beaten two nights before. In the early morning at 30 degrees below zero, the RCMP had found her, unconscious, trying to keep warm by curling up in the doorway of the post office. She was dressed in only a light sweater and jeans.

Julie said, "I seen her at this pot party the day before. When I saw her come through the door, I left. I don't want no more arguments with her. I'm glad she's out of the apartment. She's too crazy right now." The day after the party, Julie said, she had heard that Selena was in the hospital. She went to see her after the hospital said that Selena was conscious enough to talk.

"Jeeze, Eliza, both her eyes are black, and her breasts and back are all bruised and scratched."

"What about the cops?" Eliza asked and bit her lip. She couldn't control their shaking. She sat at the table and pulled her dressing gown closer around herself.

"Cops know about it. Before I went in her room, I heard a cop talking to the nurse in the hallway. 'Just as well we don't lay a charge,' he says, 'it's a waste of our time.' Waste of time! You know what else he said? 'Who do you think would believe *her*?' as if she's some scum or something."

"Was she... raped?" Eliza asked. Julie nodded and Eliza drew in a sharp breath.

"Worse than that, Eliza." Julie put her hand over Eliza's. "The doctor says maybe more than once. Selena can't remember nothing, where she was or who she was with. Nothing to go on to lay a charge."

"No shit," Eliza said quietly. She stood up and lit the gas under a pot of old coffee. Her hands were shaking, and she dropped the match.

"Guess what I heard the old White bitch in the next bed say about her," Julie said eagerly. "She says, 'My husband's dead and gone and look where I am, next to her,' she says. Then guess what she says? 'He always told me never even *to walk on the same side of the street* as people like that.' Can you believe it?"

Eliza's fear and shock bubbled over in laughter. "Never to walk on the same side of the street as Selena, eh? Maybe she'll get gonorrhea from breathing the same air as her or something!" She covered her mouth. Her laughter mixed with the tears running down her cheeks.

"Well I showed that old bag, eh? I got right up and pulled the curtain shut around Selena's bed when she said that. And I gave that decrepit Whitey a real dirty look I can tell you! Anyhow, she's left now, the old bitch, dead I hope."

"Did Selena ask you to come here?" Eliza asked, pouring them coffee.

"No. No, she didn't, Eliza. I asked her if she wanted me to, but she told me just to leave her alone. She said if it wasn't for me she wouldn't even be there. Kind of pissed me off."

"Oh, Julie, you know she doesn't really mean that. She loves you a lot."

"Lena's so damn stubborn. You know how she is. So I came here anyways," Julie said. She finished her coffee and said briskly, "Here's some money for a taxi. But that's all I can do," and gave Eliza ten dollars. "I don't want nothing more to do with it, especially if the RCMP get involved. I don't know who she left the party with, but I know most of them guys and I don't want to get nobody into trouble. I gotta stay away from shit like this or my boyfriend Darryl will kill me." She opened the door to leave and said, "Rape, for Christ's sake! What'll she get into next?"

Eliza appeared at the door of Selena's hospital room the next morning with a paper shopping bag of clothes, a pair of her old boots in her hand, and a parka borrowed from Gus over her arm. Selena lifted her arm and covered her face. She said thickly, "Please, Eliza, don't say anything. Just give me the clothes and get lost."

"Not on your life, baby," Eliza said firmly. When she was in the taxi coming over to the hospital, Eliza had told herself she would pretend that the swollen bruised face with the blackened eyes that she knew she would see in front of her did not exist. She held her breath as Selena carefully put her feet on the floor and avoided turning the wrong way while she slipped off the high bed in pain. "I'll go and call a taxi for us," Eliza said, putting the bag and parka on the bed and the boots under the chair. "You get dressed."

"Never mind. Just leave me alone. I'm OK."

In the hallway, Eliza brushed away tears before she could see the numbers on the pay phone. When she returned, Selena was lying on her bed, half dressed. She was shaking with the effort of dressing herself in the nauseous fog of withdrawal, too sick to argue with Eliza's tight-lipped instructions.

When they got to the trailer, Eliza put Selena in her bedroom. For days, she turned away anyone who came to visit and spent her days nursing Selena with light soup and indomitable cheer. She left the trailer once to go over to Gus's to pay him to buy food for them. She slept only briefly. Day and night she sat at the table, sewing beaded jewellery, listening to her radio programs carefully turned down so that she could hear any noise from the bedroom.

Happier than she had been in years, Eliza wiped up vomited soup from the floor and helped Selena walk to the slop pail or to the outhouse. They talked in brief spurts, only about the details of Selena's care. Eliza was relieved that Selena didn't complain about anything.

Four days after she came to Eliza's, Selena was able to sit and eat a real supper. Eliza smiled broadly across the table. "It's so good to see you up and around, baby! And your face is so much better." She cleared away the dishes. "Now, let's talk about Christmas. I love Christmas, don't you?" she lied. "And it's only five days away, can you believe?"

"Guess I'll stay here. Too cold to go anywheres else." It was forty-three below and CBC said it would probably stay cold over the holiday.

Eliza sat down and looked concerned. "Of course you'll stay here with me. Where else?"

Selena walked towards the bedroom. Eliza said carefully to her back, "I went over to Gus's and made a phone call for you today..."

Selena stopped by the bedroom door, turned around. Her eyes narrowed and she asked, "Yeah? What about?"

To get it all out at once, Eliza said, "I called the Sprucewood Centre to see if they could take you." She had called the alcohol treatment centre three times to get advice on what she should do.

Selena's eyes widened. "You did what?!"

"They said..." Eliza cleared her throat, "They said that they would take you. But only if you want to. And if you can stay sober for the next week. Until after Christmas."

"You didn't have any right to do that! You bitch! What business is it of yours what I do with my life?" Selena stomped into the bedroom and Eliza heard her stuffing clothes in a paper bag and putting on her boots.

At the bedroom door, Eliza pushed the curtain aside. Her lips quivering with the effort, she said, "You know, you could die next time, Selena. That makes it my business." She had never said anything to anyone as firmly as that in all her life. Selena swore in disgust as she pulled on her parka, brushed past Eliza, and slammed the door. Eliza's insides twisted in pain. She could hardly breathe.

For a long hour, Eliza sat on the couch smoking and wondering what she could have said that would have been better. The counsellor at Sprucewood had told her that Selena may react with complete denial of the seriousness of her situation. Eliza had prepared herself for telling Selena, thinking over what she would say, how, when...but no scene that she had come up with had the perfect ending to it. She just wasn't smart enough to help her baby.

Forcing herself up slowly from the couch, Eliza locked the door that was never locked. Somehow it felt safer to shut out the world that was so puzzling and made her so exhausted. She undressed and crawled into the bed that Selena had made her home for days. She felt completely empty inside. She could smell Selena's special cologne when she brought the covers up to her face and she breathed it in for a long time before she finally closed her eyes and fell asleep.

Three hours later, Eliza thought she was dreaming when she woke to heavy pounding on the door. Selena's muffled voice was yelling, "Eliza! For Christ's sake, open up! It's cold out here!" Eliza stumbled out of bed in case the dream was real, and opened the door. Selena came in with a rush of cold steamy air and stood in front of her, shivering. "God! About time! It's fucking cold." She threw her purse and paper bag on the couch, took off her parka, and threw it on top of the other things.

Eliza opened her mouth to say something, but Selena lifted her hand in a gesture to keep her silent. Eliza recognized the movement as coming from her own father. Selena said, "OK. OK. I'll do it. Shit. Just to show you." Unsmiling, she said, "I'll go to your goddam Sprucewood."

Eliza nearly tripped as she swept across the room. She threw her arms around her daughter: "Oh, baby, baby, baby...I'm so happy! That's the best Christmas present you could ever give me!" Selena did not resist the hug.

For the next few days, they hibernated from the cold and dark outdoors and pretended it wasn't a holiday. They ignored the persistent knocks on the trailer door from neighbours who called, "It's Christmas!" "Come on, join us for a drink!" "You sick, Eliza?" until Gus opened his door across the way and yelled, "Shut up! Just leave 'em alone!"

Eliza and Selena made it through Christmas in the Flats without a visitor except for Gus and without a single drink. When they weren't asleep or reading old magazines, they sewed beads for hours, quietly smoking and listening to Christmas carols on the radio. Eliza did not want to spoil the comfort they felt, so she kept herself from talking about anything personal. She wanted them to be safe from everyone, including themselves.

On Christmas Day, Eliza gave Selena a necklace made completely of copper beads that she had secretly made when Selena was asleep. Selena gave Eliza a pair of long sparkling silver earrings that she had bought for herself. Gus came over that night with a pair of woolen mitts wrapped in brown paper for Eliza and a platter of leftover turkey and dressing somebody had given him. Eliza made gravy, boiled up potatoes, and mashed some turnips and carrots. They lifted glasses of ginger ale as a toast. Gus and Selena smiled and nodded when Eliza said, "To the best Christmas I ever had."

CHOICES

SPRUCEWOOD ALCOHOL TREATMENT CENTRE, WHITEHORSE, Y. T.

NOTE TO FILE: Maclean, Selena

12/15/73

Selena's mother Eliza Maclean has requested information a few times by phone about having her daughter enter our treatment. She was advised to keep her sober over Christmas and she could be admitted in early January if she was willing. GB

1/8/74

Selena admitted. Appears to have been sober for a couple of weeks. No physical signs of withdrawal and in reasonable health. Not on any drugs for now, but has experimented. Initial assessment interview and group educational work went well. Family background supportive. Prognosis: very good. GB

Jan 12/74

<u>My Story</u>
by Selena Maclean.

OK Mr. Barnes you tell me I got to write this down, to help me think about my <u>HISTORY OF DRINKING</u>. Wow!! I never done anything like this before but nobody has to read it but me and you right? So here goes. "I'm Selena and I'm a alcoholic." You said if I have trouble to start that's a good start. Like AA.

I'm in Whitehorse right now at Sprucewood. But I'm really from Dawson. When I look back it's a real short time, like a dream, the time since I left. Like it all happened to somebody else, like the time before Christmas I was beat up--and I was RAPED! I bet you didn't know THAT, ay? I landed up in the hospital. Most of the time, I just don't think about them things. Like it wasn't my life. It's easy to do that. My real life was in Dawson where things were better. I wasn't in trouble there.

Me, I grew up different than alot of kids, with my grandfather. They call him Indian Dave Maclean, a famous trapper around Dawson. He was real strick but he loved me alot. I was his whole family, he told me that all the time. My real mother and my real father are Indians, even though my grandfather is white. You figure it out!! Anyway, I call him Pop because he's like my real father. He's the best person I ever knew. I had a neat life with him. I never thought things could go wrong when I was young. Then there was Grandma Thomas too. When she was alive, I spent alot of time with her, learning to do Indian sewing and I stayed with her at Moosehide. Maybe you don't know, that's our old Indian village down the Yukon River from Dawson. She died in 69 when I was 19. She gave me her cabin in Moosehide and I still got it. I cry when I think of her, so I don't want to say nothing more about her. She was my real father's mother. He's the chief in Dawson right now. I don't see him and his wife Rosie much. But that's my family too. They said so. Maybe I'll go back someday.

I grew up there in Dawson with my best friend Julie Fuller. I call her Jules, and I always think of her name as <u>jewells</u>. She's presious like jewels to me. Even when we get mad at each other like now. We were so close all that time we grew up. Best friends. Those were fun times, when we were playing around in the old buildings left from the Klondike Gold Rush days. Man, I really loved it when we pretended to be Klondike Kates and stuff!! What a trip! Jules is tons of fun, full of life, while me I'm pretty shy when I'm sober. I always let her lead me around, from the time we were kids. Wow, has she got alot a guts!! She got us into trouble sometimes, fun trouble, you know. She'd fight for me too when those snobs in Dawson picked on me. She comes from a huge family, a real tough bunch, them Fullers. There's <u>tons</u> of drinking in her house, let me tell you. Her mom's Indian and her dad's a Whiteman. She never told me about it, but the whole town knows that her dad sleeps with his daughters. He wouldn't pick on my Jules, though. She wouldn't let him. A teacher, she was mad at us, said one time that Jules and me, we were two sides of the same coin, I guess meaning that we were both the same. We talked about it lots after that teacher said that. I always thought we was different. Now I think that maybe we're alot like each other deep down even if we are different. You know what I mean?

Yours truely, Selena

Thanks for your story so far, Selena. I'm glad you are thinking about some of the ideas we have talked about. And the things you said about your family and Jules are really important for me to know. So now let's hear more about your drinking. What made you start? We need to look at what the patterns may be, so you can learn to stop before you begin again, OK? Greg

Jan 13. Dam cold out today, 45 below. Ice fog too. Glad I'm indoors.
OK, Greg. I can call you Greg, ay? So now you want to know about my drinking. Well, you know what? I was the only one in Dawson who <u>wasn't</u> drinking when we was kids. I started to drink at Grandma Thomas funeral I was so unhappy. OK so maybe it's like you guys say, "you can always find an excuse for starting to drink" so mine is maybe Grandma dying. I learned that anyways in here already, what are excuses and what are reasons. I think it probly would happen anyways, my getting drunk. Everybody drinks real heavy, all my friends and their families. It's a way of life down in Dawson. And Whorse too for some people. So why should I be any different, ay?
Before Grandma died, Michael and I broke up. (Michael taught me how to spell his name right. Most people write it Micheal, but that's wrong) He was real neat, my HERO. He was the social worker in Dawson. Real cute, nice eyes, short and blond, different from the other

guys. I couldn't hardly believe that he wanted to go out with <u>me</u> when he asked me one day!! He even got <u>fired</u> because of me!!! What a drag! He wasn't allowed to go out with me because Pop and me, we looked after my twin brothers. They are Welfare kids. Stupid, eh? What business is it of them what Michael and I did? I thought he, that's Michael I mean, would help me through anything bad, just like my Pop had up till then. I was even gonna marry Michael. I never told anybody that except him. But he left me instead. Said I was too young or something. It hurts me to remember him. I'd still be real happy to be with him. But maybe Julie's right. She always said I depended on him too much. Need to stand on my own two feet, she says, like I use to. Losing him and Grandma are the hardest things I ever been through and both things happened at the same time. That same time I started drinking, so maybe there's my reason, not excuse. The two of them and Pop were my whole life. I thought they would always be there for me, all of them for ever. Pop and Michael and Grandma. I keep telling myself they are all gone from my life. It's strange and hard. And Jules too now I guess. Even she's too mad at me to take me back I think. Right now anyhow. And Pop too probly doesn't want me to come home. Those are all the people that are closest to me and I don't have them no more. Now there's just me. I'm not close to nobody I guess. For now anyways.

------XXXX-------XXXXX------XXXXXX----

THEY ARE <u>NOT</u> KISSES GREG!!!!

This is after lunch. My hands sore but I want to say something. I been thinking about it, if I'm a real alcoholic. When I see that here on the paper it's like its somebody else I'm talking about. But maybe I have to take "ownership" of it like you guys say, ay? Before the pain will go away. I don't know. It's right, one thing what you guys say--I know you have to <u>accept the things you can't change and change the things you can.</u> I kind of like that saying, but it's kinda hard to choose what to change. So maybe writing down my story can help me decide what things I got to change and what I got to accept, ay? That's a big job, I'm only 23. It's hard for me being young. I guess I'm the youngest person in here right now. I know you told me I'm lucky I'm ready to sober up now instead of years from now like lots of other people but they aren't the same like me at all, man. The rest of them slobs in here is a real drag, been drinking for years. And they got no willpower. I had willpower once and I'll get it again. I got some good things going for me, like I was OK before in Dawson. Maybe that was the real me.

Bye. Selena

What a great beginning, Selena! It's really interesting for me to hear some more about your family and about Michael. How about tonight after supper writing a bit more? I am very interested in the fact that you said you were one of the few kids not drinking. What made you choose NOT to drink?

Greg B

Jan 13, night. Dark only at 3:30 today, getting more lighter again.

Hi Greggy!! OK, OK, drinking! Well Jules started me you know. She gave me my first real drink, right behind the church in Moosehide. On the same day as Grandma's funeral. It was vodka and orange, and tasted just like juice. She was the one who turned me on to booze and to dope too not much after. I was drinking and smoking dope, party party every weekend in Dawson by the time Jules asked me to go to Whitehorse and live with her. I guess that was a coupla years after Grandma died.

What made me NOT drink when everybody else was? Man, that's a hard one to answer and I'll have to think about that. Pop was dead against it, even though he drank some himself. He scared me to hell about going overboard with it. He still scares me. I'd have a hard time going back home. And knowing that my mother was such an asshole because of booze makes me sick. I remember the smell of it at Julie's house made me just about throw up, talk about being sick. I think most of all, though, it was Grandma Thomas. She never talked about people's drinking. She just lived a sober life, one of the few people who did. And she kept up the old ways and taught me how to sew. She always had faith in me, that I would be OK, without any lectures. She gave me a lot of time when she didn't have to. I wanted to be just like her. She was above all the Dawson shit. That's why I loved going to Moosehide with her I guess. We got away from things, into the old Indian ways.

But everybody boozing it up around you all the time doesn't help. And it's good for me, a fun trip, drinking. Makes me feel like I'm pretty, and you get lots of friends. And the kids in Dawson accepted me when I drank instead of giving me a hard time about thinking I'm better then them. Man were they mean sometimes! But when I got drunk, I wasn't no longer goody two shoes who thought she was too good for everybody else with my social worker boyfriend Michael, the guy who left me like I said. The booze made me forget alot of bad things like the three twisted fingers on my right hand. Even if you didn't see them Greg, you could probly tell they are crippled by my awful writing. I got them when my mother left me to freeze to death for God's sake in our cabin at forty below so she could drink downtown with her shit friends. <u>Shes</u> totally drunk most of the time, talk about drinking. I'm not like her.

Now I have to go to bed. I been at it all day & my hand is real sore. And this makes me so sad I want to cry. I'll do it tomorrow.
Selena

Hi Selena! I've had a couple of days off and I was really disappointed to see when I got back that you did not finish your story. I know we talked about a lot of these things but sometimes it's really good to write them out, too. You can think more about what's important then. How about it? Tell me why you get sad thinking about Dawson. And tell me more about your mother.

GB

Jan 15, Sprucewood. Warmer today, only 40 below. Ha! Ha!

OK, "GB"!! You say I gotta finish this thing, so here I am again, a good little girl. One thing I gotta say, the food is rotten in here. Cant we just have a pizza once in a while? I asked the cook but she said no it's too expensive. See what you can do, ay? I'm hungry all the time.

Why am I sad thinking about Dawson? You'd be sad too if you had my life now. You know, I used to be different, used to do everything right, pretty good at school, had a job cooking, looked after my brothers, never partyed and I was young too. You're suppose to get smarter as you get older but maybe I was smarter then. I gotta figure that one out I guess. I miss the old Selena. She was stronger, you know, where now I can't get it together nomore. I'm too sad about everything--Grandma, Michael, Pop--I thought being away from Dawson things would change for the better, but it made it worse I guess. It's real hard to think about me in Dawson, like another life, another person. I wish I could figure out this Selena that I am now. It's scary that I might not get the old Selena back, be her again. Maybe I can if I try hard? I'm glad Grandma Thomas can't see me now. I'm sorry, Grandma. Real sorry. I think she can hear me, you know, even dead.

But like I was starting to tell you, there is some good things about drinking. e.x. I was having bad dreams before Michael and I split. I even talked to Grandma Thomas about them, the dreams. But they ended when I started drinking you gotta believe it. Sometimes I can sleep all night when I'm blasted. And when your awake, life's just a party. What's so wrong with that I wonder if it doesn't get out of hand. I was going <u>onward and upward</u> as Jules says. Its a trip when I smoke a joint, too. Wow! It reminds me of how I felt that time in Moosehide when I saw that white caribou I told you about, my Indian guide, I guess you could call him. It's awful hard to describe how I felt then, but smoking pot is close to it so anyway a joint now and then couldn't be all bad, ay? Maybe when I drink I'm just trying to get that feeling again, like when I saw the caribou. Pop hated my drinking when he found out about it. But he's getting so old that I can fool him about what I do. Anyhow, when I was working in Dawson at the Westminster, he needed the money I made so he didn't go too far bitching at me about my partying. I made sure I reminded him about that (the money) whenever we had a fight. Like you said the other day, he's probly scared that I'll end up like Eliza, a useless drunk. But I'm gonna fool him. All of you. That will <u>never happen to me</u>. I would never leave a baby in a cabin at forty below to freeze and go out drinking like she did for one thing. When I drink, I got more sence then that stupid shit mother of mine and all her friends.

My hand's sore. Back tomorrow. Bye from Selena.

Jan 16/74

See, told ya, man! (Next day, in case you didn't notice, GB)

Here's a drinking story, Greggy. You asked for it. My mother Eliza is the title.

When I came up from Dawson, I was real surprised at how many bars you got. And lots of them open til 2 in the morning. Infact there's something like over twenty places to drink somebody said. I guess <u>you</u> know that! STUPID ME, ay? Anyways, it's great - you can pick and choose the music you like to booze to. Right on, man. I don't like the 98. It stinks and it has that lousy cowboy music. Our crowd goes to the ones that are more hip, better music, like the Bamboo. They play ROCK an ROLL, lots of Beatles and Rolling Stones, right up to date. Ever been there, GB? You can go and not drink, too you know. Some time I'll take ya. (joke, right?)

My mother--that's Eliza Maclean, you know her, she phoned you about me--she's a regular in the 98. She has a man she sometimes sleeps with in one of the other hotels I think. When she needs a little cash or a good meal. She's been on Welfare for as long as I can remember. What a drag. She's got a boney face not like other Indians and her hair is still just as black as can be, like me. Everybody says we look the same. She was pretty a long time ago, kind of like Elizabeth Taylor type, you know. Me too. She still likes to look good, takes care of herself, makeup, earrings, permanent in her hair. But you can tell she's ruined by the booze and of course she's lots older too. 15 or I guess 16 years older than me. She's small, like me only even shorter. She's like a nervous little rabbit, skinny, always has a cigarette. Sometimes when I see her, I wonder how she stayed alive all this time.

The first time I saw Eliza (I don't call her mom) after I moved to Whorse, it was in the 98. I was with Julie. We were dancing all that night, pub crawling and drinking beer. It was some kind of boring holiday--Easter or something I think, and we were just tired of nothing to do, just hanging out. Somebody gave Julie a couple of joints, and she wanted to toke it up in the bathroom at the 98. We were walking from the Whorse Inn to the Shannon to meet somebody. Julie couldn't wait to get to the Shannon, so we had to go into that dump, the 98. We just came out of the bathroom, and Julie says to me, in her loud friendly voice, Hey, look, there's your

Mom, over there by the juke box. Eliza was with a Whiteman and a native woman, some cousin of hers I think. Julie starts walking over. Julie should of knew that I wasn't gonna be happy to see Eliza. And that pair that she's with all the time. How can she be friends of them? There a real drag, <u>always</u> in the bar, or you see them begging for money outside the door. I bet you never see them in Sprucewood. Too late for them. Eliza too.

Anyways, Eliza saw me when I tried to get by between the tables. I pulled Julie away and pretended I didn't see. I didn't look Eliza up when I came to Whorse and I wasn't in any mood to see her then neither. Man, I'm sick and tired of her! I'm ashamed of alot of what shes done to our family, me and my twin brothers. The twins were taken away by Welfare. God knows whatever she done with them to get them taken away.

Anyways, she stands up, waves her cigarette at me and her chair falls over behind her! She's always so embarasing. She yells, Hey, Selena, baby, come over here. I heard you was in town. And Hi Julie! Hey, great to see you guys! Shit like that. Everybody heard. <u>"Selena Baby!"</u> She's the only person in the world ever called me that. I tell Jules let's go. I try to get away. She's stinking drunk as usual. Julie likes everybody, even her own screwed up family. She tells me I better say hello at least. I tell her as plain as day without yelling, I don't want to. Get that through your thick head. I got out the door in a hurry. Right there on the sidewalk, I yell at her--You know she's always there on Saturday night. Why the hell'd you want to go in that place for anyway. She says never mind, Lena, let's just forget it. She waves her hand in the air as if that would make it go away. Julie never likes arguing. She just wants everything to be nice and quiet. So I say, Why should I forget it! Now Eliza saw me, I say, it pisses me off real bad. Why'd you let her see us? You're always so fucking loud, Julie. I call her Julie to her face only when she makes me mad. So Julie says, she already knows you're here. She even says she told Eliza ages ago that I was in Whorse. She says Eliza's my family even if I don't like her. She looks at me as if she's better than me or something.

That woman is not my family. My family is my grandfather in Dawson, and he won't have nothing to do with her. Me neither. I tell her that. You might want to stick around shit like that I say to Julie, but I've got better things to do with my life. Then believe it or not, she says to me Yeah, like looking for work, eh? Try that sometime. She never said nothing about me looking for work before. I never seen her so mad at me before. I helped Julie out with the rent when I first came, but its true she paid all the rent a coupla times. I spent everything I had from Dawson eating out, and clothes, having a good time like she said we would. Most of it was Julie's idea too, I just went along. Anyways, then some guys Julie knows come up to her and they ask her to go up to the KK. There was this wild group from Fort St. John playing in the bar, the Alaska Highway Kings. Julies friends had to drive up the 2 Mile Hill to get there, but one guy had a car. Julie didn't ask me to come, so I just left them without saying nothing and walked to our apartment. No one gave a shit, even Julie.

It makes me mad to think about this. Mad and tired. I'm sick of this now, it's a real drag, man. Whats the point to write all this crap anyways? SM

Well, Selena, the point is that you have to take a good look at what you have been doing. For instance, you say your mother drinks too much. Is that a reason for you to choose to drink, or just an excuse? Are you blaming her for your own problems? You have to figure these things out if you are going to stop and make the right choices. What happened after you left Julie outside the 98? Please write some more.

Greg

Jan 17/74. Good breakfast today, like Pop used to make. Finally! Warmed up. 30 below. Yuk yuk.

Hi Greg!! I'm over my mad from yesterday. I'd like it better if you guys let us out of here once in a while. Why can't we just go to a movie, come home after? Ask them, ay Greggy?

So here goes. After I took off from Julie, I made up my mind to take the job barmaiding in the Capital Hotel somebody told me about. Maybe it's a good way to make alot of money with the tips, working the bars, but I figure it must be a drag, so I didn't really want to work there. Your sober when everybody else is having a good time and when you get off work and are ready to party, they're all passed out, right? And in the daytime, your time off is when all your friends are working except the other staff from the bars. You must get sick and tired of the same old faces pretty quick. It's a lousy social life. They don't like you to drink neither, some of them bars. Specially if your working. Some customer says have a drink and you gotta take a tip instead.

So the night I decided I'd go for the job at the Capital anyway I came home early, prepare myself, you know. About midnight, from a house party. Some guy started a fight over a new white girl in town and the cops were called and I was disgusted with them all. I was gonna tell Julie that I decided to take the job at the Capital after all. I went into the bathroom, and guess what I found. This NOTE. I kept it cause I'm gonna throw it back at her some day. I found it in my purse when I was getting ready to come here. I'll tape it on the page here. (makes it longer, right? joke, GB.) Sorry it's so wrecked. Anyways, you can tell she can't spell worth a dam.

Selena--

Im leaving this on the toilet where I know youll see it. because from the sounds of things last night you will be sick some more this morning. Im fed up with you coming home drunk every night and then not looking for work the next day. You have been in Whorse for over 3 months, and you have never lifted a finger to look for work, and you ow me *rent money. I like my fun, but you go to far, I told you that a couple times, but you were probly to blasted to hear me. Maybe this will smarten you up. Darryl wants me to live with him, and that's what I'am going to do, you can leave right away, he will just move in here. I'm at his place right now. You can go and be with that dumb Jerry that you think is so cute.Julie*

Whos she to talk about drinking!! For Christ sake! I just kind of snorted when I got that note. She wouldn't really kick me out I didn't think. Not when she found out that I was gonna work at the Capital. I figured that if I took the job at the Capital, then she'd let me stay for awhile until I got paid. And by that time, everything would be OK again. She never stays mad for long, and she'd probly talk Darryl into it too, my staying with them. Julie never came home all that night. That was the first time I got hard liquor in the liquor store, that next morning. I just got my Indian card with my new Band Number from DIA to prove that I'm 21. I just walked right in and bought a bottle of vodka. I was very selfconsious about it, but no one was surprised or even asked for my ID. It was easy. The lady didn't even seem to know I existed. It helped. You know sometimes its a real drag, everybody knowing everybody else and everything you do, like in Dawson? It's kinda nice to not know people sometimes. You know what I mean? You can hide. After I bought the vodka, I went home and had a couple, waiting for Julie. I was gonna get down to the Capital but I phoned there and said I was looking for work and I'd come in later. Better not to go in drinking, ay?

Julie never came, and I spent the rest of the day drinking the bottle and playing loud music on Julie's stereo, waiting for her to come home. I got so mad at her!! She wanted me to leave and I wanted to fight with her. I had it all planned. I would tell her about the Capital job as my final parting shot. Then she would get all soft like she does, and let me stay. It would all be fine in the end. But I think she changed with that boyfriend of hers moving in.

She came home from work and I guess found me naked in the bathtub, passed out. <u>That</u> I have to admit was pretty stupid of me. I don't even remember having a bath I was that far gone! The water ran out of the tub. Was I stupid drunk! She and Darryl got me onto the couch and I kind of woke up when they were putting my nightgown on me. I remember telling her what a good friend she was, taking care of me all the time. I really love her, you know. The next morning, I got up after they left, and my things were in boxes and paper bags right by the door. She didn't have to leave me a note. I got the hint all right. Some friend she was!

But you know, I feel real bad about Jules. And I guess she was right in a way. I'm just trouble these days. But I tried my best. Man, what more can I do? Not my fault Julie fell in love with Darryl and didn't want me round her place, right? So, Greg, tell me what I did wrong, ay?

SM

Selena, I'll just ask you this question: why did you choose to go and buy that bottle instead of looking for a job? GB

Jan 19, morning.

Missed yesterday. It was Sunday. Gotta have one day off, ay, GB?

Anyways, I told you why I bought the vodka. Julie made me do it, kicking me out like that. I was pissed off. Yeah, OK! I admit it - that was pretty stupid, looking back, I already said that. But it was like something took over in my head. I wanted to do something wrong, to hurt Julie, or maybe myself too. I sure hated myself the next day. I had a hangover like never before. Wow, my head pounded like a hammer, man!! It wouldn't go away, even with lots of aspirins. I drank a beer from the fridge, then I got dressed and went downtown. I was kinda shaky, it was weird. I had to wear sunglasses because the sun was so bright and it bothered me so much. I didn't know what to do. I didn't know nobody good enough in Whorse to ask if I could stay with them. We had only saw Julie's friends. And I didn't want to give her the satisfaxion of knowing that I had to go to her friends for help. No way.

But I did go to look for work, Greg, even hung over. When I got to the Capital, the manager was real snotty. You know what happened? He said because I didn't show up yesterday, he gave the job to somebody else. He gave me a big lecture - blah blah blah - some shit about being reliable until I told him to go to hell. You know what? The woman he hired musta been 40, with dyed red hair and chewing gum all the time. Man was he desprate. He didn't care who he hired. Anyway, I should of knew better. I don't stand a chance to work there, being Indian. They never hire Indian barmaids in there. I ordered a beer, and sat at the bar. I was as depressed as I would ever be in my life. What was I gonna do now. I had to find a place to live. Then in the mirror, I saw Eliza come in the door with this man and woman she was with in the 98, those ones I hate. I turned away and tried to ignore her, but she saw me and came over. She was all bubbly and excited, calling me <u>baby</u> and introducing me to her friends. She was sickening, man. She says, my only daughter, from Dawson. Isn't she pretty? Like me when I was young. All that crap. I was too depressed to care who I was with, so when she said to join them, I did. We moved over to a table in the back, and when we got settled, Eliza asks, so, where you working, honey? Staying with Julie? I said I got no job, and just got shafted there in the Capital. And I guessed I didn't have a place to stay neither. How come, she asks, all worried-like. I say, Julie kicked me out last night. And then, dam it all, I started crying, right there, in front of everybody. <u>Dam it all!</u>.

Probly if I didn't cry, I wouldn't be with Eliza now. I took off to the bathroom and slammed the door. I threw cold water on my face, and I combed my hair over and over until I thought they left. When I came back to the table to get my coat, Eliza was alone. She looked real worried. She grabs my hand and says she sent them away cause she wanted to talk to me alone. My poor baby, she calls me. God how she makes me sick with that baby crap. I pulled my hand away. She wasn't happy about that, but she says, Come and stay with me for awhile, baby. Baby. She always calls me that and it makes my skin crawl. I got a place, a little trailer, not much, she says. Whiskey Flats. You're welcome. Stay as long as you want. I'd love to have you, y'know. I told her the idea was stupid. Who wants to live in Whiskey Flats if they got a choice? Later on she says I always loved you, no matter what. She told me that once when I saw her when she went to Dawson, too. I hate her. She couldn't look after me when I was a kid. Why should I have to be with her now? I hated the thought of even being alone with her in the bar, but I stayed at the table. I guess I hoped somebody would show up. Maybe a friend of Julie's, somebody who could help me, or even Jules. She'd be her usual self, say sure, come on back.

We spent the rest of the afternoon there, drinking, sometimes with Eliza's friends, sometimes alone. I talked to her friends but not to her. Once when we were alone, she tried to talk to me about Pop. You know, Daddy has been a good father to you, she says. She says she's glad about him looking after me. But he can be mean, too, she says. She says he treated me different from her, can you imagine. It makes me sick to hear her talk about my Pop. I don't want to be reminded that he was her father too. I just told her, Look man I got enough on my mind without talking about Pop, stop being a drag. I told her he was a hell of alot better to me than she ever was. And if you don't shut up, I'll leave, I says. That felt real good. She was quiet after that.

I was getting more madder at Julie too, dumping me like that. I decided I'd get out of her apartment soon as I could. She'd be sorry. I always took her the way she was, even coming from that lousey family of hers. Why can't she accept me the way I am? That's what being friends means, doesn't it, Greg?. Taking people the way they are, not trying to change them. Later on we got hungry and Eliza convinces me to stay with her. I tell her only for one night. She has some moose stew at home she says. We take a taxi so I can get my things from Julie's in case she just throws them out on the street. I just hoped Julie would be there. I was gonna tell her off dammed good. Then it would be over, and I could stay there, see? She always ends up being the one who gives in. But Julie wasn't there. And I could see some of Darryl's clothes in the closet. My things were still by the door in boxes and bags. She was switching from me to him, I could see it then. I didn't even leave her a note that day I left I felt so bad. What could I say?

Maybe I was wrong, what I did, not paying rent, not looking for work too serious, I see that now. I seen Julie a couple times since then, across Main Street. I had to turn around so I wouldn't bump into her. I felt too ashamed, you know, and what could I say to her? She's been good to me, always was. Pop said I was too stubborn for my own good, just like him. And yeah I guess Jules came and saw me when I was in the hospital. But I told her to get lost. She left before I could say I didn't mean it. Eliza said

Jules went to see her and paid for her taxi to come and get me out of the hospital. When I get out of here, I'll tell Jules how sorry I am. I swear.

I thought it was only for a night or two, staying with Eliza, but it turned out to be alot longer. She owed me anyways, after the way she left me in Dawson. Eliza will get me drinking when we're together I know, even if we didn't drink over Christmas. I'm here to get away from her and all that crap. If I could do it in Dawson, I can do it here, right?

This whole thing has took five days to write and I don't want to write no more. It's too fucking hard. So here it is. That's all, GB.

Good bye. Selena.

NOTE TO FILE: Maclean, Selena

Uncompleted treatment. Miss Maclean left Sprucewood Centre 01/20/74, saying that she would sober up on her own. She was angry at another client when she left but we hoped she would return. At this writing, her whereabouts are unknown and clients say they have seen her drinking downtown. Denial of her addiction is obvious from her written history and her statements in group, but she showed some good insights about the people in her life which I believe came from the writing. Underneath the bravado I have sensed fear, and I believe she wants to change. She has a lot going for her: young, good support with friends and family, and a stubborn pride in herself. A good candidate for sobriety, given time and luck. She may find courage to choose to change if she returns to Dawson.

File closed 01/30/74

<u>Gregory Barnes</u>
Caseworker

JAN'S LAST WISH

Jan tried to pull the hospital covers closer to his chin, his long pale nails scratching the white sheet without effect. "Eighty-six years...long enough to live," he said. "No use to nobody no more. Even to myself." Curled under his unshaved chin, his translucent fingers appeared as if they belonged to someone else. "Damn cold in here," he grumbled. His scant white hair was soaked with sweat.

"Sixty-five bloody years in the Klondike and you still don't know how to get warm old man?" his friend Dave chuckled, rubbing his full beard. He was being too loud. He stood up abruptly and his long legs nearly pushed the chair over. Stripping blankets from the other bed, he spread them over Jan's spare body. Jan smiled and began coughing with shallow, quick breaths.

They were on the second floor of St. Mary's Hospital, the formal building that had housed the headquarters of the Northwest Mounted Police during the gold rush in Dawson City. Dave looked out the window at the junction of the Klondike and Yukon Rivers below so he didn't have to think about knowing that Jan would not be put into the nursing home on the ground floor.

Leaving the hospital, Dave trudged gravely home up Church Street to Eighth Avenue. He passed weathered grey frame houses and shops left empty from a better time in Dawson City. Jan was only twelve years older than Dave. He knew those years would go by too quickly.

The next day, the head nurse phoned Dave. Jan had died quietly in his sleep at noon. Dave rushed down to the hospital and insisted on being the one who lifted Jan out of the bed onto the hospital cart that would take him to the basement. With the nurse and orderly fussing around, Dave reached under the sheet covering his friend and neighbour of twenty-eight years, braced his heavy frame, and lifted. Jan weighed less than the sack of flour Dave had at home. He could feel his ribs against his arm. The sheet slipped off Jan, flowing around Dave's legs to the floor. Dave stood for long moments between the bed and the cart looking at the gaunt face that was finally without the torment of illness. He closed his eyes and thought of their hunting trips together, playing cribbage all night, helping each other get wood in the fall. Where did all that go so fast?

Dave tried to bury him the way Jan had long ago said he wanted: no fuss, no trying to find relatives, just plant him in the ground and then have a few drinks to his memory. But Jan was a member of the Yukon Order of Pioneers, and the president said the Order would take over the funeral arrangements even though Jan hadn't been to meetings for years. Dave had nothing to do with the Pioneers, and suspected them of questionable secret rituals. He heard that they voted on whether to admit new members, by passing around a hat. You threw in a white ball if you accepted the new man, a black one if you didn't. Even one black ball meant you couldn't join. Dave found their rules "medieval" he said once to Jan.

At the Anglican church service for Jan, one of the Pioneers laid a new purple and yellow fringed sash across his folded arms in the coffin. Then he was taken up the Dome Road to the section of the graveyard with "YOOP" across the gate. Besides Dave and the minister, six men stood around the hole in the ground. Jan had led a quiet life alone. In the July sunshine, the Pioneers' sashes, slipped on over seldom-used suit jackets, made bright diagonal patterns across the chests of the men standing three on one side, three on the other. Their bare grey heads bowed while the minister said a prayer. Dave shuffled his feet and his eyes narrowed as the solemn YOOPs did their duty for one of their own. Churches and all them so-called benevolent organizations, a waste of time. No time of day when you're alive and need it, but claiming your soul when you kick off. Dave shook his head and made himself remember the good times with Jan; it was life that mattered, not death.

Afterwards, Dave went straight to the liquor store and bought a bottle of the dark rum that Jan drank at Christmas. It was after midnight when he fell into bed, the half-bottle of rum on his bedside table. His tears surprised him.

Years before, Jan had made Dave promise to burn down his cabin when he went. "You can have the land," he had said. "Makes a good extension for your garden. But the cabin, just burn her down, eh? Get rid of everything." Jan reminded Dave of that promise while he was in the hospital. It made

Dave uncomfortable, but he had nodded and said, "Sure thing. Maybe I'll get the fire department to do it. Good practice."

Now the RCMP were telling Dave he had to search Jan's cabin for some evidence of a will. That new red-headed cop had come to Dave's the day after the funeral and said it would be easier on everybody if they could find Jan's will. There was the cabin and the lot, and the old Ford pick-up to consider. Jan had kept everything in good shape, so even if whoever was in the will wanted to sell, it was all worth something. Dave searched his memory, but he knew Jan hadn't said anything to him about a will. What if there were relatives in Sweden who had to be informed, named in a will if he found one? He didn't give a hoot about keeping the property for himself. It was just that the whole rigamarole was trouble for everybody. Jan wouldn't have wanted to be a nuisance.

The hospital staff weren't able to find the key to Jan's cabin in the pockets of his clothes, so Dave would have to break the lock. He had put off the job until he got the letter from the Territorial Agent a few days after the cop's visit. The letter assured him in polite language that he would not be charged with breaking and entering, that he did not need to make an inventory of the possessions, just look through the cabin for anything that would indicate he had living relatives or a will. The letter went on too long, and more or less ordered him to do the search. Dave had resisted. He was never one to take orders. Today he had to get to it, a final thing he could do for Jan. He stood at the window of his cabin with the last of the dark rum in his mug of morning coffee and gazed out at Jan's two-room white frame cabin across the lane. He had spent countless evenings there, drinking the pungent homebrew that Jan made and kept in the root cellar under the kitchen floor. When Jan became sentimental about Sweden during those long evenings together, Dave would ask him why he came to the Yukon when he missed the old country so much. That would always get him talking. Over the years, Jan had added a little more each time to his story.

Two generations ago in Sweden, a romantic twenty-year-old Jan had experienced the miracle of falling in love with sixteen-year-old Ana Stefansson. Jan said, more than once, "She was not so beautiful, but she was nice and fat." The Stefansson's owned the fish canning company and a lot of the rest of the village where Jan's ancestors had fished for centuries. Ana was their only daughter and they had given her a good education. "Even so young, she used to play the organ in the Lutheran Church," Jan said proudly. "Won some prizes in Stockholm for playing, by Yesus." Her parents allowed Ana to see Jan. "We'd walk home together after church on Sundays. It was a good match for us Ericksons, but we were just fisher folk, not rich enough for them Stefanssons, no sirree. There was never talk about us getting married. I could tell that they were going to turn her against me before too long, yah, I could tell...," Jan would say, slowly shaking his head every time.

In the national newspaper, Jan read about gold mining in Alaska. A second Klondike, they said. The Panhandle of southeast Alaska looked like it would be country just like Sweden where he could make his fortune twice as quickly, digging for gold and fishing. "I dreamed of coming home with a pocket full of gold nuggets. Marry my young bride, yah?" He told Ana his plans, and asked her to wait for him. She wanted to go to the university and study music. She would wait for him. "So I saved for months, borrowed some money from my father and spent it all to cross the Atlantic." He worked his way through the Panama Canal, and finally sailed into Juneau on a fishing boat.

He sent enthusiastic letters about Alaska back home to his waiting Ana. "I was real careful. Didn't tell her the truth about the cold, the long distances, the isolation. But I didn't learn the English too quick. Had lots of trouble getting work because of the English." Dawson City sounded promising for work, so he headed over the White Pass by train into the Yukon. "Oh, how I hated to leave the Pacific! When I got here, I even took jobs because they were near the water, yah? Labouring on the creeks, the gold dredges, when I couldn't work on the river boats. Saved every penny. Every penny. Didn't drink, didn't gamble, stayed home when all the other fellas were out having a good time." He tried his hand at placer mining, "Like all the idiots," he said. "Went into working a claim with Peter Larson. 35 Above Discovery on Bonanza."

After five years, he saw it would take a lot longer than he hoped to make his fortune, and he still wanted Ana. "So I wrote to her to set a date. I stretched the truth a bit. Even borrowed money to look like I'd struck it rich. I thought to go back, get married, then bring her over here, yah? Once we got married, then I'd tell her we were coming back North. Who could argue then, eh?"

"Including Ana", Dave had commented.

"Waall, I'd be the husband then, see? Not Ana, not her family, none of them could say nothing," Jan had said, looking away while he tipped his bottle up to finish his brew. "Guess all's I can say is that I wanted her too much to worry about what she wanted. Didn't get a chance anyhow. Not a bloomin' chance."

He never received a reply from Ana after three letters saying he was coming home to marry her. His mother wrote him that Ana had married the village minister weeks before Jan's first proposal letter had arrived. Jan never again had a woman in his life if it looked like it might last. He said he didn't trust them. "And as if that wasn't enough, the next summer, Peter Larson and I lost all our money on that damn piece of frozen ground, after working day and night for months in the muck and cold. All my savings and the money I borrowed went into that damn sluicebox and down the creek. I was in debt to the bank for the first time in my life, too." He was "miserable bitter." He never told anyone about Ana for years, but by the time Dave built his own cabin across the lane from Jan, he was fond of telling the romantic story of his youthful quest for gold and his failed romance. "And, you know, kind of a penance, I guess, when you look at it. I never again tried to deceive anyone on purpose. Brings bad luck, that does. Don't pay, neither, yah? In the long run, I mean." Dave had never heard anyone say a bad word about Jan. He had paid his penance well.

Draining the last of the rum and coffee from his mug, Dave picked up the crowbar he had dug out of the back shed the night before. At Jan's cabin the hasp came off the door jamb with one pull. He pushed open the door. Stepping inside, he shivered a little in the still, cool air of the kitchen. It smelled vaguely of cabbage. The place was as neat and clean as he knew it would be. There were no dirty dishes on the table, and all Jan's outdoor clothing was hung up neatly on the wall beside the door. The rocking chair in the middle of the room had the years of Jan's sitting imprinted on the green corduroy cushion.

There was only one place a will might be: in that old tin biscuit box Jan kept on the shelf over his bed. Dave took off his boots and placed them side by side at the door. He tried to shake off the feeling that someone could see him and paced self-consciously into the back room. He hadn't been inside Jan's bedroom before, though you could see straight into the room from where they always sat beside the table in the kitchen. It was dark. He had forgotten that the electricity would be cut off, and he hadn't brought a flashlight. The one window at the back was half-covered by a blind. He raised the blind and saw the black tin box on the shelf above the bed. He had seen Jan put his bills and receipts into it. With the box under his arm, Dave looked around the room. No, there was no other place that important papers might be. So that he wouldn't have to come again to check, he pulled open the drawer in the bedside table. Hunting magazines. Pipe tobacco. A small glass jar full of pennies. When he shoved the drawer back in, the alarm clock fell over, startling him with the sharp ring of the metal bell. He sat the clock upright. The fall had made the clock start ticking again. It had stopped at midnight. Or was it noon? Dave remembered that Jan had died at noon.

"Stop spooking yourself and get out of here, you old fool," Dave said aloud. "Just doing as I'm told, Jan. Don't you get funny on me now."

Dave pounded the hasp back into the door jamb with the crowbar. He wondered if there was any of Jan's home brew left in the root cellar. Probably would be. Maybe he'd come back for some later. He knew Jan would have hated to have it go to waste. He'd have to come over again anyway, with the tin box, to put it back on the shelf.

Relieved, Dave walked down the lane. What the hell was he going to do about Jan asking him to burn his place down? Probably all kinds of red tape involved in burning property inside city limits. Bah. Jan's foolish talk. With all the complications about wills and relatives, who knows what crimes the cops might nail him for. Forget that promise, Jan. Just don't haunt me over it, eh? Dave chuckled as he opened his own door.

Dave sat at the table, wishing now he had picked up some of the cool bottles from Jan's root cellar to keep him going while he had to go through the dead man's personal things. He sat the tin box in his lap, lifted the lid, and scooped several papers from the top. He sorted the bills into piles: from the grocery store, electric light company, one from the garage for a new muffler on the Ford, all stamped "paid", a large brown envelope full of cancelled cheques and pension notices.

Dave took another fistful out of the box and noticed a blue envelope with foreign stamps amongst the papers. He couldn't remember Jan ever talking about getting letters from Sweden. He looked for the return address. Could be the name of the village Jan was from. He slipped the one folded page out. All in Swedish. Of course it would be. No date, but the paper was old, marked with smudges as if it had been handled a lot. They would have to find someone to translate if the letter looked like it had relatives' names in it. There was another blue envelope with Swedish stamps. Not opened. Another one, sealed too. Strange. Dave sat with the three letters in one hand. Who would keep letters for years but not open them? Well, unopened letters weren't his business. He put them on the table.

Where the hell would a will be? What would it look like anyway? He reached for the last of the papers in the box and his arm brushed the table.

The uneven pile of grocery bills floated to the floor. He reached down to pick them up. "Damn it all!" he shouted as the tin box clattered on the wooden floor. Several papers drifted under his chair.

He stood up, moved the chair, knelt on the floor, and began shuffling the papers together. An old brown photograph caught his eye. He picked it up. A wedding. A slim man, shorter than the bride, frowned into the camera. Must be a brother; sure looked like Jan. She was smiling, a big plump blonde. He turned the photograph over. On the back in Jan's hand was written: "Jan Erickson. Ana Erickson."

SLEEPING FOREVER

It was Julie Fuller's chance to be happy, to get away from her family. "They're dragging me down," she told Selena. "I'm divorcing all of them, headed down the road," she said with a wave of her hand south. Proudly, on her own, she left Dawson City and went to the vocational school in Whitehorse for a whole year. She took the hairdresser's training, and graduated as an apprentice, like she always said she would. She even got the job she wanted at Kut 'n' Kurl on Main Street in Whitehorse where regular customers ask only for her.

She has her own apartment, lots of clothes, and friends. She meets Darryl Mason at a dance and soon afterward, they begin living together in her apartment. She can't believe that anyone as attractive and as street-smart as he is might be interested in her. He's from north of Edmonton, part Cree, taller than any of the Yukon natives, and strong. Julie calls him "My tall, dark, and handsome hunk." She loves every inch of his body. They have lived together for nearly two years and are looked upon as a permanent couple by their friends. Life is finally giving Julie what she deserves.

Darryl never talks to anyone about himself. Julie doesn't even know his age, although he is obviously about ten years older than she is. She has made up a birthdate for him because she loves to celebrate and to give him things. Sometimes she shifts the date of his birthday, or adds another one, so that they can have a party. His birthdays are their private joke. Darryl drinks a lot, but so does Julie, and everybody they know drinks too. The drugs he sells are another thing; she worries about that, even though he sells only to people they know. He introduces her to cocaine which she likes. She takes a few hits of LSD to please him. They laugh a lot.

A friend of Julie's who has spent some time in Edmonton says she thinks Darryl is married and has a couple of kids there. When Julie tries to ask Darryl questions about his life in Edmonton, he tells her it's none of her business. Once he yells at her: "If you don't shut your face, this guy is long gone." She tries to apologize, but he disappears for two weeks. When he comes back, he says he had business in Edmonton. She is terrified to ask him anything more, afraid that he will leave for good. It makes her sad sometimes, but it's easier for her if she's like the monkeys she saw once in a picture book at school: she hears nothing, sees nothing, and speaks nothing.

The second winter they are together, Darryl wants to put sheets of clear plastic on the inside of the windows of the apartment to keep out the cold. When they spread the plastic out on the carpet to cut it, Julie finds herself talking about a movie she saw once, where a woman spread plastic garbage bags around the room. It was to catch the pieces when she shot herself. "I wouldn't want to leave a mess, either," Julie says. "Nobody should have to clean up something like that." He says he thinks she's nuts.

After they finish the windows, Julie tries to tell Darryl about her brother Paul, about how she had to clean up her parents' bedroom after the cops had left, when he shot his head off. Darryl shouts at her: "For Christ's sake, Julie, I don't want to hear any more of this shit! Forget it!" He grabs his jacket. He opens the door, looks back, and says, not without concern, "You're sick, you know. Go see a shrink or something." She thinks maybe he's right. She has been really depressed lately.

****

The front door had crashed, shaking the two-storey frame house in the North End of Dawson City. Julie's eyes opened to the freezing blackness before she was fully awake. By the phosphorescent numbers on her clock she saw it was close to three o'clock in the morning. The bars had been closed for half an hour. She heard her two nieces whimpering in their sleep from the mattress on the floor beside her bed, but the other three children on the far side of the room were silent. Shuffling past the ladder nailed to the wall that gave access to the top floor, her mother and father grumbled complaints at each other and went into the back bedroom downstairs.

Julie shifted onto her side and yawned. It was the week before Christmas. She had to get up for school in the morning. Maybe she could skip school. It was so near the holidays. If neither of her parents got up, she would be responsible for looking after the younger ones. Two of her older sisters were gone to Whitehorse; the other two lived in Dawson apart from the family with boyfriends. She would have to light the fire, wake the kids up, make breakfast, get them dressed, find something for their lunches. Then maybe she could catch some sleep after that if she stayed home. She was always so tired.

In the room below, Julie heard someone throw something soft (a parka? Blankets?) to the floor. Her mother's hoarse voice came through the floorboards in the winter cold. "I thought you bought a bottle to bring home, Caleb, you cheap asshole. Where the fuck is it?" Julie heard the rasping of a cigarette lighter. Her mother said, louder, but through her lips, pinched to hold the cigarette: "Or do I have to go out and get some myself?"

"Go to sleep, for God's sake, Mary Ann. I gotta go work in four hours," her father said, his voice sullen. "You've had enough, you stinking Indian." The bedsprings creaked as he climbed into bed.

"Shit on that, Whiteman!" Mary Ann shrieked. "Gimme the money then!" Julie's nieces stirred, awake but silent.

Caleb mumbled, "Go to hell."

From the one other room upstairs Julie's older sister Kathy said, "Shit!" Everyone listened intensely to feet shuffling around in the room below. There was a brief silence. Then something hit the wall with the sound of breaking glass.

Their father's muffled voice said, "Put out that damn cigarette and get into bed." Through the cracks in the floor, the girls saw the light go off below them.

Crawling into Julie's single bed, her two nieces hugged her, front and back. It was crowded, but Julie felt warmer with them in bed. She whispered to the dark: "Just leave, Mom, just leave." Then they could get back to sleep. Sometimes she wished she could sleep forever, she was so tired.

With her foot, Julie pushed one of the girls' legs off her own under the covers. They were already asleep in the warmth of her bed. She turned on her back, brushing her fine brown hair away from her cheek. She tried to distract herself by thinking about her hair. Her pale colouring and freckles were inconsistent with the Athabascan bone structure of her face. She had been teased all her life for being a "white Indian". She thought of her face as flat and boring. Although it was not in fashion, she used makeup heavily around her eyes to give them some drama. When she became a hairdresser, she'd learn what she could do about her looks. She would know more about makeup then.

In the room below, bedsprings creaked with the weight of an adult sitting down roughly. Her mother muttered, "You never let me have any fun. Fuck you, old man! I'm going over to the party." The light switch chain tinkled against the naked bulb as she pulled the string hanging from it. "Damn this parka. Zipper never fuckin' works...where the hell's my other boot?"

They were all awake again upstairs. A streak of light swung across the roof above them, back and forth across the ceiling, back and forth, from the light hanging in the bedroom below. Julie imagined her father's frowning face as he searched for the string to turn the light off. He said, "It's 40 below out there. Don't be so goddam stupid."

A new sound below. Heavy footsteps. It was Paul, stomping across the floor from his small room at the back into the doorway of the other bedroom. Over his mother's protesting voice, he yelled: "Stop your goddam fighting!" Something thumped onto the floor. "There's your goddam boot, now get out of here if you have to."

Good. Now it'll stop. Paul was two years younger than Julie, the first boy of the nine children, and the best looking child, darker than the rest. Everybody said he would be important one day. Even their father listened to him. He had a special place in the family, a kind of perverse bargaining power over their parents. Last year, in one of their drunken fights, Julie heard Mary Ann tell Caleb that Paul wasn't his real son. Julie didn't know whether she should believe it or not.

Caleb yelled, "Leave your mother alone!" Feet scraped the floor. "Maybe he's hurting Grandma," one of the girls whispered, wonder in her voice. The scraping stopped.

Julie heard Paul say slowly and deliberately, the words coming through his teeth, "You guys quit your goddam fighting right now...or...or *I'll shoot myself*!" Julie sucked in her breath. He had never said anything like that before.

Her mother's coarse laugh made Julie's ears ring. "Go ahead, Smartie, you just do that!" Mary Ann yelled. The bed gave a loud groan as she stood up. In the silence there was a little click. Julie sat up abruptly.

"No Paul! Don't!" Caleb demanded. The bed creaked. "No! Oh, no!" A loud blast echoed through the frozen house. Caleb moaned, "No! Oh, God, no!" Julie was climbing down the ladder. She didn't remember pushing away the screaming girls who clung to her, or shouting at them, "Just stay here!"

Paul had done it. Right there in the doorway of the bedroom. Julie's father had grabbed the rifle--too late--from Paul's hand. He stood immobilized, his back to Julie, the rifle hanging at his side. His legs framed Paul's body on the floor so that Julie couldn't see above Paul's waist. When he turned, Caleb's face and chest were bright red. His underwear, soaked with blood, gleamed with a strange light. Her mother was slumped on the floor between Paul and the bed. There were bits of flesh and bone stuck to her open parka. She had one boot on, and the other was still in her hand. She scraped the floor with her legs, trying to sit up. The expanding pool of blood made her slip.

An hour later, Caleb told the RCMP that Paul had thought the rifle wasn't loaded, that he was only trying to scare them. But everyone in the house knew the guns were always loaded, a habit from living in the bush. Caleb had warned them about it many times. He locked his guns in the shed after that and kept the key in his pocket. Some of the town gossips had said, glee and shock in their voices, that Mary Ann admitted she handed the gun to Paul. Julie made herself think it was a lie.

Paul was not the first to do it. Julie knew all the other young men in Dawson who had shot themselves. In the weeks after Paul did it, none of Julie's friends wanted to talk about how people shot themselves, not in the kind of detail she needed. They talked more about how to have sex with somebody than how to shoot yourself. She was left with having to imagine every detail about what would happen. *He shot his head off* is all anyone said about them. She was haunted by questions: How did Paul do it? Where did he aim it? At his forehead? How did he reach the trigger? Did he lean over on top of the barrel? Do you put it in your mouth? Or under your chin? And what happens when you do it? Would you feel anything? No one would speculate with her. When she asked a friend what he thought, he looked off in the distance and said, "Too heavy, man. Forget it." She tried to forget it, but she needed to know these things first.

If Julie had wanted to, it wouldn't have been hard to find a shotgun or a rifle in Dawson. All her relatives hunted. She had never gone hunting alone, but she supposed she could make up some story about somebody else needing a gun. That would satisfy them, if she had wanted to get a gun. She could buy her own ammunition. She could say it was for her father. No one would question that.

In the early morning, Julie began to be startled awake with the click of a rifle's safety catch. She would sit up in bed, shaking and sleepless. She wondered if she had really heard the sound or dreamed it, and listened for it again. She heard crying sometimes, and waited for someone in the bedroom below to do what Paul did. *Commit suicide.* They never said those words at home.

Julie's Aunt Jane froze to death coming home from a party in February, less than three months after Paul died. She fell into the snow in front of the door to her house, the key still in her hand, ready to open the door. After the funeral, Julie heard her sister Kathy saying to their youngest brother, "Auntie Jane was passed out. She didn't even feel the cold, so don't worry. It's called hypothermia. If she was awake, she would have been very cold and shivering at first, but then she'd just go into a kind of warm sleep forever, in Heaven." It was an easy way to die, everyone said.

Julie started to keep track of time passing by adding up the number of months since Paul shot his head off. Five months after Paul did it, Auntie Jane's daughter Brenda did it. Julie heard the story from her cousin, Brenda's brother, right after they found her. He sat in the Fuller's kitchen, crying and holding a bottle of rye carefully against his chest between long drags straight from the bottle. He said a friend of Brenda's noticed there wasn't any smoke coming out of her chimney after two days and got the landlord to break into the house. "She was at a party, having a ball, dancing with everyone, a couple days ago. Then she goes home, lights all these red candles in the bathroom. She runs a bath, even puts bubble stuff in it. She undresses, gets into the tub. She drinks a bottle of vodka. The bottle is there, in the tub. She slices both her wrists with a kitchen knife, down to the bone, can you imagine? The knife's there, too, in the tub." He said the candles burned down to thick red drips over the toilet. Several times he said, "There were pink bubbles. It was weird. Pink bubbles, all along the sides of the tub." Brenda's blood coagulated in the cool water around her, a red velvet bed.

Slicing her wrists like Brenda wouldn't be as messy as shooting herself, Julie decided. If she did it like Brenda, she would just lie in an empty tub and let the blood wash down the drain. All you needed was razor blades. Or maybe one of those sharp knives that they used in school to make stencils. The teacher didn't see when Julie cut her arms and wrists in school, making herself bleed. Julie knew that you were supposed to cut them along the veins, not across, because it was faster.

****

Julie wakes suddenly in the early morning. She thinks she has heard the sharp click of a rifle's safety catch. But she is in her apartment in

Whitehorse, away from all that. "Darryl? You there?" She rushes out to the livingroom. She finds it empty, and realizes that she expects to see her brother Paul sitting there with a rifle, both hands holding it under his chin. It has been seven years, nearly to the day, that he did it, just before Christmas.

Julie has been to the doctor a few times, hoping to be pregnant. She has had two miscarriages. She tells him how anxious she is to have Darryl's son. At one visit she says, "I just can't seem to get to sleep lately. I don't have any energy. All I want to do is sleep all day, and then I'm awake all night. Is there something you can give me?" She has gotten several prescriptions for sleeping pills from him over the past months. She gets the prescriptions filled, but doesn't use them, counting the pills so that she won't be asking for them too many times. The pills are hidden in two plastic cases that are for tampons, in her purse. No one will look there.

Knowing she has chosen to die is like the time she had a secret love affair, or when she lost her virginity. It is a comforting secret, and thrilling because no one else knows about it. She wants to keep the good feeling she has now, so she sometimes takes a couple of uppers while she is working at the salon. She watches herself laughing at things she wouldn't have found funny before. The difficult customers with their petty comments and impossible requests for a perfect hairdo don't bother her any more. Her boss even complements her on being easier to get along with, like her old self again, and jokes with her about Darryl.

After work Julie stops in at the Taku bar as usual. In the mirror behind the bar, she sees herself joking with an attractive man who is leaning over her shoulder. The man had once been charged with raping two women who had passed out at a party. The charges had been dropped because the story each woman told was different. He is very popular amongst the men in their crowd. She doesn't usually speak to him; he frightens her. But this time she feels safe. She smiles, watching him make his way, laughing and punching some of the guys' shoulders, down the line of friends sitting at the bar. From the corner of her eye, she sees the smiling reflection of herself in the mirror looking at him. Strange. She can't feel her body sitting on the stool. The real Julie must be there in that other room, in the mirror.

Peace washes over her walking home in the early evening. The bright gold-pink sunset paints the snow with an eery light as if from within. It's so pretty; the dirty slush has changed completely. Her heart flutters in anticipation.

Inside the apartment, she locks the door and puts a chair under the door knob. She has never done that before, but somehow it seems the right thing to do. She knows Darryl will be away for most of the night. At first he will look for her in the bars. But he never likes to wait for her. Once he starts playing pool, he won't even phone her. He'll be home early the next morning.

Undressed, Julie smiles to herself as she puts her clothes away neatly in the drawer. She slips naked into the bed. She needs a glass of water for the pills. She gets it from the kitchen, adding some whiskey to the water. Before she goes back to the bedroom, she puts her favourite Frank Sinatra cassette on the stereo, called "I Did it my Way." That song always gives her courage. It's the fifth one on the tape. Will she be asleep by the time it comes on, she wonders.

From the drawer in the table beside the bed, Julie pulls out a photograph album and lays it on the bed. She searches in her purse for Selena's school picture and puts it in the album. She wants to think about better times. She sits in bed, the glass in her hand and the dozens of pills beside her. At first she takes the pills one by one, then in small handfuls. With each swallow, she pulls pictures out of the album and looks at them. She makes herself think something good about each person she sees. There's her sister Kathy, standing near their father's boat on the Yukon River, with Selena. She remembers taking that picture. They had gone down to Moosehide village with Selena that day. Her last conscious thought is that right now she is too sleepy to go with Selena downriver like she wants. She'll see Lena later, in Moosehide. Right now she wants to lie in bed and sleep. She is so tired, she wants to sleep forever.

****

It is 3:00 a.m. when Darryl Mason unlocks the apartment door. The door moves a little, but hits something. Damn! He can just see through the open space. Julie has put a chair against the door. It must be wedged up under the doorknob. What the hell's she up to now? Maybe she's got some man in there? No, she couldn't be that stupid. He goes outdoors, finds a long stick that will fit through the partly opened door, shoves it through against the chair leg, and pushes hard twice. The chair falls and he stumbles in. "Julie!" he calls as he wanders down the hallway to the bedroom. "What the hell are you doing, you stupid woman?" He still has the stick in his hand. For a moment, he has a vision of beating her with it, teaching her a lesson for trying to keep him out.

He turns on the light in the bedroom. Julie's under the covers, with some photographs spread around. He hits her twice on the legs with the stick. He laughs. "Wake up, bitch!" he shouts, and throws the stick across the room. Sitting on the bed, he takes her by both arms and shakes her. It makes her head wobble. She must have taken something. Probably mixing booze with downers again. He told her not to do that, especially when he wasn't around. He shakes her harder. He pulls the blankets off and tries to make her sit up in bed. That usually works, but her naked torso gives way. She falls forward in his arms. He pushes her away. Her head rolls on the pillow and he notices that her eyes are half-open.

"Shit!" He's worried now. He goes into the kitchen, finds a cooking pot, and fills it with cold water. Back in the bedroom, he throws the water on her. She doesn't move. He reaches over and puts his hand near her mouth. No breath. He pulls his hand back as if it were burned. "Fuck!" He stands by the bed, stunned. She must have killed herself.

He should have seen trouble coming. For months he has been putting up with her talking about her brother shooting his head off. She was always tired, never wanting to see friends, ever since she lost that last baby. He told her she should see somebody about it, get some pills or something. She worried him.

This is the last thing he needs right now with the cops hanging around. Just that night, a man that he suspected was an undercover drug cop had asked him too many friendly questions in the bar. It made him think he should split town. Now he would have to go. He should have left a long time ago, but he had waited for the good times to come back. In the back of his mind, he had been afraid of this.

He grabs a duffle bag from the closet and shoves some clothes in it. Can't take too much. It'll look suspicious. He picks up the bag and walks toward the bedroom door. Something's not quite right. He looks at the body lying on the soaked blankets. He wishes he hadn't thrown that water on her. When they find her they will know someone did that, maybe trying to revive her. Maybe they'll think he tried to kill her, for Christ's sake. Maybe gave her drugs, overdosed her. How could he prove he didn't do it?

Darryl takes the cooking pot into the kitchen, puts it in the cupboard, and places the chair that Julie had used back at the table. He goes into the bedroom, reaches in his pocket for his lighter, and lights a cigarette.

He thinks about how she would light his cigarette in that bed after they made love, leaning over him to reach for the ashtray, her breasts teasing him. Why, Julie, why fucking kill yourself? They had some real good times together. She never did ask for much, just that he not hit her. Maybe he should have listened to her a bit more, even gotten her some help. But she was too quiet lately, never talking the way she used to. He stands there, frowning at her, cigarette smoke drifting between them.

Got to get out of here. He throws the cigarette onto the bed and snaps his lighter. Holding the dry corners of the blankets one by one, he lights them. It takes them awhile to start, but he is patient. A photograph on the bed seems to come alive as it curls and blackens. He picks up his bag and goes down the hall. Dense grey smoke is just reaching the bedroom ceiling when he slams the apartment door. He tries the knob to make sure it is locked behind him.

ENDINGS AND BEGINNINGS

Eliza Maclean always said that Whiskey Flats, facing Grey Mountain from across the White Pass railway tracks and the Yukon River, was the best place to live in Whitehorse. Only people on welfare or pensions lived there, in lean-to's, shacks, old log cabins, and trailers in the 1970's. The respectable City Fathers had big plans for The Flats so they wanted to get rid of the mixture of squatting Indians and poor Whites. If the City didn't put in any new water or electricity lines, they thought that everyone would eventually disappear. They were mistaken.

Eliza's tin trailer came up the Alaska Highway twenty years before. "It's not the Ritz, but the price is right," Eliza would say. She paid no rent, thanks to an old boyfriend. He moved Outside a few years ago and gave it to her. Gus, who lived next door, said it must have been painted shit yellow to scare the bears away. It was warm enough in the winter if she put a blanket over the door. Gus let her haul water from his outdoor tap and he strung up an extension cord so she could get electricity from his cabin. Eliza paid for her part of the power when she got her welfare cheque and she cleaned up his place once in awhile. "Sure needs it," Eliza told him every time. "Wouldn't even have my dog sleep in that mess."

Gus and Eliza listened to the Western music squealing from her little green transistor radio on the table while they played cribbage. She never missed the afternoon show, the "Rootin' Tootin' Truck Drivin' Beer Drinkin' and Mom Show", with Willy Tucker. It came from Inuvik in the Northwest Territories.

"Inuvik!" Gus said, "I been there. About as far away from cowboy land as you can get. I'd like to see them cowboys trying to run a dog team across the Mackenzie Delta flats some day."

"Forget it and deal the next hand, will ya?" Eliza said. She played the radio all her waking hours. The music made her feel good when she was down in the dumps. CBC was like a good friend. It kept her up on the latest local news and weather. She could send messages on Outpost Message Time to reach friends. She pictured in her head what the disk jockeys looked like if she didn't know them and she was a devoted fan of her favourite announcer, a cousin of hers, Jim Anderson. She laughed till tears came down her cheeks when Jim played tricks on the new guys, like making them read the news when it was about Aishihik. Nobody from down south could read that right the first time if they weren't told how.

Eliza sang along with Hank Snow. "Movin' On" was one of her favourite tunes. "Makes my feet just want to get up and go somewhere else, somewheres down that old Alaska Highway, eh?" she said.

Jim Anderson broke into the music. They had found a body in an apartment downtown and the apartment was on fire. That was all Jim said. Hank started singing again from the beginning.

"That Jim!" Gus said, throwing down a card. "Gets a kick out of interrupting in the middle of a song I figure. He could wait till the end. Makes him feel important to butt in when something exciting happens, I guess."

"Imagine! Burnt up!" Eliza said. "Gruesome, eh? Must've passed out." She threw down a card. Gus grimaced at it. He picked out one of his cards and scratched his jaw with it. He kept a week-old growth of beard that itched until he finally gave up and shaved. Eliza took a sip of cold tea and punched out her cigarette in the overflowing ashtray. "Wonder who it is," she said.

"That body in the fire? Well, let's just hope it ain't somebody we know," Gus said seriously. They knew everybody. He shook his head. "Look at those cards will you?! Looks like you're taking my whole damn pension cheque this time, Liza." He wouldn't say her whole name, *E*-liza. She had given up trying to make him say it ages ago. Liza sounded like some cow. They played for a quarter a game. Pay-up was on Sunday nights and Eliza was ahead a dollar and a quarter. Gus hated to lose, but he pretended it was all right if she teased him about being a poor sport. "You're so damn lucky today," Gus said.

With broken match sticks stuck into the moose antler cribboard that Gus made for her last Christmas, Eliza counted out twelve points that she didn't need. She said, "No luck, Gus, honey, just smarts." She pointed to her forehead with a wink. Gus was too old to take anything like that as flirting. He was safe to be around.

Lighting a cigarette while Gus shuffled the cards, Eliza said, "Bet that guy in the fire was smoking in bed. Ya know, I never do that. Even in my real drinking days I never did, eh? Too dangerous."

A few minutes later, this time between songs, because he knew he already had everyone's attention, Jim Anderson said on the radio that the body was found lying on a bed and the bed was almost completely burned up around it. Eliza chuckled, "Told ya. Smoking in bed. Stupid."

Then Jim gave out the address: 310 Hanson Street. "Oh my God... my God... that's Julie's place!" Eliza shouted, standing up. Her chair overturned and her cards were on the floor. "It might be my baby! In that bed! Selena!" Her eyes searched Gus's face, hoping he would tell her it wasn't Selena. "Julie's her Dawson friend. She used to stay with her for Christ's sake. I gotta go find her, know if she's OK." She grabbed her coat and purse and headed for the door.

Gus was by the door. He put his arm out to stop her. "Take it easy, will ya?" he said. She hesitated for a moment, wondering what to do next, where to go to look for her. "I don't understand you, Liza. You done so much for that girl already and what does she do for you? Nothin'. You found out she didn't even stay at Sprucewood after all the work you did to get her in that place." Eliza hadn't seen Selena for over two months, since New Year's, when she went to the alcohol treatment centre. They told her when she called them that Selena had left.

"You just don't understand a goddam thing, do you?" Eliza said. "You wouldn't, would you, you old fart. Haven't never had kids." She put on her coat and stuffed her purse under her arm. Maybe she would need the picture of Selena that was in her wallet, the one where she looked like a younger Eliza.

"Well it sounds to me like she don't really care about her drinking, even after gettin' beaten up and ending up in the hospital like she did," Gus said.

"That's the last straw! You think it's Selena's fault somebody beat her up?" Eliza pointed her cigarette in the direction of downtown. "That could be my daughter lying there all burnt up, damn it! Burnt up!" When she said the words, her throat squeezed tight and she nearly threw up with panic. "This has got absolutely nothing to do with her drinking, for Christ's sake. I gotta find her." Her heart pounded and she was breathing hard.

She remembered it was wet out, muddy with spring snow melting. She sat down to put on her boots. Gus started to say something about Selena might have gone home to Dawson, but when Jim stopped playing music again on the radio, Eliza waved her hand impatiently in between them. "Shut up!" she shouted, more impolite than she had ever been with him. Sometimes when they pushed her, she hated every man she'd ever known in her life. They thought they knew it all. Smart asses, all of them.

Jim said, "We have a bulletin about that fire in an apartment on Hanson Street that we reported on earlier. More details were released by Sergeant Lister in an exclusive interview with us just a few..." The radio coughed. Damn static! Eliza banged the radio on the table. They heard: "... reports that apparently in the wee hours of this morning a man living in the apartment above telephoned the owner of the building complaining about smoke. The owner inspected the building, but said he thought it was the garbage being burned in the back lane behind the apartment block. By 6:00 a.m. the smell of smoke was so strong that someone called the fire department. They had to break down...fire axes..." Silence. Shuffling sound. "One moment please." Finally Jim said, "And Fire Chief Ron Vance spoke to us just minutes ago at the scene. We have that on tape."

Another man's muffled voice came on, rushed, like Eliza felt. He was talking to someone: "Yeah. OK. Pretty heavy in there, eh?" He noticed the mike. "Uh, yeah, Jim. I'm here. We had a devil of a time getting to the bedroom. Had to use oxygen masks. Just terrible. Must've burnt for hours, smouldering, you know, in that mattress."

A formal Jim Anderson asked, "Chief Vance, can you tell us anything about the body you found?"

Vance's voice became official. "The RCMP are investigating. All I can say at this time is that we did find a burned body lying on the bed. The fire was just starting to get at the wall behind the bed. Lucky we got there when we did. Saved the building."

"Yes, lucky indeed. Thank you, Chief Vance." Shuffle. Silence. Static. Eliza picked up the radio and shook it. She banged it on the table and Jim came on again: "...and the RCMP have still not released information about whether that body was a male or female. We're trying to find out for you who was living in the apartment. Stay tuned. We'll give you more as soon as we know it as we continue to follow this story." Hank Williams started to sing "I'm so Lonesome I Could Cry". Eliza's mind flashed on Selena singing that at Christmas when she stayed with her. Before she would burst into tears, Eliza threw open the door. Gus was left sitting at the table, shaking his head, his cards still in his hand.

On her way to find Selena, Eliza had to walk past Julie's apartment building. She turned the corner and from two blocks away, she saw a fire truck. There were some police officers and other people hanging around. She got closer, slopping through dirty slush from the water they had used on the fire. There was black on the outside wall of Julie's apartment, above the broken living room window. An acrid smell drifted toward her. She had to get away from looking at that black, evil hole in the wall. If she stopped to talk to anybody she knew they would tell her it was Selena they found in there.

It started to rain. Eliza hated the rain in the spring. It just soaked you through; you felt colder even than in winter. Downtown. That's where she would find Selena, in one of the bars. Eliza kept in touch with what her daughter was doing from people they both knew. She went into the first bar on Main Street, the Taku. The barmaid was from Dawson too, one of the Hanson girls. She said, "She's been in here a couple of times in the last day or so. I haven't seen her today, though." She warned Eliza, "She's pretty drunk, you know. Better stay away from her for awhile."

That's the last thing on earth Eliza could do. She asked, "Heard anything more about the fire?"

"Nope. But I figure that body has to be Julie Fuller or her boyfriend Darryl." She saw Eliza's frown and said quickly, to be kind, "Or it could be anybody else, you know. Probably some stranger. You know how Julie can't say no to anyone needing a place to flop. Oops, gotta go." She moved off to deliver some drinks. Eliza stood by the door, hoping that somebody who knew Selena would walk in. The barmaid came back and said, "Don't worry about Selena. She takes care of herself these days." She patted Eliza's arm.

Two other bars said they saw Selena in the past few days, but not that day. Eliza asked them to tell her to come home. She went to the CBC station away across town and put a message on the Outpost Message Time. Everybody listened to Message Time. "Selena, come home," that's all she said. Eliza knew that Selena wouldn't be happy to hear Eliza calling her trailer Selena's home. It just came natural for her to say that. It was still raining on the melting snow and her cheap boots were soaked. Her feet were freezing so she started back to The Flats. Every step she took made a splash and at each step she said a word, like a prayer: "Come. Home. Come. Home. Come. Home."

The next morning, two girlfriends of Selena's came around to Eliza's trailer. They had heard Message Time. They told Eliza that Selena was probably OK, just partying, but they didn't know anything for sure. Eliza went downtown and everybody she saw told her it was Julie they found in the apartment. She wanted to believe them, but she had to see Selena first. She figured her best bet was to stay at home and wait, but it was hard. Late that night, she couldn't sleep and she was sitting at the table listening to the radio and drinking beer. At night the music came from Vancouver, light jazz, a lonely sound. It made her feel sad and empty. She couldn't eat. Her macaroni and cheese dinner from hours before was still on the plate in front of her. The transistor was squealing with static so she turned it off and threw herself down on the couch to try to sleep.

The door flew open. It was Selena! Her long hair was plastered like black streaks of paint around her face and she looked even smaller than she was, standing in the doorway. Eliza pulled her inside and the rich dark smell of liquor filled the room. Selena said, "Jus' came for clothes."

Eliza picked up her empty beer bottle and threw it in the garbage without Selena seeing. "Where were you, Selena? I been looking everywhere for you. You hear my message?"

"Party. Pot party. Cool, man, on North Highway." It was still wet and muddy out and she looked like she had fallen somewhere. There was dried mud on the back of both her pant legs. She smelled like something rotten.

"I been waiting for you to come home," Eliza said. "I been looking for you for two days downtown." Selena looked like a wild animal, her unfocused eyes staring blankly as if Eliza were a stranger. Eliza had heard that people high on pot stared like that, looking at something for hours.

"S'what?" Selena said suspiciously. Selena probably thought she wanted to talk about family things. She didn't like that. Before Eliza could say anything, Selena shouted, "You lookin' for money? Haven't got none!" She flung her arm as if to push Eliza away, and started a wavering walk towards the bedroom door where her clothes were. "Just let me 'lone."

Eliza took her arm but Selena shoved her away, moving in slow motion, like in a movie. Selena tried to get into the bedroom but Eliza stood in the way with her foot against the door jamb. Eliza said loudly as if Selena was deaf or couldn't understand English, "Do-you-know-about-Julie?"

"Don't see Julie no more. Don't wanna. Kicked me out." Selena sneered. "Pisses me off with her *job*. Thinks she's better'n me." In the condition Selena was in, that was a long speech. She leaned back against the wall. Eliza wondered if Selena was going to pass out on her right there and hoped she wouldn't fall. Selena was small, but Eliza was even shorter. She'd never be strong enough to get her up off the floor.

Eliza moved away from the door. "Come over to the couch and sit down for just a minute, baby. I gotta tell you something."

"Gotta go, somebody waitin'. No time." Selena went into the bedroom, and Eliza heard rustling sounds behind the curtain.

"No time?" Eliza was angry now. "None of us got enough time, eh, just like Julie!" She went to the bedroom door and said very clearly, "She's dead! Julie's dead! She's the woman in that fire!"

"Fire?" Selena stopped throwing clothes into a paper bag.

"Oh, God, you're so out of it you...*did you hear me?* Julie Fuller...is... dead!" Quietly, Eliza said, "your Dawson friend, baby."

Selena's drugged brain took in some of what Eliza said. She walked stiffly back into the front room and stood in the middle of the room. The paper bag hung from one hand. She stared at Eliza without moving until she let her move her over to sit down on the couch. Eliza feared what Selena might do. Maybe with all those drugs, she'd have a heart attack.

"Julie Fuller is dead, baby," Eliza repeated as clearly as she could. She sat down beside her and took her hand, the crippled one. Selena didn't push her away.

Selena's face screwed up. "Jules? That's crap! Somebody else maybe. Stop the bullshit." She pulled her hand away and stood up. Too fast. She fell back on the couch.

Standing in front of her, Eliza leaned over and put her hands on Selena's shoulders. She spoke as if she was teaching her something when she was little: "It is Julie. She was in a fire. In her apartment. Her brother Bobbie told me it was her. I seen him today downtown. He was up from Dawson to stay with her." Eliza could see by Selena's face that it was more than she could take in, but she went on. "When Bobbie got to her place, it was all burnt. The cops wouldn't let him in. They took him off to question him."

Selena frowned, her eyes darting around the room. She leaned back on the couch and said, "Jules? Jules dead? No kidding!" Eliza was shocked to hear her laugh. Selena ran her fingers through the hair on the side of her head, "That's wild, man!" She covered her face with her hands. "Impossible - maybe...maybe it's me. Maybe I'm dead. Better that way." She begins a singsong without a tune: "Dead. We're dead, all dead...dead... all dead......dead."

Eliza was frightened. She had to move away from her. She stood up and went over to the sink. Goddam dope. Young kids today. Smoke everything in sight. To keep busy, she made coffee and sandwiches.

The next morning, Selena's sandwich was still on the table. When Eliza urged her to eat, Selena said she had a rotten headache. She wouldn't eat all that day, crying until she was hoarse, talking over and over again about the days when she was in Dawson. She remembered how she and Julie played hide and seek in the old deserted buildings and how Julie used to love to do her hair, before Julie left to live in Whitehorse. She wanted those times back, she told Eliza. Eliza wanted to hear the stories; they were the only ones she had from when her baby was young.

Having Selena there and caring for her reminded Eliza of Christmas, when they did things together like sewing for the first time. She needs me, Eliza told herself, like she did then, after she was beaten up. Eliza told herself she would remember not to say anything that would make her mad, or to force her into anything. She'd learned not to do that.

The next few days were long and terrible. All they did was try to find out what really happened, to sort out the truth from the rumours they heard. They caught short naps, ate on the run, made trips downtown to see people or to buy a bottle to keep them going. Julie hadn't shown up anywhere. They listened to the radio all the time, but nobody important said who it was they found on the bed. Anybody who knew Julie knew it was her apartment by the address and was convinced that it must have been her on the bed. Eliza figured that it couldn't be her boyfriend Darryl, even though he hadn't shown up either. They heard that he told some people the last time he saw them that he wouldn't be in Whitehorse for awhile, that he was going Outside. Eliza hoped that maybe Julie and Darryl had both gone to Edmonton.

Gus came over all the time. Eliza said he was just curious. The old bugger loved to gossip. Once he said to Eliza, "You know, you shouldn't encourage Selena to drink. You both should sober up for awhile, don't you think? Who knows what might happen?"

Eliza's lips pinched together. "None of your damn business what we do," she said. "Listen, I don't want her any more upset than she is already. If she wants to drink, we'll drink. At least she isn't smoking that pot or taking them shitty pills. We're doing this together. We're just fine." Gus stayed away after that.

The third night, Selena came through the door from going for groceries and Eliza said, "Here's the latest *no*-news for you. CBC says the RCMP are still not saying who it was. And they still don't even say if it was a guy or a woman."

Until then, they believed that Julie was smoking in bed, that it was a terrible accident. "There must be something wrong about the fire, or they'd say her name," Selena said. "Anyway they'd say that it's a woman, don't you think?"

"God, you're right, you know," Eliza said. "It's been more than enough time to tell the Fullers in Dawson about her. They don't need to keep it a secret. What could've happened?" With a sense of satisfaction, Eliza realized that they had both been thinking the same thing. Like a mother and daughter who were really close. ESP or something.

The next morning they listened to Outpost Message Time after breakfast in the hopes of reading between the lines for any news. All they heard was: "Freda Smith at Lake Laberge: I had a fire in the pickup when I started out. I'm OK. At Ten Mile with Connie. Sorry about last night. Come and get me. That's to Freda at Lake Laberge from Sam."

They decided Freda and Sam were fighting again and he took off on her. "Good for him," Eliza said, "A fire in his pickup is what he deserves. She should make him wait a week to get his ride home like she did last year." They both managed to laugh at the next one too: "Message to Johnny James at Canyon Creek. Send a truck in for the outhouse. It's waiting for you at the back of the RCMP in the Junction. That's from Pete, Johnny." Somebody was pretty desperate stealing an outhouse, Selena said, when there's all that good bush around.

Later Jim Anderson read the noon news and said the body was sent to Vancouver for investigation. "I never heard about that before, sending dead people Outside," Eliza said. "It makes me worried. Gotta be something wrong." Julie's friends were shocked and sad, but underneath they were hypnotized, even thrilled by the details. They would repeat the same information over and over again to each other and ask each other, *What are they looking for? What do you think they could find?*

They met with Selena's friends from Dawson a couple of times each day to share whatever information they had, in the 98 bar. The 98 was a long, narrow building, with a false front. Eliza said she thought they stuck it in the space in between after they built the two bigger buildings on each side, just nailed up the front and back and a roof. She hated the ugly dark green snap-on terry cloth covers for the tiny metal tables. They soaked up the spills so the barmaid didn't have to work too hard but they got all wet and sticky by the end of the night and she wasn't able to lean on the table. It was always too noisy for her to hear people, and the air was thick with smoke. When they went in there she felt as if she was in a bad dream, even though she had spent a lot of time there in her real drinking days. Selena said she hated it too, that she hadn't gone in there for a long time, but that's where their Dawson friends were.

They finally heard CBC give out Julie's name on the suppertime news. "About time!" Selena yelled at the radio. "Anybody who cares about it knows that it's her for Christ's sake!"

Eliza said, "It's been nearly two weeks since she died. Jesus!"

"I'll phone Dawson and find out when the funeral is," Selena said. She went over to use Gus's phone and when she came back, she said, "It's Saturday, in Dawson. I want to go."

"You have *got* to go, baby, and I'm going with you," Eliza said. "I already borrowed bus money from Gus." It had been a long time since Eliza or Selena were last in Dawson. They knew it wouldn't be easy for either of them. Selena's two brothers, the twin boys John and Jake, were living there with Eliza's father. "The boys are nearly sixteen now, Selena. How do you think they'll react to seeing me?" Eliza worried. She remembered Selena yelling at her, one time she went to see her in Dawson. She had only wanted to try to make amends.

"Pop won't be happy to see me, neither. He's still pretty sore at me for leaving home." Selena said.

"No. He sure don't like it when people leave him," Eliza said, "even when he kicks them out."

They decided they would both stop drinking the day before they left to go to Dawson, to show respect for Julie. Maybe it would make the old man happy too, Selena said.

As soon as they arrived in Dawson on the bus, the night before the funeral, Selena went to the Fuller's place in the North End to visit. She was able to stay with Pop "under the circumstances," he said. But there was to be no drinking or she would be tossed out on her ear. Eliza stayed with her old friend Jane at the other end of town.

On Saturday, a half an hour before the funeral, Eliza met up with Julie's sister Kathy and Selena walking by the old Blacksmith's Shop on the way to the Anglican Church two blocks away. Eliza heard Kathy say to Selena , "Please don't tell anyone yet about what I told you. Mom doesn't even know yet. We're going to tell her in a couple of days. Dad knows."

"What's that?" Eliza asked. It sounded bad.

Selena said, "They phoned up from Vancouver. She took a bunch of sleeping pills. Of course we won't say anything. Right, Eliza?" She frowned at Eliza.

"I know you think I talk too much, Selena. Don't worry," Eliza said, "I'll keep quiet, for Julie's sake. She was always good to me, like a daughter." She saw Selena glance at Kathy as if to say, *here she goes again*.

Kathy went on, "They said my sister was already dead for four hours when the fire started, that..."

Selena stopped walking, and broke in, "What? Dead? Four hours? Then she was gone when the fire started?"

Kathy nodded, "Yes, thank God. Wait. There's more. That fire inspector guy from Whitehorse says there's no sign that the fire was started by a cigarette. He says it was set *on purpose*."

"On purpose? What?! That's crazy, man!" Selena stared at Kathy. They all stood in the middle of the street.

"Christ. Let's get going. People are looking at us," Eliza said.

"Well I guess the RCMP don't think it's crazy," Kathy said. "They sent a cop guy up from Outside--Vancouver, I think--all the way to Dawson. He talked to me this morning."

Eliza was confused. "Christ, you mean it might be...murder?" She could hardly say the word. It sounded thick and heavy, like a foreign word, and her lips wouldn't work right. In her head, she saw somebody giving Julie pills, then trying to burn her up. Make it look like an accident, get rid of the evidence.

They walked slowly toward the crowd in front of St. Paul's without talking. Selena mumbled to Kathy, "Darryl, do you think?"

Kathy shrugged her shoulders, but her face said yes. "Just before you came," she whispered, "I found out that nobody's seen him. Somebody phoned us from Whitehorse and said that he's gone out to Edmonton. Maybe he went before, maybe after. I just wish I could get my hands on him. I'd kill him myself." Selena took her arm.

Kathy said she had to catch up with her mother, and hurried on ahead of them. Eliza said to Selena, "You know, Julie never struck me as the kind of person to be depressed. She joked and laughed all the time. Loved to tease people, make them happy. That's how I'll remember her."

"What do you mean, depressed?" Selena asked.

"Well, the sleeping pills...doesn't that mean...suicide?"

"Nobody knows anything for sure yet, just remember that."

"Well, all them damn pills you youngsters take nowadays does that sometimes, changes people's moods, makes them do things they wouldn't do if they was normal-like. And that shit Darryl used to beat her up something terrible, didn't you say? Must make anybody depressed."

They entered the church and Eliza looked around for her boys, half hoping they would be there, half not. "Will Daddy let John and Jake come?" she asked.

"I asked them. They said they didn't want to come. But Pop said they could if they wanted to. He's not coming either." Eliza was relieved. Trying to make things better just with Selena was a big enough job for her. She would think about the twins later.

Even in the summer the church was cold. Selena and Eliza sat on hard wooden pews shivering with their jackets on, looking at Julie's dark coffin at the front, the lid closed, the handles shining gold. They smelled old musty books and sour smoke from one of the huge candles that had blown out. The smoke drifted around in the air above the red and purple plastic flowers lying on top of the casket until the minister came and lit the candle again.

Eliza had never liked being in church since her time at the residential school. She always felt she was being punished for something she didn't do. And it made her think about her mother dying so long ago. Once again she was seven and sitting in the church at Moosehide beside her daddy who was crying. Would he leave her now, too? She was afraid to ask him.

The RCMP officer from Outside sat at the back with the local policeman beside him, obviously writing in a note pad. The two of them were whispering. They were keeping track of everyone who came to the funeral. It bothered Julie's father so much that he went up to them and shouted: "Get out, you bastards! Let us bury my daughter in peace!" He was drunk, but that was the first time Eliza felt some respect for him. After that the RCMP stood on the steps of the church outdoors, looking uncomfortable.

After the graveside service on the Dome, everyone left except Selena and Eliza. Selena sat on her jacket near the bright flowers on the pile of dirt that was going to cover Julie forever. Two men with shovels stood leaning against a tree, waiting for her to leave so they could finish their job. Selena stared down at the coffin deep in the ground, smoking one cigarette after another for almost an hour. Eliza sat next to her and the two women said nothing. Selena didn't cry, but she looked pale and her face had lines that

Eliza hadn't seen before. She imagined what Selena would look like when she would be older than even herself.

It started to drizzle, and Eliza finally talked Selena into leaving. Selena threw away her cigarette and they walked back down the Dome Road, not talking. Eliza thought about taking her arm, but she was afraid that she would push her away. They reached the bottom of the road and started along Seventh Avenue. Selena said, "This is where we used to toboggan. Julie nearly killed me one day when we were kids, you know. She fell right on top of me. She just about *killed* me, she was so big, eh?" She nearly smiled. "What happened, is...I killed her instead."

Eliza breathed in hard and said, "Don't you talk like that! There's enough death in the air. It's bad luck."

Selena didn't hear. She said, her voice dreamy, "No, I did. I helped to kill my precious Jules. I wasn't there for her when I should have been, when she took those pills or whatever it was Darryl did to her. I deserve to be up there in the ground too."

Eliza's eyes grew large and she stopped walking. She said, fear in her voice, "I said don't say that! Don't, eh?! Shit. It's bad luck!"

"It seemed OK, you know, safe...safe to be fighting, you know what I mean? It didn't matter. We still had all the rest of our lives ahead of us. She always forgave everyone, specially me, eh? I counted on that. I thought we could make it up later." The gravel crunched under their feet as they walked on silently across town. "Now there's no time, there's no later for us. It's the end. No time left for us." Selena's face was blank. Eliza's arms ached to hold her, to shield her from everything. But she was afraid to do anything except to grimly walk beside her.

Wherever Selena went she was faced with another memory of Julie, or another person to tell her how sorry they were. Everybody wanted to stay close to her, talk to her. They didn't know that Julie had made her move out of the apartment. They assumed that they were still best friends, which made it even harder for Selena. She said over and over to Eliza, "She needed a friend and I wasn't there." She couldn't sit still, had to keep moving. Eliza followed her, feeling helpless and depressed. Eliza asked Selena twice to ask Dave if the twins would see her. They refused both times.

Two days after the funeral, they were sitting in the Downtown bar, still not drinking. Selena said she was afraid that she would start drinking heavy again. "You know, for the first time, I really don't want to," she said.

"I want to face this with a clear head. Let's get out of this damn bar." She said she wanted to sleep.

"Well, that's a good sign," Eliza said, and left her a block away from home. "You go home now and have a good rest."

The Vancouver RCMP officer stopped Eliza that night after supper and asked directions to find Selena. She met Selena downtown the next day. Selena said that she cried for the whole hour that the cop was there. He had asked her about the argument she and Julie had. She told Eliza that she felt as if she was guilty the whole time he questioned her. "I'm scared," Selena said. "They know we weren't talking. Probably some of those so-called friends of ours in Whitehorse told them. It's like the cops think I did something to Jules for God's sake."

"I don't think so. I've got some news for you. Let's go over to the river," Eliza said. They sat on a bench overlooking the Yukon River and Eliza told Selena that she had heard Darryl had been picked up in Edmonton. They were bringing him back to Whitehorse to charge him with manslaughter.

"It's about time!" Selena said. "But how can they charge someone when the person was already dead? Maybe they think he killed her first, then tried to cover it up with the fire?"

Eliza said no one she had talked to had any answers. "Darryl's pleading not guilty. Looks like he stands a good chance of getting off."

Selena said, "I haven't been drinking, this whole time, you know that, but now Pop says it's OK for me to stay a couple more days, but then I have to leave. He doesn't like me being at his place, even if it's for Jules's funeral. He's still afraid I'll be drinking I guess. The old bugger never liked her neither. He always told me that she'd get me in trouble."

"What about the boys?" Eliza asked. She had seen them only at a distance, walking downtown.

"If they are in the house and they see me coming, they leave. They're both working at the garage for the summer. I used to have such fun with them. I like kids." Digging her hands in her jacket pockets searching for her cigarettes for something to do, Selena looked across the river. "I think I'm pregnant, Eliza," she said.

Eliza was stunned. She said nothing, trying to sort out her thoughts. She had never thought about her daughter being a mother herself some day. Selena lit her cigarette and said, "I'll need a place to stay, at least for awhile, till I'm on my feet. Come with me to talk to Pop. Tell him that I'm not drinking, that I need to stay with him for awhile."

"You gotta be kidding! He won't let me through the door. He sure as hell won't listen to me about anything."

"It's just till I can figure out what to do. You're my mother for Christ sake. You should help me." Eliza realized that for the first time Selena was talking about her being her mother without being angry, and asking for her help. Selena needed her. And she had her grandchild inside her. What could she do? They walked together to the South End. Eliza stepped nervously through the door behind Selena. She looked for the twins, but they were gone.

Dave Maclean was as polite to them as he would be to any stranger. He gave them tea. Sitting down on the other side of the table from them, he said to Selena: "So you're living with your mother in Whitehorse now?" as if Eliza wasn't there.

Selena said, "Not really." It made Eliza frown.

Dave looked off through the window at the Klondike River. He took a deep breath and said, "I have to say something to you both. The hardest thing I have ever had to say to anyone. So please listen." He turned towards the two women and Eliza's stomach churned. She could hear her heart beating inside her head like when she was small and had done something wrong that he had found out about.

Dave said, "You look like you're going the same way as your mother did, Selena. Like mother like daughter, I guess." He held his hand up and shook his head to stop her when Selena opened her mouth to argue with him. "I've heard the stories about what you two are up to, boozing it up in the bars in Whitehorse, so don't try to make up anything," he said. "And now you're involved with the police too." For a few seconds he looked straight at Selena without saying anything, his eyes gleaming behind his beard, until she turned her head away. He was always good at doing that.

"You know, I blame myself for your problems, both of you," Dave said. Restless, he stood and walked over to Selena's old bedroom door and stood there, filling the whole doorway, his back to them, his hands on his hips. He looked around the bedroom as if there was an answer in one of the corners. "I think I must have done something really wrong, to make the two of you like you are." Eliza believed he was right. He had been wrong, leaving her in residential school, and then turning Selena and the twins against her, not making them see her.

As if he was explaining it to someone else, Dave said, "I don't know why both my daughter and granddaughter drink. I wish I had some idea.

Maybe then I could do something about it, if I knew why. It must be my fault somehow. Something I did wrong, maybe. I guess I just have to live with that the rest of my life."

Selena began to say, "Pop, you haven't done anything wrong. You've done everything you can for all of us. Don't blame yourself..." He waved his hand in the air and turned around. He said, slowly and quietly, "What I do know is that both of you have to...to *get out of our lives*. We can't live with your drinking any longer. It's killing me. And it hurts John and Jake too much. I don't want them to go the same way."

Selena and Eliza sat silently. Selena took a deep breath and said carefully, "Pop, I want to stay, just for a little while. I'm not drinking now, and I promise I won't start again. Tell him, Eliza."

Eliza nodded. "It's true, Daddy. Selena's really a good girl. She needs your help."

Selena said, determination in her voice, "I want to stop. I've stopped now and I'll keep off it. I really want to, for you, for the twins, and for Jules."

"Julie!" Dave exploded, slamming his hand on the table. Eliza felt the sound in her chest. "She's the one who got you into this whole shit. Not only booze. Drugs too! Look at where she is now." He pointed up the Dome. "A black corpse in the ground! Is that where you want to be?"

Eliza heard herself say, "Daddy, please..."

Dave threw his hands in the air. "You two think all you have to do is say you'll stop drinking and then it's true. Well, I've got news for you. It takes a lot more courage and a lot more determination than I've ever seen in you two. Either one of you." He nodded his head at Selena and his beard shook with anger. "Yeah, you. I hear you were in Sprucewood. But you never even finished that. What makes you think you can do it now, eh?"

Selena looked him right in the eye and said, "I *know* I can do it! I can stop. Even if it's just to prove that you're dead wrong." Eliza saw them like two stubborn bull moose she saw fighting one time, their horns locked together.

"Come back in five years still sober," Dave said. "Maybe then I'll believe you!" His face was red, twisted.

Selena started to cry, and jumped up, holding her stomach with one hand. She ran into her old bedroom. Eliza hoped she wasn't going to throw up. She knew that if she told him Selena was pregnant, he might listen and change his mind. But she stopped herself. She wanted to be the one who would look after her daughter, see her through this birth. She wouldn't share that with anyone, least of all her father.

Father and daughter sat, listening to Selena pack her bag. Selena walked over to the door with it in her hand and said calmly, "Let's go, Eliza." Eliza walked past her through the door. Selena began to follow, but stopped and looked back. "Bye, Pop. I'll come to see you. I promise. Even if it is five years from now. I'll always love you. No matter what happens." Eliza heard the echo of herself saying something nearly like that a dozen years before, to Selena from that same door.

Dave sat at the table, his back partly towards the women, looking out the window. Eliza could see by his shaking shoulders that he was trying not to cry, his hand tight over his mouth. Or was he trying to stop himself from calling Selena back, Eliza wondered. He had lost his wife, his daughter, his only granddaughter, and was risking losing his great-grandchild although he wasn't aware of it. And all he had ever done was what he thought was best for all of them, all his life.

MOTHERLESS CHILDREN

I know if I listen to it, and do what it says, I'll go crazy. I can't tell if it is a man or a woman. It's never around our cabin in Dawson, or when I stay at Moosehide, only when I'm out in the real bush. I dream about it too. When I was little, I was so afraid of it I would sometimes pee in my pants running back to our camp from the bush when I heard it. I wouldn't tell anyone in case they thought it was my fault, that I caused it. As I grew older, I worried that they might just laugh at me. I know I am the only one who hears it. It sneaks up on me when I'm thinking about something else, not paying attention. Funny thing, though, if I remember to think about it ahead of time, it doesn't come. But sometimes I forget to do that. When I finally told Grandma Thomas about it, years ago, she said it was probably a bushman, but I don't really believe in bushmen. It's only the old Indian people who have seen them. I think they are gone now because young natives like me never see them. It's been a dozen years since that voice came to me, as long as the time that I have been away from the real bush.

My father Walter and my stepmother Rosie are hunting for moose and caribou. It's a dark wet day in the middle of August at our camp along the Dempster Highway north of Dawson City.

The rain has eased off, and Annie is bored with sitting in the tent. So we take Walter's old black Lab, Randy, and wander along a shallow nameless creek that twists through the North Klondike valley. We look for pretty stones and lost feathers. Without warning, a rough voice comes through the thick willows along the creek bed. It whispers in a high rasping singsong, "Seleeeena, come to me, Selena. Come seeee meee." A shiver, a sharp memory, shoots through my body as if someone has grabbed me from behind. I had forgotten about it. That's why it's back, trying to get me and maybe my little girl, Annie, too.

I stop walking and hold my breath. Randy stands very still, sniffing the windless air, and whines. I have to pretend nothing is wrong, for Annie. She is a few feet ahead of me. Just as I am going to call her, she turns around and says, "Mommy, I'm scared. Are there any bears here?" Before I can reply, three ptarmigan, their wings chopping the air, burst out of the willows directly in front of us with a loud flapping noise.

My legs are shaking. I can't breathe. I try to control my lips and to keep my voice calm as I say, "No! No bears. They don't come here." I have to talk, have to erase my terror with sound. "Not enough fish in the creek Grandpa said, remember? They eat berries now, higher up. Remember? He told us that."

"Seleeena, come on...." The voice is right there, beside us! Randy barks three times, staring into the willows.

"Shut up, Randy! Shut up!" I yell at the dog without thinking. My voice shakes, but I have to ask Annie, "Do...do you hear anything, Annie?"

"I think I hear a bear, Mommy. I think he's following us."

Sometimes she has too much imagination. I should know better than to ask her. "There aren't any bears! Didn't I tell you that?!" I sound angry, louder than I want to be. I know she can hear the fear in my voice. I never shout at her. She stands still in the shallow water, five years old, in her little red rubber boots, sucking on her bottom lip to keep from crying.

"Oh, my poor little Annikins," I say and splash over to her. "Come here, Sweetheart, give Mommy a big hug." She raises her arms and I lift her up and cling to her. I yell into the bushes, "Go away, Mr. Bear. Go away *now*!!" Randy runs over to us and barks in support. We all listen in the silence afterward, my eyes scanning every direction. The only thing we hear and see is a cluster of small birds on the water's edge. They complain sharply, strutting back and forth on their spindly legs, mad at us because we are near their nests. If the birds are there, we must be OK, I tell myself.

Annie whispers in my ear, "He's gone now, Mommy. You scared him. I can't hear him anymore."

I turn a full circle with Annie's arms clinging to my shoulders and her legs around my waist. With relief in my voice, I say, "Yeah. I can't hear him either. I think we did scare him off, you know." I put her down and try to sound confident, saying, "We're a couple of brave warriors, eh?" Randy trots down the creek bed and licks up a drink of water. He looks satisfied.

"Is it supper time yet, Mommy? I'm hungry," Annie says, her dark eyes looking up at me from under her yellow rain hat and black bangs.

"Yep. Nearly. Let's get back to camp. Too cold and wet today to walk anywheres, right?" We slop through the creek and join a gleeful Randy wagging his tail, waiting for us to decide where we are going. Annie gives him a hug around the neck, he licks her face, and I laugh in relief. "Come on, let's race!" I call, and running hand in hand, we splash through the water, making lots of noise all the way back to the tents.

After supper I put Annie to bed in our little pup tent, and lie with her on the foam mattress. I love that time of the day. She cuddles warm and quiet beside me, the muffled voices of Rosie and Walter drifting in the air, the sweet smell of campfire smoke reminding me of home-tanned moosehide and Walter's smoked salmon. Lying here with Annie curled around me, I let myself wonder what life was like before she came to me. She is a living miracle. She was conceived in my drinking days, when I was raped the second time. I don't remember who the man was. Such a dreadful act, and yet it held this gift for me. It's like a dream, or something that happened to someone else, those terrible times.

My grandfather Pop was the centre of all my young life. The last time I saw him he told me that my drinking was killing him. He gave me a challenge, not in so many words, but he meant that if I stay sober for five years he would see me again, but not before that. I know he is stubborn enough to keep his word. It's been more than five years and I have been sober all that time, but I haven't had the courage to see him. I don't trust that this life I have now, this peace, will last.

"Tell me 'nother story about Great-grandma Thomas, Mommy. She was Annie, too, right?" Annie pleads. She has asked me that so many times! But I always want to talk about that wonderful woman and she knows it.

"Yes, she was Annie Thomas. You've got her name, my little Annie Maclean. But you know that, you silly little rabbit," I say tickling her under the sleeping bag. She screams in mock protest and giggles. I bring back images of my own childhood for Annie, and Grandma Thomas' cheery round face smiles encouragingly at me once again while we sew beadwork in her kitchen or cut up salmon on the river bank at Moosehide. I am beginning to be able to let my mind go back to those wonderful days of my growing up in Dawson without feeling the pain and guilt of being responsible for its loss. So many of my memories are on the Yukon River, fishing in the summer at Moosehide, travelling over the river ice with our scrappy dog team, the excitement we felt when the river broke up in May.

For awhile I see little Annie as myself, listening to Pop telling me the familiar stories about his life in the bush with his Indian wife.

Annie is safely asleep, wrapped around her favourite stuffed toy, a soft grey and white husky dog that Walter gave her. For awhile, I am relieved. It is hard, being reminded that I haven't talked to Pop for so long, that he hasn't seen Annie except at a distance on the street. He was right when he said I thought it would be easier than it would be to quit drinking. I still feel shaky about being able to handle any stress without a drink in my hand. I will always be grateful that Walter and Rosie took me and Annie in, giving us so much support without question. But the time is getting close when I will have to go back home to Pop to face some of the things I did to him and my younger brothers. And to myself.

Golden shafts of light pierce through the pink and grey clouds, casting an eery light, making dark shadows that grip the rounded Twelve Mile River valley. At the far end of the valley, the jagged teeth of the black Tombstone mountains bite through a layer of low clouds. I join Rosie and Walter in front of their tent where they are sitting on logs around the campfire drinking tea. Looking up at the sky, Walter says, "Rain's stopped. Looks like tomorrow'll be clear." He leans down and gives Randy a scratch behind the ears. "Be a good day to move up around Jensen's camp. What you think, Fritz?" Even Walter can't remember exactly why he gave Rosie that pet name. He's the only one to use it.

I sit on the log beside Rosie. She adds three spoons of sugar to her tin cup of tea from the old mayonnaise jar on the ground. She stirs the tea thoughtfully, and decides: "Good idea. Selena says George and Betty stopped by today, headed home. They already got their moose. Said they saw a cow up that way yesterday, near the road. Coupla caribou too."

"Must be new snow at Jensen's, after this weather." Snow will make tracking much easier. Walter's smile under his worn red baseball cap takes up the whole of his round face as he turns to me. "Want to try out that old rusty rifle of yours, Lena?"

For the four days that we have been there, I have stayed in camp reading and playing with Annie and Randy while Rosie and Walter walked the valley. "My gun's not the only thing that's rusty, Walter," I say, "I haven't been out hunting for years." I lean past him and pour myself tea from the blackened pot on the fire. The tea is boiled, bitter. I add lots of sugar.

"Hmmm. Time to start again maybe?" he says and I can feel him looking at me.

"You'd probably have better luck with Rosie along instead." I force a smile.

"Tired of my old lady hanging around! Complains too much all the time!" Walter says with a laugh, "Isn't that right Fritz?" He looks up at Rosie's large frame as she stands up to gather our supper dishes. Walter is being about as persuasive as he will ever get, and I know he isn't comfortable with trying to talk me into going. I should *want* to go, in my own time.

"Well, you're too darn fast, you and those long legs of yours," Rosie counters. She looks at me with a playful frown, "Just poops me out, that man," she says. "Me, I'm gettin' too old to go all day." Rosie is two years older than Walter and she plays it up when she needs to.

"What about Annie?" I ask, poking at the fire with a stick. I know the answer.

"Been awhile since I had a little girl to play with," Rosie says, "I'll stay in camp with her while you two youngsters get us a moose. Besides, I need a rest from the old man. He complains too much!" she laughs and punches his shoulder.

Walter pretends to fall over and says, "Hah! See how she treats me, Lena? Strong woman, my old lady, and boy is she mean!" He looks at me. His eyes glitter with delight under his heavy eyebrows. "Too bad she's so darn slow in the bush. Gotta trade her in some day. Need me a young one."

Rosie says, "Sure! Any day! She'd keep you on your toes, you old fart. Make you pay your way." She pulls his baseball cap down over his eyes and we both join her laughter.

Walter is right about the weather. The next morning there is a clear sky. The sun promises a warmer day but we know the clear sky means colder weather, maybe snow. A mist clutters the valley bottom but it is burnt off by the time we pack up. Sand flies close in on us in the morning dampness, crawling into our noses and ears. We haul our camping gear over the old side road, avoiding wet grass and puddles.

When we get to the pickup parked a few hundred feet away on the highway, Randy is already in the bed of the truck, his tail eagerly wagging. His feet make a metallic drum beat as he paces in anticipation of the ride. We jam ourselves into the cab, scratching new insect bites. Rosie says, "Whew! Close that door quick, Walter. Don't want any more of them little buggers in here. Had enough out of me, them things." Annie climbs onto my lap. Walter teases the motor to life and we settle into silence, bumping along the gravel surface, splashing through a puddle here and there, watching the country change. From the Tombstone mountains, we curve through the high North Fork Pass and on down to the wider, flatter Blackstone River Valley. The treeless mountains, red with tundra bushes and topped with new snow, move away from the road, inviting us to come further. From here, the rivers flow north to the Arctic Ocean.

"Great-grandma Thomas used to tell us about the old days, Annie," Walter says, "when us Trondek Indians came up to meet the people from Fort McPherson around here. The Gwitchin came down this way to hunt in the fall, long time before there was a highway. We shared feasts with them. Ate caribou till we dropped, sang songs, danced to the drums. They'd camp around here until there was enough snow to go home to McPherson on their dogsleds."

"Sometimes I feel like they're still here, you know, like I can hear them, when it's quiet." Rosie says. We all nod.

"This is where they looked for Dawson girls, too," Walter laughs. "Yep. Prettier girls in Dawson than up North. They got more than caribou on those trips, eh Fritz?"

"Shush, you dirty old man," Rosie giggles.

A little later Annie turns to me and asks with excitement, "You gonna get our moose today, Mommy?" Silence from all of us. She is challenging fate; it's bad luck to say ahead of time what might happen, especially in a hunt.

"Better not let Mrs. Moose hear you say that," Walter chuckles. "She'll just take her little calf and run in the other direction with him right into those mountains over there."

"Just like I would do with you," I hug her.

"Yeah, let's not tell her we're coming," Annie says, "Then we'd be hungry all winter."

The highway winds closer to the Blackstone River. Rosie shouts and points across Walter's face, "Look! Medicine plants, over there! Stop this truck!"

Walter jumps on the brakes and we tumble out of the cab while Randy flings himself across the road and up a little hill. He crouches behind some dwarf birch bushes and waits patiently for a ptarmigan to fly away so he can chase it. Walter brings his gun out from behind the seat and says, "Come on with me, Annie, time you learned how to kill your dinner. Let's look for tracks in the mud." He slings the gun over his shoulder.

"OK, Grandpa!" Annie eagerly takes Walter's free hand and they climb over the rocks lining the river. Randy gives up on the ptarmigan and runs over, trotting close behind them. Rosie rattles around in the camping gear and finds a small shovel, a digging fork, and a cooking pot. She hands me the pot.

"Grandma Thomas told me this is where the medicine always is," I say, following Rosie. She walks determinedly across the road. I imitate Grandma's voice: "Good for *an-y*-thing: sore head, stomach flu, cons-i-pation..."

Rosie smiles. "She was right. Real good stuff. But it's got to be picked at the right time of year, like now, just before real freeze-up. See them over there?"

"I never came here with her when she picked it. Show me."

Rosie points at some plants rising above the low juniper. They look like fireweed but without flowers. "It's all over the place," I say. "Look, some over there, too." I point to the side of the hill.

"Nope. Just down here. Wetter here." She is on her knees, turning over the thin rocky soil with the digging fork.

"How come that's different stuff over there? Looks the same to me. The leaves are the same, Rosie."

Rosie triumphantly lifts a clump of fat bright orange roots from the ground. "This is why. Try digging up some of that other stuff." I take the shovel and do as she suggests. I am disappointed to see that the plants I choose have long, skinny grey roots trailing off the stems. Rosie won't explain how she knows which are the right plants, even if she can. She believes I am smart enough to find it out by experimenting for myself, learning the Indian way.

"Try over there behind those willow bushes. Should be some there." She points with her digging fork.

I take the shovel and walk across to the willows. At the first crunch of the shovel into the soil, I hear it. "Seleeena, Seleeena, come here. Come seee meee, Selena." It is in the willows, but I can see right through them and there is nothing there. My body feels so weak I can't dig. I have forgotten it again, and there it is. I stand, frozen. "Come, Selena, come seee meee, Seleeena," it says again. I look over at Rosie's large round back. I can see she is digging hard in the ground, but she is close enough. She should be able to hear the voice. "Seleeena, come on..." I don't wait to hear anything more. I throw the shovel into the willows and shout, "No! Go away! Leave me alone!" I turn to run away and see that Rosie is hurrying towards me.

"Did you hear it?" I cry.

"No. What? A bear? Did you hear a bear?"

In my confusion and embarrassment, I say, "Yeah. A bear. I think I saw a bear in the bushes."

"Selena, you can see for miles," she says, pointing to the wide open valley with the medicine root still in her hand. "You'd see the bushes moving a long time before you could see any bear. You know that." She walks over to the willows, picks up the shovel, and comes back to me, looking concerned. "What's really wrong?" she asks, "You look scared to death, child."

I slump to the ground and burst into tears. "I'm going crazy, Rosie. I hear things. I hear things, in the willows."

"What things? What do you hear?" She kneels down beside me and puts her arm around my shoulders.

"I used to hear it when I was a kid, too. Not in town. Not in Moosehide. Only in the bush. A voice. A voice whispers to me. It calls me and says to come. I think it wants me to see something."

"Bushman!" Rosie says with certainty. "Funny, though. I didn't think they would be this far away from town. They like lots of kids around to tease."

"Do you believe that?"

"Well, the old people say it's true. I never seen any. I think some of them was maybe old sourdoughs, you know, left over from the Gold Rush, living in the bush, gone crazy looking for gold. I think maybe they had kids that still live in the bush."

"Rosie, do you think I'm crazy?" I whisper.

"No, no, no! Don't ever say that! You'll *make* yourself crazy by talking like that." She smiles and pulls me closer to her. "I'll talk to Walter tonight. He'll know what to do." We go back to the road and see Walter and Annie climbing up the river bank with Randy.

"Don't say anything to Walter yet. I don't want to scare Annie," I say.

She nods and puts the pot full of roots and the shovel in the back of the truck. She calls to Walter, "Any tracks?" He shakes his head and she asks, "Got some pennies? I don't have nothing in my pocket." I watch, puzzled, as he silently comes over to us and hands her some change from his wallet.

"Too bad. Don't have no tobacco these days," he says, looking at me significantly. Rosie sniffs. She finally talked him into quitting cigarettes last New Year's. "Guess I'll have to be useful and gather some wood for later," Walter says, walking away. There will be no wood above tree-line, farther up the highway.

"Come with me, Annie, you should see this," Rosie says, beckoning to her with the digging fork. I follow them back to the broken ground and watch as Rosie puts a penny into one of the small holes she had made and carefully covers it with the scattered soil and dead plants. "We have to leave something for thanks. Sometimes we leave tobacco, but pennies will do."

Grandma Thomas told me the same thing once when we were in Moosehide but I had forgotten. She seldom told me anything more than once. I was supposed to remember, and now I did. "Make it look as if nothing was took," Rosie says to Annie, giving her some pennies, "or it'll be unhappy and won't grow again." She lets Annie do the rest.

"Do we pray, now, Grandma?" Annie asks seriously when she finishes.

"This is praying, sweetie," Rosie says, and pats the soil where Annie has filled in the hole. "Indian praying."

Walter drives slowly along the Highway. His eyes scan the rolling waves of red and green tundra in the Blackstone Uplands. The shallow Blackstone River cuts through a valley lined on both sides with strange olive and brown mountains. They are shaped like pyramids with rows of rock jutting out near the tops. The outcroppings remind me of the wedge of petrified mammoth's tooth Pop keeps on the window sill. He told me he found it one time in the sluice box when he was helping someone placer mining. As a child, when I lifted the heavy stone tooth and held it breathlessly against my cheek to feel its ridges, those ancient lives came dangerously close. Now the mountains with their teeth draw me into that prehistoric time.

We all lurch forward as Walter abruptly stops the truck and jumps out. Reaching for his gun and small packsack behind the seat, he says tensely, "Come on, Selena, time to test your eyes." He is famous for seeing game when no one else has.

Rosie and Annie spread themselves across the seat as I get out and put on my warm jacket. I wait without moving, standing by the truck, trying to remember everything I should know. Walter silently digs my old gun out from under the camping gear, fills it with shells and hands it to me. He calls to Rosie through the open driver's window, "Put that useless dog in the front will you, Fritz." Randy jumps enthusiastically into the cab when Rosie opens the passenger door. It's a treat for him and Annie. He licks her face as she scratches his neck and laughs.

Walter turns to me. "Remember how you put the safety on?"

"Uh huh," I say, and click it on awkwardly. What if I do something wrong, shoot somebody? I worry if it will still work OK if I use my little fingers for shooting like I used to because of my crippled right hand.

"Come on, then," Walter says. He is a different person. Serious. Demanding.

Paralleling the highway and the Blackstone, I follow Walter's lead as quickly as I can over the uneven tundra. The soaking wet plant-covered mounds, like sponges, give way to our weight. My feet ache; my arms are heavy with the weight of the gun. I want nothing more than to be back sitting in the warm pickup.

After several minutes, Walter stops abruptly. "Shhh. He's right over there, see?" he says in a loud whisper. He points with his gun toward a cluster of stunted spruce beside the river.

I can't see anything. Walter says, "Caribou. By himself. Get back to the highway. Other side. I'll stay here." I do as he says. Climbing the river bank, I finally see the caribou standing in the shallows. His delicate antlers, almost as large as his body, bob up and down as he bends to munch lichen and to drink. I move out of sight, my heart pounding. Walter shakes some willows and I hear the caribou reluctantly taking four or five steps towards me in the water. He lifts his head, listening, and trots across the road toward me. I hold my breath and click the safety off. The gun is light as plastic as I raise it. A thrill of control rushes through my whole body. I work my two smallest fingers around the trigger with old familiarity.

"Seleeena, Seleeena, come here. Come seee meee." The voice is rasping, behind me, hidden in the ditch. Without thinking, I whirl around and shoot blindly into the ditch. "Go away!" I shout desperately and throw my gun to the ground. The echo of the blast clears and I can hear the caribou splashing in the river, away from us. Walter fires a shot. Then another.

Walter is on the road. "Wounded!" he shouts. "I'm going after him. Get back to the truck. Bring it here." He shifts his packsack, disappears over the bank, and is gone.

I stand for a long minute in disappointed silence, exhausted, tears flowing down my cheeks. I pick up the gun and its weight pulls on my arm. I remember to put the safety back on. Then with fright I think, *It'll call me again if I don't get out of here.* I am shivering in the cold wind, and start walking back to the truck. In a few minutes, I hear a motor and our pickup comes into view from around a curve in front of me. Randy's black head is pressed against the side of the cab, peering from the back, his tongue hanging out of his mouth in excitement. Rosie stops, rolls down the window, and her head pops out in front of Randy's. "Thought I heard some shots. They're out there, eh? Did you get it? Cow moose?"

"Wounded. Male caribou," I say. I walk around the box of the truck, empty my gun and place it on top of the gear in the back. I pull open the passenger door, and get into the cab.

"Good!" Rosie smiles eagerly. "Walter'll be back in a little while. Won't let him get too far. He's fast in the bush, that man."

"Mommy, mommy, you got our caribou!" Annie bounced proudly on the seat beside me.

"No, honey, it was Grandpa's shot."

"What?" Rosie looks at me, puzzled. She puts the truck in gear. We drive for a few seconds and she says, "He told me he was going to let you get it, Lena."

"Well, he did let me. But I missed by a mile. Sorry," I mumble.

"Oh. Well, need a little practice, that's all. Come on, we got lots of work to do before this wind gets up too much." She steers the pickup off the road into a flat clearing left by the highway crews. An Arctic tern complains with sharp cries about our presence near her nest. She swoops over Randy and he ducks out of her way. The exercise setting up the tents helps me feel a little better. I boil some water on the gas stove; we will save the campfire wood we brought with us for warmth later at night. Annie gets the tea things ready, and we eat a cold lunch of canned meat sandwiches, sitting silently on the camping boxes. The caribou and Walter are the only things on our minds but we don't speak of them.

The wind gusts fiercely through the valley, rising steadily as the afternoon passes. Annie and I are warmly cuddled in our tent two hours later and I am reading her a story when we hear Randy's bark and Rosie's excited call over the flapping sides of the tent, "He's here!" We scramble out.

Walter is walking slowly towards us, gun in one hand, leaning into the wind, a burlap hump on his back. Rosie yells, "He's got it! Caribou ribs tonight, kids!"

Annie cheers, "Grandpa, Grandpa!" and runs up to him.

I watch as Walter puts down his gun, leans over and gives her a cautious hug. "Careful, honey, I'm pretty dirty right now." When Walter stands up, Randy jumps with his paws onto his chest, sniffing the blood on his jacket and over his shoulder at the burlap bag. Rosie hurries up to Walter to untie the bundle on his back and it falls with a thud. She pulls it apart, kneeling on the ground.

"Get that dog out of here, Selena," Rosie says with her back to me. I pull Randy away and tie him to the pickup. "Look at that fresh meat! My teeth are just aching. Can't wait to get into it," Rosie laughs.

Smiling, Walter looks across Rosie's back at me and says, "Told you our daughter would bring us luck, Fritz." I hurry away, my insides heavy. I pour Walter a cup of steaming tea. I keep myself busy with the gas stove, getting the dishes and cast-iron frying pans ready for the thick steaks we have all been waiting for. When they are slapped into the pans Randy whines in excitement. The pungent smell and the sizzle curls around, energizing all of us for the work ahead.

We spend the short afternoon caring for the meat, skinning it and dragging it to the highway before dark. We all have jobs to do. Randy is harnessed and slowly pulls the carcass over the bumpy tundra, encouraged with shouts from Annie who pulls on his leash ahead of him. Then by the gas lantern, we hang it on a frame made of poles that Walter had ready in the truck. It is past midnight when we finally wash up, eat, and throw ourselves into bed. We are so busy we haven't even started the campfire.

Overnight, the wind dies down. The sun warms the valley by the time the smell of caribou ribs frying wakes Annie and me late the next morning. The calm weather means that the sand flies and mosquitoes are heavier than usual, and Rosie builds a smoky campfire with green willow branches to keep them away. The lazy morning is spent swatting insects as we do small chores and make idle talk. Randy chews a leg bone and sleeps where he is, tied to the truck to keep him away from the meat. Annie plays with her toy husky. We hear her pretending it's leading a dog team to Fort McPherson, bringing home a caribou.

"Had enough caribou meat for today. Want to get us some grayling for a change?" Walter asks me late in the afternoon. I know he is never tired of caribou, and at this time of year the grayling are not the best. Reluctantly, I agree. He wants to talk.

Rosie says, "Annie, how about you and me seeing what we can do about finding those cranberries Auntie Betty said she picked when they camped here?" She picks up a plastic container.

"Will you keep the bears away, Grandma?" she asks. My heart sinks. Have I made her as afraid of the bush as I am?

"You're darn right. But you gotta help by making lots of noise. Anyways, by now we smell so bad no bear in his right mind would have us!"

"Yeah, we need a bath."

"Tomorrow, honey, we'll be home," she says, taking Annie by the hand. "Remember running water? A warm bed? Electric light? Just turn on a switch...I wonder what cooking with an oven is like..."

"Grandma! You know! You got a oven." I hear Annie giggle as they wander off, "You just tease."

Walter and I take fishing rods and walk up the river to a small eddy full of rocks. We cast our lines. Both of us know it's not a good spot for fish. For long minutes, the only sound is our muted swearing at a couple of pestering black flies. I can't stand the silence and finally I say, "I'm real sorry I didn't get that caribou, Walter. I made a lot of work for you."

He laughs. "Well, you know, it always helps to aim at the thing you're gonna shoot at."

"You saw?"

"Mmmm. Heard too."

"Heard me?"

"Yep. Yelling at something: 'go away!'"

I hold my breath. "Did Rosie talk to you?"

"Yep. Voices, eh?"

I reel in my line, sit down hard on a rock, and say, "I must be going crazy, Walter. You know, I used to hear it when I was a kid. I thought it was just a bushman then. Walter, do you think I'm crazy?"

Walter reels in his line. He comes over, sits beside me on the ground, and drops his fishing rod. He pulls a length of grass to fiddle with, and looks into the distance. "Nope. Nobody's crazy till they think they are." He waits for that to sink in and then, looking at me, says, "Do you think you're crazy, Selena?"

I hesitate. "No. Not really. But I think I will go crazy if I do what it says."

"What's it say?"

"It wants me to come to it." I'm breathing hard. I can't seem to get enough air. "To see something."

"Might be a devil. God sends us devils to test us."

"You know, funny thing is, if I think about that voice ahead of time, it doesn't come. It sneaks up on me when I'm not ready for it, in the bush."

"Sounds like a devil. Lots of devils in booze, you know."

"But I quit."

"They wait. Come out later, when you're sober. When you're boozing, you're so full of the devil he don't need you. He got you already!" Walter grabs the air in front of him.

"Do you think it wants me to drink again?"

"Maybe."

We sit in silence. After awhile, Walter says, "You know, you're very special to God. Like Ma was. She knew that, too. She told me she could see God in you."

"What? Me? I'm not special. I was only special when I was with Grandma. She made everyone special." We sit silently thinking about that dear old woman, still so much alive in our hearts. What would she think of me now, I wonder, a drunk like my mother, afraid of my shadow, not even able to hunt properly?

I say, "Walter, you heard Grandma that day in the hospital. Her last words to me. *'Never forget you Indian. Indian.'* I think I know what she means, now, but how am I supposed to be Indian, when I'm so messed up?"

Walter says, "My ma she help people see themself, I think. What they are. What they can be. It's her power." Walter doesn't hear himself talk about her as if she is still with us. He is listening to her and repeating what she says. "Your Grandma say...God send some people special things... to help...to help specially children who don't have mothers...motherless children. He make them stronger...stronger than the rest. She say she send you that white caribou that time she die...that spirit, to be with you rest of your life, to help you."

We are both silent for a long time, listening to the river and the birds, until he stands up and says in a determined voice, "Maybe God send this devil to help make you both strong mothers, you and your own mother too. Eliza. She never really had a mother too." My mother. A hopeless drunk until the last few years. Walter never talks about her. He wanted to marry her once, Grandma Thomas told me, but she wouldn't.

"But I don't feel strong at all!" I protest. "I'm even scared of the bush now. Never was before. Before I drank."

"Now you're sober, maybe time to get strong again, be Indian, for Annie," Walter says.

We pick up our fishing gear and start walking back to camp. He says, "A good thing, you know, this devil coming." He stopped walking, smiled, and thrust his fishing rod in front of us like a sword, his eyes sparkling under his baseball cap. "You just got to fight him off, eh? Face him down. You're strong now. My Ma and your Annie, they both help you. You just watch. It's in you. You just can't help it."

As we walk silently back, I can feel Walter's certainty and love surrounding me, a warm blanket against my own cold fear. It is like the comfort and support that Grandma Thomas gave me, freely, whenever I needed it. Like when she sent the white caribou. I should do whatever I wanted with it, she said. He never came to me again. Maybe because that was when I started drinking, at Grandma's funeral. Maybe I can get the caribou back, find the peace I had then.

Rosie teases us when she sees us coming: "What, no grayling? What we gonna eat?"

"We caught something better than fish," Walter says, smiling.

"Well, now, that's good. That's good." Rosie chuckles.

That night before we go to bed, I lean over Walter's shoulder and whisper in his ear for the first time in my life, "'Night, Daddy." He squeezes my arm, unable to speak.

That last night on the Dempster beside the Blackstone River, the voice comes again in my sleep, like it has many times before. I dream that I have to pee, and I am walking to an outhouse. It's in a place I remember from when I was little, but I haven't seen for a long time. The voice is in the willows along the path, telling me, in that singsong, "Seleeena, come. Come and see. Come and seee meee." Every other time if I dreamed about the voice, I would run away and wake up. But this time I make myself see what it is, that voice. I walk toward it. My heart pounds like a drum. There is a scrawny man we kids used to call Spider crouching in the grass on his haunches, smiling. Both his arms are beckoning me to come closer. His pants are down on his ankles. He grabs my head and pushes it into his groin. I wake up choking, trying to scream. As I toss around, Annie's sleepy voice says, "Mommy, you OK?"

"Yes, Annikins, I'm OK. Just a bad dream. It's over now."

She wraps herself around me, saying, "I love you, Mommy," and falls asleep again. I lie awake for a long time, staring into the darkness. I can see Spider. It was him. He would wait for me, when I was young, by the outhouse, calling me, making me do things that made me throw up. He's dead, now. He drowned in the Yukon River, falling out of a boat when he was drunk, years ago.

Relief slowly overtakes the fear left from the dream. I listen to the Blackstone River rushing by. Every once in awhile I hear a watery clunk as a stone rolls over with the current in the shallow riverbed, sounding like a raven talking. My own voice assuring Annie echoes in my mind, "It's over now; it's over now. Just a bad dream." I have a vision of black stones being washed away to the Arctic Ocean. I know it really is over.